THE YEARE'S
MIDNIGHT

THE YEARE'S MIDNIGHT

ED O'CONNOR

CARROLL & GRAF PUBLISHERS
New York

Carroll & Graf Publishers
An imprint of Avalon Publishing Group, Inc.
161 William Street
16th Floor
NY 10038-2607
www.carrollandgraf.com

First published in the UK by Constable,
an imprint of Constable & Robinson Ltd 2002

First Carroll & Graf edition 2002

ISBN 0-7867-1028-4

Printed and bound in the EU

For Mum, Dad and Alix

CONTENTS

Blasted with sighs, surrounded with teares,
Hither I come to seek the Spring,
And at mine eyes, and at mine eares
Receive such balms, as else cure everything.

John Donne, extract from *Twicknam Garden*

Part I

A Bath of Teares

1

Twilight drained from the sky in sudden streams. The ground felt damp. December winds had chilled the soil but had not frozen it. Crowan Frayne had hoped for a harder surface. Frozen earth makes no sound. Mud squelches and clings like an ugly memory. No matter. Frayne thought of forcing his face into the ground, to impress his image upon the earth. The idea amused him. He could peer down on the dead as God peers down on the living.

Tonight he heard music; voices abstracted by time. As if the piano in his mind was strung with the spirits of the dead, producing exquisite notes of pain at his every delicate keystroke.

The spot he had chosen was well concealed at the base of a dark cluster of elm trees. He could see the house clearly. The lights had come on an hour earlier. The garden – half illuminated – was small and neat. Flower beds huddled against the wooden panelled fence. In spring they would surge with colour but now they seemed skeletal and forlorn.

Frayne could make out the image of a woman beyond the windows. Young, tall, lean. She would be strong. He would have to be cautious. Finding her had been a Providence. Chance had dealt him an unexpected and brilliant hand. Lucy Harrington had fallen through his letter box.

He checked his watch. Not long. The details could not be left to chance. Precision was everything now. The house was old, a recently gentrified nineteenth-century cottage. The back door was ill-fitting, with an old-fashioned lock. He had already checked. The lock could be dealt with easily. None of the nearby cottages overlooked the garden directly. He would have privacy.

And time. She would need to leave by 7.50. The reception would last two hours at least. Time enough. An upstairs light threw a square of light onto the gloomy lawn. Crowan Frayne

3

squeezed the flower in his left hand until his fingers were stained violet. He picked a scalpel from his selection of medical instruments and gently sliced the skin under his left eye. A spot of blood bloomed on his face. He spoke quickly and quietly as a single dark tear rolled down his cheek.

'Let me power forth
My teares before thy face whilst I stay here.'

The words evaporated with his breath in the cold air. He became still. A hole in the night.

The cocktail dress fitted perfectly but Lucy Harrington was unhappy. Her shoulders were too big and her boobs too small. She wondered if she should have been a cyclist instead of a swimmer. Maybe a blouse would have worked better, been less unforgiving. She glanced at the clock. 7.52. There was no time. The reception started at eight and New Bolden was at least a ten-minute drive. It would have to be the dress. She straightened its soft lines and dabbed her favourite Issy Miyake perfume onto her neck. Satisfied, she grabbed her car keys and hurried downstairs.

Frayne caught his breath as the front door opened and Lucy Harrington emerged, silhouetted against the hall light. He knew that she couldn't possibly see him, but he still felt conspicuous. As if the heat of his excitement created a variation in the texture of the night. She turned and double-locked the front door (as he knew she would) and walked quickly to her car. Her breath ghosted against the car windows as she fumbled with the lock.

This excited Frayne. He remembered that Donne had contorted the view of Aquinas that angels were spiritual entities that created bodies of air to assume visible properties. How did it go?

'Then as an angel, face and wings
Of air, now pure as it yet pure doth wear . . .'

4

Perhaps Lucy Harrington would be an angel. He would help her.

The headlights blazed accusingly in his direction. Frayne sank low to the ground, until he feared that the earth might absorb him alive. The car spluttered to life and spat light against the ancient curtain of the woods. Inside the vehicle, Lucy Harrington cursed her vanity as her high heels slipped on the clutch and the engine stalled. Eventually, the yellow Fiat began to move away and, after a moment, passed within a few feet of the spot Crowan Frayne had just vacated.

It was a housebreaker's trick. It only worked on older dwellings. New buildings had security locks fitted as standard and required different treatment. But, this time, Crowan Frayne's research the previous night had proved correct.

He knelt at the back door. The cold stone grated at his kneecap. Moving rapidly, he withdrew a piece of card from his equipment bag and slid it under the back door, directly beneath the keyhole. The card in place, he carefully fed a narrow steel meat skewer into the keyhole until it stopped against the key that had been inserted from the other side. He held the skewer in place with his left hand and with his right picked up a hammer. He hit the skewer firmly once and heard the key fall gratifyingly from the lock inside. Smiling, he withdrew the card with great care from the crack underneath the door. Slowly the key emerged. Frayne snatched it up, inserted it into the lock and turned it. The whole operation had taken less than a minute. He was inside.

The warmth hit his face like a breaking Mediterranean wave. The door clicked shut behind him. He locked it and for the first time felt a flash of fear. Crowan Frayne placed his anxiety in a box: he would open it later.

The Civic Centre was crowded with journalists, local residents and dignitaries. It was hot and airless. Lucy Harrington found the atmosphere stifling. Still, this was what it was all about. All those lonely winter mornings in the New Bolden swimming pool, the pain of weight training, the sacrifice of a social life. She tried to enjoy herself and concentrate on what the Mayor was saying.

'Few districts can boast their own Commonwealth gold medallist.' New Bolden's bald mayor paused for emphasis and breath. 'Lucy's achievement has put our town on the map.' A firework display of camera flashes flared across the room as Lucy smiled a shy, embarrassed smile. The mayor continued, his forehead sparkling wet under the lights. 'A personal triumph, yes. But one in which we can all share with a great degree of great pride. As the name suggests, New Bolden is a new town and Lucy is the first of its new generation of young people to make a real mark on the world. I therefore ask you to raise your glasses and toast the new Commonwealth 100-metre freestyle champion ... Lucy Harrington.' A noisy toast. A ripple of applause. Lucy Harrington rose nervously to her feet and fixed the audience with a grateful blue-eyed gaze.

'I suppose a swimmer should never be out of her depth, but public speaking has always terrified me.' Indulgent laughter. 'I'm determined that this speech won't last longer than my race did so that gives me about a minute to thank everyone. Swimming can be a lonely sport and athletes, almost by definition, have to be selfish individuals. But when I stood on the blocks last weekend I knew I had all of New Bolden right there with me. That feeling is hard to top.' Lucy Harrington paused and looked around the room: the wallpaper of unfamiliar faces, the flashes from the press cameras. Suddenly she felt very tired.

It was 11.07. He had expected her back by now. However, Frayne was unconcerned: this had always been the variable and he was prepared. The time had passed quickly until now. He had familiarized himself with the house. He had checked and rechecked his instruments. Now he sat quietly and read. Lucy Harrington's bedroom smelt vaguely of flowers and vanilla. A car rumbled up outside.

Crowan Frayne put his book away.

*

A weary Lucy Harrington slammed her front door shut against the cold. She dropped her keys on the hall table and kicked off her shoes. She leaned against it for a second as fatigue began to build up behind her eyes. Then, just as she was about to enter the kitchen, she heard running water. The bath. She must have left a tap running. She swore quietly as she hurried upstairs and strode into the bathroom, expecting the room to be awash. It wasn't. Water gushed noisily from the cold tap but the bath was less than a third full. She hesitated. Was she going mad?

As she bent over the bath and turned the tap off, Crowan Frayne stepped quickly up behind her and smashed a hammer into the back of her head. Blood spat against the tiles and Lucy Harrington slumped to the floor. He hit her again, harder. It was important to be certain.

It was done in a moment and she had hardly made a sound. Frayne worked quickly. He was well rehearsed. He rolled her onto her back and pushed back her left eyelid. The pupil was dilated, black and unseeing. He brought in his equipment box and withdrew a scalpel, scissors and a set of forceps. This was the critical challenge. He anticipated no problems removing the eyelid but severing the lateral ciliary muscles that supported the eye in its socket would be awkward. He didn't want to damage the eyeball. That was vital. He saw his own face bloated and floating in Lucy Harrington's dead black pupil. He addressed the darkness softly;

> 'On a round ball
> A workman that hath copies by, can lay
> An Europe, Afrique, and an Asia
> And quickly make that, which was nothing, All.'

Conditions were cramped and he needed more light. There was a metal reading lamp in the bedroom. No need to rush. He had plenty of time.

2

10 December

Rain drummed against the bedroom window. Through the chink in the curtains, Underwood watched the droplets merge and stream downwards, sometimes flaring with yellow from the brightly burning street lights. He was grateful for the central heating but sweated beneath his T-shirt. He had kicked the duvet off an hour previously. To little effect. He found he had problems catching his breath. During the day, he scarcely noticed, except when battling up the stairs to the station canteen. However, at night, in the stuffiness of a centrally heated bedroom, he increasingly found himself short of air. Sleep rarely came easily to Detective Inspector John Underwood. Ugly dreams flew at him out of the darkness. He found it harder to drift off when he was alone, impossible when he was angry.

The alarm clock glowered at him. 3.17. Julia had been due back at midnight. He had last tried her mobile an hour ago. It had been switched off and that was always a bad sign. He knew he was being punished but couldn't understand why. Maybe it was *because* he couldn't understand why. Eighteen years of marriage seemed to have driven him and Julia further apart. Familiarity didn't just breed contempt. It bred unfamiliarity.

He was getting annoyed now and mainly with himself. Thinking is the undoing of the insomniac. Once his anxiety generator had been switched on, Underwood knew he would end up tracing the ripples of paint on the ceiling. Sometimes, if he was lucky, the ripples would wash together in waves of exhaustion and he would sink: but not tonight. His throat was dry. He reached for the can of Pepsi that he kept on the bedside table.

A car drew up outside. He peered through a gap in the curtain. A minicab: another bad sign. Where could she have been until 3.17? New Bolden was hardly Monte Carlo. Once the pubs cleared out at 11.30 the only action was at the kebab van. His mind raced. None of the alternatives was appealing. Julia stepped from the car and hurried inside.

He heard her climbing the stairs. She was trying to be quiet. He counted her steps. The fourth stair was loose but he heard no sound. She must have stepped over it. She was trying not to wake him up. Why? Thoughts ricocheted through his brain.

It's after three in the morning. She doesn't want me to know when she's coming in. Why? Because married women don't stay out this late unless they're fucking around. She doesn't want to wake me so she can lie tomorrow about the time she got in. Why would she lie? Because she doesn't want me to be suspicious. But if she's lying, then I bloody well ought to be suspicious.

The bathroom light clicked on. He heard the sudden, brisk rush of the shower. A very bad sign. She had taken a shower before she went out. 'Why would she have two showers in a night?' His thoughts were spiralling and they kept spinning back to the same sharp, uncomfortable point. Underwood tried to block the thought from his head. He would not allow himself to think like that. *Two plus two does not equal six. Do not pass go. Do not collect two hundred pounds.*

The shower stopped. Julia opened the bedroom door, ever so quietly. She fumbled for her nightdress at the foot of the bed and cursed softly. Underwood could smell wine. He tried to breathe in and out with studied regularity. The bed creaked slightly as Julia slipped under the duvet. Then she lay, still as a corpse, until she was convinced that Underwood's breathing pattern was authentic. Satisfied, she finally let her body relax. Underwood's stomach had curled into a tight ball of frustration. His wife was playing games with him. And she smelled like a stranger. He was thirsty again but knew that reaching for his can would rupture his tactical advantage. Instead, he half-opened his eyes and tried to concentrate on the random collisions of raindrops against the black glass.

3

Breakfast was strained. Underwood savoured the bitterness of an instant coffee. Julia hid behind the *Telegraph*. He knew it was just a matter of time now. The clock was ticking on their marriage. What would he do then? He felt like a wounded animal: he wanted to crawl away and embrace the comfort of oblivion. The idea seemed increasingly appealing.

'So when did you get in last night?' He tried to make his opening salvo breezy. There was a brief pause. He sensed his wife collecting her thoughts behind the newspaper.

'I'm not sure, to be honest. Quite late. Maybe half-one, two o'clock.' That was clever; use a small admission of guilt to mask the bigger lie. Give the interviewer what he thinks he wants to hear and defuse the situation. Smart. He'd heard it a thousand times before, from more accomplished liars than his wife. Still, he had to concede that she was getting more adept by the day and this had been going on for weeks.

'Hmmm . . . late one. You must be knackered. Where did you get to?'

'Madeleine and I went to the Haydn recital at St Peter's: the Bellini Piano Trio. We had dinner at Marco's at ten and then went for a bottle of wine at her place.' Julia lowered the paper and looked straight at him. 'We both got drunk and fell asleep in the living room.'

It was undeniably plausible. Madeleine certainly liked a drink. Julia's deliberate eye contact was calculated to convey sincerity. The sequence of events was a bit too ordered, though. It reminded Underwood of the well-thought-out, unrealistically symmetrical alibis offered by novice criminals. He hoped he was wrong. In the terrible chaos of life, he knew that guilt usually cowered in the details.

'What did you have for dinner?'

The phone rang. Julia jumped slightly.

'Fusilli Alfredo.'

Had she answered too quickly? Underwood's train of thought had been derailed. He stood up. Julia seemed to breathe a silent sigh of relief. He was aware of her gaze trailing him across the kitchen, like that of a nervous cat tensing itself in anticipation of an attack. Acid fizzed in Underwood's stomach. He picked up the receiver.

'Double six two four.'

'Sir, it's Dexter.' DS Alison Dexter had a sharp, loud London accent. Underwood winced slightly. Bad news coming.

'Morning, Dex. What's up?'

'Shit start to the day, sir. We've got a stiff.'

Underwood was too tired to make the obvious joke. Besides, he knew that you didn't flirt with DS Alison Dexter; it was like falling into a thorn bush. In any case, a flirty joke with his assistant would have ceded some of the moral high ground to Julia and he wasn't prepared to do that. This was the endgame of their marriage. Tactics were all that remained.

'Male or female?'

'Female. Mid-twenties.'

'Sex thing?'

'Not sure yet.' She paused. 'You should come quickly, sir. I think it's that Harrington girl.'

'The swimmer?' Underwood groaned inwardly. He had read the papers. New Bolden's local heroine was fast becoming a national celebrity. This was going to be a nightmare.

'Yeah. Someone really messed her up.'

'OK, Dex. Seal the place off. Get Forensic out there. The press will be all over this like shit on a bed sheet. Try and keep a lid on it.'

'That's going to be difficult, sir. They're already here.'

Underwood took down the address and grabbed the heavy blue jacket that he wore for work. He downed the remains of his coffee and turned to face Julia. She still hid behind the *Telegraph*, wide-eyed, not reading.

'Three-seventeen,' he said.

'Sorry?'

'Me too.'

She watched him leave. A bitter tide of guilt and frustration surged within her. She no longer had the energy to swim against it. Julia Underwood was exhausted.

4

Hartfield Road snaked out of the richer suburbs of New Bolden into Cambridgeshire's cheerless flat countryside. A cold mist hung over the Fens. Underwood drove north towards Ely, trying to block the previous night from his thoughts. His chest felt tight. The damp didn't help.

The journey to Fawley Close took him ten minutes. The four old cottages nestled at the southern edge of Fawley Woods. Previously occupied by farmworkers, a forward-thinking landlord had renovated the cottages a few years previously. They had been sold to young couples; mainly office professionals and teachers who worked in New Bolden or Cambridge. Lucy Harrington with her lottery grant cheque had been a recent arrival.

A police squad car blocked the entrance to the cul-de-sac, its blue lights twirling hypnotically. A few spectators had gathered nearby. Underwood parked on the main road. He could see DS Dexter outside one of the cottages; her dark hair was severely cropped. She seemed to bristle with authority. Dexter dealt in certainties. Underwood envied her.

The unforgiving air slashed at his lungs as he approached. There were puddles and, at the roadside, leaves crushed brown with mud that softened underfoot. Underwood coughed painfully as he approached.

'Sounds nasty, sir.' Dexter's bright green eyes were watery with the cold.

'It is. I'm getting old.'

'You already are old.'

Underwood appreciated the joke despite his discomfort. Maybe it was an intimacy. 'Thank you, sergeant. What have we got, then?'

'A mess. A journalist at the *New Bolden Echo* got a call at

7.30 this morning. Man's voice told him that Lucy Harrington was dead and gave him this address. Journo called our duty sergeant.'

'Did the guy have an accent?'

'Nothing obvious. The journo's over there if you want to speak to him.'

'I'll see him later. What else?'

'We got here after eight. Her car's in the drive.' She gestured at Harrington's Fiat. 'Tried the door and called her phone. No reply. So we went in.'

'Any signs of a forced entry?'

'None. Apart from ours, of course. New Bolden CID – interior devastators.'

Underwood smiled. Dex was a live wire. The Met had been right about her. She continued, encouraged: 'Inside is horrendous. The body is in the bathroom. Forensic are up there now. There's blood everywhere. It looks like a slaughterhouse. The killer left the bath taps running, so the whole place is awash. Upstairs is flooded. Getting decent forensic evidence is going to be a nightmare.'

'Clever if he meant it.' said Underwood thoughtfully. Dexter seemed uneasy.

'There's something else, sir.'

5

Ten miles away. A small terraced house. There are flowerpots outside but the flowers are withered and dead. The curtains are drawn for privacy, respect and celebration. Crowan Frayne sits on the patterned carpet in the living room. He sits cross-legged like a child. There is a plaster under his left eye. He still has blood under his fingernails. He will need another bath. He is tired but quietly triumphant.

In front of him is a photograph of an old woman. She is smiling. Her hand rests on the shoulder of a small boy who might be Crowan Frayne. Next to the photo frame is an African violet. Its flowers are richly coloured. He has nurtured it. Some of the flowers have fallen. There are violet petals on the carpet.

From his inside coat pocket, Frayne takes a small, polished wooden box. There are small brass letters screwed onto the lid. They spell out 'V. A. Frayne.' He places the box carefully on the carpet. Slowly, and with curious respect, he opens the box. It has a purple silk lining. It holds Lucy Harrington's left eyeball. There are two remaining spaces in the box. Frayne is satisfied. The back and sides of the eyeball are damaged. His forceps have gouged unsightly scars on each side. An occupational hazard. His first operation. Next time will be tidier.

He closes his eyes. He is on the desert planet where he likes to hide. Sand is all around him, sand and mountains, rocks and sky. The sand is black and the mountains have eyes: the rocks talk when the sky replies. Ahead of him, lying on the sand, is a giant mathematical compass. Its pointed steel legs glitter though there is no sun. He climbs over the compass and walks to the giant flea that winks within him. It is as high as a building, purpled and turgid with the blood of a billion innocents. The flea belches blood.

'Marke me,' says the flea.

The flea jumps over a giant grand piano that changes colours like the sand. The piano stool is two metres high. Frayne climbs up and stands on the white keys that soften like glue. The lid is heavy, so heavy, like lifting an ocean. Eventually he moves it and looks inside. A billion souls, stretched and screaming, sing their agony and absurdity back at him. The lid smashes shut.

He is back in his living room, Lucy Harrington's eye in his hand. He licks its smooth surface as if it were a highly polished jewel.

Underwood clipped the standard-issue plastic covers to his shoes and entered the house. It was old-fashioned inside, with white-painted walls and dark exposed beams. The carpet squelched unpleasantly underfoot. He looked up the stairway. Water and blood streamed down. The carpet had previously been blue but was now horribly stained and smeared with blood. He had never seen such a mess at a crime scene. The smell was terrible: a mildewy, damp deadness. Dexter was right. The chances of finding hair or DNA evidence from the killer would be small.

Police pathologist Roger Leach stood at the head of the stairs at the entrance to the bathroom. He was a heavy man, bearded and thickset. His habitually ferocious expression softened slightly as he saw Underwood gingerly clambering up the narrow staircase.

'Need a hand?' Leach smirked. 'You look rather strained.'

'Feeling my age.' Underwood was out of breath.

'You're younger than me.'

'Only just.' The carpet gave up more blood. Underwood grimaced. 'This is like a horror film.'

'It doesn't get any better, I'm afraid. I haven't seen anything like this before.' Leach heard Underwood's rasping breath. 'You sound a bit ropy, old man. I might be having a look inside you soon if you don't get some exercise.' Underwood finally joined him at the doorway and looked in.

'Jesus Christ.'

'That was pretty much my response.' Leach moved carefully into the bathroom. Underwood stayed at the door.

Lucy Harrington lay on her back, still wearing the black cocktail dress from the previous evening. She lay in a terrible slush of blood and water that seemed to have engulfed the entire room. The bath brimmed with water, its taps finally turned off. Harrington's face was unrecognizable, streaked red and distorted. Her right eye stared blankly at the ceiling. Her left eye was missing, the socket black with blood.

Underwood felt his stomach tighten. He bit his lip. The smell was getting to him. He looked up from the body. On the back wall of the bathroom the killer had written a short sentence in what looked like blood. The lettering had run down the white tiles and Underwood struggled to make out the words:

'Draw not up seas, to drowne me in thy spheare,' he mouthed quietly.

'Freaky, isn't it? Very Jack the Ripper.' Leach had crouched over the body and was carefully inspecting the wound at the back of Harrington's head.

'Any idea what it means?'

Dexter had arrived at the bathroom. 'Some mad shit from the Bible, I expect. An eye for an eye and all that,' she said without enthusiasm.

'Sounds more like Shakespeare to me,' Leach replied.

'So what else have we got here, Roger?' Underwood was becoming increasingly uncomfortable. He wanted to get away from the house quickly.

Leach leaned back on his haunches and thought for a moment. 'All this is subject to the post-mortem, of course.' He gently turned Harrington's head so they could see the wound in the back of her skull. 'Cause of death: massive blow to the cranium with a blunt instrument. Must be metal to have done this much damage. The entry wound is ragged at the edges but is basically round, about an inch and a half across. Hammer, I'd say. Or a steel pipe. Your boy bashed the back of her brains in.'

'One blow?'

'Two, maybe three. The lights went out immediately after that, I'd say. Looking at the blood-spray pattern on the tiles above the bath, my guess would be she was bending down over the bath when he clocked her. She fell forward, face first, and then he flipped her over.'

'What about the eye?'

'Well, it's hard to say – he's taken most of it. Judging by the nature of the damage to the socket, I would say that he started very carefully but got increasingly frustrated. It's a tricky pro-

16

cedure and our boy is no surgeon. He's cut through the ciliary muscles tidily enough but the eyeball was eventually wrenched from the socket. The optic nerve and a chunk of the eyeball were left behind.'

Underwood frowned. 'You don't think our man's a medic, then?'

'No. At best, he's a well-read enthusiastic amateur.'

'Time of death?' Dexter asked the obvious question that Underwood had missed.

'Expensively educated guess – eight to ten hours ago. Can't be certain before the post-mortem. The water has mucked up her body temperature. Mine too, as it happens.'

'She was out at some reception until elevenish,' Dexter observed. 'Probably got home at about eleven-thirty. Assuming she didn't stop somewhere first.'

Underwood had seen enough. 'OK. We'll assume death was around midnight until we get the PM results. I'll get Harrison to start the house-to-house.'

'John, you should understand that getting reliable forensic is going to be damn' nigh impossible. Marty Farrell is dusting for prints where he can but my hopes aren't high. I've never seen such a fucked-up crime scene. Whoever did this is smart – ' Leach looked around him despairingly ' – and very ill.'

'Do what you can. Dex, make a note of that writing before it slides off the wall. Find out if it means anything. He's trying to tell us something.'

'Fair enough.' Dexter flipped open her notebook and carefully wrote down the strange text.

'I'm off to find that journalist.' Underwood shot a final glance at the bloody mess that had once been Lucy Harrington and cautiously made his way downstairs.

17

George Gardiner stood outside the cottages, rain beginning to prick at his bald head. He was trying to fight off impatience with the knowledge that he was at the centre of the biggest story New Bolden had ever seen. It beat the crap out of the car accidents and crimes against cats that he usually ended up reporting on. He consoled himself with a Marlboro Light and leaned against the bonnet of a squad car. Underwood emerged from the house.

'You George Gardiner?' the inspector asked.

'About bloody time.' Gardiner jabbed at Underwood with his glowing cigarette. 'I've been waiting for an hour. It's bloody freezing. Without me, you buggers wouldn't even be here.'

Underwood felt the smoke sting at his lungs, scratch at his throat. He coughed. Gardiner smirked.

'Tell me what happened, then.' Underwood was running low on patience too.

'Got a call on the news desk at seven-thirty. Some of us do a full day's work.'

'Get on with it.'

'Bloke asked for me by name.'

'Why you? Are you the crime reporter or something?'

'No. There are only four of us on the news desk. We're hardly the *New York Times*. Perhaps he appreciates my prose style. I picked up the phone and this geezer says that Lucy Harrington is dead and he gives me her address.' Gardiner looked up at the house. 'This address. I asked him who he was and he said I should concentrate on his great conceit.'

'Conceit?'

'That's what he said. He sounded like an arrogant bastard.'

'Did he have an accent?'

'Not that I noticed. He didn't say much. He hung up. I called you lot.' Gardiner pulled out his notepad. 'Now, if you're finished, I'd like to ask you a few questions. We've all got our jobs to do.'

'There'll be a press conference at the station. Before you piss off, I want you to talk to one of my officers and get them to write down exactly what this bloke said to you. Do you know DS Dexter?'

Gardiner sniffed. 'Looks like a dyke?'

'I won't tell her you said that.'

'You can if you like.' Gardiner blew cigarette smoke into the cold East Anglian morning.

'Just tell her what you told me.' Underwood walked away. He felt drained and it was only nine-thirty.

'Thanks, by the way,' the journalist shouted. 'Thanks for nothing.' But Underwood had gone.

8

There was a narrow side alley next to the cottage, sandwiched between the kitchen wall and the high wooden garden fence. Underwood edged around to the back of the house, realizing again that he had to lose some weight. He was struck by the garden's simplicity: it was virtually all lawn and flower beds. Low maintenance. Lucy Harrington was obviously a reluctant gardener.

All of the back windows were intact and shut. There were no obvious signs of entry. The back door was locked from the inside. He thought for a moment. Lucy Harrington's killer had surprised her upstairs. He had almost certainly been inside the house when she'd arrived. He hadn't used the windows or the front door. There was no other way into the house: he had to have used the back door. But it was locked. What did that actually prove? Only that the killer didn't leave that way. Maybe he found another key somewhere. Underwood looked around for a loose paving stone or a brick under which Lucy Harrington might have concealed a spare key. He saw nothing obvious. He rejected the idea. A single woman living alone was unlikely to leave keys lying around outside. He looked again at the back door.

It was heavy and needed repainting. There was a single large glass pane in the door. The house was set slightly higher than garden level and Underwood climbed the three concrete steps. He studied them carefully. Rain would have washed away any residual mud from the killer's shoes. In any case, he hadn't seen any mud inside the house. He crouched on the top step, noting the crack between the bottom of the door and the kitchen floor. Something caught his eye. Wedged against the foot of the door frame was a tiny purple flower petal. Was it significant? Doubtful. Underwood thought of his own house: all sorts of crap got stuck under doorways, especially those that backed onto gardens. Still, it was something. He looked down the line of the fence at the colourless flower beds; it hadn't come from there. He picked the petal up between his thumb and forefinger and bagged it.

'Any thoughts, sir?' Dexter emerged effortlessly from the narrow alleyway.

'Assuming she didn't let him in the front door, and I don't believe she did, he had to come in through here. But the door's locked. Have you got a pencil?'

Dexter handed over one of her small notebook pencils. She always carried two. Underwood took it and forced it into the keyhole. The space was tight and he was concerned that the pencil might snap. After a moment of awkward fumbling he managed to wedge the end under the tip of the key. At the third attempt, Underwood managed to lever it from the socket. There was a soft clunk on the other side of the door as the key fell to the floor; just as it had ten hours previously.

'Bingo,' said Underwood.

'That's an old trick, sir.' Dexter was unimpressed. 'Why not just break a window? There'd be less risk of cocking up.'

'But more risk of her noticing it when she got home. He planned all this very carefully. He wanted to be in the house waiting for her. He wanted her to come upstairs. There's a good chance that if she'd come in and seen a broken window she'd have twigged that something was up.'

'Makes sense.' Dexter was annoyed she hadn't thought of

that. Something else was troubling her. 'How did he know she lived here? Maybe he knew her; a boyfriend or someone she'd met.'

'You think a jealous boyfriend would bother to hack her eye out?' Underwood said dismissively. 'Or write all that rubbish up on the wall?'

'Why not? He might be trying to confuse us.' Dexter looked around at the small cluster of houses. 'I mean, if he didn't know her, it's not an obvious place to come looking, is it? Way out here in the arsehole of beyond.'

Underwood felt instinctively that the killer hadn't known Lucy Harrington personally. His rational mind sought for a reason. It was the timing. If he had known her, Underwood reasoned, her killer could have knocked on the front door whenever he wanted and strolled right in. Why wait until a night when everyone in New Bolden knew that Lucy Harrington would be out somewhere else and force an entry? *Everyone in New Bolden.* The thought niggled at him.

'There was a newspaper article about her recently, wasn't there?' he asked.

'Lots. All the local rags ran a feature on her winning that medal. Big news for a tinpot town like New Bolden.' There was still something of the cockney snob about Dexter, Underwood thought to himself.

'Not as big as this, though,' he said.

'The reception was well publicized,' Dexter continued. 'Anyone in New Bolden who can read would know that Lucy Harrington was going to be in the Civic Hall at eight p.m. So that narrows it down to you, me and the mayor.'

'Behave.'

'Sorry, guv, but I don't see what you're getting at.'

'I don't think he knew her. There's something else going on here. He's got some kind of fucked-up agenda. I think he saw a newspaper article, got horny about it and started planning. He's very thorough. Leaves nothing to chance. Still, neither should we, I suppose. Put together a list of her friends and family. People she knew socially, people she trained with.' It sounded pathetic. Underwood knew it would be a waste of time. He looked out at the dense clumps of trees, darkly entangled beyond the back fence. Dexter read his mind.

'There are footpaths through the woods, aren't there?' she said. 'Some lead out to London Road, some don't go anywhere at all and some lead on to Hartfield Road. I wouldn't fancy finding my way through there in the dark. You think he came in that way?'

Underwood had started to walk across the lawn, his eyes fixed on the grass. 'I certainly think he left that way. Do you remember that article we all got from the police shrink about mental maps and criminal activity?'

'Vaguely.' She looked left into the near distance as she always did when retrieving information from her memory. 'It was about how individuals make their own mind maps of areas where they live. A place looks different based on your own perspective.' She was warming up as the article came back to her. 'So, if you ask a Londoner to draw a map of London, they'll put their own locality nearer the centre of the map than it should be and make the Thames look straight instead of bendy because as far as they're concerned it is.'

'Something like that. Most rape cases occur within five miles of the offender's home.'

'This isn't a rape, as far as we know.'

'No. But how would you know about these woods and pathways . . .'

'Unless you were local.' Dexter finished the sentence.

They looked more closely at the fence. There was a small amount of blood, a streak at the corner. Underwood gestured toward it. 'He came out over here and into the woods. Somehow he knew where she lived. He knew she was going out at eight p.m. and wasn't going to be back quickly. That gives him bags of time of to muck about with the back door, get inside and then do whatever it is he does to prepare himself.'

'Put her knickers on and dance about, probably.'

'Get the uniform plods to do a sweep of the paths behind the house. Our boy might have dropped something on the way out. I think that's unlikely but it was dark and he was in a hurry.

22

We'll need to find out where these paths emerge onto London Road and Hartfield Road. Check for places he might have parked a car. Someone might have seen something.' Underwood was short of breath. The cold air dug at his chest again. He coughed painfully, covering his mouth with cupped hands. His eyes filled with water. Dexter watched him closely for a moment before tactfully withdrawing to the house. Underwood hacked again. This time he had blood on his hands. It wasn't Lucy Harrington's.

9

Southwell College, Cambridge meant different things to different people. To Shelley, it had been a 'medieval mediocrity'. To tourists, its sprawling gardens and curious chapel made it a convenient diversion en route to The Copper Kettle. To its undergraduates, it was a kind of baroque holiday camp. To Dr Heather Stussman it meant recognition. Or, at least, a decisive step towards it.

She cast her gaze around the ancient Combination Room, where the Fellows of the College took their meals. Even now, at lunchtime, the room seemed dark and oppressive. The steward had nurtured a raging fire in the sculpted stone fireplace that now threw strange shadows against the oak-panelled walls. Stussman was too close to the fire for her liking and was starting to get uncomfortably warm beneath her academic robes. The food was extremely rich and Stussman could feel her heart racing. The gloomy oil portraits of previous college masters stared down disapprovingly at her. Southwell only had one other female Fellow, a particle physicist, and she appeared so infrequently that Stussman assumed that the resident misogynists had shooed her off. The male Fellows treated her with a mixture of disdain and a kind of horrified curiosity. Still, she had expected a degree of hostility.

'Who are you?' the wolf-eyed Professor Dixon boomed at her from across the table, peering over his half-glasses.

'Heather Stussman. We met last week, Professor Dixon, at the Master's drinks.'

Dixon seemed surprised. 'What do you think of our Master?' he asked.

'I found him delightful,' Stussman replied. 'He has been very helpful to me.'

'Of course, he's a raging queen, you know,' Dixon opined learnedly. 'A terrible poof. I only voted for him out of a misplaced sense of irony. Sadly, so did everybody else and now we're stuck with the old fraud.'

Stussman was aware that another fellow, Dr McKensie, was eyeing her as he chewed his *noisettes de chevreuil Cumberland*. He reminded her of a hyena coveting a corpse.

'You're the new English Literature research Fellow, aren't you? The woman,' he asked between delicate mouthfuls.

'That's right.'

'Extraordinary world, isn't it, Roger,' he said to Dixon, 'that we should have an American researching English Literature?'

'I guess the world is moving on. We're no longer divided by the same language,' Stussman said quietly. Her collar felt uncomfortably tight.

'Do you know what we call a female Fellow here?' McKensie beamed. Stussman could feel the hyenas closing in around her. Other fellows were starting to tune in to their conversation.

'I'm afraid not.'

'A fellatio!' McKensie squawked triumphantly. There was a ripple of laughter. Even Stussman managed a smile.

'That should be pronounced fell-ah-tee-oh,' she responded. 'But maybe you are unfamiliar with the concept.'

'Whereas you, clearly, are not.'

'What exactly is your speciality?' asked Dixon. He was still confused.

'The metaphysical poets – John Donne in particular.' Stussman put her fork down. She was not enjoying her first formal lunch.

'Your book proved rather controversial,' said McKensie.

'You can't make an omelette without breaking a few eggs,' she said, trying to be cheerful. The blank expressions deflated her. She continued, 'I'm surprised you've read it, Dr McKensie.'

McKensie was sprinkling salt onto his sautéed vegetables. He looked horrified. 'Oh, Lord. Not all of it. I made it to chapter three.'

'What did you think?' It was a dumb question. She regretted it immediately.

'I thought your naivety was endearing.' Conversation over. McKensie turned away, no doubt relishing the tang of his own acidity. Stussman fumed inwardly, attempting to console herself with the knowledge that these terrible people were only a means to an end. Cambridge still carried more academic clout on a CV than did the University of Wisconsin – for the time being, anyway. She retreated mentally into the subject matter of her forthcoming lecture series, Donne's songs and sonnets. 'The back of your mind is a good place to hide,' her father had once told her, 'but the back of a poet's is better.' *Batter my heart, three person'd God / As yet but knocke, breathe, shine and seeke to end / Your force, to break, blowe, burn and make me new.* Not for the first time she marvelled at Donne's verbal dexterity and manipulation of metre. She returned to her *noisettes de chevreuil Cumberland*.

10

Dexter set up the Incident Room with her characteristic speed and accuracy. Her ability to focus was almost frightening to Underwood. All he had over her was experience, and every day Dexter was eating into that advantage. Underwood knew that it wouldn't be long before she wanted to move on; before she realized he was holding her back. He wondered if Julia felt the same. Maybe he was paranoid. He was certainly scared. Scared of being alone. Underwood had never been alone before. He knew he would be soon: alone with himself.

The room was filling rapidly. Dexter had co-opted three

detective constables to work with Harrison and herself on the house-to-house enquiries and two secretaries to work on the phones and the cross-referencing of information. A large white board had been put up at one end of the room. Dexter had pinned on it a picture of Lucy Harrington – obtained from the girl's parents in Peterborough – next to the official crime-scene photographs. She always did this in a murder case. She liked people to remember that the victim was a person, not just a name or a set of horrific photographs. It was smart psychology but the juxtaposition made Underwood uncomfortable. Dexter had also attached cut-outs of recent newspaper articles about Harrington's gold medal. Above them was a large blue paper sheet detailing the known facts of the case. Underwood and Leach were standing in the centre of the semicircle of plastic desks. There was a polite white noise of chatter. Marty Farrell, one of the scene-of-crime officers, was leaning back against a radiator. He offered Dexter a cigarette. She refused.

Underwood was finding it increasingly difficult to order his mind. Julia infected his every thought like a virus. Drawing energy from some hidden reserve, he eventually addressed the room.

'Let's get started. Lucy Harrington, twenty-six years old, single. Famous swimmer and local celebrity. She leaves a reception at the Civic Hall last night at around eleven o'clock. Drives home. It takes about fifteen minutes, assuming she didn't stop anywhere. We don't think she did.

'Once inside the house she was attacked from behind and killed. The body was found in her bathroom this morning after a tip-off, presumably from the killer, was received by a reporter at the *New Bolden Echo*.

'I have asked Sergeant Dexter to put together a list of Harrington's family and acquaintances. However, this is a particularly unusual assault: almost ritualistic in certain aspects. We should consider the possibility that we might have a serial murderer on our patch.' Underwood nodded at Leach who cleared his throat and began his report.

'Post-mortem has confirmed that time of death was sometime between eleven last night and one o'clock this morning. I'm afraid I can't be much more accurate. The body and clothes were partially immersed in cold water. Cause of death was massive trauma to the brain following at least two sharp blows to the back of the skull.'

He held up a grisly picture of the back of Lucy Harrington's head. 'The occipital bone was impacted here, pretty much on the line of the lambdoidal suture. The diameter of the wound was approximately two inches. I would guess that the murder weapon was a steel hammer, a metal pipe or something very similar. Death would have been almost instantaneous. Considering what happened next we should be thankful for small mercies, I suppose.

'After inflicting these blows, the killer turned the body over and surgically removed the victim's left eye. This would have taken some time.' Leach brushed the sweat from his brow as he continued. 'He tried to do it scientifically at first but eventually resorted to brute force. I would guess one to two hours. Presumably after he had completed the operation, the killer turned on both bath taps and flooded the room. The search for forensic evidence is ongoing, but we don't hold out much hope.'

A hand went up. DC Jensen: she was blonde and attractive. Heads turned quickly.

'Was there any sexual interference, sir?' she asked Underwood.

'Apparently not,' he replied.

'The victim was found fully clothed and there does not appear to have been any sexual violation. We can't find any bite marks, semen or saliva residues from the killer. Although I should point out that the water prevents us from making any final conclusions,' Leach added.

Underwood took over again. 'There are woods at the back of the property. My guess is that the killer came out the front door and made off through the back garden, climbed the fence (there are traces of Lucy's blood on it) and legged it through the woods.'

He paused for breath. 'Uniform are sweeping the woods but as yet they've drawn a blank.' He moved to a large map of the area that Dexter had pinned to the board at the far end of the room. 'The paths through the woods end at these points.' He gestured at the five red stars on the map. 'Three come out on London Road and two on Hartfield Road, here and here. If he drove – and bearing in mind that he was covered in blood afterwards, I think he had to – then he must have parked near one of these locations. I want you to check with the locals, see if anyone saw a car or a van parked nearby.'

DS Harrison had been carefully making notes, his face furrowed with ever-deepening lines of confusion. He looked up at Underwood. 'Guv, I just can't get a handle on this. What's his motive? It's clearly not a burglary gone pear-shaped. It's not a sexual assault, as far as we know. If he just wanted to kill her – you know, like a domestic gone haywire or something – then there are much easier ways to do it. And why did he screw with her eye? The Doc said that takes time. Time means risk. He must have really wanted it.'

'A souvenir,' Dexter suggested. 'I've read that some of these sick bastards like to take something that belonged to the victim. So they can relive the event afterwards.'

Harrison was unconvinced. 'Yeah, but why not a lock of hair or some of her clothes? Much easier and far less messy. I think this guy has a seriously twisted imagination. I reckon he's going to do it again.'

Underwood nodded. 'The eye obviously has some special significance for him. The killer also wrote some text on the bathroom wall with some of the victim's blood. Have we figured out what it is yet, Dex?'

'Not yet, sir.' She flipped open her notebook and read aloud: 'Draw not up seas, to drowne me in thy spheare.'

'Water,' said Harrison. 'He flooded the place, didn't he? Maybe it wasn't just to corrupt the crime scene. To drowne me in thy spheare. "Spheare" could mean eye. Draw not up water to drown me in your eyes. Don't drown me with your tears. Sounds like a love song.'

The image of the blood-blackened eye socket and the filthy, thick water flashed across Underwood's mind. Eyes. Water. Blood. Harrison had made a connection of sorts. It was something. They were up and running.

'Dex, get Harrison to help you find out where that text comes from.' Dexter nodded and shot a dark look at Harrison. She was irritated that he had made a connection she had missed. Underwood's request implied that Harrison was more likely to source the text than she was. That rankled. However, now that the savage peculiarities of the murder had become clearer to her, she did agree with Harrison on one thing: this was just the beginning.

11

Heather Stussman left her rooms in Southwell College's Osbourne Court and headed for the porter's lodge. It was late afternoon. The interminable East Anglian rain had finally passed. Sunlight was starting to drizzle through the fragmenting grey clouds, glinting in the large puddles of rainwater that had gathered in the corner of the Court. The rain had scared off the tourists and the old college was wonderfully quiet. The air was clean and sharp like newly cut glass: maybe things were starting to look up.

Mr Johnson (the head porter) nodded curtly as Stussman entered the lodge. He didn't speak. Presumably he was as unimpressed with her as McKensie and Dixon had been at lunch. Her pigeonhole was crammed with mail: university flyers, adverts for music recitals, a letter from her publisher, two personal letters – one from her mother in America and another written in a spidery hand she did not recognize. She stuffed the wedge of paper into her rucksack and headed out of the lodge up Trumpington Street. She turned left at the Silver Street junction and crossed the river over Silver Street Bridge, catching a waft of beer from The Anchor on her way.

Her lecture series, 'Reconstructing Donne', was based on her recent book. Stussman had set about the academic orthodoxy on the Metaphysical Poets with a ferocity she was beginning to regret. The *New York Times Book Review* had pretty much caught the critical response: 'Stussman's attack on poststructuralism is memorable more for its vigour than its rigour.' The others weren't much better. 'Try to avoid meeting Dr Stussman down an intellectual dark alley,' warned the *Washington Post*: 'her vitriol is fatal at ten paces.'

Both of these reviews were better than the one in the *Sunday Telegraph*, which had described her as 'bereft of empathy, temptingly putdownable and probably certifiable'. The controversy had sold more books than she had ever expected. Her lecture classes were extremely well attended. However, she had clearly got the bird from the grey-hairs at the English Faculty who had given her the highly unpopular five p.m. lecture slot. Perhaps she was being paranoid. She doubted it.

The faculty site at Cambridge was a spectacular architectural horror. The dismal cluster of buildings resembled an old Eastern Bloc military hospital. The lecture rooms were no better. They were small, badly ventilated and uncomfortable. Stussman longed for the airy auditorium at the University of Wisconsin, with its remote-control slide projector and sound system. Still, at least the room was full and not many lecturers could claim that distinction. She noticed that for the second week running her audience was mostly male. Next time she would wear trousers.

'Last week, we talked about the intellectual context of metaphysical poetry. We talked about its associations with the religious uncertainties of the sixteenth and early seventeenth centuries and with the rise of humanist philosophy during the Renaissance. Today, I'd like to consider the anatomy of metaphysical poetry. In particular, the intellectual and stylistic devices deployed by the poets to force home their points. If we accept the view that many of these pieces were composed for a highly specific coterie audience, then we need to understand what that audience was looking for. Foremost among the literary devices used was the "conceit". Who can explain that to us?' There was a shuffling of feet and a couple of nervous coughs. She had expected this. British students were notoriously taciturn. She pointed at a shaggy student in the front row who seemed to be

30

fixated on her ankles. 'How about you?' He jumped slightly and sat up in his chair.

'Well, a conceit is a kind of metaphor. A clever image used to make an argumentative point.'

'Good. A conceit is a metaphor or simile that appears at first glance to be unusual, improbable or even shocking. However, as the poet develops the image, the reader is gradually persuaded of its intellectual value.' She heard a few students starting to scribble notes. The sound was always rewarding. *Screw the New York Times Book Review.* 'John Donne famously compares a humble flea with a marriage bed. He is trying to seduce a woman and bitterly complains that because the flea has sucked his blood and his lover's it has enjoyed a closer intimacy with her than he has.' More scribbling. She was beginning to relax. Next week she would try making a joke.

It was dark when Stussman left the Faculty. The reflected lights of Queen's College wobbled brightly in the black Cam as she retraced her steps across Silver Street Bridge. There was a lot of traffic in Cambridge, far more than the small town deserved, and Stussman was soaked with spray from the roadside puddles by the time she arrived at her rooms. She could hear her phone trilling sharply behind the door. She fumbled with the key and stepped quickly inside, making it to her cluttered desk just in time.

'Heather Stussman.' There was a faint crackle of electricity. Then she heard the voice that would come to haunt the silent spaces of her existence.

'Your book is promising.'

'Pardon?'

'The newspapers have mistaken your originality for careless-ness. Sadly, your obsession with logical clarity seems to have dulled your empathetic reflexes.'

'I'm sorry. Who is this?'

'Did you receive my letter?'

'If you don't tell me your name, I won't know if your letter arrived or not.'

'It would have arrived this morning,' the voice said simply.

Stussman paused. This was getting weird. Her mind chewed over the alternatives: a practical joke, maybe. It was probably Mark, an ex-boyfriend from Wisconsin now researching Milton in Edinburgh. He could do all sorts of funny accents. She reached into her rucksack and pulled out the envelope, still unopened, that she had received earlier in the day. She wedged the phone between her right cheek and her collarbone and tore the envelope open. Inside was a neatly folded piece of writing paper.

'What does the letter contain?' said Crowan Frayne.

'A line of poetry.'

'You recognize it, of course?'

'Is this some kind of joke? If that's you, Mark, I'm going to kick your ass.'

'Tell me.' The voice was insistent. Stussman could feel the frustration rising within her.

'It's a fragment from "A Valediction: Of Weeping" by John Donne.'

'You are familiar with it?'

'It's all in the book, Buster – maybe you should read it more closely.'

'I read it voraciously,' Frayne said. 'I am a poet. Watch the evening news.'

'Who *is* this?' Stussman's patience had never been her strongest feature and now it evaporated completely in the sudden heat of annoyance. Whoever this was, it wasn't Mark.

'Explain it to the police.'

The line went dead. Stussman slammed the phone down angrily and closed the door to her rooms. It was probably some student trying to freak her out. Or one of McKensie's cronies. She looked out of her small window across the dimly lit courts of Southwell College and its braying cabals of students. Car headlights crawled interminably up Trumpington Street as the early-evening rush hour tightened its grip on the ancient city.

Heather Stussman felt very alone.

12

Underwood sat at a desk in the Incident Room. A list of Lucy Harrington's known friends and local acquaintances lay in front of him. Harrington's parents had managed to provide most of the names that afternoon before heading back to Peterborough. None of the names struck him as particularly promising. Most of the people they belonged to were female and none had criminal records. Lucy Harrington was a serious-minded athlete and her social circle was limited, consisting mainly of her fellow swimmers. Underwood felt that the curious and savage circumstances of the case would require more complex treatment. They were hunting a predator.

Dexter was opposite him, frantically writing a crime-scene report. She had brought in an electric lamp from home and Underwood found its hard white light hypnotic. He was a rabbit in Dexter's headlights. Now she was tiring him out and he was finding it hard to concentrate. A brief conversation with Julia ten minutes previously had done nothing to improve his mood. She was apparently going to the cinema with her sister.

Underwood didn't believe her. His stomach flipped again. He had to find out what was going on. He had learned to beware the banal, suspect the plausible. His wife was a good liar: too good, in fact. Underwood dealt with liars all the time. He recognized the symptoms.

'Have you got a minute, sir?' DC Jensen was standing at his side. Dexter tensed visibly. Underwood wondered for a second if his sergeant was the jealous type. He crushed the thought. *Jealous of what, exactly? Don't flatter yourself, pal.*

'We are continuing the house-to-house, sir. Nothing as yet. We're going to work up one of those "Did you see anything?" major-incident posters for motorists and put them up on Hart-field Road,' Jensen said.

'And London Road.' Dexter shot across Jensen's bows without looking up. Jensen ignored the detective sergeant and continued.

'Harrison and I have been going through the newspaper articles that were printed after she won her medal.'

Dexter swore under her breath. She had been planning to do that herself.

'Good,' said Underwood. 'What have you got?'

'There's an article in the *Echo*, sir,' Jensen waved the paper in front of him, 'Can I read you a section?'

'Go ahead.'

'It's just one paragraph, actually.' Jensen sat on the edge of Dexter's desk and read aloud. ' "Lucy Harrington returned home today after a triumphant Commonwealth Games. Lucy won the hundred-metre freestyle in a new European record time, narrowly defeating Australian world champion Suzy Baker-Douglas. Lucy, of Hartfield Road, Fawley will be guest of honour at a Civic Reception on December 9th. Tickets available from the Town Hall." '

'So?' Dexter put her pen down firmly. 'I imagine they all say much the same thing.'

'They don't, actually.' Jensen smiled, ever so sweetly. 'This is the only one that says where she lives.'

'It doesn't give her address, though. Hartfield Road goes on for miles. She lived in a cul-de-sac off the main road anyway,' said Dexter dismissively. 'There's no mention of that.'

Underwood shook his head. He was getting the point. 'Think about it. Hartfield Road, Fawley.' He got up and walked over to the map board. 'Fawley isn't a village or a town. The area only has that name because of Fawley Wood.' He pointed at the green smudge on the map that represented the woodland behind Lucy Harrington's house. 'The implication of the article is that Harrington lived somewhere along the Hartfield Road as it cuts through the wood. If you look, there are only two groups of houses in this section of the map: Fawley Close and Sherling Drive. It wouldn't have taken our man long to figure out which one she lived in.'

Dexter thought for a second. 'Who wrote the article?'

Jensen checked. 'George Gardiner.'

'That's the journo the killer called this morning,' Dexter said.

'If the killer read the *Echo* then he's almost certainly local. It's delivered through the letter box.'

'Well done, Jensen.' Underwood watched the detective constable as she walked away. The double helix of desire and despair twisted darkly inside him. He tried to crush it. 'Dex. We should pull up records of people arrested for burglaries in the county over the last five years. The way our boy gained access to the house suggests to me that he's done it before. If he's local, he might already be in our system.'

'Right. That'll be a long list,' she said tightly.

'What's up, Dex? Jensen gets your hackles up, doesn't she?' Underwood asked.

'Off the record?'

'Always.'

'Jensen is a slag. She screws around. She thinks she knows it all. She's a bright girl but you should see her off duty – ' Dexter was warming to her theme ' – staggering around the pubs with a fag in one hand and a double gin in the other.'

'Doesn't make her a bad person.'

'It makes her a bad *police* person. You don't become one of the lads by screwing them. The way she behaves affects the way the other coppers look at me.'

'That's your imagination.'

'When I was a uniform, back in London, I was sent to Coventry by my entire relief because I wouldn't sleep with any of them. That's the mentality we have to deal with. I decided that if I was going to be a serious copper, then I should behave like one. If a bloke slags around he's a hero. If a girl slags around, she wrecks her own reputation and makes life twice as hard for the rest of us.'

Underwood went quiet. He thought of Julia again: cold and uninterested. Screwing another man and enjoying it. Laughing at him. He was angry that somehow the thought excited him: as if it had injected life into their dead sexuality. Dexter sensed her boss's change of mood and switched the subject. She was learning how to play him.

'This case, sir. Have you ever seen anything like this before?'

'Not really.' Underwood stood and pulled his jacket from the back of his chair. 'But I've got the feeling that it's going to be a long winter.'

Dexter watched him leave. They were both flying blind. They would have to learn together.

13

The railway line cuts into the northern suburbs of New Bolden, through the city's new retail and industrial parks and then on towards Parkway station. The line has become much busier in recent years, following New Bolden's growth both as a commuter station and as a business-development zone. A number of software and logistics companies have sprung up in the city, taking advantage of the new sites and financial incentives that the city council has made available. Their hi-tech, smoky glass buildings back onto the railway line, reflecting the tired faces of rail passengers as the crowded commuter trains for London flash past.

The line is old and unsuited to the increase in traffic volume. The fencing is rusted and broken in places. At some points, it has ceased to exist altogether. Sometimes, at the weekends or during school holidays, children crouch in the overgrown hedgerows and hurl stones at trains as they accelerate out of New Bolden.

Tonight, however, the area is deserted apart from a cluster of swallows huddling together for warmth on a steel pylon and Crowan Frayne who walks in the centre of the southbound track. It is almost nine p.m.

This section of track is long and straight. He can see two miles in both directions. He has plenty of warning, plenty of time to avoid oncoming trains. There is a small risk that he might encounter maintenance staff working on the track but he is unconcerned. Granite splinters crunch hard underfoot. Crowan Frayne stares ahead. There is blackness on either side.

Blackness above. Only the path ahead is lit, the rails stretching endlessly to the horizon. He has walked three miles from his house and is nearing his destination. He has decided not to drive. His car is not distinctive but he does not wish to attract attention. Eyes are everywhere. Like the dead.

New Bolden Cemetery sits next to the main line. It is a huge sprawling place that predates the new town. Frayne finds its proximity to the railway unfortunate. He thinks of the dead jarring in the ground with every express train; two trains an hour in both directions. Fifteen minutes of blissful oblivion between each disturbance. There is a splintering fence half swallowed by hedgerow. He is over it quickly and inside. The cemetery is dark and vast. There are trees that seem to ache with cold. Most of the graves are terribly overgrown. Tall, unkempt grass obscures the inscriptions on many of the headstones.

Crowan Frayne moves like a ghost along the dark pathways. He is not afraid. He is energized by the concentration of nature. There are elemental forces focused here: disease, war, fire, flood, life, birth, death. He feels a strange energy, as if the numberless infinities of the dead have risen and surged up within him. There is a quieting as he moves deeper inside. Crowan Frayne looks at the star-strewn sky. He is familiar with the constellations and the bright spots of planets. He listens for the harmonies. In this place he can sometimes hear the Harmoniae Mundorum: the harmonies of the planets.

He is familiar with the writings of Pythagoras and Aristotle. He is attracted to the idea that each of the planets produces a particular musical note determined by its distance from the Earth. This celestial music is the most beautiful sound imaginable and is so exquisite, so rarefied, that is beyond the comprehension of ordinary mortals. He has explored the Pythagorean notion of musical intervals expressed as simple numerical ratios of the first four integers: octave 2:1, fifth 3:2, fourth 4:3. In this context, the relative distance between the planets corresponds to a musical interval.

Frayne remembers Kepler's attempts to 'erect the magnificent edifice of the harmonic system' and one occasion attempted to recreate the sound himself. He spent considerable time translat-

ing the distances of the various planets from the sun into musical intervals that could be applied to a piano keyboard. He applied the same logic to the largest asteroids in the Solar System – Ceres, Pallas, Juno and Vesta – and even tried to work in variables such as orbital velocity that were not available to Kepler in the seventeenth century. In a fury of excitement he transcribed the notes into a repeating musical pattern and recorded it. The result was frustratingly discordant: a leaping, falling cacophony. He has blamed the failure on mathematical miscalculations and is determined to correct his errors. However, behind the silences of this place, he sometimes hears snatches of the Musica Mundi: brief, distant but heartbreakingly beautiful.

His grandmother's grave is at the far side of the cemetery. It is one of the newer plots. The area is not yet overgrown but Crowan Frayne tears any weeds from the ground. He eats the colourful ones. He is a regular visitor. The headstone is black, marbled and inscripted with gold text. 'Violet Frayne 1908–1999, beloved mother and grandmother: One short sleep past, we wake eternally, and death shall be no more. Death, thou shalt die.' Crowan Frayne chose the inscription himself.

He speaks to his grandmother for a while, sitting squat on the cold earth. As is his habit, he recites two or three of her favourite poems from memory and tells her how his own studies are progressing. He can feel her reaching out for him and drives his hand into the damp soil as deeply as possible. The music is much louder now and its colossal beauty wells up within him, tearing at his soul. He begins to cry. He can hear Violet's voice – encouraging and learned – floating between the notes of time and space. He will be with her soon.

A train clatters behind him as Crowan Frayne smoothes the soil that he has disturbed. An hour has passed. It is time to leave. He has lots to plan: a thousand variables to pitch and sound. He steps over another grave as he leaves. He does not allow himself to read the headstone. He tries to beat away the bad memories that rise from the soil and scratch at his ankles.

14

Underwood had left the station and driven to the end of his own road. He had a clear view of the front door of his house but remained in the car. He waited. There was a debate on Radio Four about the ethics of genetic engineering. He listened without hearing. Shortly after nine a minicab drew up at his house and Julia came out. He couldn't make out what she was wearing but he saw her best necklace sparkle briefly against the porch light. The minicab drove off and indicated left at the end of the street. Underwood thought for a second. He felt curiously excited by the experience. He started his engine and followed.

He tried to rationalize his feelings. He felt a degree of guilt, even shame that he had fallen so far; that he doubted his own wife's word. However, he felt impelled by the inherent justice of his cause. This would settle the facts of the matter. The rest was about conscience and he knew he could handle that. The cab's lights glowed ahead of him. He kept a reasonable distance but was not uncomfortable. He knew Julia wouldn't be expecting a tail.

The cab turned towards New Bolden town centre; Underwood knew that the cinema was in Argyll Street. There was a one-way system so they would have to turn left at the end. On cue, the cab indicated and swung into the line of traffic. Underwood held back; two cars behind them. Eventually the cinema loomed brightly ahead and the cab pulled up in front of the foyer. Underwood quickly veered into a side road. He pulled up with a decent view of the entrance to the cinema. Julia climbed out of the cab and rushed inside. Underwood sat back in his seat, suddenly aware that his shirt was soaked with sweat. So she had been telling the truth. His heart sank slightly. He was uncertain whether to feel ashamed or relieved, both or neither.

He started the engine and was about to drive off when Julia emerged from the front of the cinema and jumped back into the cab. The car promptly leapt out in to the traffic and drove off.

Underwood was shocked. He began to feel sick and flattened the accelerator, breaking into the stream of cars to a raucous cacophony of hoots and shrieking tyres. He closed on the minicab. The driver had moved into the right-hand lane of the dual carriageway. Underwood's mind was working rapidly, trying to calculate possible destinations and explanations. Maybe Julia's sister hadn't turned up and she was going to collect her. But Sarah lived at the southern end of town and they were heading north-east. What was up there? Nothing, really. It was a wealthy residential area: detached houses and Land Rover Freelanders.

The traffic melted away as the two cars left the centre of town. Underwood was careful to hold back. Wide leafy avenues replaced the dual carriageways and Underwood realized that they were only a mile or two from Fawley Woods. He thought of Lucy Harrington: torn up on a mortuary slab. He should be hunting her killer, not checking up on his wife.

Fuck Julia for making me do this: creeping about, degrading myself. She has hammered me into something pathetic.

The cab pulled up about one hundred metres ahead. Underwood stopped outside a large mock-Tudor house. It was tasteless in its mockery. The double garage smirked at him. He watched his wife step out of the cab. She paid the driver and then, without waiting for change, scrunched up the expensive-looking gravel driveway. This time, the cab drove away.

Underwood stepped out of his car and walked briskly up the other side of the street. He was careful to stay in darkness all the way. The trees provided a shadowy camouflage against the street lights. He stopped opposite the house in time to see Julia ring the doorbell. Underwood's chest was burning but he dared not cough. Instead, he stared in morbid fascination. The door opened. A man appeared. He quickly stooped to gather Julia in a vast hug and drew her inside. The door shut. Underwood was horrified, his darkest fears confirmed. Should he confront them, knock on the door and demand to see his wife? Was she in danger? Would he have to fight for her? Could he be bothered to fight for someone who clearly no longer loved him? No. There were other ways. At least he had the advantage now. The

40

endgame was truly under way. He stepped out of the shadows and crossed the road. There was a blue BMW in the driveway. He took out his notebook and wrote down the registration.

A light came on upstairs. Underwood started and was sick into the road as terrible imaginings flooded his mind. When he thought that they might overwhelm him, he coughed the bile from his throat and headed back to his car. Why couldn't he cry? He felt that he should. He now knew for sure that his marriage was over. That the years he and Julia had shared had been utterly meaningless. All he felt was emptiness and a hot spark of rage. Underwood unlocked his car and climbed inside. He stared into the rear-view mirror.

Lucy Harrington's mutilated face gaped back at him.

15

At roughly the same moment, Dexter turned along Fawley Close and parked. Three of the four cottages had their lights on. Only Lucy Harrington's remained shrouded in darkness. The police cordon was still in place around the house, which had been locked and sealed.

Dexter had no plans to go inside. Her mind had been working overtime since Jensen had showed them the newspaper article that had given general details of where Lucy Harrington lived. As Underwood had said, there were two roads in the area that fitted the information given by the article: Sherling Drive and Fawley Close. Dexter tried to imagine herself in the killer's position. 'I have rough information about where my target lives but nothing specific. I know she lives in one of two roads but I need to find out which road and then which house. Lucy Harrington is not in the phone book.' Dexter looked again at the map. Sherling Drive had two entrances and ten houses. Fawley Close had only one entrance and four cottages. 'I have a fifty-fifty chance but one road is much easier to watch than the other. I would choose Fawley Close first because if she lived there I could find her quickly. If she didn't, I could rapidly eliminate the four houses.'

The logic was compelling and, on a whim, Dexter had driven to Lucy Harrington's house. It was getting late. There were no street lights and she had only the lights from the houses and her torch to guide her. She started at the front door of the cottage and looked across the entrance to the cul-de-sac at the woodland beyond. 'If I was watching this road,' she thought, 'where would I hide? I need a good view in both directions, I need to be able to see the front doors of all four houses.' She walked out onto the roadway. She stood at the centre of the rough semicircle formed by the four houses, directly facing Hartfield Road and the woods beyond it. 'Our man knows the woods.' She remembered – she was a little afraid now – that serial killers often returned to the scene of the crime to relive the fantasy. The trees looked vast and ominous. Woods had always made her uneasy. Still, in for a penny . . .

She crossed Hartfield Road and stood at the fencing that marked the edge of the woods. There was a stile leading to a public footpath about fifty yards down to the right. She discounted the area next to it. The killer would have wanted to steer clear of that. She looked to her left. The hedgerow was pretty dense but he could have crawled in anywhere. She climbed over the fence. The cold mud squished over her work shoes.

'Bollocks.'

She cursed the countryside for the thousandth time and looked at the entrance to Fawley Close. She suddenly felt vulnerable with the vast black expanse of woodland behind her. Maybe this hadn't been such a good idea.

Dexter had had a nightmare when she'd been a child and it had stayed with her. She was running in a field that had become a wood. The woods became darker and darker as she ran further in. The trees were high, so high she couldn't see the tops. The bark was rotting and twisted. The woods became an abomination. Insects snapped at her feet, the ground became gluey and she couldn't run. Then she heard it. A terrible noise behind her: pushing trees aside, screaming and grunting. She dared not look round but she could feel her pursuer closing in. She threw herself at a tree and began to climb as fast as she could. The branches and bark splintered in her hands and she slipped as she scrambled upwards. The thing was behind her, snapping at her ankles – she could feel its breath against her skin. Then, as she finally reached the top of the tree, she looked down to see the hellish creature below her – and she fell. Smashing through the branches, rushing ever faster towards the ground.

Then she had woken up.

She was wide awake now, though. Dexter shone her torch around her. Nothing. From where she was standing she could see only two of the cottages. That was no good. She moved carefully along the line of the fence, stumbling slightly on the uneven ground. A third cottage came into view. She pushed back a sapling branch and sidestepped a tree stump. Finally, the dark shadow of Lucy Harrington's home appeared.

It seemed as good a place to hide as any. Dexter shone her torch at the ground. Twigs, leaves, mud. Ahead of her and slightly to the right was a small clump of hedgerow, pressed up against the wooden fencing. Some of the branches had been broken away and lay on top of the mud. She moved towards them.

A large beech tree loomed above her, a thick root clawing into the soil next to the hedgerow. She leaned against the tree. The bark was damp and rough. It felt cold and dirty against her skin. Dexter looked more closely at the root. It was twisted and pock-marked with age. Rainwater had pooled darkly at a point where the root divided in two. She flashed the torch at it; there were tiny black leaves floating on the surface. She picked one up. It was a flower petal.

Dexter remembered that Underwood had found and bagged a flower petal at the back door of the cottage. Was it coincidence? Had the killer left the petals behind him? As far as she could see there were no flowers in the area around the tree stump. She doubted whether the petals could have been blown there: the base of the tree was sheltered, surrounded by other trees and hedgerow. She withdrew an evidence bag from her pocket and carefully dropped the flower petals inside. It was something.

The cold and blackness was getting to her; she felt the trees closing around her. She remembered her nightmare. Time to go. Dexter had a hard rational brain and didn't scare easily but she was starting to feel increasingly tense. She stumbled along the line of the fence as quickly as she could and crossed the road to her car. She had scared herself but felt exhilarated. Fear can come as a rush. She checked the back seat of the car for madmen before she drove off.

It took her ten minutes to get to the station. There would be no one in the crime room now. Dexter bounded up the stairs. She would compare the flower petals she had collected with the one Underwood had found. What if they matched? What did that prove? That the killer liked flowers? The thought seemed ridiculous. She opened the door of the crime room and retrieved Underwood's evidence bag from a locker at the back of the room. She dropped the two bags on her desk and flicked on her desk light. Using the tweezers she kept in her top drawer she withdrew a petal from each bag. They were the same. Or, at least, they were the same colour. Purple. She knew that they probably wouldn't be able to get a print from either sample but she felt a flash of triumph. If the killer had left the petals behind, he hadn't expected them to be found. He had made a mistake.

Satisfied, she rebagged the evidence, sealed it back in the secure locker and left the room. She locked the door behind her and headed along the corridor. There was a light on in Underwood's office. The door was slightly ajar and she looked through. Underwood was asleep. He was leaning forward onto his desk, his head resting on his arms. Dexter hesitated, deciding whether or not she should wake him. It was past ten. 'Guv . . .' she said softly. No response. Dexter watched him for a second. Her boss was breathing heavily, his breath rasping against his ribcage. She would leave him alone. Underwood twitched slightly: maybe he was having a dream. Dexter hoped it was a happy one.

16

The room was warm and sumptuously furnished. Julia Underwood sat with a glass of South African Sauvignon in her hand. It had been intended to steady her nerves but had made her feel worse. The music wasn't helping either. Chopin's Nocturnes were her favourite and she guessed Paul had chosen the CD deliberately. She recognized Opus 15 No. 1 in F major. Moravec's piano work was exquisite; the notes seemed to drop through time like tears onto ivory. Ravel had famously described the Nocturnes as 'deeply felt poems of despair'. Tonight, as they wrenched at her, she truly understood why.

Where does the pain come from? Regret? Anger? Disappointment? The things we have done. The things we will never do. The people we leave behind. The people we bring with us. The things we have said. The things we bury inside. The hurt we make for others. The hurt they make for us. The weakening of our bodies. The strengthening of our prejudices. Living up to our expectations. Living down our failures. And Time. Julia knew that for sure. *The time we have wasted and the time that we have yet to destroy.* Was she saving her future or destroying it absolutely? She kept biting down on the thought like an angry fish that had taken the bait and the hook kept driving deeper into her brain.

She was having an affair; she was one of those women you read about in the problem pages of magazines whose misfortune you smirked at. She knew that her husband suspected something was wrong. Despite his failings – his insensitivity, his pigheadedness, his carelessness with himself and others – she knew you could only fool John Underwood for some of the time.

'You have to tell him,' said Paul, reading her mind. 'It's the only way now.'

'I know, but it's not as easy as that.'

'Nothing worthwhile ever is.' He took her hand. Julia shivered. He felt warm. Paul Heyer. He was her lover. HER LOVER.

The thought was absurd. She was a woman on the cusp of middle age. People like her didn't have lovers. They had headaches and gardening gloves.

'It's been eighteen years, Paul. You can't just throw it away.'

He was getting frustrated with her. 'You already have, Julia. It's a dead marriage. The rest is paperwork. And courage'

'You've been through all this yourself.' She didn't feel at all courageous. The prospect of telling John she didn't love him any more made her feel sick. 'This is all new to me.' She was crying. 'I don't know what to do.'

He smiled softly at her. 'You're right, I have been through it myself and it's pretty horrible. But I'll tell you one thing: I have never regretted it. If you've got a cancer you don't pretend that everything's all right and hope the problem goes away. You cut it out.' He could see she agreed with him. 'We can't go on like this, can we? I am tired of all this lying and sneaking about.'

'Me too. And I'm sure he knows that something's wrong. He's too sharp not to have noticed something.'

'All the more reason to tell him now. He'll find out sooner or later. Isn't it better that you do it on your own terms?'

'You don't understand, Paul. He's not well. He's depressed or something. I don't know how he'd cope if I wasn't there. He's hopeless. Like a child sometimes.'

'You can't think like that. It kills me to see you like this. Let's be clear. You don't have to worry about money. You don't have to worry about having somewhere to stay. You just have to be brave.' His voice was quiet but insistent. Paul Heyer was a patient man and he was in love – but he was too old to mess around. Life was like business: profit or loss. She either wanted to be with him or she didn't. Julia cradled her glass and glanced at the clock nervously.

17

Heather Stussman's bedside clock beeped once at midnight. She was awake and worried. She had seen the news and wasn't sure how to react. The phone call earlier in the day seemed unreal now. She wanted to think it hadn't happened. She was afraid. She had checked and double-checked the lock on her doors. The college gates were locked at nine. She knew she was safe. What should she do? She had tried calling Mark and her mother but had got no reply. She would have to figure this one out for herself.

A man had called her, told her to watch the news and explain it to the police.

She had dismissed him as a crank, a practical joker or an irritating colleague. Then she had seen the news. A local girl murdered. Was this what the guy had meant? She hadn't made the connection at once. The images of the cottage, of police cars, of the ambulance had all flashed across her TV screen. It didn't click until the newsreader had mentioned Lucy Harrington's name for the second time. Then she knew that she would have to call the police.

18

11 December

Underwood woke slowly and painfully, uncertain where he was. A phone was ringing. He ignored it. There was a pain in the back of his neck and he had chronic pins and needles in his left arm. He sat up at his desk. It was morning. There was movement in the corridor outside. Harrison pushed the door open. He seemed surprised.

'Sorry, guv, I didn't think you were here.'

'I hardly am.'

'I didn't mean to barge in. I heard the phone ringing. I didn't think you'd be in yet.'

'What time is it?'

The phone had stopped ringing. 'Six-forty-five,' Harrison said.

'Jesus. Do you always get in this early?' Underwood's eyes felt like bricks wedged into his head.

'Mostly. I jog in, then shower here.' Joe Harrison was tall and athletic, the only black CID officer in New Bolden. Underwood knew that Harrison had been a victim of racial prejudice within the force in the past. Some people would have lost heart: Harrison just seemed to get tougher, more determined to succeed. He was a year or two junior to Dexter, another refugee from the Met. They would make a formidable partnership one day – assuming they didn't kill each other first.

'Jogging?' Underwood asked. 'What for?'

'It's habit, really,' Harrison continued. 'I never sleep well. Do you want a coffee or something?'

'Milk. Two sugars.' Harrison rushed off. Underwood recalled the previous evening's events. An exhausted sadness gnawed at his heart. Did he really care any more? He wondered where Julia had spent the night, what she had done with the man he had seen. Underwood was falling through emptiness, clutching at branches that wouldn't bear his weight. He had to clear his head. Who was this fucking bloke anyway? Who was this fucking bloke who was fucking his wife? He flipped open his notebook and looked at the car registration number: S245 QXY. More than just a number. The code to his misery. He decided he did care. A lot. It would be a long day for everybody.

Harrison returned, carrying two steaming coffees. He placed one on the desk. Underwood watched him carefully.

'Did we get anything from the house-to-house? Didn't anybody see anything?' the inspector asked.

'Hardly anything.' Harrison sat down, 'A woman who lives off London Road – you know The Crescent?' Underwood nodded as he sipped his coffee. 'She says that a white van was parked in her road from seven that night and had gone the following morning. We asked at the other houses but no one else saw a thing.'

Underwood scowled. 'This coffee is disgusting. Did the woman see the driver? Can she give us a description?'

'No.'

'Marvellous. Did she know what type of van? Can she remember the registration?'

'Only that she thought it looked like an RSPCA van. She was worried they might have come for her cat.'

'What do the RSPCA inspectors drive? Those small Sherpa things?'

'Not sure, guv. I'll check it out.' Harrison pulled a Post-It off Underwood's pad and scribbled a note to himself.

'It's not much but it's a start. If he has a van like that he might be a plumber or a joiner.'

'If it's our man.' Harrison seemed doubtful.

'What about this bloody poem thing? The text on the wall? Any joy there?'

Harrison shook his head. 'Dexter is going to the library this morning. She's got an old squeeze who works there, apparently. I left it with her. She seemed a bit tense. I didn't want to step on her toes.' He left the statement hanging. Underwood got the message. 'I better get on, guv.' The detective sergeant stood and stretched. He was still wearing his jogging gear.

'Before you go.' Underwood handed over the piece of paper on which he had written Paul Heyer's registration number. 'There was a call last night after you'd gone. Some woman. Wouldn't give her name. She said she saw a car driving down Hartfield Road late on Monday night. BMW, she thought. She had to swerve to avoid it. It's probably just a pisshead on a magical mystery tour but it might be worth checking out.'

'Bit weird. The fact she got the whole number, late at night.'

'Who's to say she got the *right* number, though? As I say, I doubt it's anything but we should check it out.'

'Fair enough. I'll run it through the computer.' Harrison left the room and closed the door firmly behind him.

Underwood smiled to himself. He was taking a calculated risk. Still, Harrison would come back with a name and that would give him an advantage over Julia. Maybe he would pull the bloke in for questioning and rough him up a bit. It would be interesting to hear his alibi for Monday night. There was a cruel symmetry in all this that amused him. He felt his chin. He needed a shave. It was grey outside. Dawn was beginning to streak against the sky. The phone started ringing again. He got up and walked out of his office along the corridor to the gents. The phone jangled faintly behind him as he closed the cubicle door. It was their wedding anniversary in three days. Maybe he'd ask for a divorce then: more symmetry. Underwood felt mucus crawling up his throat, saliva creeping across his dry tongue. He leaned over the pan and was sick.

19

Dexter drove away from the library car park. Her librarian contact, Dan, was an ex-boyfriend and was far less attractive than she had remembered. She smiled bitterly to herself and wondered why Fate always cast such tossers in her direction. Still, despite his lack of personality, Dan had been extremely helpful: he'd recognized the line of text immediately and had recited the rest of the piece. He was arrogant with his intelligence. It was a fragment from a poem by a writer whom she had never heard of. She was none the wiser in reality but at least they had identified the source. Underwood could figure out the rest.

Dexter considered calling him on her mobile. She decided not to. It was as if she needed to tell him face to face. She felt that if she called him it would somehow detract from what she had discovered. In her absence, Underwood would most likely call in Harrison to discuss the information. Then the line of responsibility for turning up this piece of evidence would be blurred. She would get no recognition. Female officers needed recognition more than the men. They had more obstacles to overcome: they had to attach themselves more aggressively to success stories or risk being overlooked in the general orgy of backslapping. She wondered if she was making excuses.

Dexter had always felt an inexplicable need to prove herself to Underwood. *Prove herself.* Was that the right way to express it? No. It wasn't so much proving herself as wanting to please him. The thought made her shudder. Dexter had tried to purge herself of flirtatiousness, of the clinginess she so despised in some other female officers.

She turned her car along the dual carriageway that swung alongside New Bolden Parkway station. Was she any different from Jensen? The WPC overtly flirted with male officers, even slept with some of them. Didn't Dexter's own desire to please Underwood grow from the same emotional root? She wondered what that was. Insecurity? A perception of inferiority? Absence of a paternal influence? She almost made herself laugh at that last one. Dexter hadn't known her own father so she didn't regard herself as an expert. However, Underwood didn't strike her as much of a father figure. He was weak, even vulnerable in many ways. She often felt that she was carrying him, nursing him through his insecurities and inefficiencies. Her mind flipped the question over. Perhaps it was some misguided maternal instinct in her. The thought made her shiver. She wondered if she was going mad.

Dexter tried to clear her head, to focus on other things. She always found it hard to concentrate first thing in the mornings. Maybe because the previous night's dreams and nightmares were still close: still swimming near to the surface in the back of her mind. Her head was a wrecking ground early in the morning: thoughts and emotions scattered without meaning, ideas that were once beautiful smashed to pieces.

Concentrate. She stared through the dirty glass windscreen at the white lines sliding beneath her and the stretch of grey tarmac arcing to the right ahead. She tried to build a logical structure. This was always her reaction to concepts she couldn't understand. It usually worked. *A girl is killed with a hammer. Why? Ease of execution.* Dexter tried not to smile at her unintentional pun.

A hammer blow to the back of the head will undoubtedly put the victim down quickly. Possibly even kill them immediately. That's what happened to Lucy Harrington. She was a strong girl, an athlete. Maybe our killer didn't fancy his chances face to face. Is he physically weak? The killing blow would have happened very quickly. Maybe the act of killing doesn't excite him. The eye. That's why he killed her. That's the key to all this.

Dexter pulled up at a traffic light. There was a scruffy-looking man with a silver nose-stud selling roses at the roadside: five for three pounds. *Flowers. Flowers are important to him. Does he deliver flowers? Is that how he found Lucy Harrington?* She discounted the idea. It was too obvious, too easy to trace. The killer was too smart for that. *And then there's the poem. Written in blood on a white-tiled wall. Very melodramatic. A cliché, almost. The killer wants us to read the poem. Why? How can a poem written four hundred-odd years ago be important? Eyes, flowers and poetry: another interesting bloke, another messed-up limp-dick.* A car hooted behind her. The lights had changed.

She came back again to the image of Lucy Harrington's eye, gouged from its socket. She stopped and corrected herself. It hadn't been gouged. What had Leach the pathologist said? The killer had tried to do it scientifically and had eventually resorted to brute force. There was method in the madness. He had researched his subject carefully. *What instruments would you need to remove an eye? A scalpel to cut and forceps to pull the eyeball from the socket. What else? Leach didn't think our man was a doctor so where did he get the instruments he needed?* Was he from a medical family? A long shot but it was a possibility. *Where do you buy medical instruments? Are there shops? Trade fairs, maybe?* She made a mental note to check.

Dexter pulled up outside the station and hurried inside. The desk sergeant nodded curtly at her as she swiped her access card and hurried upstairs. Underwood's office was on the third floor and she was glowing slightly by the time she arrived. Underwood was standing with his back to the door, staring out of the window. He had his coat on. His hair was a matted mess, Dexter noted despite herself.

'You all right, sir?' she asked.

Underwood turned and smiled faintly. His eyes were blackened at the edges and he looked exhausted. 'I'm fine, Dex. Full of flu.'

'There's a lot of it about.'

'There always is.'

Dexter prepared herself. 'I've got some good news, sir.' She pulled a folded piece of paper from her back pocket. 'The writing on the wall at Lucy Harrington's house.' She savoured her moment of triumph and watched Underwood's face closely as she spoke. 'It's from a poem. My friend at the library photocopied it for me. The poem's called "A Valediction" . . .'

' "A Valediction: Of Weeping" ' Underwood cut her off. He picked up a note from his desk and read aloud, 'Written around 1620 by John Donne.' He looked up at her. Dexter tried to disguise her disappointment. She failed.

'Pardon my asking, sir, but how the bloody hell did you find that out?' Dexter was angry. Life only stole things from her when she started to get excited about them.

'I'll tell you in the car.' He picked his keys off the desk and tossed them over to Dexter. 'You're driving.'

The car crawled out of New Bolden in heavy traffic and turned towards Cambridge. Underwood sat in the front passenger seat, increasingly aware of the sweat soaking his back. He felt empty: as if the only thing that defined him now was his illness and exhaustion. So this was how it felt when you eventually realized your life was meaningless. He had spent years preparing for the moment but it still stung him like a hornet. His mind wandered through the previous night's events. He would call Harrison later about the licence plate. Dexter half-turned to him as they finally broke free of the traffic and settled at a comfortable seventy miles an hour.

'Are you going to tell me what's going on, sir?'

'I received a call this morning at eight from a Dr Heather Stussman. She's a lecturer at the university. She was pretty freaked out. She thinks the guy who killed Lucy Harrington telephoned her yesterday.'

Dexter was shocked. 'What makes her think it's our bloke?' She was finding it hard to concentrate on the road.

'She got a letter in the post, a letter containing a line of poetry. Then yesterday afternoon some bloke called her, asked her if she'd received his letter and told her to watch the news. He didn't mention Lucy Harrington but guess what the line of poetry was . . .'

'Draw not up seas, to drowne me in thy spheare?'

'Bingo.'

'But the writing on the wall isn't public knowledge yet. How did she know our man was talking about Lucy Harrington?'

'That's a very good point. I guess we'll find out.'

'Why did he call her? Who is she, anyway?'

'She's an expert. Fellow of Southwell College. She published a book on John Donne's poems last year. She's quite a big fish. American.' Underwood frowned as the hulk of New Bolden power station loomed beside them. 'He told her to watch the news and explain it to the police.'

'Explain it to us?'

'Fucked-up or what?'

They approached Cambridge from the north, passing the entrance to Girton College then turning left onto Chesterton Road. The ring road slowly brought them around the city, with Dexter zigzagging energetically to avoid cyclists until they swung right at Parker's Piece and crossed into Lensfield Road. Southwell College was at the southern end of the city, backing onto the river. On instructions from Underwood, Dexter parked outside the Fitzwilliam Museum and the two of them walked up to the Southwell porter's lodge. Dexter shivered. It was always cold in Cambridge at this time of year, just as it had been in East London.

Southwell College was a mish-mash of architectural styles reflecting the building's spasmodic evolution through the centuries. The sixteenth-century first quad was lined with flower boxes and was far more attractive than the dark Victorian court that had grown up behind it. Like many of the colleges, the desire to expand had also encouraged Southwell to build a monstrous, modern accommodation block. It sat uneasily next to the college gardens like an uninvited guest at a family reunion.

The porter directed Underwood and Dexter to Stussman's rooms in the second quad. Dexter slowed down diplomatically at the foot of the old wooden staircase and allowed Underwood to take the lead. She knew he was more likely to have difficulties with the ascent than her. Stussman heard them approaching and was waiting at the entrance to her rooms on the first-floor landing.

'Inspector Underwood?' She held out her hand.

Underwood was impressed. Stussman had thick black shoulder-length hair and brilliant stone-blue eyes. She had a firm handshake, too.

'Pleased to meet you, Dr Stussman.' Underwood was trying not to gawp. 'This is Detective Sergeant Dexter.'

'Nice to meet you, sergeant,' said Stussman. No hand was offered this time. Dexter didn't mind: she was used to that. Stussman led them inside. The living room had the typically chaotic feel of an academic's office. One wall was entirely dedicated to books, from floor to ceiling. Dexter ran her eye across the titles: lots of poetry books and biographies. She didn't recognize many of them. On Stussman's desk was a vast glacier of paper that was threatening to spill onto the carpet. Her computer was an old-fashioned Apple Mac that seemed to be feeling its age. There were two armchairs: Underwood fell gratefully into one. Dexter remained standing.

Stussman was leaning against her desk. Underwood's eyes moved along the firm lines of her legs. Julia had great legs too. Desire and despair ambushed him again: the double helix burned in his heart. He cleared his throat.

'Dr Stussman. For Sergeant Dexter's benefit and my own, could you talk us through yesterday's events and explain why you called us?'

'Sure. I received this letter yesterday.' She handed Underwood the envelope. He held it carefully at the edges. Stussman continued, 'I didn't open it at first. I got a call just after six p.m. when I got back from giving a lecture.' She lit a cigarette. She seemed shaky. 'The guy on the phone asked if I had received his letter. I guessed it was this one so I pulled the envelope from my bag and opened it. He asked me if I recognized it. I said I did and that is was a line from "A Valediction: Of Weeping".' Stussman looked over at Dexter. 'That's a poem by John Donne.'

'I know,' Dexter said sharply.

'He told me that I should watch the news and explain it to the police. Then he hung up.'

'Did he have an accent?' asked Underwood.

'He was English. Beyond that I wouldn't really know.'

'What did you do then?' Dexter asked.

'Well . . . nothing, I'm afraid. I thought it was a practical joke. The academic world is a very spiteful one, Sergeant Dexter. My papers have proved pretty controversial. I assumed someone was trying to freak me out. Then, late last night, I saw the news.'

'About Lucy Harrington?' Underwood was watching her closely.

'Yes. Then I panicked. You see, the name Lucy Harrington is significant. In the context of John Donne's poetry, that is.'

'How so?' Dexter had started making notes.

'Donne was one of a group of English poets writing in the late sixteenth and early seventeenth centuries. The group subsequently became known as the Metaphysical Poets.'

'This is your area of expertise?' Underwood asked, his gaze drifting.

'Yes. My doctoral thesis was on the stylistic variations between Donne and his contemporary, George Herbert. I recently published a book on the life of Donne.'

'What does "metaphysical" mean?' Dexter was confused.

'Literally, it means "beyond physics". The Renaissance was an intellectual revolution that encouraged writers and philosophers to question the accepted principles of scientific and religious thought.' Stussman noticed that Dexter had stopped writing. 'The Metaphysical Poets tried to address intellectual issues that were beyond the ability of science to explain.'

'Such as?'

'Love, life, spirituality, God, death. Take your pick. The

poems were tightly argued explorations of the ideas surrounding these "metaphysical concepts". John Donne is the best known and most able of all the metaphysical poets.'

'You say these poems are arguments?' Underwood was struggling to understand.

'Yes, most of them. Remember that during the sixteenth and seventeenth centuries, the written word was less important than the spoken one. Few people could actually read. In fact, Donne's poems weren't published until after his death. During his lifetime the poems were generally read aloud to friends, groups of like-minded intellectuals.'

'You said that the name Lucy Harrington was significant?' Dexter asked.

'That's when I made the connection. You see, Lucy Harrington, or Lucy Harrington, Countess of Bedford, to give her her full title, was one of Donne's patrons. One of his coterie of intellectual friends, you might say. When I heard the murdered girl was called Lucy Harrington I realized that this was what the guy on the phone wanted me to know about. I got scared and I called you first thing.'

The information sent a shiver of electricity down Underwood's spine. This was the first indication of why the killer had selected Lucy Harrington. The choice of victim had been troubling Underwood: there were easier targets everywhere – schoolkids, the prostitutes behind New Bolden Station. Why risk attacking such a high-profile target unless it meant something special? He suddenly felt that the balance had shifted slightly in his favour. Or had it? After all, the killer had wanted this to happen.

'Dr Stussman, I'll need you to provide us with a list of Donne's associates. People like Lucy Harrington: patrons, girlfriends, the people who were close to him.'

'No problem.'

'The line of poetry that was sent to you was also written on the wall of Lucy Harrington's bathroom. That isn't public yet. Keep it to yourself,' Underwood said.

'Jesus Christ.' Stussman shuddered. 'Do you think this fucked-up bastard is going to come after me?'

'Let's not get carried away,' said Underwood. 'Is there anyone you can think of – a student, someone who knows you – who might want to do something like this?'

Stussman shook her head. 'No one. A few dodgy ex-boyfriends . . .'

'I'm sure,' said Dexter unnecessarily. Underwood fired a withering look in her direction. 'Haven't we all?' she added quickly.

'The man who phoned you, he asked you to explain the poem to us. Could you do that, please? Maybe something you say might be useful. Assume that neither of us knows anything about this,' said Underwood. Stussman turned and retrieved two pieces of paper from her desk. She handed a piece each to Dexter and Underwood. She tried to collect her thoughts.

'Here's a transcription of the poem. I'll read it to you. Follow along in the text. As I said, Donne intended that the poem should be read aloud.' Stussman began to recite the poem from memory. Her gaze floated to the window as she spoke and fixed on the spire of the college chapel.

'Let me power forth
My tears before thy face, whil'st I stay here
For thy face coines them, and with thy stampe they beare,
And by this mintage they are something worth
For thus they bee
Pregnant of thee;
Fruits of much griefe they are, emblemes of more
When a tear falls, that thou falls which it bore
So thou and I are nothing then when on a divers shore.

'On a round ball
A workeman that hath copies by, can lay
An Europe, Afrique, and an Asia
And quickly make that which was nothing All,
So doth each teare,
Which thee doth weare,
A globe, yea world by that impression grow,
Till thy teares mixt with mine doe overflow,
This world, by waters sent from thee, my heaven dissolved so.

'O More than Moone,
Draw not up seas to drowne me in thy spheare,

58

Weepe me not dead, in thine arms, but forbeare
To teach the sea, what it may doe too soone;
Let not the winde
Example finde,
To doe me more harm, than it purposeth;
Since thou and I sigh one anothers breath,
Who e'r sighes most is cruellest, and hasts the others death.'

Dexter looked at Underwood and shrugged. Stussman caught the movement out of the corner of her eye. She took a deep breath.

'A valediction is a poem that is concerned with saying goodbye. In Latin, "vale" means farewell. In this poem, Donne is saying goodbye to someone he is in love with. The poem is constructed around a conceit: an elaborate metaphor. It's a common device in metaphysical poetry. In this case the conceit is that the tears of each lover bear the image of the other.

'Look at the first verse: "Let me power forth my teares . . . For thy face coines them and thy stampe they beare". In other words Donne is saying "Let me cry, my tears will have value because they contain your reflection."

Stussman took a swig of coffee from the mug on her desk and sat down in the spare amchair. She was directly opposite Underwood now and addressed her comments to him.

'But Donne doesn't leave it there. He develops the idea. This is the argumentative element of the poetry that I mentioned earlier. He draws in a sexual image: "For thus they bee/ Pregnant of thee" – the tears are bulging full of his lover's image. Imagine the shape of a pregnant woman. Then, like ripe fruits of pain ("emblemes of grief") they fall to the ground.' She looked Underwood straight in the eye. 'Are you with me?'

'Just about,' he lied.

'In the second verse the argument moves into phase two. Do you know what a microcosm is?'

Underwood shook his head. Julia had called him intellectually flat-footed once. Now he knew what she had meant.

'It's a miniature representation of something large: like a room representing the whole universe or, as we see in the second stanza, a tear representing an entire planet. Donne says that "A

workeman . . . can quickly make that which was nothing All".
In other words, through the prism of his argument the tears may
be seen as a globe, a world of their own. He then injects the idea
that as the tears of the lovers mix together, the imaginary world
they created is destroyed by a biblical-style flood: "This world
by waters sent from thee, my heaven dissolved so".'

'A biblical flood?' Underwood remembered the terrible mess
at Lucy Harrington's house: the bloody water that had washed
away and corrupted all residual evidence. Harrison had had a
similar notion the previous day. Underwood looked at the page
and concentrated on the third verse.

'So the last verse is the one that contains the line he wrote on
the wall: "Draw not up seas to drowne me in thy spheare."' He
struggled to understand. 'He's saying that his lover is like the
moon and controls the tides?'

Stussman nodded. 'Almost. Donne is saying that his lover is
more powerful than the moon; that the power of her will is
greater than that of nature itself; that she can draw up oceans of
tears that can destroy worlds.'

'Eyes. Water. Blood,' said Dexter quietly.

Stussman turned to her. 'Does that help? I mean, does what I
said have any bearing on what happened to the girl?'

'It might do. There are certain common elements.' Dexter
didn't look her in the eye.

'Like what? If you tell me I might be able to help you.' Said
Stussman.

'I doubt it. In any case, we can't reveal important details of
ongoing investigations to the public.' Dexter's eyes remained
glued to the page of notes she didn't understand.

'I am hardly the public. And I do have a vested interest in you
catching this guy. He knows where I live, after all. He has
selected me already.' There was an edge to Stussman's voice
now. Dexter noticed it. So did Underwood.

'I have a question, Dr Stussman,' the inspector asked. 'Do
eyes have any special meaning or significance in metaphysical
poetry?'

'Eyes?' Stussman hesitated momentarily at the implication of
the inspector's question. 'Well, yes, in a number of ways. We

have alluded to the idea of microcosms already. In "A Valediction: of Weeping" the microcosm was in the tears of the two lovers. In other poems, Donne uses eyes to similar effect. Entire universes or planets are compressed into the eyes of a lover.

'There's a poem called "The Good Morrow", for example. Donne awakes and sees his own reflection in his lover's eyes: "My face in thine eye, thine in mine appears/ And true hearts doe in the faces rest/ Where can we find two better hemispheares/ Without sharpe North, without declining West?". Do you see what he's doing?'

Underwood shook his head. Stussman continued, 'Each eye is a hemisphere – half a world. Together, the two reflections make a whole new world; a perfect construction without the hostility of a frozen north or the sunsets of "declining West".'

'A bit Spandau Ballet, if you ask me,' said Dexter.

'What else, Dr Stussman?' asked Underwood. He was making extensive notes and was not looking forward to making sense of them later.

'There is something else that strikes me. Remember the line from "A Valediction: of Weeping" that I was sent: "Draw not up seas to drowne me in thy spheare." As I said, that line is about the power of the human will. Humanist thought during the Renaissance emphasized the importance of the rational human mind in contrast with divine belief systems. In the poem "The Sunne Rising", Donne is lying in bed with his lover, addressing the sunrise. He implies that his will, expressed through closing his eyes, is more powerful than the sun: "Thy beames so reverend and strong/ Why should'st thou thinke?/ I could eclipse and cloud them with a winke/ But I would not lose her sight so long". Maybe your killer thinks that by using his rational mind he can create a new world.'

'A rational mind wouldn't do what he's done,' said Dexter dismissively. 'This guy's a fruitcake.'

'Don't underestimate him. He's been very careful, methodical almost,' said Underwood. 'He thinks he's being rational. Everything that's happened so far he has willed. Maybe he believes he is a force of nature. We're here, aren't we? He willed that. Now it's happened.'

'Am I in danger, Inspector?' Stussman asked. 'I feel like I don't want to be here any more.'

Underwood considered for a moment. 'The honest answer is that I don't know. My instinct is to say no. This guy, whoever he is, has chosen to communicate with us through you. For whatever reason, he thinks that you understand what he's about. I'd like you to stay here. He may try to contact you again. For safety's sake, I'll arrange for a uniformed officer to be outside your door from this afternoon. We'll tell the porters to lock the college gates early and only to admit people that they recognize. You should tell them the names of all your visitors in advance so they can check them as they arrive. This is a pretty secure room. You're on the first floor and the door is the only way in. I would recommend that you stay in college as much as possible. Is that feasible?'

'I guess so.' Stussman considered. 'The only times I have to go out are for my lectures and the next one isn't until the middle of next week. I can eat in college.'

'Do that.' Underwood scribbled three numbers on a piece of paper and handed it over. 'You can contact Sergeant Dexter or myself on either of the first numbers if he calls you again or if anything else occurs to you. The last number is our fax. We'll contact Cambridge police now and make sure they put a guy on your door today. Are you okay with that?'

Stussman looked at the numbers on the notepaper. 'Not really, but I guess I don't have much choice.'

'You'll be fine. If we think that you are at risk, if the guy threatens you on the phone or something, we'll put you in a hotel or a safe house.' Underwood stood up. 'Thank you for your help. I don't pretend to understand everything you said but I get the gist.'

'If I think of anything else I'll let you know.' Stussman suddenly felt very small. Vulnerable. Maybe Underwood sensed it. He shook her hand again, more gently this time. He held her grip for a moment too long, as if frozen for an instant by those crystal-blue eyes. Dexter turned away and briskly walked to the door. For a split second, Underwood felt that there might be an ounce of beauty in the universe after all; reflected in those eyes, maybe even he could be beautiful. The moment vanished. He walked away, hoping that the killer of Lucy Harrington hadn't seen Heather Stussman's photograph.

20

Harrison was already on his fifth coffee and it was still before midday. It had been a fairly productive morning and the benefits of working a case with WPC Jensen were not lost on him. Aesthetic advantages aside, she was an enthusiastic worker and keen to make an impression. She was also a willing fetcher of cappuccinos. He would take her out for a beer soon: she looked the pub type. Harrison wondered if her flirtatiousness would get her into trouble one day: he hoped he was there when it happened.

The two of them had spent the previous three hours following up leads from the preliminary house-to-house enquiries. Mrs Edith Jackson, an elderly homeowner in The Crescent, London Road had previously told Harrison that she remembered a white van – like an RSPCA inspector's van – had been parked outside her house the night Lucy Harrington had been murdered. It had disappeared by the following morning. Jensen had spoken to the RSPCA that morning and determined that their inspectors generally used the white Ford Escort 1.8d. She had then downloaded a picture of this type of vehicle from a Ford dealer website and on Harrison's advice had then driven up to The Crescent. Mrs Jackson wasn't confident but agreed that the van she had seen looked very similar to that in the photograph.

It was something, but Harrison found it hard to get excited. Even if the van had been driven by Lucy Harrington's murderer, they had nothing else to work with: no registration plate, no description of the driver. There were thousands of white Escort vans across the country; hundreds in the New Bolden area alone. Underwood's tip concerning the BMW seen on the Hartfield Road didn't seem a much better bet. He had called the DVLA and had them process the registration through their central computer. It had thrown back a name and address in New Bolden: Paul Heyer, 17 The Blossoms. Harrison knew the area: detached houses mostly owned by affluent business types and located about two miles from Lucy Harrington's cottage.

He cross-referenced Heyer's records with the New Bolden and Cambridgeshire police records. Heyer had been fined for two minor speeding offences in the previous five years. He was hardly a 'ten-most-wanted' candidate. The records showed that Heyer was a local property developer and a director of the New Bolden Chamber Orchestra. 'Pillar of the community,' mused Harrison; it looked like another dead end. However, he was experienced enough not to assume the obvious and if Heyer had been in the area that night he might have seen something. It would be worthwhile speaking to him.

On Dexter's instructions Jensen had started compiling a list of all those arrested for housebreaking in the New Bolden and Cambridge region over the previous five years. The list was pretty extensive, covering Peterborough, Cambridge, New Bolden and Ely as well as the rural districts. There were just under a hundred names of suspects with arrest records still living in the county. It would take time to check them all. Jensen decided to wait and tell Underwood herself. She would cross-check to see if any of them owned white Escort vans. They probably all did.

Jensen also began to sift through the huge pile of unsolved burglary cases, looking for similiarities with the break in at Lucy Harrington's cottage. It was a tedious task that Harrison had happily delegated. Many of the crime reports were incomplete or contained only scant details. Making connections was going to be tough. However, Jensen had already claimed the biggest success of the morning. She had fielded a call from the forensic laboratory. The lab confirmed that the flower petals found by Dexter the previous evening matched the petal Underwood had found stuck under Lucy Harrington's back door. They were *Saintpaulia ionantha*: African violet petals, probably from the same plant. Harrison now knew for sure what Underwood and

Dexter had suspected: that Lucy Harrington's killer had waited in the woods outside her house for her to leave and then gained entry by the back door.

'Why carry flowers around with him, sarge?' Jensen asked. 'You'd think he'd have had more important things on his mind.'

'My mum grows African violets,' Harrison replied. 'Kind of an old people's thing, aren't they?'

'Don't ask me. The only flowers I know are roses.' Jensen smirked.

'So you're used to little pricks, then?'

'Have to be, working here.'

Jensen was sharp. Harrison liked that. He would push it one step further. 'You're obviously hanging round with the wrong people.' This time Jensen just smiled at him. He hadn't enjoyed work this much for ages.

'I'll get some more background on these flowers, then,' she said eventually, 'see where you can buy them locally – that sort of thing.' Jensen had come over all businesslike now. Harrison knew when it was time to back off. He was in no hurry. The chase was invariably more enjoyable than the main event. The phone rang. Jensen answered and handed the phone to Harrison.

'It's Underwood, sergeant. Sounds like his mobile.'

Harrison took the phone from her. 'Hello, sir. Anything interesting?'

'Confusing,' said Underwood. 'Any joy on the van or that licence plate?'

'We are pretty sure the van was an Escort 1.8d. Beyond that it's anybody's guess. No one else saw the bastard.'

Underwood's voice softened slightly. 'What about the BMW?'

'Licensed to a Mr Paul Heyer. 17 The Blossoms. Local business type. Couple of driving fines but nothing more serious than that.'

'Get him in.'

'You sure, guv? Sounds like a non-starter to me.'

'I'll see him this afternoon. You and Jensen pick him up.'

Twenty miles away, Underwood clicked off his mobile phone. So his rival's name was Paul Heyer. *Mr and Mrs Paul Heyer.* The thought ricocheted around his mind like a squash ball. *Paul*

and Julia invite you to a barbecue . . . Paul and Jules At Home.
He screwed his eyes shut. Julia would be worrying about him by
now; wondering where he was, why he hadn't come home or
called. *Fuck her,* he thought bitterly. Let her suffer. The suffering
was only just beginning and he was going to make the most of
it. The suffering was all he had left. This afternoon he would
look into the eyes of the man who was screwing his wife.
Underwood wondered what kind of nightmare world he could
create from the reflections he would see in them.

21

Julia Underwood lay back in the bath. There was a pain behind
her eyes and anger in her belly. She had hardly slept. Every
passing car, every creak and rattle in her old house had made
her jump. She had returned from Paul's place before eleven the
previous evening steeled with resolve; prepared for the confrontation that he had compelled her to undertake. But John hadn't
been there. Progress came only with pain. She understood that.
Like childbirth, new life only came with agony. Julia knew that
it was probably too late for her: once she would have liked to
have children. Now she was glad that she hadn't. She shuddered
at the new dimension of complexities that a child would have
brought to her current situation.

   In the darkest moments of her despair over the previous six
months, Julia had often thought about killing herself. Sometimes,
if she was standing at a station, she would imagine falling in
front of the approaching train; progress only came with pain.
She had thought of taking pills: there were two boxes of parace-
tamol in the kitchen and John always kept a bottle of vodka in
the cabinet. She had thought of cutting her wrists: in the bath,
probably, to dilate the blood vessels. The last option appealed to
her most; there was something beautifully ironic about leaving
the world the way you came into it: in blood and water. Riddled
with fear and self-doubt, torn between conflicting responsibili-

ties, Julia Underwood had stared into the abyss and found nothing. That scared her the most: the nothingness of her life, the nothingness of her death. She had been alone for eighteen years. She would not be alone any more. She had read a line in a women's magazine once: 'If you can save one life, make it your own.'

She had called her husband four times in the previous twenty-four hours. Two calls to his office, two to his mobile. She had left recorded messages and text messages. No response. Julia understood what was going on. John always retreated from confrontation; rather than take up the exposed ground of an argument, he preferred to launch a kind of intellectual guerrilla warfare. This usually involved long periods of absence or silence bookended by occasional fusillades of invective. It had been going on for eighteen years and she was tired of it now. At least there were winners and losers in arguments. In the war of attrition that was her marriage, everyone had lost out.

Julia looked at her body. She would be forty in five months' time. You could tell the age of a tree by cutting it in half and counting the lines. Julia could count her lines all too easily. Sometimes she felt like she was trapped in another, unfamiliar body, the body of a stranger. It wasn't that she was fat: her weight fluctuated but it never soared beyond her control. It was more that she just looked exhausted: baggy and exhausted. She looked like a crumpled suit someone had left hanging in a wardrobe for eighteen years.

When she had started seeing Paul, Julia had avoided over-dressing. She had chosen her plainest, smartest, most sexless clothes. From early in their relationship – God, how she hated that word – she had fantasized and panicked about sleeping with him in equal measure. She had feared the moment when he would look on her naked for the first time; feared that he might in that instant feel he had been misled or had made a terrible mistake. 'At least,' she had reasoned, 'if I dress like a frump he won't be surprised.' She needn't have worried.

She had met Paul at a concert in the New Bolden Theatre. It was a charity fund-raising event. The orchestra had played Ravel's orchestration of Mussorgsky's *Pictures at an Exhibition*.

Paul had introduced himself at the interval. He was a director of the orchestra. They had talked about Mussorgsky. Julia remembered snippets about the composer from school but Paul had talked freely about Mussorgsky's early life in St Petersburg and his training with Balakirev. Julia felt in that instant that her life had changed gear: that she was being *engaged*; he had assumed intelligence in her, he had taken an interest and opened the door to a different world. A rarefied world of music and conversation. In that moment she was lost. At the end of the performance Paul had invited her to a recital of Mussorgsky's *Songs and Dances of Death* in Cambridge the following week. It didn't sound particularly romantic but she was intrigued. He was polite and softly spoken. She had accepted.

And here she was. Six months down the line, on the verge of leaving her husband. She wondered how much John already knew. He had a dark, perceptive intelligence that she understood only too well. He suspected something was wrong, that was clear enough, and his natural pessimism had probably already led him to believe the worst. Julia climbed out of the bath and towelled herself dry. She put some cream on her legs – their skin always seemed to dry out so quickly – wrapped herself in her dressing gown and went upstairs. Her clothes were lying on the bed. The bed she and John had shared for eighteen years: the bed where neither of them could sleep.

She dressed quickly and packed a few clothes and toiletries into a bag. Her purse and passport were in the bedside drawer. She removed them, along with her mobile phone. She placed a sealed envelope on the bedspread and, after a final look around, Julia Underwood left the house. One suitcase wasn't much to show for eighteen years, she thought bitterly. She would stay at Paul's that night and then decamp to her mother in Worcester for a couple of weeks. She had to clear her head and concentrate on the way forward. Progress through pain.

22

Underwood was trying to draw disparate threads of thought together. His meeting with Stussman had been memorable for two reasons: Stussman herself and the reason she had offered for the killer's selection of Lucy Harrington. Underwood had been unable to push the memory of Stussman's stone-blue eyes away from the front of his mind. They had bored into him with the kind of ferocious intelligence he usually found intimidating. She had talked with gravity and conviction about a subject Underwood had previously thought to be the preserve of old men and bespectacled undergraduates. She carried the quiet confidence that only the marriage of natural intelligence and hard work can forge. Underwood realized he envied her: someone so young and in command of their subject; so imbued with life.

Then there was Stussman's comment about Lucy Harrington. The name was important. Lucy Harrington, Countess of Bedford had been John Donne's patron four hundred years ago. The killer had chosen her because of her name. Why? It didn't make any sense. Then there were the flowers. 'African violet petals,' a smiling Jensen had told him half an hour previously. What was all that about? The fact that flowers are often associated with death seemed inadequate to him. There had to be more to it than that. The petals weren't left anywhere near the corpse. The killer had not intended them to be part of the crime scene. It was almost as if he was carrying them around with him. Why? For comfort? Did he like the smell?

Stussman had said one other thing that had rattled him. He checked his notes: he had written her comments down carefully – 'Maybe your killer thinks that by using his rational mind he can create a new world.' He had read several articles about how serial killers create a fantasy world for themselves and then live out increasingly ferocious recreations of that fantasy. The killer of Lucy Harrington had removed her eye and scrawled a line of poetry on her wall. That line had originally been written by a poet four hundred years previously, a poet whose patron had been someone called Lucy Harrington. There was an obvious circularity but what kind of fantasy did it denote? Underwood gave up as he started coughing again.

There was a knock at the door. Jensen entered. She waited for the inspector to recover his composure.

'Sir, we checked with the phone company. The call to Dr Stussman was made from a payphone on the B692 north of Cambridge. Marty Farrell has been to check it out but he says that there are no usable prints. Cambridge police have agreed to watch the kiosk for us in case the killer uses it again.'

'He won't,' Underwood said abruptly. 'He's not an idiot.'

'Sergeant Harrison asked me to let you know that he has a Mr Heyer in interview room one.'

'Thank you, Jensen.' Underwood's heart skipped a beat. *So, he's here.* Underwood had crawled out on a limb and was worried it might snap under him. Perhaps it would be better to let Harrison handle the interview: ask the obvious five questions and let the poor bastard go. Then he thought of Julia giving herself up to this man, the man who was trying to destroy his life. It was more than morbid curiosity: a cold hatred chilled his blood. He had the power. He had the advantage.

Paul Heyer was confused. He sat in the claustrophobic whiteness of interview room one racking his brains for any reason why he might be there. He hadn't committed any offences that he was aware of: a couple of speeding misdemeanours but that was in the past. Maybe it was something to do with his business: property development was a murky world sometimes but he had always tried to act honourably. Perhaps it related to a client or more likely an employee. That was probably it.

'Will this take long, sergeant?' he asked Harrison. 'I don't mean to be awkward but I am supposed to be in a meeting at the council offices in an hour.'

'That depends, Mr Heyer,' Harrison replied.

'On what, exactly? I still don't know why I am here.'

'It depends on how long Inspector Underwood wants you to stay.'

'Underwood?' Heyer suddenly felt acutely uncomfortable. What was all this about? He thought of Julia. The door opened and Underwood walked in. Harrison turned to the recording machine.

'One-fifty-five p.m. Inspector Underwood has entered the room.'

Underwood circled the table and sat down directly opposite Heyer. He was scared, exhilarated and sickened – all at the same time. So this was the man who was fucking his wife. He wasn't much to look at. Thin, not very well built. Affluent, though, that much was obvious. Underwood looked at Heyer's hands. They were smooth, hairless. He wondered if they smelled of his wife. He tried to remain focused.

'Mr Paul Heyer?' Underwood's gaze locked on the papers in front of him.

'That's right.'

'Of 17 The Blossoms, New Bolden?'

'Correct.'

'Do you know why you're here, Mr Heyer?'

'No idea, I'm afraid.'

'Do you read the papers?'

'Regularly. Would you mind telling me what this is about?' Heyer looked at Harrison whose face remained expressionless.

'So you've heard of Lucy Harrington?'

'Of course.' Heyer paused for a moment. 'What are you implying?'

'I'm not implying anything. "The Blossoms"? Do you like flowers, Mr Heyer? Gardening?'

Harrison leaned forward slightly in his seat and looked at Heyer more closely. The man suddenly seemed on edge.

'As much as the next man. Have I been arrested for gardening?'

'Where were you between eleven p.m. and two a.m. on the night of December the ninth?' Underwood checked his notes again. He didn't need to. Heyer opened his mouth to speak and then hesitated.

'Mr Heyer?' Harrison prompted.

'I was at home.'

'At home?' asked Underwood. 'Are you sure about that?'

'Absolutely.'

'Can anyone verify that, sir?' Harrison asked the question for him. Underwood bit his lip to stop smiling. A film of sweat had spread across Heyer's brow. Underwood suddenly wanted to force his fountain pen into Heyer's eye.

'No. I was alone.'

'Can you remember what was on TV?' asked Harrison.

'No. I don't watch television. I listened to music all evening.'

'With a lady friend?' Harrison watched Heyer intently.

'No. As I said, I was alone.'

'That's very interesting. You see, we had a call yesterday from someone who claimed to have seen your car – blue BMW with licence plate S245 QXY – on Hartfield Road very late on Monday night,' said Underwood. He had grown in confidence as the interview had progressed and was now looking Heyer directly in the eye. 'Said you were going extremely fast and they had to swerve to avoid you.'

'That's absolutely ridiculous.'

'You *have* had a couple of speeding convictions, Mr Heyer,' Harrison added, consulting his notes. 'Maybe you'd had a few drinks and can't remember the details. It happens. We know how it works. Businessmen work under a lot of pressure these days.'

'Look.' Heyer was getting annoyed. 'There has been a mistake here. I was in all Monday night. By myself. Your information is wrong. I didn't take the car out all night. Actually, you can check my phone records if you like. I made a couple of calls from the house quite late that night.'

'Thank you, Mr Heyer. We might just do that,' said Harrison. Heyer hoped they wouldn't. The only call he had made after eleven had been to order Julia's minicab home.

'You can understand our concern, though, Mr Heyer,' said Underwood. 'A well-known local girl is murdered, your car is reported to have been in the area and you don't really have an alibi.'

72

'There has been some mistake here. I came here in good faith. I don't understand how this has happened.' Frightened though he was, Heyer decided to go on the offensive. He was beginning to see the light. Underwood obviously knew exactly what he'd been doing on Monday night. He had to talk to Julia. 'I think, if you wish to continue this interview, that I should have my lawyer present.'

'No need, Mr Heyer.' Underwood sat back in his chair. 'I don't have any further questions. That was very helpful. If you could provide us with an itemization of your phone calls that night, we'll check them out with the telephone company.' He paused as Heyer stood up. 'I'll be in touch.'

Heyer turned to face him. 'I think someone is playing games with you, Inspector.'

'You know, it's funny,' Underwood said. 'That's just what I was thinking.'

Harrison led Heyer from the room. Underwood looked up at the clock on the wall.

'Interview concluded at two-oh-six p.m.'

It had been an enjoyable ten minutes. He had derived great pleasure from making Heyer wriggle in his seat: local notable he might be but Heyer wasn't a very adept liar. Harrison didn't miss much and Underwood was sure he would have picked that up. A couple of minutes later the detective sergeant returned to the room. He looked thoughtful.

'What did you make of that, sergeant?' Underwood asked.

'He's hiding something. That's for sure,' said Harrison. 'I don't know, though, guv. He doesn't strike me as the type.'

'We shouldn't jump to any conclusions.' Underwood could tell his sergeant had suspected Heyer had been hiding something. 'Let's have a look at his phone records and see if we can dig up any background on the bloke – his business, his friends. Before we discount him, I want to be sure we've looked under every bloody rock in his garden.'

'Will do.'

Underwood thought of Julia, imagined her perfume clinging to Heyer's jacket, her hands on Heyer's smooth pale skin. He felt a sting of jealousy but also strangely calm. Underwood had looked straight into the eyes of his darkest suspicions and had felt no fear: just cold hate. Hate was a positive emotion. It was a harbinger of action. Maybe it was time for a chat with his wife.

Part II

Multiplications

23

Crowan Frayne sleeps intermittently through the afternoon. His mind throws off sparks like a Catherine wheel. Shallow sleep is the realm of dreams and Crowan Frayne wades through nightmares that cling and pull him down. He is in a wooden ship, rolling across a dark, undulating sea. He is watching the sky. Mapping the stars that smudge like raindrops against night's endless black panes. Dimension and distance gnaw achingly at his consciousness; he seeks pattern and accord where there is none. He is drawn by the asteroid Chiron. It completes its orbit of the sun once every fifty years despite the gravitational whirlpools that distort its progress: one blinding flash of clarity, one mathematical completion in a human lifetime. He imagines Chiron's music as a brilliant deafening glissando that completes and repeats its slide once every fifty years.

He sees distant planets, constellations and asterisms; flickering stars that may already be dead. Perhaps he is dead: perhaps his senses and awareness are mere corruptions of light and time distorted by the vastness of space. Others can map and record his dying light but he has long since collapsed into an oblivion that only mathematics can comprehend. Multiplication upon multiplication above, below, behind and beyond: multiplications of vastness upon emptiness upon chaos upon time. What gives us substance? Self-perception? Will? There are submicroscopic particles that only mathematics can identify: reductions upon reductions upon compressions. Higgs-Bosun particles give us mass and form. Ultimately, our existence is tangible only at a subatomic level. Crowan Frayne knows there is music in the tiny rotations of electrons, neutrinos and quarks. It is infinitesimally acute like a white-hot pin in the brain. He is awake for an instant. Winter sunlight pricks at his eyes but he can eclipse it with a wink; like the curtains hide the garden.

There are flowers in the garden and the grass is overgrown. Crowan Frayne is a child who plays knee-deep in grass alone.

He pulls grass from the ground with the soil that bore it. Soil is where we come from. Soil is where we go. Death gives soil its richness. Death is how we grow. Nothing is ever destroyed, it merely changes form: even Isaac Newton. Crowan Frayne travels along the spider's web of carbons and proteins that simplify us; the interlocking spirals of acids that reduce us to chains of numbers. Every dead thing is simplified in the soil and drawn up within us as particles of food and fluid. We are rich with the dead. Imbued with the dead. The dead are everywhere: drawn into flowers and trees, the water in rivers, the air we breathe. They interlace us, bind us together. We assimilate the molecules of the dead into new living structures. Nothing ever dies, it merely changes form. Crowan Frayne feels the molecules of the numberless dead sing within him. If mass can exist only at the subatomic level, he must be a billion dead things wrought into newness; forged into one by mathematics and will. Every thought, pain, memory and instinct of the dead is bound within him. He is a multiplication of everything that went before, of everyone who preceded him. The dead liveth for evermore . . .

He sees the war memorial in the older part of New Bolden cemetery. It is a white marble wall carved with the names of those who fell 1939–45. He likes to visit sometimes. Arrayed before the monolith are approximately two dozen gravestones, crosses stained grey by exposure to the polluted acidic air and soot from the railway. Frayne has taken cuttings of some of the flowers that grow there: roses, mainly blood red and bone white. He has learned many of the names and can converse with them as friends. Sgt P. Whittaker, Pvt. E. Plum, Cpt. J. Vigor. Specks of dust blown into oblivion. Frayne sees politics, war and conquest as essentially organic: no different in essence from packs of animals jockeying and fighting for territory or food. Sharks tearing apart seal pups: machine guns tearing up soldiers. The Spanish Armada was carried like a disease by the wind that eventually flung it to the bottom of the sea. Human affairs ultimately reduce to basic organic functions: birth, survival, death. The rest is poetry, mathematics and will.

Crowan Frayne sits up and pushes back the hair that has become stuck to his forehead. There is a cold swaddle of sweat around him. He feels exhausted but he faces a long, important evening. The power of his rational mind will draw up the energies that are buried within him. He will be ready. He rises and walks to his desk. There are Saintpaulia ionantha plants around his work. He has transplanted them from pots to his grandmother's graveside and back to pots. In this time they have flowered spectacularly. He knows that the petals and delicate stems are now as much imbued with her form as he is with her memory. As he touches the petals he feels like he is holding hands.

He sits and extends his mind around the day's events. Planning and the rational will has brought him so far. All that remains is concentration and energy. He has already mapped the constellation of possibilities. After the Providence of Lucy Harrington had thunderclapped across his consciousness he had begun developing his argument. He is uncertain where the next woman lives. However, he knows where she works; he has watched her and constructed patterns of probability. A shark can smell blood in the water from three miles away. To Crowan Frayne human vulnerabilities are even more obvious.

'Twice or thrice I lov'd yee / Before I knew thy face or name.' In 'Air and Angels' Donne speculated that human souls exist together as angels before their physical conception. The death of the body returns the soul to its original angelic state. The cycle is inspirational to Frayne: beauty returning to beauty through the ugliness of existence.

Lucy Harrington may now be an angel again. The Providence of her name had detonated an explosion of terrible possibilities in Crowan Frayne's mind. He had researched extensively, sifting through his books and his own copious notes on John Donne. He marvelled at his own intellectual arrogance: the extraordinary yoking of opposites. Perhaps Stussman would understand. He wondered if she could, truly. Her breathtakingly original study of Donne had filled Frayne with hope and purpose but he doubted whether even she could anticipate his conceit. Stussman was a technician of language; a surgeon, brilliant but pitiless.

He now had a selection of names to choose from. He expected

that Stussman would soon develop a similar list. However, the identification of the coterie was merely a preliminary, like the smoke that, when viewed from a distance, puffs silently from a starting pistol before the explosion cracks out and the race begins.

Elizabeth Drury would become an angel. The name itself was the broken-hearted soul of pity. A tragic acquaintance of Donne: the fifteen-year-old daughter of a patron, she had died prematurely of some unknown disease. Now Crowan Frayne would give the name a new significance: extol it beyond even Donne's own achievement in 'The Anniversairie'.

He had started searching for an Elizabeth Drury even before he had visited Lucy Harrington. The strongest arguments are fully constructed and sounded before they are articulated. There were ten 'Drurys' in the telephone book, none with the initial 'E'. He toyed with the idea of calling each and asking for Elizabeth on the off chance that there might be a wife or a daughter. That struck him as clumsy: they had to be a more efficient way. He then went to his computer and downloaded a UK people-finder program available on the Internet. He entered 'Elizabeth Drury' and New Bolden as the search parameters. His search provided no results. If there was an Elizabeth Drury in the area, she was almost certainly ex-directory. He would need to be more resourceful.

The New Bolden town library is an impressive building on three storeys. It was built in the mid-eighties after a series of cash donations from some of the computer and logistics companies that had relocated to the town from London. In the front lobby is a grey plaque that was unveiled by a minor member of the royal family when the library first opened. The library is modern and extremely well stocked. Crowan Frayne is a regular visitor. He does not hold a library card, preferring to steal the books that excite his curiosity. He tends to work in the Reference Room: a quiet annexe on the second floor away from the rustling carrier bags of pensioners, the raking coughs of the unemployed

80

and the grim squadron of wailing babies that often make Frayne want to rip his own stomach out with the carpet knife he always carries with him.

He uses the library's large resource of literary criticisms and certain history books of the Renaissance. It was here on an opaque, foggy morning that he discovered Reconstructing Donne by Dr Heather Stussman of the University of Wisconsin. There was a striking picture of Stussman on the inside back cover. Intrigued, he dug out back copies of the TLS and the Literary Review and finally unearthed a critical review of the book. It was spiteful and, in Frayne's view, idiotic. The author, Professor Arthur Spink of Exeter University, subsequently received a human stool in the post: carefully wrapped in tinfoil inside a Tupperware container tied with a silk bow. The accompanying note simply said 'Cunt'. However, Spink's review had provided him with one piece of useful information: Stussman was a visiting Fellow at Southwell College, Cambridge for the current academic year. Frayne had been shocked by the discovery. Cambridge was only twenty miles away.

It was while Frayne was searching for other publications by Heather Stussman that he chanced upon Dr Elizabeth Drury. The library had recently installed a state-of-the-art computer system that enabled the user to search for books across a network that linked all the libraries in the area – including the University Library in Cambridge, one of the few copyright libraries in Britain. Using this system, Frayne had learned the title of Stussman's doctoral thesis and obtained copies of two academic articles she had written when she'd still been in America.

After a productive session at the computer, he was struck by an idea. He returned to the first page of the 'bookfinder' pro-gramme and clicked twice on the 'Master Name' box. The likeness of a typewriter keyboard appeared on the screen. Using his mouse to guide the screen arrow he clicked in the name 'Elizabeth Drury' and tapped the return key. The screen blanked for a second before a white dialogue box containing the follow-ing text appeared:

Search results: *One match*
Author: *Drury, Elizabeth J.*
Title: The Weight of Expectation: Obesity and Self-Image
Class Mark: 678.094' 081
Year: *1992*
Material Type: *Non-Fiction*
Language of Text: *English*
Copies: *1*

Frayne fingered the petals in his jacket pocket and hurriedly noted down the class mark. The simplicity of the process had dazzled him. He walked to the health-care section of the library and quickly located The Weight of Expectation: Obesity and Self Image. *It was a thick, well-thumbed hardback with a picture on the front cover of a young woman wearing a leotard and holding a mirror. Frayne wondered if there were chocolate fingerprints on the inside pages. The photo and accompanying paragraph of author's details were helpful: 'Dr Elizabeth Drury was educated at University College, Oxford and Guys Medical School. She is a leading international dietician and runs the Drury Clinic, a private medical practice in London. She has published a number of articles on the psychological aspects of obesity.* The Weight of Expectation *is her first book.' However, it was the last piece of information that excited Frayne the most. 'Dr Drury has lived in Cambridgeshire for ten years.' Frayne never understood why authors included such pointless personal detail: perhaps Dr Drury felt that announcing she lived in Cambridgeshire somehow enhanced her intellectual credibility. In any case, he now had all the information he needed to find her: a drop of blood had plopped into the water. He noticed that the book also contained an extensive bibliography: that might prove useful.*

Directory Inquiries gave him the phone number of the Drury Clinic. He called immediately and asked the receptionist for the clinic's mailing address.

'17 Mayfair Crescent, SW1.' She had an Australian accent. He liked that. He didn't know why.

'Very helpful – thank you. Is Dr Drury's husband available?' asked Frayne.

'Husband? There must be some mistake. Dr Drury isn't married.'

'I do apologize. I'm confusing doctors with dentists,' said Frayne flatly.

'No problem. You have a nice day now.' But Frayne had already gone.

The following day he took the train from New Bolden to London and then the Underground to Leicester Square. After a brisk ten minutes' walk he was in Mayfair Crescent. It was a busy road, cluttered with traffic and expensively suited professionals. There were double yellow lines on both sides of the street. He guessed that Drury came in by train. If she lived in Cambridgeshire that meant she probably came into Liverpool Street and then across town on the Central Line. She was wealthy, though, Frayne mused. Maybe she took a cab. That would be problematic. The entrance to the Drury Clinic was impressive. White Doric columns topped with an ornately carved lintel: smoked-glass doors with golden handles. They might have self-image problems but Drury's clients were clearly rich.

The clinic closed at six p.m. A dozen or so staff, secretaries mostly, filed out shortly after. Frayne didn't see Drury until six-thirty. She left the building with another woman and they parted company with a reassuring hug: 'Client,' Frayne thought to himself. Drury walked to the edge of the road and looked intently in both directions for a cab. It was a cold night in London and the wind whipped up bitterly from the Thames: piercing and hard.

Drury lost patience and started to walk. Frayne followed at a distance. Drury was tall, blonde and elegant. She wore a dark red full-length coat that was easy to spot despite the bustle of early Christmas shoppers. She walked up Haymarket to Piccadilly and descended into the Underground station at Piccadilly Circus. Frayne got closer: the crowd was thick now and he felt anonymous. He caught a glimpse of himself on a security monitor at the top of an escalator: coat collar up, baseball hat tightly pulled down. He managed to suppress a smile. Drury took the northbound Piccadilly line to Holborn, as he suspected

83

she would, and switched to the Central Line. Frayne smiled to himself: Liverpool Street.

The concourse at Liverpool Street was a sweaty, bumping chaos. Dozens of tired eyes gazed up at the departure-announcements board: many squinting to read its impossibly small text. Drury paused below the board next to a group of foreign students who were sitting on rucksacks and eating baguettes. She saw her train on the board and quickly turned towards Platform 5. Frayne saw that it was a Cambridge train. Drury hurried ahead of him and stepped carefully into a first class carriage: she had broken heels on the footplate several times in the past. Frayne walked past the carriage without looking inside and boarded the packed adjacent standard class section. It smelled of beefburgers and the warm fug of commuters. Through dirty glass panes he could see into first class.

The train shuddered out of London, moving slowly through graffiti-sprayed cuttings and the rapist's paradise of Hackney Marshes. Soon the city receded and the black sky seemed to drop to the ground like a falling curtain. The train emptied gradually. The extra comfort this afforded was outweighed in Frayne's mind by his own increased visibility. Harlow came and went and soon the flat blacklands of Cambridgeshire yawned enormously in both directions. They had to be close now. Drury had put down her newspaper and seemed to be assessing her profile in the dark window. She tugged gently at the skin that hung from the angle of her jaw. After an hour the train began to drop off the last handfuls of commuters at each of the small village stations that nestled against the last stretch of line before Cambridge. As the train groaned into Afton, Drury stood up and walked to the door.

She stepped cautiously off the train and clicked briskly in her high heels along the platform. There were two or three other people between her and Crowan Frayne. She walked into the car park and used her remote to beep off the security system of her grey Audi TT.

Frayne held back and pretended to jangle his own car keys at the door of a nearby Renault Clio. The Audi roared to life and

84

growled expensively along the line of cars. Crowan Frayne made certain not to look until it had gone completely past him. Then he wrote down Elizabeth Drury's licence plate number on his hand and walked back into the station. He took a local train into Cambridge and then changed for New Bolden.

Once home he wrote down the following details: 'Wednesday. Office 6.30. 7.17 from Liverpool Street, first class carriage. Afton station 8.22. Grey Audi. EDR92.'

The next morning he called the Drury Clinic and spoke to the same Australian receptionist. He used a name that he knew Drury would recognize.

'Good morning. My name is Dr Thomas Stiglitz. I am a professional acquaintance of Dr Drury's.'

'I'm afraid she is with a patient at the moment.'

'Can I make an appointment to see her? I am in London for two days next week and would like to visit her at the clinic. I'm calling from the United States.'

'I'll check her diary. Which day did you have in mind?'

'December the eleventh.'

'What time?'

'Six o'clock.'

'That should be OK. She has a five-thirty but I could bump that forward.'

'If you could. As soon as I've seen Elizabeth, I'm heading back to LA.'

'Can I check the spelling of your name, sir?'

'Stiglitz.' Frayne checked the bibliography of The Weight of Expectations, which he had opened in front of him, 'S-t-i-g-l-i-t-z. I am from the University of Los Angeles at Berkeley.'

'Thank you, sir. That's all booked. Have a good day now.'

Elizabeth Drury was surprised and delighted when she saw the new name in her diary.

'Stiggy! I haven't spoken to him in five years.'

'He sounded like a real nice guy,' said Sally the receptionist from behind a steaming café latte in a cardboard cup.

'He is. Kind of brilliant, too.'

Elizabeth Drury went back into her consulting rooms with a

85

smile on her face and marvelled at how the world seemed to get smaller every day. Miles away, in a darkened living room, Crowan Frayne closed the copy of The Weight of Expectations that he had stolen from the New Bolden library and threw it in the bin.

A week had passed since Crowan Frayne had arranged the meeting. During that time he had been active: planning, researching. He had cleaned Lucy Harrington's eye thoroughly and spent considerable time enjoying its dead blueness. He had expended much time the previous evening delicately cutting away residual muscle and raggedness from the surface of the eyeball. He wanted it to be smooth as glass.

He had also washed and checked his collection of medical instruments. When the exceptional brilliance of his conceit had first sparked across his brain he had quickly taken stock of the equipment available to him. Kitchen knives and carpet cutters seemed to him cumbersome and witless tools for such an important exercise. He had rooted through his grandfather's garage in search of more delicate knives and found instead two steel-headed hammers. He realized these would be useful. One was small enough to be concealed in the sleeve of his jacket.

The question of cutting instruments had perturbed him. He needed small, light and razor-sharp knives, along with other specific equipment like forceps. There were no stores in New Bolden that sold medical equipment. He wondered if Cambridge with its University medical faculty and Addenbrokes Hospital might be a more likely hunting ground. He quickly realized that there were no medical equipment suppliers in the region that sold over the counter. Frayne was frustrated. What were his alternatives? Stealing equipment from the hospital or the university was a possibility that he quickly discounted. That would be a highly risky undertaking: both locations were always crowded with people and, Frayne mused, probably protected with video-camera surveillance. It was too big a chance to be taken.

Then Frayne had an idea. He remembered that the essence of his work was beyond science and history, filling the gaps *between knowledge and belief. Like his conceit, he would need to transcend time. Or fold it. He had turned on his computer and linked up to the Internet. After typing in the search terms 'antique medical instruments', half a dozen options had appeared on his screen. One of them seemed especially promising. An antiques shop in Hampstead, London called Lieberman's. Its home page promised 'antique furniture, paintings, works of art, and glass, antique surgical equipment.' Better still, there was a section of the website devoted entirely to Lieberman's collection of medical and scientific items. There were photographs of three boxes of surgical knives dating from the nineteeth century and, to Frayne's great delight, an ophthalmic surgery kit from 1840. He had driven to London that same afternoon and after trying unsuccessfully for an hour to park in Hampstead had eventually left his van in the car park of Jack Straw's Castle and had walked down Hampstead High Street to Lieberman's.*

The shop was tucked away in a side alley behind the entrance to Hampstead Tube station. A woman worked alone inside. She was middle-aged, quietly elegant with greying blonde hair. Frayne noticed her silk scarf: it was beautifully styled, with azure patterns that sharpened her porcelain-grey eyes. He started when he heard her sudden phlegmy smoker's cough. The entanglement of beauty and ugliness jarred in him. Using information he had gleaned from the website, Frayne managed to sound like something of an expert. He said he was looking for an antique medical kit as a birthday present for his father: a prominent London eye surgeon. The woman had made the connection herself and told Frayne that she had the very thing. She disappeared to a darker and, judging by the increased frequency of her coughing, dustier section of the shop, returning with the small ophthalmic surgery kit Frayne had seen on the website.

It had been made in 1840 by John Weiss (later of Weiss and Son) of The Strand, London. The small black leather box bore Weiss's name and crest. The inside was lined with red silk and contained twelve ivory-handled scalpels, a selection of grisly surgical scissors, four small clamps for holding back the eyelids,

87

some long needles with hooked ends, a pair of forceps and two L-shaped scraping implements. There was also a set of spindly metal surgeon's magnifying glasses that clamped around the patient's head and enabled the surgeon to look deep into the eye. The kit was in immaculate condition, a unique set. Frayne had picked up one of the scalpels. It felt almost weightless and beautifully balanced in his delicate grip. The cutting edge had lost some of its sharpness but Frayne knew that, with care, it could be restored. 'Makes you shudder, doesn't it?' said the woman, smiling. 'What those poor people must have gone though.' Frayne had politely agreed with her and paid the eight hundred pounds asking price in cash.

Tonight he would visit Dr Elizabeth Drury in her house near Afton. He had no intention of keeping Dr Thomas Stiglitz's appointment at The Drury Clinic. However, when Dr Stiglitz failed to turn up he reckoned that Drury would rush to catch the 7.17 from Liverpool Street. He had effectively cleared her appointments for that evening: she had no other reason to delay in London and he could predict her timetable accurately. He would be in the car park at Afton station waiting for her. Before then he would need to focus carefully on poetic expression.

Donne had commemorated Drury's premature death in 'The Anniversaries'. However, in 'A Feaver' the poet had attempted to wrestle with similar concepts, particularly the exaltation of the dead woman to the status of a celestial entity and the reduction of the world to the status of a carcass. 'A Feaver' was more concise but related to Elizabeth Drury only in its roughly equivalent thematic content. Frayne was confident that Dr Stussman would make the connection. If she didn't, he would enjoy explaining it to her personally.

24

When Paul Heyer returned home at three o'clock that afternoon, Julia Underwood was already waiting for him. She had poured herself a gin and tonic and was sitting on the edge of the sofa, her suitcase resting pathetically and accusingly in front of her. She jumped when she heard his key turn in the door and she ran out to embrace him.

'Paul! I was worried. I thought you'd be here.' She was shaking.

'So did I.' He took a step back from her embrace.

'Where have you been?' she asked, her eyes seeking a clue in the lines of his face.

He wasn't sure how to answer. 'I have been in a police interrogation room, being grilled by your husband.'

'By John? Why?' Julia was shocked: she felt as though a terrible weight had dropped in her stomach.

'I don't fucking know. A police car turned up at lunchtime. They asked me to go to the station where I had the pleasure of being interrogated by your husband. He was asking where I was on Monday night.' Heyer was shaking, partly with rage.

'But you were with me on Monday night.'

'Of course I was. He knows, Julia. Don't you see? He's playing games, trying to frighten me off, I suppose.'

'Did he mention me? Did he say anything?' Her heart was leaping and pounding.

'No. He kept asking me about the dead girl: the swimmer. He said my car had been seen on Hartfield Road that night. He implied I was a suspect.'

'But you were here, with me.'

'I know I was here. He's making the whole fucking thing up, trying to put the wind up me. You should have told him, Julia. It's all gone up the wall now. I think he's lost it completely.'

'I left him a note today,' Julia said, misery welling inside her. 'He won't answer any of my calls.'

'Well, now we know why, don't we?'

'How could he know about us? Nobody knows.' She was crying.

'I have no idea.' Paul poured himself a large Scotch at the sideboard and gulped it gratefully. 'But he knows, all right. I could see it in his eyes: pure bloody hatred. He's made up some cock and bull story about the car to get me in there. Frighten me. Well, if he tries it again I'll have my lawyer with me and we'll have the bastard for harassment and fabricating evidence.' There was a rage in his eyes that Julia hadn't seen before. It frightened her. 'You say you've left him a note?'

'Yes, but I didn't mention you. I told him it was over and I had gone to stay with my mum.'

'You have to speak to him, Julia. It's out of hand now. He has lost the plot.' He took another giant swig of Scotch and relented slightly. He looked at the suitcase. 'Still, at least you're here.' He sat beside her on the sofa and put his arm around her.

25

Heather Stussman had spent the morning drawing up a list of names. She went back through her own research on Donne and flipped through some of the more compelling biographies. She reasoned that the killer would use names that were directly associated with Donne's poetry and so she discounted a number of the poet's casual relationships. And yet, if the killer had focused on the notion of a coterie, an audience of like-minded intellectuals, wouldn't he also have included contemporaries of Donne? Other poets such as George Herbert or Thomas Carew? If so, the list would be enormous.

She focused on the *Songs and Sonnets*, Donne's letters and his religious poems. Stussman began to divide people associated with these pieces into categories: dedications, patrons, relatives and subject matter. After an hour she had put together the following list:

Dedications/Letters/Friends	Patrons	Relatives
Lucy Harrington	Lucy Harrington	–
		Ann More (wife)
		Lucy Donne
G. G Esquire		
Henry Goodyere		
		Anne Donne (sister)
Cecilia Bulstrode		
	Sir Robert Drury	
Elizabeth Drury		
Susan Vere		
Rowland Woodward		
Henry Wooton		
Ann Stanhope		

It was by no means a full list. It was not even a list of all those closest to Donne. However, it was a decent enough collection of people directly associated with Donne's writings.

Pleased with her efforts, Stussman printed the list off from her computer and left her rooms. There was a uniformed police officer from the Cambridge Police HQ at Parker's Piece standing guard at her door. She explained to him that she was only going to the college office and he let her go alone. She faxed the page through to Underwood with a brief accompanying note: 'We discussed the potential significance of names. Attached is a summary list of some of Donne's acquaintances. Yours, Heather Stussman.'

She bumped into Dr McKensie as she left the office. He seemed amused. 'Well, well! Who's a naughty girl, then? Word is that you've been entertaining the police all afternoon. There's a frightfully good-looking young officer standing guard outside your door. We *do* like a man in uniform. What on earth have you been up to?'

'Just leave it, McKensie, I'm not in the mood right now.'

He carried on regardless, his gaze boring into her like lasers. 'Professor Dixon wondered if it was tax evasion. I suspected it was for crimes against academic convention. Are you under house arrest? Can we expect a visit from the FBI?'

Stussman pushed past him. McKensie grinned at her retreating back like a hungry dog. 'Do let me know if I can be of any help. I have friends in the House of Lords should things progress to court.'

'Go fuck yourself, McKensie.'

McKensie smirked: the girl certainly had spirit. He called out after her, 'I frequently do, dearie. Though I doubt I could manage it as effectively as you have.'

26

Underwood sat in his office. He had dialled Julia's number into his mobile but had not quite mustered the courage to call her yet. The interview with Heyer had been revealing. He had looked into the stranger's eyes, the same eyes in which his wife saw some hope, some knicker-wetting false hope, and he had seen fear. Not many people were frightened of Underwood any more; it felt refreshing. Heyer had been afraid because he had something to hide and Underwood knew fully what that was: the impending destruction of his, Underwood's, marriage, the corruption of his wife. It had been sweet to watch Heyer squirm but now he would have to be more careful. Still, despite everything there was a sadness nagging at Underwood's heart. Whatever acidic gloss he daubed over the situation, however he tried to blot the thought from his mind, Paul Heyer had struck Underwood as a fundamentally decent man.

Jensen was at the door. 'Sir. Have you got a second?'

'Come in.'

'I have put together the list of people arrested for housebreaking in the area as you requested. It's pretty long, I'm afraid, over a hundred names.'

'I thought there'd be more, to be honest.' Underwood was only half-interested. 'We seem to spend half our lives chasing burglars.'

'I've only gone back five years, sir. There'll be a lot more if I extend the search.'

'No, let's start with that. Cross off people aged under twenty-five and over forty-five. See how many that leaves us with.'

'What's the logic there, sir?'

'As I understand it, most serial killers are aged between twenty-five and forty. What they do requires planning and control. Characteristics of an older man.'

'I see.' Jensen tried not to smirk and scribbled a note on the page. 'Everyone's calling him a serial killer but he's only killed one person so far, sir.'

'One that we know about. They'll be more if we don't get our shit together.' Underwood thought for a second. 'The likelihood is he's white too, so take out members of all other ethnic groups.'

'Why do you say that?'

'Serial killers tend to stick to their own.'

'I'll get on it. Shall I run the remaining names through DVLA and see if any of them own a white Escort?'

'You might as well but we still don't know for sure that our man even drives a white Escort.'

'OK. Forensic identified the flower petals, sir: the one you found at the Harrington girl's back door and the ones Dexter found in the woods by the house.'

'Go on.'

'They're African violets.'

'Violets?'

'*Saintpaulia ionantha*,' Jensen said after checking her notebook. 'Pretty common, I'm afraid. Old ladies like them, according to Harrison.'

'Are there any nurseries or flower shops around here?'

She had anticipated this and flipped her notebook open again.

'Two shops in New Bolden and a nursery out near Feldreth. Worth checking, sir?'

'Probably not, but let's roll the dice. Take a trip round them. Ask a few questions. You might be able to turn something up.'

Dexter brushed past Jensen at the door. She had a habit of breezing in when Jensen was alone in the office with Underwood.

'Excuse me, sir,' said Dexter, brisk and businesslike. 'We just got a fax of possible names from Dr Stussman.'

'Is that all, then, Jensen?' Underwood asked.

'Yes, sir.' She hesitated, 'Do you mind if I hang on for a second, sir? I'd be interested in what the detective sergeant has to say.' Jensen smiled sweetly at Dexter.

'Be my guest,' said Underwood.

Dexter bristled. She spoke quickly, hoping Jensen wouldn't be able to follow her train of logic. 'Stussman said that Lucy Harrington's name was important. The name is the connection with the writing on the bathroom wall, the same text that Stussman received in the post. Four hundred years ago someone called Lucy Harrington was a patron of the poet John Donne.'

'I asked Stussman to send us a list of other individuals connected with John Donne,' said Underwood to Jensen.

'There're thirteen names on the list,' Dexter continued, 'eight of them women.'

She handed the fax to Underwood. He ran his fingers through his hair as if to push back the tiredness; some strands came away in his hand.

'None of the names are that common, I suppose,' he observed. 'That's the good news.' He scanned the fax carefully, then shook his head. 'I don't know, Dex, this seems a bit far-fetched to me: all that stuff about coteries and like-minded individuals. The killer would be taking a huge risk if he limited himself to this list of names. He's probably guessed that Stussman has made the name connection.'

'Two things, sir,' said Dexter. 'For whatever reason, I think that he *wanted* Stussman to give us the names. Remember, she said he told her to "explain it to the police". He wouldn't do that if it was likely to make him vulnerable.'

'What's the second thing?'

'I was thinking, sir: there's no risk to him at all if he's already done one of them.'

Underwood looked outside. It seemed to get dark by mid-afternoon. He hated December, the deepest, darkest pit of the year. 'Let's get cracking, then,' he said quietly. 'You two go through the list together. See if any people with those names live locally; use telephone directories, the electoral register, police records. Get someone to do a news run on the names. Our man likes to read the papers, doesn't he?'

Dexter and Jensen exchanged a none-too-happy look and trooped out. Underwood looked at the list in front of him. Old-fashioned names. He noticed that Lucy Harrington was in two categories, 'Dedications' and 'Patrons'. Scanning down the list he saw that no other name was entered in two columns. Except Drury: Sir Robert Drury and Elizabeth Drury. Was that significant? He searched on his desk for Stussman's phone number. His desk looked like a tornado had torn across it. He found the scrap of paper and dialled. The phone rang once.

'Heather Stussman.' There was a nervous edge to her voice.

'Dr Stussman. This is John Underwood, from New Bolden CID.'

He heard her relax. 'Thank God. Every time the phone rings I have a baby.'

'No contact from our man, I suppose,' asked Underwood. Why did he feel nervous?

'Nothing. Your friends at Parker's Piece have sent my body-guard over, though.'

'Good. You're perfectly safe there, Heather.' Underwood knew that the words sounded empty. He also knew that he had called her by her first name and felt a tired thud of excitement. Desire and despair.

'I guess so. I just feel kind of exposed.'

'I need to ask you a question about the list you sent to us.' Underwood was trying not to think of an exposed Heather Stussman but it was a compelling image.

'Shoot.'

'Robert Drury and Elizabeth Drury. Were they blood relations or husband and wife?'

'Father and daughter. Is that important?'

'I'm not sure. Other than Harrington, Drury is the only name that appears in two of your columns. Bearing in mind what happened to Lucy Harrington, I thought it might be worth checking out.'

'OK.' Stussman paused for a second to take a sip of coffee. 'It's a sad story, actually. Sir Robert Drury was a wealthy Suffolk landowner who had participated in the Cadiz expedition – you know, singeing the King of Spain's beard and all that. Poets like Donne were dependent upon wealthy patrons like Drury or Lucy Harrington and Donne made a concerted effort to win favour with Sir Robert. In 1610, Sir Robert's fifteen-year-old daughter Elizabeth died of some infection – we don't know exactly what. Now, some commentators believe that Donne used the death of the girl to ingratiate himself with Sir Robert.'

'By writing about her?'

'Yes.'

'Jesus Christ.'

The penny dropped. Stussman's hand felt clammy against the phone. 'My God, John, you think he's going to look for an Elizabeth Drury?'

'If he hasn't found her already. I'd better go. Call me if anything else occurs to you.'

'Will do.'

Underwood hung up. He was attracted to Stussman but instead of stimulating him it just impaled him on the spike of his own worthlessness. He recalled a phrase: 'Despair is easy to manage, but hope destroys you.' Who had said that? A terrible weariness was seeping into him: a miserable sense of resignation. Perhaps he was going to die: they said animals wanted to be alone when they sensed their own death. Now, suddenly, Underwood just wanted to go home. Lucy Harrington's killer was playing a game that required energy and Underwood had none left. He walked through to the Incident Room where Jensen and Dexter were arguing about how best to apportion responsibility for locating the owners of names on the list. Underwood summarized his conversation with Stussman, telling them to concentrate their immediate efforts on the names Robert and Elizabeth Drury.

Dexter sensed a new sadness in her boss as she watched him leave: he had suddenly looked very small, pathetic almost. Outside the Incident Room Underwood was trying to blot Julia from his mind. Would she be waiting for him at home? He couldn't bear to think of her, soiled by a stranger: except, of course, Heyer wasn't a stranger any more. For a split second, Underwood occupied the space where Julia's lips touched Paul Heyer's and their pressure crushed the breath from him. It was only when he had returned to his office and cleared his clagging chest that he remembered Stussman had called him by his first name.

Dexter began with the telephone directories, just as Crowan Frayne had done, and turned up the same ten names in Cambridgeshire. Unlike Frayne she called each of the numbers in turn. It was a laborious process and after an hour and a half she had only got through to four of the ten numbers. No Elizabeths or Roberts but plenty of confusion and hostility. She became frustrated and handed over the task to Jensen who grudgingly accepted and spent the remainder of the day angrily listening to interminable ringing tones in empty houses.

Dexter began to sift through electoral registers. She began with New Bolden and after an hour had drawn a complete blank. With a heavy heart she had turned to Cambridge and eventually found a Robert Drury, living on Bentley Road. She immediately called and learned from a cleaner that Mr Drury had been taken into Addenbroke's for observation after a kidney failure. Mr Drury was eighty-six. Dexter ploughed on: she knew that the electoral registers weren't perfect. For a start, they were out of date and didn't seem to have been amended for two years. Secondly, although they broke out family composition they did not include the names of people below voting age. Underwood had told her that the original Elizabeth Drury had only been fifteen when she died.

Police records were equally unhelpful. There were no Drurys whatsoever on file. 'Law-abiding folk,' mused Dexter. 'Not even a shoplifter.' She thought about the killer. He had found Lucy Harrington in a newspaper. A public data source. The likelihood was that he would look for Elizabeth Drury using other public sources: that would make it harder for the police to trace him. He was probably using something like a telephone directory or a newspaper.

Belatedly, Dexter remembered Underwood's request for a news run. The County Police Headquarters in Huntingdon has access to a computer software program that could search for names and headlines in the local and national press. She looked at the clock: it was after six. The information office would be shut by now. She cursed herself for forgetting and left a voice-mail message on the enquiry number requesting a two-year text run on Robert Drury and Elizabeth Drury for first thing in the morning. Dexter walked into Underwood's office to tell him that the news run would be delayed: the office was empty. Dexter returned to the Incident Room and watched her reflection in the window: the blackening sky pawed at the glass. Maybe Underwood had gone home: she hoped so – he looked crumpled. She settled in for a long night with the electoral registers for Ely, Peterborough, Huntingdon, and the rural constituencies of Waterskill, Holton, Evebury and Afton.

27

Dr Elizabeth Drury gave up waiting for Thomas Stiglitz at 6.45 that night. She was disappointed not to have seen her old acquaintance but was determined not to sit around in an empty building all night waiting for him. After all, Stiglitz had told her assistant that he had a plane to catch that night: perhaps he had been delayed elsewhere and had decided to go straight to the airport. Still, it would have been nice of him to call. Fortunately, she got a taxi almost immediately outside the clinic and jumped out at Liverpool Street station at 7.15 exactly. The train journey was as stuffy and unpleasant as always. Drury was mildly irritated that people who obviously had standard-class tickets were standing in first class. Still, at least she had a seat.

There was a tall dead-eyed youth standing with his back to her. She tried to blot out the electronic tippy-tappy of his personal headset and rustled her newspaper in annoyance. There was no peace anywhere. No quality anywhere. She felt life in Britain had been dumbed down and dragged to the lowest common denominator: the National Gallery had become filled with what seemed to her to resemble a football crowd. Conversely, she had read that football crowds had become flooded with people who used to go to the National Gallery. Paying for a first-class ticket now meant you could sit in sweltering, sweaty heat with a man's backside next to your face for an hour and listen to the machine music that was battering his brain cells. 'There is no beauty but the self.' She had written that sentence to conclude *The Weight of Expectation*: now she was beginning to believe it.

The cold air and stillness of Afton station was a huge relief: like diving into an ice-cold swimming pool on a stifling day. After the cramped tin-can suffocation of the train, even the inside of her Audi felt like a luxury leather armchair. She flicked the ignition and before driving off chose some music: *Miserere mei, Deus* by Allegri. She closed her eyes for a second as the piece started, still the most beautiful choral arrangement she had ever heard. She secured her seat belt and reversed out of the parking space. It was a shame that she had not been able to see Stiggy, she mused as she pulled away: his work on the genetic inheritance of the characteristics leading to obesity had influenced much of her own thinking. She turned left out of the car park. Twenty yards behind her, Crowan Frayne switched on his headlights.

Drury's Audi sped out of Afton village. Frayne's Escort van had trouble keeping up. He didn't want to get too close but he had to stay in visual contact since he had no idea where Drury lived. The roads narrowed as the two cars headed out into the countryside. Blindman's Lane twisted and rose across farmland. The ploughed fields on either side looked like bottomless black pools to Frayne but he knew that they were alive with the intermingled dead of a thousand generations. He kept about a quarter-mile behind Drury: his eyes fixed on the rear lights of her Audi in the near distance. Suddenly, they disappeared around a bend in the road. Frayne accelerated: he didn't want to lose her in the maze of lanes. He was already uncertain of his bearings.

As he rounded the bend he saw the Audi turn down a narrow driveway off to the right and approach a large house that stood incongruously in the open country around it. It was almost certainly a converted farmhouse. He drove past and parked up a farm track at the entrance to a field about half a mile along the lane. The van was out of sight of the main road: he took a calculated risk that nobody was likely to come out to the field at that time of night. He strained his eyes, peering into the darkness ahead of him: no cattle or sheep, just a barren field.

He was uncomfortable. He had found the house but knew nothing about it. A house that size, so isolated would almost certainly have a burglar alarm: probably a very good one. He knew for sure that Drury had plenty of money. Frayne decided to take a closer look at the buildings before he made his final approach. He could double back to Drury's house along the edge of the fields. He didn't want to risk being caught in the headlights of an oncoming car on the road. There were patches of hedging he could use for cover where the field met the lane. He needn't have worried. Blindman's Lane was seldom used for anything other than farm traffic and he made it to Drury's driveway without encountering any cars.

He found the darkness comforting: it penetrated him, empowered him. He was the darkness: the blind, encompassing night. It was cloudy and he could not make out any of the constellations he knew so well. He could hear them, though: muffled and obscured by the tumbling grey clouds but unmistakably beautiful. His gaze focused on the house. He could make out the downstairs lights clearly. There was a gate leading onto the gravel driveway. Drury must have closed it after he had driven past. A large open lawn stretched in front of the house. There were clumps of trees at the back of the buildings that might have provided useful concealment but to get there he would either have to cross the lawn or pick his way across the adjoining field. The ground looked as if it had been recently ploughed and Frayne rejected the idea of stumbling blindly across the heavy mud, carrying his equipment. More promising were the two large beech trees on the left-hand side of the driveway. There was also a line of hedgerow behind them. If he moved carefully, he would be virtually invisible against it and could rest at the foot of each of the beeches if necessary.

Frayne crossed the road and clambered over the wooden gate. Keeping to the left, he moved quickly towards the house, hugging the rustling black wall of privet. He could see the house more clearly now. It was large, square with high sash windows and a heavy wooden door. Drury's car was parked at the front of the house about twenty yards from the doorway. He crouched at the foot of the first beech to consider his options. He ground the violet petals in his left hand and held his palm to his face, breathing in the thick musty scent. The situation didn't look promising: the house seemed very secure. There was a security-alarm box above the front door. He moved closer, wanting to get a more detailed look: he knew that some people put dummy boxes outside their houses to deter burglars, thinking that the implied presence of an alarm system would be enough. He had reached the second beech tree and could still not make out the box clearly.

Crowan Frayne sat back on his haunches. He had been caught out trying to cut security-system wires before. Many of the modern alarms incorporated fail-safe systems that went off immediately if tampered with. It was a huge risk. He needed to be certain. He moved from behind the tree and stepped forward. He was suddenly illuminated in brilliant white light. He jumped, dived down to the gravel and crawled to the side of Elizabeth

Drury's Audi. Security lights. He cursed his stupidity: he should have expected this. Still, the car hid him from the sight of anyone in the house. He waited.

Elizabeth Drury looked briefly out of her living-room window at her driveway bathed in light. She was used to the security lights now. Her cats frequently triggered the system when they played outside at night, as did the local foxes who regularly raided her rubbish bins. She saw nothing and returned to her book.

After what seemed an age the lights blinked off. Crowan Frayne relaxed and allowed himself a closer look at the house through the car windows. He could see the alarm box and noticed immediately that it was wired. He just stopped himself from swearing aloud, afraid his rising breath would betray him. Breaking in through a door or a window would be extremely dangerous: Drury might even have a system that contained a silent trigger to the local police station. There had to be another way. He looked again at the front of the house through the expensive prism of the Audi. His gaze hunted frantically for weaknesses and found none. Then something on the side window of the car caught his eye. It was a sticker.

Satisfied that he had not been detected, Frayne hurried back to the relative safety of the fence and considered his options. There was a way to do this but it would take time and a degree of risk. It was now well after nine o'clock. He decided to return at midnight. He believed that Dr Drury was an early riser; given the length of her daily commute. He flitted along the edge of the driveway and was quickly over the road, through the hedgerow and retracing his steps back to his car.

There were only two pubs in Afton village and Katie Hunt was under age. Steve Riley was just eighteen. They had spent an hour together in The Farmer's Boy before they had both grown tired of Coca-Cola. Steve suggested they should go for a drive to find somewhere more private. He was excited at his own boldness: it was only their second date. They had kissed in the car park of the pub, then again inside the car. She tasted of lemon. Steve realized that she had been sucking the lemon slices in her drink.

As they drove out of the village into the darkness, Steve's mind raced through the alternatives. It was difficult to concentrate with Katie's hand on his thigh but he tried hard. At the junction of Afton High Street and Blindman's Lane he paused for a moment. Then he had a flash of inspiration and turned left out of the village.

From some distance Crowan Frayne saw the car coming: its headlights cast a short, uncertain beam out into the sprawling darkness. He crouched against a hedge and waited. He heard the car's engine getting louder, the noise growling through the air. His mind worked through the alternatives: other than Drury's house there was nowhere obvious to stop on this road. If Drury had been expecting visitors she would have left the gate open. No. It had to be through traffic. He waited for it to pass. Two minutes later, Steve Riley's Fiesta flashed past the spot where Crowan Frayne was hiding, its occupants seeing nothing unusual through the wall of darkness that stared back at them. Frayne was rising to his feet again when he heard the car slowing down.

Steve Riley turned along the farm track. The soft ground seemed to squish under the car. Katie giggled as they bounced on the lumpy turf. Steve slowed and peered out through the windscreen: his headlights picked out the back doors of Crowan Frayne's white Escort van.

'Looks like someone's got the same idea as us,' he said.

'Maybe it's broken down.'

Steve stopped a few feet short of the Escort and climbed out. He walked up behind the van, following the trajectory cast by his own headlights, and looked through the back windows. There was no one inside. He could make out a couple of wooden boxes in the back section but there were no signs of life. He turned back to face his own car and shrugged: Katie shrugged too, although he couldn't see her. Steve walked back and jumped back inside.

'There's no one there. Must belong to some farmworker. I think there's tools in the back,' he said. 'Do you want to find somewhere else?'

'This is fine.' Katie leaned forward and kissed him again. Lemons. Steve put his hand onto her jumper, quickly working his way round to cup one of her breasts. There was no point wasting time.

Ten yards away Crowan Frayne, a hole in the night, watched them. He was uncertain how to proceed. He was tempted to leave them. But if they remembered his van, they might remember the number of his licence plate and Frayne wasn't ready for the police yet. Did he dare let them go? 'Shit.' He hadn't planned the Drury woman carefully enough. He had chosen an unsafe place to prepare and now he had scuppered himself. He had two options: abort the Drury woman completely, wait for the couple to leave and drive quietly home. Or he could act now.

Steve Riley had his hand down the front of Katie's jeans. There wasn't much room to manoeuvre in the car but he was pleased with the way things were going. Her mouth was alive and willing as he kissed her hard and long. He had fancied her for months and had imagined this moment a thousand times already. He knew exactly what he was going to do next, though he thought he might have to push her seat right back to manage it. He reached across her, trying to find the seat-release lever. She took his hand and pushed him back gently.

'Steve.' She was giggling again – he liked that. 'I need to pee.'

'You're joking.'

'I'm sorry. But I've really got to go.'

'Where? We're in the middle of fucking nowhere.' He couldn't conceal his disappointment. He hadn't imagined this.

'I'll find a bush. I've got to go.' Katie clicked open the car door, did up her jeans and swung her legs out into the cold. She stepped tentatively into the dark, squinting. There was a flat plateau of grass about ten metres away: behind the car, off to the left. She didn't want Steve to see her. The ground was hard to negotiate and uneven. Katie stumbled forward. Finally she reached the raised bump of grass she had chosen and unbuttoned her jeans. Before she could crouch, Crowan Frayne stepped from the darkness and struck the back of her head a terrific blow. She saw an explosion of light, then fell to the ground without a sound. Her body twitched in shock as life began to ebb out of her. Frayne kneeled over her and struck her hard again. Twice.

A minute passed. Steve Riley was getting impatient. He wiped condensation off the rear-view mirror and tried to see out of the back window. He couldn't see Katie. Suddenly he felt sorry for her; she was alone in the darkness. He was being selfish. He opened his car door and stepped outside.

'Katie? Are you all right?' he called into the void.

'Katie's fine now,' said a soft voice behind him.

Steve turned towards the noise. Something struck him, a glancing blow to the forehead. He reeled against the side of the car, falling backwards, his feet slipping on the mud. He could make out the shape of a man in front of him. He knew that if he went down he was dead. Something flashed above him and smashed into his face, breaking his cheekbone. He felt his teeth splinter and blood rush across the unfamiliar sharpness in his mouth. The impact sent Steve Riley toppling into the mud. As he tried to lift himself the third blow came. This time he didn't move.

Crowan Frayne dragged Steve Riley's dead weight back to the Fiesta and hauled the body onto the back seat. There would be blood everywhere. He was pleased that he couldn't see anything. He was panting. The effort had drained him. This was ugliness. This was not poetry. He opened the door of his own car and took out a torch. He hurried back to the spot where he had put the girl down. Crouching, he rolled the woman onto her back and shone the torch into her face. Her eyes were wide open in shock. They were brown. He cursed his bad luck and dragged the dead girl back to the car. With an effort, he placed her inside and found the keys in the ignition. It was important that he got rid of the bodies quickly. He started the engine and reversed down the track.

28

Underwood sat in the wreckage of his life. On the bed that was his everywhere, he sat as nothing. Julia's note had hammered what he already knew like a rusty nail between his eyes and into his soul.

> *John: It is obvious to me that our marriage is over. It would be obvious to you too if you cared to look. I have tried to call you, tried to speak to you but you have refused to let me. This is the only way.*
>
> *I will be staying with my mother for a couple of weeks. I will contact you after that to discuss arrangements. I have a solicitor; I recommend you get one as well. It will make things easier.*
>
> *I never wanted this, John. But my life has been empty for some time. I could cope with you, with the uncertainty and the stress of your job if you made an effort to connect with me. You are not the only person who feels. You seem to have given up on both of us. I am not prepared to give up on myself yet. I have met someone else.*
>
> *Please see a doctor.*
>
> *Julia*

So there it was: the final proof of his failure. Infallible eyewitness testimony. The written word was cruel and unforgiving: it found you like a bright light would. Underwood's head boiled and throbbed. He felt it might implode. He had become a tiny slick of pain in a vast pointless universe. John Underwood slumped on the floor, his back to the bed. '*I have met someone else.*' The epitaph to eighteen years of marriage; twenty-two since they had first started dating. '*I have met someone else.*' Simple and effective – like a gunshot.

His gaze fixed on Julia's dressing gown, still hanging on the wardrobe door: maybe she thought she didn't need one any more, maybe this Heyer fuck had bought her a new one. He got up and opened the wardrobe: a line of Julia's dresses still hung inside, a neat battalion of her shoes at the bottom. Her underwear still lay in the top drawer of the dresser: bitch probably didn't need it any more. Underwood fetched a suitcase from their spare room and started piling her clothes in. It took five minutes and the bulging case didn't shut properly. He dragged it downstairs and slammed it into the boot of his car.

5 November 1975. The date he knew he loved her. He had known her for a year. She was in the class below him at school. Clever girl, university bound. Straight black hair to her shoulders, big serious eyes. She was the star of the school play and he used to watch her rehearse, pretending he was helping out with the set or the lighting. Julia had to sing 'Somewhere Over the Rainbow'. She had a beautiful voice: it rose and fell effortlessly. John Underwood sat in the lighting gantry and watched her unseen, gobsmacked with awe. He resolved to ask her out.

5 November 1975. School Bonfire Night. They had built a huge pyre on the unused sports pitch behind the gymnasium. It was always a big event: parents and children together. There was even a guy that the art department had painted to look like the headmaster. Julia Cooper went with her parents. John went alone. He had bought a hot dog and gone hunting for her in the firelight flickering across a crowd of chattering faces. He had found her by the bonfire: staring into the flames with those big green serious eyes, the warmth of the fire on her face. Her parents were talking to the headmaster and his wife: probably about Cambridge University admissions policy. Julia stood alone. He threw his hot dog into the fire and approached her,

*wiping the grease from his chin. She was holding a paper cup of
tomato soup: it steamed pleasantly in her mittened hands.*

'All right, Julia?'

'Hello. It's John, isn't it?' *Her brow furrowed slightly. Was
she intrigued or embarrassed?*

'Good fire.'

'Great.'

'They've got some good fireworks later. They've spent three
hundred pounds this year.'

'I'm looking forward to that.'

'That's Mr Hodges, isn't it?' *He pointed at the lopsided
flaming effigy that was causing much amusement.*

'It's really funny. It looks just like him. Except it's not so fat.'
She laughed, looking straight into his eyes, and he was lost.

*A cheap firework phutted and whizzed overhead. People
began to move away from the fire to get a closer look. Julia
looked awkward suddenly.*

'Better go, I suppose,' *she said.*

'Oh yeah. You don't want to miss anything.' *He had to move
quickly, think of something.* 'I liked your singing today. You've
got a really good voice.'

'Thank you. Will you be at rehearsal tomorrow?' *She didn't
seem embarrassed at all.*

'Yeah. See you there.'

'See you there.'

*John hadn't bothered watching the fireworks. He walked
home feeling that God had lit the touch paper to his soul. The
following day he found out that Julia Cooper had snogged
Danny Lynch after the fireworks. It was the big gossip of the
school. The bottom fell out of John Underwood's universe. He
cried for her in the school toilets. But he was a lost cause. He
wouldn't give up. A month later, on the last night of the school
play, he asked her out.*

Twenty-five years later, John Underwood stood on the driveway
of Paul Heyer's mock-Tudor detached house and poured a can
of paraffin over a suitcase full of his wife's clothes. He knew she

was inside the house, probably caressing a fucking wine glass. Bitch. She could stare into this. He lit the corner of one of her blouses with his cigarette lighter and stepped back. The paraffin ignited with a gratifying *whoompf*. For a few seconds he watched the fire start to take: the flames quickly licked three or four feet into the air. Things had come full circle. John Underwood walked away and was quickly swallowed by the darkness.

About a minute later Paul Heyer threw open his front door and sprinted into the night. He had a washing-up bowl full of water and flung it over the blazing suitcase. The air was acrid with smoke and he coughed as it stung his eyes and throat. Julia Underwood followed him and threw a saucepan of water at the fire. The combination worked and the pile of clothes steamed poisonously. She recognized the address tag on the suitcase.

'Bloody lunatic,' said Paul.

'Oh God.' Julia put her hand to her mouth.

'Can you hear me?' Paul shouted into the night. 'You're a bloody lunatic.'

The night just listened.

29

12 December

The whole process had taken nearly two hours. Crowan Frayne had driven for about two miles before he had found a suitable place. He hadn't seen a single car in that time. Nothing had broken the nervous monotony until the headlights had picked out a steel gateway. Frayne had climbed out of the car and looked into the field beyond. It was large and sloped downhill for about half a mile. Away, at the bottom edge of the field, Frayne thought he could make out the dark outline of a wood.

It looked like a grazing meadow for sheep or cows. Thick

grass. It would have to do. He untied the gate, climbed back into the car and he drove through. He closed the gate behind him – no point taking unnecessary risks – and after a quick look along the road in both directions he climbed back into the car and turned off the headlights. Gently, he came up off the clutch and the Fiesta lurched awkwardly forward, gathering momentum as it began to jar and bump down the slope. Frayne could hardly see a thing but found the experience exhilarating: flying invisibly through the rushing blackness. Coins rattled in the glove compartment as the car bounced along the lumpy ground. Frayne could see the line of trees approaching and began to brake slowly: Katie Hunt's body slid forward and thudded onto the floor of the car. Frayne briefly flicked the headlights back on and off to check his position and slowed to a stop.

He got out of the car and walked into the trees. It was hardly a proper wood, more a cluster of elms that separated two fields. However, there was a gully about ten feet deep that cut sharply down to a narrow stream. Frayne returned to the car and released the handbrake. He pushed hard against the frame of the driver's door and, after a second or two of straining against the car's inertia in the mud, the Fiesta began to move.

As it moved onto the harder ground at the edge of the trees the car began to pick up speed. Crowan Frayne pushed it over the brow of the gully and then stepped back, panting as the Fiesta crashed nose first into the stream. The car was out of sight: invisible from the road and, Frayne guessed, undetectable unless you walked right up to the edge of the gully. Satisfied, he jog-walked back up the gradient to the steel gateway. This time he climbed over the gate and began to make his way back towards his van, staying on the tarmac but close to the edge of the road.

In the thirty minutes it took him to get back to his vehicle, Frayne saw only one car and was well concealed by the time it passed him. He was sweating heavily as he sat down in the driver's seat of the van but he felt a strange sense of satisfaction, as if the hoarse minstrelsy of the spheres had become amplified, blending in with the thumping blood in his head. He had taken a terrible risk and had derived no real pleasure from the act, but he had preserved the integrity of his conceit.

Had not Donne sacrificed rhythmic and stylistic beauty to sustain the logical structures of his poetry? Few would say Donne's work was aesthetically pure. Quite the opposite: his style was rough, his language almost violently colloquial. Frayne looked in the rear-view mirror. There was a spray of blood and flecks of mud on his forehead. Donne's reputation was based upon his wit and logical argument: the yoking of extraordinary opposites, the brilliant unravelling of metaphysical conundrums. History had forgiven Donne his stylistic abrasiveness: Frayne was confident that the beauty of his own conceit had not been violated. Stussman would understand. Like the divine children in the oven, it would remain unblemished.

He switched on a torch and looked himself over. There was more blood all over the front of his jacket and gloves. His boots were caked in gluey mud. Fortunately, he carried a spare set of over-clothes in a carrier bag in the back of his van. The ugliness from which his poetry emerged necessitated such precautions. He took off his gloves and placed them in a spare plastic bag. Then he stepped outside the van and removed his outer garments: the night air bit and nibbled at his skin, his hands fumbling at the bloody buttons.

He kept a bottle of mineral water in the car. Now he poured its contents over his hands and face, wiping clear most of the blood and dirt. He wondered if the water would facilitate an osmotic reaction on the surface of his skin: if the subatomic markers of the girl and the boy had been drawn within him. Were they now jostling for position in his brain with the other assimilated dead? They were thick in his thoughts so perhaps they did now live within him.

There was a grey boiler suit in the carrier bag, along with a clean white T-shirt and underwear. Frayne was chilled to the marrow and it took some time before his body began to reabsorb the warmth it had at first given up to the rough material. He collected his thoughts. He would need a carpet knife, a torch, a hammer, and a pen and paper. His leather gloves were dirty but still functional. In any case, he would use rubber gloves for the operation. He pulled the equipment together into his toolbox and left the car. It was late now and Frayne knew that there was little likelihood of encountering any other traffic on the lonely country road.

He stepped out onto the black tarmac and marched to a steady rhythm, down the gentle gradient towards Elizabeth Drury's house: 'You violets, that first appear' – light beat, hard beat, iambic foot – 'By your pure purple mantels knowne / Like the proud virgins of the yeare / As if the spring were all your own / What are you when the rose is blowne?' He realized that he had spoken the words aloud to the attentive darkness. The scrap of verse had been from Wooton's throwaway poem on the Queen of Bohemia. Still, it had a nice nursery-rhyme swing to it. 'Sir Henry Wooton, you appeare / By your childish structures knowne / Inside my head but once a year / As if the darkness were your own / But I've a knife and you're alone.' Much better.

Frayne quickly climbed the gate of Elizabeth Drury's garden and stole along the fence line to her car. The lights were off in the house now and he was less worried about triggering the security lights. They drenched the front garden with radiance as he dashed from the darkness and took up his previous position behind Elizabeth Drury's car. He used the light to note down the address and phone number on her window sticker. He just made it in time before the lights clicked off again. He slipped his small notebook and pen back into the breast pocket of his boiler suit and withdrew the carpet knife from his toolbox.

Elizabeth Drury slept fitfully. The security lights hadn't really woken her but they dragged her into an unrefreshing shallow sleep. She dreamed that she was having liposuction. That the machine couldn't be stopped. A man with no face loomed above her. It was painful: the thing sucked at her legs, then at her arms and chest, pulling fat from her muscles, muscles from their bones, bones from their sockets, organs from their mountings. The pain was a terrible, sweet release. The machine went quiet and she could see herself pulled inside out, floating in liquid fat in a cylindrical glass tank. Then she was looking out of the tank at the man with no face. She couldn't breathe. The machine was beeping a warning, beeping a warning. The flow had been reversed, she was being sucked out of the jar, sprayed across the wall in bloody chaos. She sat bolt upright in bed. Her alarm clock shrilled at her. 5.45 a.m. It was still dark outside. In a clump of bushes across the road from the house, beyond the front lawn and the sleeping car, Crowan Frayne watched the front bedroom light click on.

Drury showered and wolfed down a bowl of muesli. Her cats mewed hungrily at her, demanding food and attention. 'You're such a porker, Misty,' she muttered through a fog of near-wakefulness at her particularly insistent tabby. 'You're going to need laxatives at this rate.' Drury smiled as the cat whimpered pathetically and rubbed itself against her bare ankles. What was the point? Cats know which buttons to press.

At 6.30 she closed her front door, double-locked it and crunched across the gravel to her Audi. As the security lights came on she saw that the car seemed slightly lopsided. She walked around the front of the bonnet and squinted at the wheels on the passenger side of the vehicle. Both tyres were flat. She swore loudly and hovered for a second, uncertain what to do. She was about to swear loudly again when she remembered the hundred pounds she paid every year to National Car Recovery Services. She took her mobile phone from her handbag and dialled in the emergency rescue number on the NCRS sticker in the car's side window.

'NCRS,' a male voice said eventually.

'Hi there. I have two flat tyres on my car. Could you send someone out please?'

'Name and address, please?'

'Elizabeth Drury. The Beeches, Blindman's Lane, Afton, Cambridgeshire.'

'You say you've got a flat?'

'Two flats. Could you please hurry? I have a meeting in London.'

113

'We'll send out a local recovery team straight away.'

'How long will that take?' She began making her way back to the house, fumbling for her keys.

'Within half an hour.'

'OK. Thank you.' Elizabeth Drury unlocked her front door and stepped back inside the house. Irritated, she turned off the house's beeping alarm system and slammed the front door behind her.

In the near distance, Crowan Frayne emerged from the shadows and hurried back to his van.

30

Four miles away, in a pebble-dashed terraced house in Evesbury, Suzie Hunt rolled out of her underpopulated double bed and put on her slippers. She yawned out the dry fumes of a hangover and lit the remainder of the cigarette she had half-smoked the previous night. The smoke warmed her and sharpened her senses, turning on the lights in her head. It had been a late night. She worked part-time in the Coach and Horses on Evesbury High Street and she had stayed after hours. Half a bottle of vodka, a lot of fags and a flabby shag on the Snug Bar sofa with Fat Pete the landlord had left her feeling empty. Mrs Pete had been asleep – drunk – upstairs the whole time. And that mused Suzie bitterly, had been the only vaguely exciting thing about the whole experience.

Thursday mornings were the worst for her. She always stayed late at the pub on Wednesday nights and on Thursdays she worked earlies at the supermarket in New Bolden. It was a long shift, longer with a hangover. On Thursdays Suzie felt every one of her thirty-six years – and some. She wondered what time Katie had got in. 'Dirty little slag. Out all hours like an alley cat: just like her mother.' Suzie almost managed a smile as she pulled on her dressing gown and left the bedroom. The landing was cold and only partially carpeted. She banged on Katie's bedroom door as she walked past.

'Wake up, you dirty stop-out.'

There was no response. Suzie shuffled downstairs and filled a kettle. The noise rattled her. She moved to the fridge and took a long glug from a half-pint of milk. The fluid chilled her as it crawled down her throat and she shivered hard. Her head had started to ache quite badly now, though the gurgling of the kettle promised imminent relief. Still no sound from upstairs. 'Little madam.' Suzie leaned out of the kitchen and aimed her voice up the stairs.

'Wake up, you lazy cow!'

The kettle boiled and switched itself off. Suzie poured two cups of tea, both with two sugars, and trudged exhausted back up the stairs. She put down one cup in the bathroom and started running herself a bath. The other she took into Katie's room. The bed hadn't been slept in. Suzie Hunt felt a hot surge of anger.

She picked up the phone in her bedroom and called Katie's mobile: it rang for an age before switching to answerphone:

'This is the Vodafone recall service. The person you have dialled is unavailable. Please leave a message at the tone.' *Beep.*

'Where the bloody hell are you? You ain't arf gonna catch it when you get back, my girl. Call me as soon as you get this message or I'll bloody well brain you.'

She hung up, feeling useless and sad. She hated getting ready for work by herself.

31

Elizabeth Drury tapped her finger on the windowsill, mild irritation seeping in at the edges. Twenty minutes had become twenty-five. She had already eaten two doughnuts. She dialled her office number and got Sally's voicemail:

'Sally. It's Elizabeth. I have had a total nightmare. Flat tyres on the Audi. It's 7.40 now. There's no way I'm going to be in before ten. Can you call Danielle at my publishers and cancel my meeting. I'm on the mobile if anything urgent crops up.'

She couldn't understand how her tyres had gone flat. Perhaps she'd driven over something at the railway station: there always seemed to be a carpet of shattered glass in the car park. Both tyres, though? Vandals, maybe: kids too old to stay at home and too young to be in a pub. Had she driven home with two punctures? She shuddered.

A van had pulled up at the gate, its headlights throwing shadows across the lawn. A man, about thirty-five, got out and released the catch, pushing the steel gate back into the clip, fixed in the ground that held it open. Elizabeth Drury jumped up and put her coffee cup on the ledge of the hatch that connected her expensive new living room with her expensive new kitchen. She heard the van pull up at the front of the house and a door slammed. Footsteps scrunched on the gravel. Through the small frosted-glass pane in the front door she saw the recovery man checking the side of her Audi. She opened the door. The man stood up.

'Mrs Drury?'

'Miss.'

'Sorry about that. I'm from NCRS. I see you've had a bit of a disaster.'

She stepped out onto the drive, the cold air niggling at her. 'Bad car day. I can't understand it. They seemed fine when I drove home.'

'And they were flat when you came out this morning? Weird.' The mechanic lay down at the side of the car and checked under the arch of the front wheel. He peered at the brand-new tread. 'Actually, you haven't got a torch, have you, love? I left mine back at the garage.'

'Er – yes. I think so. It's in the kitchen somewhere. Will this take long?'

'Depends. Some clown might have just let the air out. If so, I'll pump them up and you're on your way. If they're both punctured you'll need two new tyres. I'll be able to see better with the torch.'

Elizabeth Drury scrunched back into the house, grateful for the warmth of her hallway. She kept a heavy-duty torch in the cupboard under the kitchen sink: rural locations were prone to power cuts in winter. She heard the front door snap shut and sensed someone behind her. She stood quickly and stared into the unblinking shark eyes of her mechanic.

'What are you doing? You frightened me,' she gasped, holding out the torch. Her eyes weren't really blue. They were closer to grey, like the smooth stones licked to perfection by the sea.

'I mourn with the widowed earth and will yearly celebrate thy second birth,' said Crowan Frayne as he grabbed her neck with his gloved right hand.

Elizabeth Drury, grey eyes wide with fear, panicked and lashed out with the torch, smashing Frayne squarely in the face. He staggered back, his nose bleeding, and she pushed past him, running into the hallway. He caught up with her just as she made it to the front door and dragged her, kicking and screaming, to the ground. She tore at his face and hair. She was strong and it took him some time to turn her over onto her front and push her face into the carpet. She screamed wildly, arms and legs flailing. One of her shoes fell off in the struggle and Frayne couldn't stop himself from laughing at her stupid, stockinged feet. But now he had taken control. He held her face down with his left hand and had time to take a deep breath of her rich perfume before withdrawing the bloodstained claw hammer from his pocket. She stopped moving after the fourth blow, her body suddenly limp, the back of her head a tangled mess of blood and bone.

'Bad hair day,' said Crowan Frayne.

He sat back, exhausted by the effort. The car scam had worked. He had called the NCRS breakdown line five minutes after Elizabeth Drury, claiming to be her husband and giving the correct address. He told the female telephonist that his wife had overreacted, that he could reflate the flat tyres himself and there was no need to send an NCRS recovery van after all. The telephonist had thanked him for calling back so quickly and cancelled the booking: there would be no charge. She then described the new NCRS all-inclusive international rescue package that covered the overseas motorist for 'almost all continental breakdown eventualities'. He had told her to send the details by post.

It had been a long night but Frayne's head was alive, sparking with possibilities. The glittering, persuasive second stage of his conceit was looming. It was tangible now: the wrong could soon be corrected. The numberless dead cheered his daring, every particle of his being vibrating with their applause. He dragged Elizabeth Drury's body to the foot of the stairs. A yellow-eyed tabby cat watched him politely through the wooden struts of the banister, its head tilted inquisitively to one side.

'She to whom this world must it self refer / As suburbs, or the Microcosme of her,' said Crowan Frayne to the cat between gasps.

'Shee, shee is dead; shee's dead; when thou know'st this / Thou know'st how poore a trifling thing man is,' the cat replied.

Dawn was finally breaking up the night sky into fragments. Frayne tried to clear his head, to restore his focus. He left Elizabeth Drury's broken body at the foot of the stairs, opened the front door and walked outside. He drove his van around to the side of the house so that it would be invisible from the road and quickly returned to the warmth, carrying his ophthalmic surgery kit. He needed to work accurately and fast: Elizabeth Drury would be missed.

32

Dexter arrived in the office early. Even Harrison hadn't arrived yet. Maybe he had been up late: Dexter had seen Jensen leave in Harrison's car the previous night. Was she jealous? She tried to focus on the pages in front of her.

They had finally got through all the Drurys in the phone book. There had been no Elizabeths and only one Robert, an old age pensioner. She had been through most of the electoral registers, with only Peterborough and Evebury and Afton remaining. She looked at the clock: the information centre at County Police HQ in Cambridge opened at eight and Dexter wanted the news run before Underwood got in. At one minute past eight she called. The phone rang for an age before Dexter finally got through.

'It'll take about twenty minutes,' said a tired voice at the other end. 'Do you want me to e-mail it?'

'Yes, but fax it too, it's urgent.'

'They all are, love.'

Dexter bought herself a ditchwater coffee from the machine and began trawling through the electoral register for Peterborough. Jensen and Harrison came in together at ten past eight. Dexter didn't look up. The pair seemed to be giggling at some secret joke: she imagined it would be at her expense. She ignored them. Other officers began filing in: the level of conversation rose. Dexter covered her ears with her hands and tried to concentrate. Then a dialogue box popped up on her computer screen. It said, '*You have new mail.*'

Her computer took an age to shift to her e-mail inbox. At the top of the list was a new message from 'Paul@infocent_CamPHQ.org.net.' She clicked the attached Word document open. There were four news stories attached, the search term highlighted in bold. Each headline was dated and cited the source newspaper. She scrolled down the page:

'Rats Invade Theatre Royal, **Drury** Lane: *Evening Standard 5/11/98*'

'Mayor Resigns, **Drury**, Missouri: *International Herald & Tribune 6/6/99*'

'The **Drury** Clinic's Recipe for Success: *Daily Mail 8/12/98.*'

'Roger **Drury**, Violinist dies at 89: *Daily Telegraph 4/2/99.*'

There was nothing obvious. Dexter clicked on the third headline and the story popped up on her screen. Before starting to read, she took another swig of coffee, its bitterness searing her throat: her breath would be terrible.

119

The Drury Clinic's Recipe for Success

The fat of the land is proving profitable for one London company. Paddington-based dietary consultants the Drury Clinic are moving to more salubrious offices in London's Mayfair Crescent. The private clinic was founded in 1993 and now boasts a number of show business celebrities amongst its clientele.

The Drury Diet runs a psychological self-help guide for people with weight problems. The clinic offers counselling programmes and discussion groups that attempt to develop its patients' self-esteem. Patients are then invited to draw up their own diet plan in conjunction with a nutritionist and a psychologist.

'The Drury plan changed my life,' said Melissa Wyatt-Faulkner, host of TV's Can't Stop Cooking! 'It introduced me to the thin person I knew I always was at heart. Fat is all in the mind.'

They say the proof of the pudding is in the eating and the Drury Clinic certainly seems to have hit upon a successful recipe: its Mayfair Crescent offices have cost the company 2.6 million pounds. 'It's a calculated risk,' said Cambridge-educated founder Dr Elizabeth Drury, 37, 'but this will carry the clinic into the twenty-first century and enable our clients to benefit from truly world-class facilities.'

Dexter immediately picked up her phone and got the number of the Drury Clinic from Directory Enquiries. A dry panic was beginning to overtake her. There was no reply: an answerphone clicked on: 'You are through to the Drury Clinic. Our opening hours are nine a.m. until six p.m. If you'd like to make an appointment—' Dexter hung up. She thought for a second and called Underwood's mobile. It rang for an age before she heard the inspector's voice:

'What is it?'

'Sir. It's Dexter. I've found an Elizabeth Drury.'

'Who?' He sounded hungover, half-dead.

'The name Dr Stussman gave us. There's an Elizabeth Drury in London. She runs some clinic for fat people.'

'A clinic?'

'Yes. But it says she was educated in Cambridge. She might still live up here somewhere.'

'Is she on the electoral register?'

'Not for Cambridge or New Bolden. I haven't been through all the others.'

'Call her clinic and get her number.'

'I've called them already. It opens at nine.'

'Well, call them again then.'

The line went dead.

The next half an hour lasted an age. Eventually Dexter got through to the clinic at five minutes to nine. An Australian receptionist told her that she had just had a message from Dr Drury and that she had been delayed at home. There was no reply on her mobile so she was probably on her way in. Dexter asked for Drury's address. The receptionist suddenly became defensive and said she couldn't give out Drury's home address over the phone, even if Dexter was a 'fucking policeman'.

'Just tell me the name of the fucking town, then.' Dexter was losing patience.

'Afton. In Cambridgeshire.'

Dexter turned back to her computer and called up the electoral register for the Evebury and Afton constituency. The screen scrolled down at a painfully slow rate. The she saw it: *Drury, E. The Beeches, Blindman's Lane, Afton, Cambs, CA8 9RJ.*

'Christ.'

She grabbed her keys, jumped out of her seat and ran from the Incident Room. The door slammed behind her.

'What's rattled *her* cage?' asked Harrison.

'Time of the month,' mouthed Jensen silently.

33

John Underwood, aged forty-two, lies half-dead on his empty marital bed. He has chronic inflammation of the pleural membrane of his left lung and is in considerable pain. Most of a bottle of whisky still lashes at his stomach and his head. He is torn in pieces, ulcerous and rotting from the inside. A corruption of a man. His radio alarm has clicked on and he listens to a traffic report, too tired to turn it off. The booze has made his legs ache, the poison crawling through his marrow, nibbling at his joints. His mind is falling through memories and time, looking for a hook to cling to. *'Time goes by so slow-oh-ly / And Time can do so much.'*

Yorkshire. September 1981. Their first holiday together. More of a long weekend. Three days walking in the Dales. The weather had been damp and cold. Ingleborough, Wernside and Penny Ghent in one day. The twenty-five miles on rough ground, the two-thousand-feet climb in inadequate boots had made his joints scream and his feet raw with blisters. But it had been fantastic. Clean air in his lungs, the vast silence at the peak of Wernside, waving at the motorcyclists in the winding country lanes, the thick, sweet smell of cattle. He had taken Julia's photo next to the Ordnance Survey point on top of Ingleborough: she had stuck her tongue out. The last five miles had killed him. She was lighter and fitter than him and he had problems keeping pace despite his longer legs. The pain was excruciating – only the image of a warm pub and comfy sofas kept him moving forward.

As they climbed the last hill into Ribblesdale, Julia suggested they sing a song. He laughed at first but joined in quickly: there was something about her beautiful rising and falling voice that had once made him want to improve himself to bind with her in whatever way he could. As they climbed the last hill into Ribblesdale Julia suggested they sing a song. He laughed at first but joined in quickly: there was something about her beautiful rising and falling voice that had once made him want to improve himself to bind with her in whatever way he could. He didn't know all the words to 'Greensleeves' but followed her lead:

Alas my love you do me wrong
To cast me off discourteously

And I have loved you so long
Delighting in your company

Underwood opened his eyes. The dream had made him cry. With an effort he rolled out of bed and, wobbly on his feet, headed for the bathroom. The song still reverberated around his head. Only now, hungover and ill, it began to irritate him. Especially the dreadful, insipid chorus:

'Greensleeves was all my joy
Greensleeves was my delight'

He would call her today and wring the tune from his head.

34

Crowan Frayne had taken his time with Elizabeth Drury and the results were very gratifying. He had taken the left eyeball with care and considerable precision. His experience with the Harrington woman had been helpful. He had used two of his four clamps to hold back the eyelids of Drury's left eye while he toiled; he had also used a smaller, lighter scalpel this time, which had reduced the collateral damage to the eyeball itself.

Two hours of concentrated effort, but it had been worth it. After all, Michelangelo hadn't painted the ceiling of the Sistine Chapel with a roller. Elizabeth Drury's eyeball now nestled comfortably next to Lucy Harrington's on the silk lining of Frayne's wooden box. The image excited him enormously. As did the texture of the eyeball: the sclera was springy, tough, elastic. He had imagined the eyes would feel like glass: rigid and fragile. Like his conceit the eyes were perfectly formed, fully evolved structures. Two-thirds of his argument was now complete. Only his logical denouement remained.

He washed his instruments carefully in the bathroom sink before replacing them in the instrument case. He checked to make sure that every item of equipment had been returned to its correct resting place. Was he taking unnecessary risks? Drury's mobile had already rung three times. Perhaps it was now time to go. He was reluctant to leave the house: it had been a fitting theatre for his poetry. Drury had excellent taste : there were a number of antique clocks and prints on the walls. To his delight, Frayne had even found a series of prints depicting anatomical drawings by Leonardo da Vinci hanging in what seemed to be Drury's office. He took them from the wall and placed them on Drury's bed next to his instruments and his hammer. He would need to make two trips to the car now.

The gate was open and Dexter swung her car through in one smooth movement. She peered through the windscreen at The Beeches: it was certainly an impressive building. She crunched up the gravel drive and came to a halt next to the Audi TT with two flat tyres. The front door of the house was open but there were no signs of life. Should she radio for a squad car? She decided not to and walked up to the front of the house.

'Hello?' she called through the open door. 'Elizabeth Drury?' Silence. Dexter hesitated, then stepped inside. 'Is anybody here? It's the police.' She looked down: there was blood on the carpet and a long red smear leading up the stairs. A cold rush of panic, then excitement. She should definitely call for a squad car now. She looked up the stairs: she had to know for sure. This was her discovery; the credit should be hers. Besides, she reasoned quickly, Drury might still be alive. 'Inspector Dexter' – she liked the sound of that. She took a deep breath and began to climb the stairs, her heart pounding.

Crowan Frayne stood flush to the wall at the side of the house, deciding what to do. He had put the framed prints in the back of his van. He knew he should make a dash for it: drive away while the policewoman marvelled at his poetry. He was shocked that they had made the connection with Elizabeth Drury so quickly. The woman had been awkward enough for him to find. Stussman was obviously alert to the notion of a pre-selected audience. Perhaps this policewoman was also worthy of admission.

He tried to reason clearly. It was too risky to delay. He should leave now. There was a good chance that she hadn't seen his car. He could be away before she realized what had happened. That was the most sensible option. He was about to get back into his van when he remembered that he had left his hammers and, more annoyingly, his medical instruments on Elizabeth Drury's double bed.

Dexter, driven on by nervous excitement, fear and curiosity, pushed open the door to Elizabeth Drury's bedroom. Bath taps. She heard the water running and, with a terrible sense of inevitability, stepped over the bloodstains on the carpet and pushed open the door to Drury's lush en-suite bathroom.

Elizabeth Drury lay half-submerged in a bath of bloody water. Dexter felt her stomach contract but she wasn't sick. She felt paralysed, unable to move. The woman was fully clothed, dressed for work. Her left eye had been removed and the socket stared emptily up at the ceiling. The water was thick red like some terrible soup and Dexter, inching closer, could see the edge of the impact wound in the side of Drury's skull. The collar of the dead woman's jacket was torn. Had she fought her attacker? Dexter shuddered at the thought. She followed Drury's dead gaze to the ceiling, where in hideous red letters she read the following:

'For in a common bath of teares it bled
Which drew the strongest vitall spirits out.'

Steam from the hot tap was already making the text run. She took her notebook from her handbag and, with a shaking hand, wrote down the words. Then she noticed there was blood smeared on the lid of the toilet. Dexter took out her handkerchief and delicately turned off the bath taps, trying hard not to corrupt the fingerprints she knew wouldn't be there. Then, with the same hand, she lifted the toilet lid.

Inside was a dead tabby cat. It had been placed sitting upright in the toilet pan, its tail in the water, its head bleeding and hanging down and to one side. Both the eyes were missing. Wedged between its forepaws and its bulging belly was a piece of white card, carefully inscribed in flowing red handwriting:

> 'Or if when thou, the world's soule goest,
> It stay, 'tis but thy carkasse then,
> The fairest woman but thy ghost
> But corrupt wormes, the worthiest men.'

Dexter knew she had to call for help now. Her early excitement had been replaced by a nagging fear and a sense of isolation. She stepped gingerly over the bloodstains on the bathroom floor and back into the bedroom. It was only then that she noticed the strange black case on the bed. And the two hammers. As she began to panic something hit her hard on the side of her head. She lurched against the bedroom wall, barely conscious. She could make out the dark image of a man. He was tall. She couldn't fix her eyes on him: the room was moving around her. She knew she musn't go down. Something struck at her again and she fell, hitting her head against the frame of the bathroom door. Darkness.

Frayne crouched over her, confident that the woman wasn't getting up. She was breathing, though, moaning softly. There was a cut in the side of her head. He opened her bag and withdrew her police ID. Alison Dexter, Sergeant. Cambridgeshire CID. A number. A barely recognizable photograph. He sat back.

'Alison Dexter.' The name meant nothing to him: it was a colourless name. It scarcely resonated with poetry. And yet, she had found the Drury woman. She had found *him*. Crowan Frayne was impressed. He reached over and pushed back Dexter's left eyelid and considered. Green eyes. Unfortunate. And yet, perhaps there *could* be a role for her in the final ecstasies of his argument. A child in the oven. The idea appealed.

*

Images. A man standing over her. Pain banging at the side of her head, warm above her eye. Panic. Was he killing her? Had he taken her eye? Please, no. Not her eyes. She tried to see. Lights, images, the room spinning. She tried to move: no response. He was over her, speaking: 'Bedtogotobedtogo'. Gibberish. Noise. See his face. Try to see his face. He was moving. He was gone. 'Stupid cow, you stoooooopid ca' – her mother's voice. The room spins. Sickness. Nausea. 'Come on, Ali, got to move.' She hauled herself to the side of the bed and blinked, trying to decipher the chaos. She was alone. She could see. Relief. She climbed the side of the bed and got to her feet. She could hear a car. Gravel scrunching. Bedtogotobedtogo. She scrabbled in her bag for her mobile phone. 999.

35

Heather Stussman's phone rang at 10.30 that morning. The voice filled her with dread.

'Write this down.' He sounded dry, irritated, tired.

'Who is this?'

'You know who it is. Don't waste time. Write this down. It's your starter for ten.'

She picked up a pen. 'Go on.'

Crowan Frayne dictated the stanza of poetry that Misty the cat had shown to Alison Dexter.

> *'Or if when thou, the world's soule goest,*
> *It stay, 'tis but thy carkasse then,*
> *The fairest woman but thy ghost*
> *But corrupt wormes, the worthiest men.'*

Stussman recognized it.

'It's from "A Feaver".'

'Correct. Ask yourself. When is the world a "carkasse"?'

'I don't understand.'

'Your list obviously worked.' The had voice softened.

'My list?'

'The list you did for the police. It worked.'

'The coterie idea? I gave them a list of names, associates of Donne's.'

'Do you think you understand?'

'I understand Donne. Isn't that why you contacted me?'

'You have a narrow window of perception. But you operate in two dimensions. You wire plugs without comprehending the nature of electricity. Do you hear music when you stand at your little window? When you look at the stars and pirouetting planets, do you hear the intelligences? The Harmoniae Mundorum?'

'I like music. I don't hear the music of the spheres, though. Isn't that just a poetic idea? A romantic construction?'

'All the meanings we attach to things that are beyond our understanding are poetic constructions, Dr Stussman. The music of the spheres is no less provable than the idea that we all exploded out from some compressed mega-atom. Poetic constructions are the only things that distinguish us from cockroaches.'

'If you say so.'

'Oh, I do,' Crowan Frayne said, 'and you will understand the nature of my conceit. When the world has become a carkasse you will understand, Dr Stussman. In the meantime, I recommend that you call your police friends to discuss "The Anniversairies" and "A Feaver". Be gentle with them: the clever one has a terrible headache.'

The line went dead. Heather Stussman ran to her door and called in the bored police constable who was standing guard outside.

Two minutes later, at the news desk of the *New Bolden Echo*, George Gardiner also received a phone call.

36

Underwood raced his car along Blindman's Lane towards Afton. Harrison had called him half an hour earlier and had told him about Elizabeth Drury and then about Dexter. Underwood had been filled with a sudden terrible sense of shame. And anger.

'Dexter has been hurt,' Harrison had said sharply. 'Seems like she caught the bastard in the act. She's lucky to be alive.'

The driveway at The Beeches was crowded. There was an ambulance, police squad cars, Dexter's car too. Dexter was sitting on the back step of the ambulance, holding a large cotton swab to the side of her head. She had dried blood on her cheeks. It looked like she had been crying as well. Underwood went straight up to her.

'Where have you been, guv?' she asked, half annoyed, half pathetic.

'I've been ill. Went to the doctor's,' he lied. 'What happened, Dex? Are you OK?'

'I'm fine.' She considered for a second. 'Actually I'm shaking like a fucking leaf and I've got the mother of all headaches.'

'She's got concussion,' said a nearby ambulance man. 'She should go to hospital for a scan.'

'Did you see him?' asked Underwood.

Dexter shook her head and winced as the pain rushed at her again. 'Not really. I found the Drury woman in the bath. I went back into the bedroom and something whacked me. I went down. He whacked me again. I didn't see his face. He was quite tall, I suppose – about six foot. He had a boiler suit on, I think. But I didn't see his face clearly, guv. I wouldn't recognize him again. Sorry.'

'Don't be silly. You should go to hospital now.'

'No, thanks.' Dexter looked at the blood on her fingertips, surprised and irritated.

'That's an order.'

'I'm not going anywhere. This is *my* party.' She wiped her

fingers clean on her skirt and tried to will the pain away. 'There were two hammers on the bed, sir, and a black box, like a little briefcase. They're not there any more. And there's more poetry on the ceiling – I wrote it down.' She offered him her notebook. 'Bastard messed her cat up, too. It's not pretty up there.'

'He took her eye?'

'Yes. Left eye, same as before. Dumped her in the bath. I turned the taps off just before he whacked me.'

'You're bloody lucky to be alive, Dex. You should have brought someone with you.'

She ignored the rebuke. It was rich, coming from Underwood. 'There's something else. I think he said something to me.'

'What?'

'This might sound stupid but I think he told me to go to bed.'

'You sure?'

'That's what it sounded like.' Dexter suddenly lurched forward in a half-crouch and was sick onto the driveway. She was swaying and Underwood had to hold her firmly to stop her from falling.

Underwood took the notebook and sat Dexter back down on the step of the ambulance. She wiped the vomit from the side of her face. He put his arm round her. After a minute or two, she stopped shaking.

His mobile rang. It was Heather Stussman. She sounded panicky.

'He called again, John. He sounded different. Pissed off.'

'I'm not surprised. My sergeant interrupted him in the middle of his morning workout.'

'Oh, God, John, were we right? About the name?'

'Dr Elizabeth Drury.'

'Christ. Is she dead?'

'Very.'

'How's your colleague?'

'She's OK.' He looked at Dexter. 'Tough as old boots.'

'I don't know what to say.'

'There's nothing to say. Your list got us very close to him. Quicker than he anticipated, judging by what's happened this morning.'

'Is there anything I can do? I feel so useless, cooped up here.'

'Write down everything you can remember from the conversation this morning. I want you to come down to New Bolden. We'll send a car. I want you to look at the poetry he's left on the wall for us here and tell us what you know about it.' He looked at Dexter's notebook. 'Something about a bath full of tears.'

'I know it. It's from a poem about the original Elizabeth Drury. The girl I told you about.'

'OK. I'll send a car in an hour or so.'

Underwood hung up and looked at Dexter. She looked very small and embarrassed. It was strange to see her bleed: it was almost like seeing her naked.

'Our man called Stussman a few minutes ago,' he said after a pause.

'He's a creature of habit,' Dexter mused.

'And that's why we'll catch him.'

He had meant the words to be a fillip. In fact, they sounded hollow. Underwood had stopped believing in most things now – even in his own bullshit.

'Are you all right, guv? You've not been yourself for a while,' asked Dexter.

'Julia's gone,' he said suddenly. 'Pissed off with another bloke. Keep it to yourself.' It sounded like an admission of failure and insecurity. It was. Dexter nodded silently and tried to think of something helpful to say. Underwood didn't give her a chance. He stood up and walked wearily into the house where Leach and his scene-of-crime officers were waiting.

37

Suzie Hunt loathed stacking. Working the till was boring enough but at least you were sitting down. Stacking tins of beans and pork mini-sausages was hard work and Suzie's hangovers were unforgiving. She was sweating beneath her unflattering work apron and her headache seemed to be sharpening with every can she put in position.

Suzie wasn't one for philosophy but on mornings like this she did begin to wonder whether there was any point to anything at all. How had she ended up here? The sequence of events was unclear. Time had mugged her.

She was single, thirty-six, screwing pub landlords by night, arranging tinned mini-sausages all day. Perhaps it was Fate. Maybe this was her punishment for enjoying herself too much, too early. Screwing up her O levels had been the beginning of it all: her endless helter-skelter slide of bad luck. Why have life-determining exams at sixteen? Sixteen is precisely the age when you are least able to cope with it. Sixteen is when pubs and boys sparkle before you like presents round a Christmas tree. How can Physics and History and Economics compete? Suzie had been an early developer – like Katie – and she had always been popular with the boys. Education was boring: those endless afternoons in stuffy classrooms staring out of dirty glass windows. She regretted it now, though. Schoolwork had been tedious but stacking shelves was soul-destroying.

'All right, Sooz?' her friend Mo was standing behind her, next to a trolley laden with packets of toilet rolls. 'The beast of burden has arrived.'

'You on bog rolls, then?' said Suzie.

'That's right, love. It's a shit job . . .'

'But someone's gotta do it!' It was their running joke. They both laughed.

'On earlies again, then, Sooz?' Mo wiped a film of sweat from her brow. There was a gap between her teeth that seemed to flare open when she smiled. Suzie had seen Mo wedge a baked bean in there once: Mo was funny like that.

'Bloody nightmare, darlin'. I'm hanging today.' Suzie stepped down off her foot ladder.

'Ooh! Late night?' Mo folded her arms in mock disapproval.

'Stayed late at the pub, didn't I?' Suzie winked at Mo: Mo knew all about Fat Pete.

'Old Mr Sausage been up to his tricks again?'

'It's a shitty job . . .'

'But someone's gotta do him!' They both laughed again.

'Beats sitting at home by meself.'

'Don't get me wrong, darlin'. I'm only jealous.'

'Don't be, Mo. I've had better. A lot better.'

'Ain't we all? Still when you get to our age any fuck's better than fuck-all. That's what I always say.' Mo shrieked with laughter. Suzie giggled too but felt a tinge of sadness: Mo looked ancient to her.

'My head's killing me,' said Suzie.

'Vodka?'

'Suzie's ruin.'

'Think yourself lucky. My cystitis is playing up like a right bugger,' said Mo reflectively. Suzie smiled. Mo was a good sort, really: not many people could make her smile on a Thursday.

'My Katie stayed out all night. Little cow.'

'You should put you foot down wiv her. It's a dodgy age. Give 'em an inch and they take the piss.'

'Kids grow up fast these days.'

'No faster than we did, girl. There's no excuse for disrespect.'

'I s'pose.'

'Be thankful she's not shoving pills down her throat.'

'She better bloody not be.'

'Oh well. I better get going. That little shit Harrap has been on my case already. Bums need a-wiping, darlin'.'

'Someone's gotta do it, Mo.'

Mo pushed her trolley slowly to the end of the aisle and disappeared out of sight. Suzie watched her with affection. Good old Mo: always friendly, always the same, game for a laugh, ready for a chat. Wanker of a husband, twat of a supervisor. But it all seemed to wash off her. Like the millions of other Moes who put up and shut up.

Suzie returned to her stacking. Tins on the shelf, tins on the shelf. So many tins: vacuum-packed; mindless, pointless. On the shelf: like her. Tins that hide and never see the light; tins in the darkness, rotting on the inside; tins that have passed their sell-by date. Opened up once and ruined for ever: just like her. Sometimes the light flickered inside her on Wednesday nights but apart from that it was darkness: behind, around and ahead.

Suzie looked up and down the aisle. There was no one about. She withdrew her mobile phone from her apron pocket and called Katie's number. It rang and rang for an age before the voicemail came on. She switched the phone off in frustration and looked at her watch: six long hours to go. She would brain that little madam when she got home.

38

Julia Underwood bagged up the charred remains of her clothes and threw them into the rubbish bin at the end of Paul Heyer's driveway. She checked the road but there was no sign of John or his car. Relieved, she hurried back inside.

She hadn't slept at all. The previous night's events had scared her. She was scared for John, for what he had done and for what he might do. She felt ashamed that she had left him a note and had not stayed to rough it out face to face. But what choice had he given her? He had deliberately avoided her calls and had refused to come home. It was pathetic. How had he found out about Paul? The thought troubled her. They had no mutual friends. Had John seen them out together? Had someone else tipped him off? Riddled with anxiety, self-doubt and shame, Julia had lain perfectly still for four hours – watching each digital minute snap past. She had sensed that Paul was awake too, which hadn't helped her. Julia wasn't used to sleeping with him yet: you get used to one person's movements and stillness, noises and silences. It had been a long, anxious night.

As she walked back through the front door, she could hear Paul on the phone in the living room. She decided to make them both a cup of tea and went into the kitchen. To her shame, she realized that she didn't know how Paul took his tea.

'Good news,' he called out after putting the phone down.

'What's that?' Julia replied, loading sugar and a jug of milk onto a tea tray.

'We're going away,' said Paul. 'I've booked it.'

Julia walked through to the living room, carrying her tray.

'Booked what?' she asked, sitting down next to him.

'A week away. In Norfolk.'

'Norfolk?'

'It's not Barbados, I know, but it'll do us good to get out of here for a few days. Sitting around fretting with your mother isn't going to achieve very much.'

'What about John?'

'I wasn't planning on inviting him.'

'I'll have to speak to him eventually.'

'Bugger John. He's had the opportunity to speak sensibly and he's decided to play silly beggars. Harassing me, setting fire to suitcases: it's pathetic, Julia. Frankly, he's bloody lucky I haven't reported him to the Police Complaints Commission: my lawyer is recommending that I should. You should feel no guilt about him at all. It's his choice to act like an arse. And his loss, too.' He kissed her furrowed forehead.

'OK.' She was coming round to the idea of some peace and sea air. 'Where are you taking me?'

'Blakeney. North Norfolk. It's only an hour and a half's drive. There's a cottage by the water. A friend of mine owns it. It's ours for a week. No charge. I've been there before. It's great.'

'It's very sweet of you, Paul. I think it's a brilliant idea. Thank you.' She kissed him hard, gratefully, on the lips.

'I need to go into the office for an hour to tie up a few loose ends and tell them what I'm up to. Will you be OK?'

'I'll be fine. Maybe I'll try and get some sleep.'

'Good idea. This will be great, Julia. It will remind us of why we're tolerating all the bad things. This is what it's all about. You may not feel like it, but you deserve a chance to get away: to clear your head.'

'I know. You're right.'

He stood up. 'I'll be back in an hour or so. Pack your bag.'

'I didn't unpack it.' She looked out of the vast living-room window across the front lawn. 'The rest of my stuff is ash.'

'We'll buy you more clothes. Clothes are easy.'

Paul left about five minutes later and Julia suddenly felt very alone, dependent. She told herself those feelings were natural;

she was bound to feel vulnerable. She was paddling in uncharted waters. It was a big house, still unfamiliar to her. The rooms were airy and uncluttered. They were vestigial traces of Paul's ex-wife here and there: a pot-pourri, a curtain tie, cookbooks. Silly things that made her feel like an intruder.

'Keep busy,' she told herself, 'keep moving.'

She unpacked some of her clothes and then, not knowing how Paul would react to her commandeering a drawer or some wardrobe space, she repacked them all again. *Find something to do.* She decided to have a shower. The warm water began to stir her brain into action and wash the tiredness down the plughole. A phone was ringing. Julia jumped in surprise: the noise had startled her. It was Paul's house phone. She let it ring and continued her shower. A minute after the ringing had stopped, it started again. Maybe it was Paul. Had he forgotten something? Had he forgotten her mobile number? She climbed out of the shower and wrapped a towel around herself. Her mobile was turned off: perhaps it *was* Paul. She sat on the edge of the bed, cold air goose-pimpling her exposed skin, and the phone fell silent. When it started ringing for the third time, she picked it up.

'Hello.' She tried to sound like a guest rather than the lady of the house.

'So how's your mother?' asked John Underwood, his voice tart with sarcasm, 'Did she sleep well?'

Julia's heart skipped a beat. 'How did you get this number?'

'I called Wife-Fuckers Anonymous. They gave it to me.'

'I'll hang up.'

'I'll call back. Or maybe I'll come round. I don't get out much these days.'

'What do you want, John?' Julia was tired of playing games. 'What was last night's little escapade in aid of?'

'Eighteen years of marriage blown to shit. That's what.'

'Don't try and make me feel guilty, John. It's as much your fault as it is mine.'

'Is it really?' He was aggressive, frightening. 'So you humping this flowery ponce is my fault, is it?'

'Don't talk like that, John. It doesn't achieve anything.'

'Oh, it does. It makes me feel a lot fucking better.' He read aloud from her note: ' "I will be staying with my mother for a couple of weeks . . . blah . . . blah . . . blah, oh, by the way, in case you are interested, I have met someone else." Thanks for letting me know, Jules, I'd never have guessed. I'd never have figured out that you creeping in at three in the morning reeking of come was anything unusual. Those Haydn recitals must be pretty fucking spectacular. I'd hate to see you after the 1812 Overture.'

She paused before replying. 'Have you finished? I met someone else because you were never "fucking" there emotionally. I left you because you were never "fucking" there mentally. And I left you a note because you're never "fucking" there to speak to. Is it sinking in yet, John? Are you getting the "fucking" picture?'

Silence.

She continued. 'You are different, John. Different from when we got married. You resent me for what I am. You resent me for what you're not. You blame me for things I don't understand. You can destroy yourself but I won't let you ruin me too. I refuse to be an inmate in the private hell that you have created for yourself for another twenty years.' She was shaking. She couldn't believe what she had just said. Her heart was smashing at her ribcage. She had said it! Finally had the courage to say it after all these years.

'What now, then?' His voice had quietened.

Julia was fired with confidence, as if a vast weight had been lifted. She was not going to hide any more. She took pride in her new-found self-belief. 'Paul and I are going away for a week. Your bonfire last night made my mind up. Neither of us can cope with New Bolden or you any more.'

'Ah, diddums.'

'Paul is furious. He wants to report you, John. Report you to the Police Complaints Commission. I stopped him.'

'Am I supposed to be grateful?'

'No. You're supposed to leave me alone. Why is that so difficult? You never usually have a problem with it.'

Silence.

'Where are you going with him?' asked Underwood eventually, as though the thought had finally hit home.

'That's none of your business, John.'

'Of course not. Why should I care? You're only my wife.'

'I'm surprised you remember.'

'Do you read the papers? Do you know what we're going through? Some maniac is ripping women's eyes out, smashing their skulls open. He nearly killed my sergeant this morning. Don't you think I deserve some respect, a bit of fucking slack?'

'That's not my problem any more, John,' said Julia.

'Maybe I'll send you the pictures. Tell you what, we'll do swapsies: you send me your holiday snaps, and I'll send you some tasteful shots of Lucy Harrington's bathroom. That'll give you and your boyfriend some food for thought.' He hung up.

Julia dropped the phone and flopped back on the bed, exhausted. How many more phone calls like that would it take before this was over? The cottage in Norfolk suddenly seemed like the best idea in the world. Paul was right. 'Bugger John'. Bugger his madness and his selfishness. The guilt was ebbing out of her. The phone call had reminded her of why she was leaving him. She was determined now, more than ever. When she next made love to Paul she would enjoy it all the more now, would give him more than she ever had before. She would scream her enjoyment into the night and hope that John Underwood heard every last gasping syllable.

39

Underwood smashed down his office phone. Fury burned within him, twisting and contorting his thoughts. He would show that polluted bitch and her ponce boyfriend, the poisonous little shit. He reached inside his drawer and withdrew his near-empty bottle of whisky. A large, hard gulp stopped his hand shaking.

The Earth depends on the gravity of the moon. Without it, the planet would topple, its axial tilt dangerously exaggerated. Wobbling like a spinning top, plunged into eternal winter.

Dexter appeared at the door, her head heavily bandaged. Heather Stussman was with her. Underwood slipped the bottle back into its hidey-hole and looked up. He even managed a half-smile as he gestured at them both to come in.

'Hello, Heather.' He hoped she couldn't smell his breath.

'John. How are you?' She could.

'You were right about the names, then,' said Underwood. 'Dexter almost got to Elizabeth Drury in time.'

'In time to get beaten up,' said Dexter unhappily.

'I don't feel very good about being right.' Stussman seemed downbeat.

'We've got a crime-team meeting in half an hour. It would be helpful if you attended,' Underwood continued. 'I should warn you, though, it won't be pleasant. There'll be the post-mortem report on the Drury woman and some nasty photographs, among other things.'

'Not squeamish, are you, Doc?' asked Dexter.

'I'm not sure.'

'I'd like you to be there,' said Underwood. 'I might get you to say a few words about Donne. Now this is clearly a serial-killer investigation, we are going to get much more press attention. Be warned, the papers will find out about you and they will pester you. Try not to tell them anything.'

'I understand.'

Dexter took over. She had found the crime scene and was not in the mood to stand on ceremony. 'I found two separate pieces of poetry in the room where Elizabeth Drury was killed. The first was written on the ceiling: "For in a common bath of teares it bled, which drew the strongest vitall spirits out."' Dexter looked up at Stussman. 'What's all that about, then?'

'It's from "The First Anniversary", Donne's poem that commemorates the death of a girl called Elizabeth Drury. As I told John yesterday, she was the daughter of a rich landowner, Robert Drury, who was acquainted with Donne's sister. Elizabeth died, aged fifteen, of some disease or other and Donne wrote "The Anniversairies" to celebrate Elizabeth's life and thereby to ingratiate himself with Sir Robert.'

'What else?' Dexter was terse. Her head was killing her.

' "The First Anniversary" is really over the top, linguistically. Donne exalts Drury to the status of some quasi-celestial power. He depicts her as the essence of all that was good about humanity and maintains that only the presence of her spirit prevented the total corruption of the Universe. By her death, Donne said that the world had become a "carcass" devoid of hope and form. "*Shee, shee is dead; shee's dead: when thou know'st this, Thou know'st how ugly a monster this world is.*" '

'When your killer called me today,' Stussman continued, 'he asked me when is the world a carcass? Twice, come to think of it.'

'I don't get it,' said Dexter. ' "When is the world a carcass?" Dead, you mean?'

'Yes. You see, Donne argues in the poem that the world ceased to retain its goodness following the death of Drury. Remember, he is trying to exalt her: "*And, oh, it can no more be questioned that beautie's best Proportion is dead,*" ' Stussman continued.

'You mean because of the death of this woman, everything else in Donne's world has lost its value?' asked Dexter.

'Be careful,' said Stussman. 'Remember that Donne never knew Elizabeth Drury personally. There is no real emotional engagement with this dead girl. In a way, she's a means to an end. He is celebrating her in grandiose language, attaching a metaphysical significance to her death that he supposes will have repercussions for all humanity. The objective is to impress the dead girl's father with Donne's wit and magniloquence.'

'Gotcha.' Dexter's mind was firing despite her headache; like a car engine racing and leaking oil at the same time. Perhaps the pain helped. The image of Dr Elizabeth Drury half-submerged in a bath of her own blood kept drifting across her consciousness. *A means to an end. No real emotional attachment to this girl,* Dexter mused. *To whom, then?*

'What was the other piece of text that you found?' Stussman asked.

Dexter read aloud from her notebook. 'Or if, when thou, the . . .'

'. . . World's soule goest, / It stay, 'tis but thy carkasse then, / The fairest woman but thy ghost / But corrupt wormes, the worthiest men.' Stussman finished the extract for her.

'How did you know that?' Dexter asked.

'Your killer read it out to me over the phone this morning,' said Stussman, shivering at the memory. 'It's from a poem called "A Feaver". I brought it with me. It's similar in its content to "The First Anniversary": again, it refers to a sick woman and suggests that her death will rid the world of its last vestige of value.' Stussman handed over the pages and read aloud:

> 'Oh do not die, for I shall hate
> All women so when thou art gone
> That thee I shall not celebrate
> When I remember thou was one.
>
> But yet thou canst not die I know:
> To leave this world behinde is death
> But when thou from this world wilt goe
> The whole world vapors with thy breath.
>
> Or if when thou the world's soule goest,
> It stay, 'tis but thy carkasse then
> The fairest woman but thy ghost
> But corrupt wormes, the worthiest men.
>
> O wrangling schooles, that search what fire
> Shall burne this world had none the wit
> Unto this knowledge to aspire
> That this her feaver might be it?
>
> And yet she cannot wast by this,
> Nor long beare this torturing wrong
> For much corruption needful is
> To fuell such a Feaver long.
>
> These burning fits but meteors be
> Whose matter in thee is soone spent
> Thy beauty and all parts which are thee
> Are unchangeable firmament.

Yet 'twas of my minde seising thee
Though it in thee cannot persever
For I had rather owner bee
Of thee one houre, then else forever.'

'It's the same as "The First Anniversary",' said Dexter. 'The world is a carcass because this girl is dead.'

From his crazy toppling orbit, Underwood watched her in amazement.

'That knock on the head must have done you some good,' he said.

Stussman ignored the joke. 'There are two other things. First, Donne again compares the woman with celestial forces like he did with Elizabeth Drury in "The First Anniversary". In the penultimate verse, he says her fevers are "but meteors": transitory, inconsequential things in comparison with her beauty which is an "unchangeable firmament". The woman is a timeless wonder, like the universe itself. I think your killer is a bit of an amateur astronomer.'

'What makes you think that?' Underwood asked. This was a specific. Specifics got people caught. Like Julia.

'A number of Renaissance writers tried to incorporate scientific ideas of the time in their works. Developments in astronomy and other sciences had significant religious repercussions and, as such, contributed to the uncertainties of the time. The man who called me this morning asked me if I could hear the music of the spheres.'

'The what?' This was a new one on Underwood. The last week had been full of surprises.

'Ancient philosophers believed that the planets each made a different noise depending on their relative distance from the Earth. Just like the length of a string on a guitar determines its pitch. They believed that the music of the spheres was the most beautiful sound in the universe. Your killer thinks he can hear music from the planets. He asked me if I could too.'

'Can you?' asked Underwood.

'Of course not.'

'What was the other thing?' Dexter asked.

'The other thing?' Stussman frowned.

142

'You said there were two other things. Celestial forces was one. What was the other?'

'Ah, yes.' Stussman looked back at the page. 'You notice the last verse: *Yet 'twas of my minde seising thee / Though it in thee cannot persever / For I had rather owner bee / Of thee one houre, then else forever.* Does that remind you of anything?'

'Not really.' Underwood suddenly found himself wandering blindly in fields of broken glass. He saw his own reflection smashed and contorted everywhere. Voices shouted back at him from every angle:

Julia's screwing another man, Julia's screwing another man. Little Johnny limp-dick. Little Johnny Lonesome.

She was unworthy of him. Or were they unworthy of each other?

'After the Harrington girl was killed we talked about the other poem: "A Valediction: of Weeping". Remember?' Stussman asked.

'I do,' said Dexter, conscious that Underwood seemed to be drifting out of the conversation.

'We talked about the power of the rational mind. That the human will was capable of anything, even metaphysical accomplishments. Well, it's the same idea again: he's saying that he would rather seize her soul for an hour than possess everything else in the universe for ever.'

Underwood heard that. The idea was compelling.

'So what are we saying here, in summary?' Dexter asked.

'The names of the victims are drawn from known members of John Donne's creative and personal circles. The killer is focused on the idea of a coterie: an audience of like-minded intellectuals,' said Stussman. 'The poems address certain common issues. The power of the rational will, the exaltation of dead or sick women, the importance of celestial forces and the notion of microcosms: shrinking concepts or physical entities of giant proportions into something that is tiny by comparison.'

'Like an eye,' said Dexter quietly.

40

Underwood stayed behind as Dexter and Stussman made their way through to the Incident Room. He could hear the other detectives gathering and picked out Leach's stentorian tones booming above the mêlée.

He had to clear his head. *Julia is screwing Paul Heyer. They are going away together.* How could he sleep for the next week knowing that his wife was getting fucked by another man? He had to do something. Jealous, impotent rage was eating at his every waking moment. He was going mad. *Got to do something; use the power of the rational will. Gain control.*

'We're ready in here, guv,' called Harrison from the Incident Room.

'On my way.' Underwood gathered his papers and walked across the corridor. Perhaps he could make something happen. He had to seize the initiative.

Part III

The Leaning Compass

41

The atmosphere was tense. The room had filled quickly and the new photographs on Dexter's board reminded everyone of the consequences of failure. Even Jensen had lost some of her natural ebullience after seeing the images. First Lucy Harrington and now Elizabeth Drury: the newspapers would tear the police apart. There would be massive pressure from above and shit invariably flows downhill. Underwood, coughing and pale, came into the room and nodded at Leach who gathered his notes and came to the front of the room. Heather Stussman stood with Dexter against the back wall: a number of male eyes watched her. She ignored them.

'OK. You all know what happened this morning,' said Underwood. 'Elizabeth Drury, thirty-seven, a leading dietician, found murdered at nine a.m. Similar circumstances to Lucy Harrington – Doctor Leach will tell you more. There are three things for us to concentrate on: one, how did the murderer find her? We almost didn't find her at all. Two, how did he gain access? The house has a brand-new alarm system, security lights, panic alarm and yet there are no signs of forced entry. Three, the names of the victims are connected. The killer seems to be obsessed with a poet called John Donne: four hundred years ago Donne knew an Elizabeth Drury and a Lucy Harrington. Dr Stussman at the back there has provided us with a list of Donne's other associates. Dexter used it and almost caught the bloke this morning. Dr Stussman, do you want to add anything on the names?'

Heather Stussman's heart jumped as the collective attention of the room turned back to her. 'Erm. All I'd add is that the killer seems to be focused on the notion of having a coterie. When these poems were written four hundred or so years ago, they were written for, and read aloud to, a specific audience: an audience that would appreciate the wit and logic of the poetry.' She noticed the blank looks and for a second thought she was lecturing in Wisconsin again. 'I am no expert on crime but I think your murderer has chosen these women – and me, I suppose – as his coterie audience. He is performing for us; he wants us to appreciate his wit.'

'Wit?' said Harrison drily. 'I don't see anyone laughing.'

'Wit doesn't refer exclusively to humour,' Stussman explained. 'In Latin, for example, one word for wit is the same as the word for salt: "sal". That's because wit in ancient Rome was associated with intellectual sharpness – salt tastes sharp, right? Likewise, to the aristocratic coterie audience that Donne and the other metaphysical poets performed to, wit didn't just mean being funny: it meant using bold, sometimes shocking images to get their points across.'

'Can you give us an example?' Harrison was beginning to get the point.

'In a poem called "A Valediction: Forbidding Mourning" John Donne famously compares two lovers with mathematical compasses. As one foot of the compass moves away from the other, so the other leans after it. This in Donne's mind reflected the soul of a lover seeking out its partner when the two are separated.' She looked around, gratified by the scratching pencils. 'Wit, you see.'

There was a silence. Underwood tried to push Julia from his thoughts and turned to Leach. 'Doctor, do you want to give us a preliminary report on the scene of crime and the victim?'

'Of course.' Leach flipped open his notepad. 'Judging from the pattern of blood dispersal I would say the victim was killed downstairs in the hallway, then dragged up to the bathroom. Her left eye was removed post-mortem, just as Lucy Harrington's was, only this time more successfully.' Leach looked at Underwood. 'He's getting better at it.' Dexter shivered. It could have been her picture up on the board. Leach continued, 'Time of death would be early this morning, say eight o'clock. She called her office at 7.40 and there is undigested breakfast cereal in the woman's stomach.'

'That's a different MO, sir,' said Jensen to Underwood. 'Harrington was killed late at night.'

'The burglar alarm,' said Dexter. 'She would have turned it off in the morning before she left for work.'

148

'Except she wasn't going to work,' Leach replied. 'Both the tyres on the passenger side of her car had been deflated. Presumably by the killer.'

'So he stopped her from leaving, then biffed her as she went back to the house?' Harrison was working the scene in his head.

'There are no signs of struggle outside the house. It looks like he attacked her inside,' Leach added.

'Why would she let a stranger into her house at eight in the morning?' asked Jensen.

Leach considered. 'Well, what would *you* have done in her shoes, Jensen? A woman living alone, you need to get to work early and you find your tyres are flat.'

'I suppose I'd call a cab,' she replied. Her mobile phone suddenly rang loudly. She scrambled to turn it off.

Dexter fired a withering look at Jensen. An idea struck her. 'There was a breakdown-recovery company sticker in her car.'

'Check it out,' said Underwood, his concentration failing him. 'Go on, Doctor.'

'Death was caused by repeated blows to the back of the skull. I would guess with the same instrument that was used to kill Lucy Harrington.'

'I saw two hammers on the bed before the guy hit me,' said Dexter. 'One was a claw hammer, the other one looked heavier – maybe a masonry hammer.'

'If he's a mason, we'll never catch him,' said Harrison. There was some laughter.

Dexter continued after a second. 'There was a case on the bed, too. A rectangular leather case: black. About so big.' She made the shape with her hands.

'That's interesting,' said Leach. 'Tell me, did it have any writing on it? A crest, maybe?'

'What are you thinking, Doctor?' asked Underwood.

'He needs to keep his knives somewhere. There were tiny indentations in the woman's head – four marks around her left eyebrow. I would guess that the killer used clamps to hold her eye open, to pull the eyelid back from the eye and hold it open. It looks to me as though your killer has got himself a proper set of surgical instruments from somewhere.'

'Where would he get them, Doctor?' The same idea had occurred to Dexter the previous day. She kicked herself for not following it up.

'There are specialist suppliers in London. It would be risky buying from them, though, since you would need a medical ID and they would keep a record of all sales.' Leach thought for a second. 'Did the case look old-fashioned to you?' he asked Dexter.

'I suppose so. I didn't see it that clearly. What are you saying?'

'I was just thinking,' Leach said. 'Modern skin clamps wouldn't have pierced the surface of the skin like these did. Your man likes history. Maybe he's been antique shopping.'

Dexter nodded and made a note. She would check it out this time.

'Anything else? Did he leave any trace evidence we could get a DNA match from?' Underwood seemed restless.

Leach paused before he spoke. He wasn't quite sure how to put this. 'There's good news, bad news and potentially *very* bad news. The good news is that Drury fought with him: there are small samples of skin under her fingernails. The bathwater didn't wash it all away. There's enough to give us a match if we catch the bloke. Whether it would stand up in court I don't know: the defence could conceivably argue that the water and Drury's blood corrupted the DNA, but let's cross that bridge when we come to it. The bad news is that there are no fingerprints anywhere – other than Drury's and Sergeant Dexter's, of course. He wore gloves all the time.'

Underwood thought for a second. 'And the very bad news?'

'Elizabeth Drury's blood is group A. Sergeant Dexter's is O-positive. There are small samples of two other blood groups at the crime scene: AB-negative and O-negative. There are traces on Drury's neck and on the bathroom floor.'

'Fuck.' Harrison got the point. 'Two other people.'

'At a guess, I would say there were traces of blood on his gloves. We know he grabbed Drury by the neck at some point as there is some minor bruising on either side of her windpipe. Not enough to strangle her, mind,' said Leach.

'And the bathroom floor?' Dexter asked.

'Perhaps he changed gloves before the operation on her eye,' Leach volunteered. 'If he was waiting outside he probably wore thick gloves. Once he went to work on the poor woman's eye he would need to be more dexterous. I guess he changed to surgical gloves or maybe rubber washing-up gloves. Again, the presence of multiple blood samples at the scene might undermine the credibility of any DNA evidence we were to submit at a trial.'

'I'm more concerned that there might be two other corpses with their eyes ripped out lying around somewhere,' said Underwood. 'Have we had anyone reported missing in the last two days?'

'Not that I can remember, sir,' said Harrison. 'We'll check.'

'He's taking more risks,' said Underwood. 'Why? He's killed two, possibly four people, in three days. That's a very close grouping. He took pains to ensure that the crime scene at Lucy Harrington's was a forensic nightmare. He stakes her place out, kills her in the middle of the night, escapes through woodland: no one hears or sees a fucking thing. Virtually no risk.

'Then there's the names. We would never have understood the significance of the names without Dr Stussman – and the killer told her to contact us, to explain it all to us. He must have known that Dr Stussman would have understood the link between the poem found at Lucy Harrington's house and her name. Presumably, he must also have known that Dr Stussman would give us a list of similar names. He took a big risk and the upshot was that Dexter walked right in on him.

'He kills Drury first thing in the morning. She's supposed to be at the office: they're bound to wonder where she is. Risk. There's more traffic in the morning, even out in Afton: more chance of being seen. Risk. Maybe he poses as a taxi driver or a repairman to get in to the house. Risk. He felt he had to kill Drury today.'

Dexter followed the logic. 'Then there's the blood. At Harrington's there's no DNA evidence at all. At Drury's there's loads – from at least three unidentified sources. Why did he let *that* happen? He is risking us making connections. The more connections we make, the more vulnerable he is: the more likely that someone sees something, or remembers something.'

151

'He put Drury in the bath, though, didn't he?' said Harrison. 'He still made some effort to corrupt physical evidence. Dr Leach said the fingernail samples might not be credible in court. That mean's he's achieved the same effect as he did at Lucy Harrington's.'

'*For in a common bath of teares it bled.*' Stussman's American accent sounded incongruous. 'At both murders he left behind text that referred to water. *Draw not up seas to drowne me in thy spheare* was the other one. I think that the bodies in the bath are more about the consistency of poetic imagery than about messing up DNA evidence.'

'Consistency of poetic imagery?' Harrison's thick eyebrows had climbed to the top of his forehead. 'Do me a favour!'

'Sure. He takes the girls' eyes, right? Eyes produce tears. Both examples talk about being swamped by tears; overcome with pain. A conceit is supposed to seem absurd at first but gradually persuade us of its brilliance, make us realize the direction of his logic. Isn't that what we're doing now? Aren't we starting to piece together what he's doing, why he's doing it? Maybe he's taking more risks to ensure we understand what he's saying.'

The room was quiet as everyone tried to absorb the significance of what she had said. Underwood got it first. 'He's running out of time.'

42

The meeting broke up. Underwood disappeared back to his office. Dexter waylaid Harrison and Jensen.

'By the way, how's that list of local B-and-E arrests coming along?' she asked.

'We've worked it down to eighteen possibles, based on age, ethnic background and nature of offence.' Harrison showed her a list of names and addresses.

'Who are these guys down at the bottom?' There was a cluster of five surnames without addresses below the main list.

'They fit the age and ethnic type and they're more or less local but they're all very minor offences; they all got warnings from the magistrates but weren't even served with sentences,' Jensen said.

'Vandalism, creating a public nuisance, nicking cars – that sort of thing. None of them actually broke into any houses,' Harrison added. 'We were going to drop them off the list at its next iteration.'

'Fair enough,' said Dexter. 'I'm beginning to think this house-breaker thing is a waste of time anyway. This guy sounds like a one-off head case to me. I doubt he's got any previous. There's no point creating extra work.'

'Once we've got a final list, we'll go round each of them and check out alibis for the ninth and this morning. Don't hold your breath, though,' Harrison said.

Dexter nodded and went off to find Underwood. Stussman had been loitering uncomfortably in the background and quickly followed in Dexter's wake. Jensen returned to her computer and called up the list of names she had worked up with Harrison. She scrolled to the bottom and, as requested, deleted the names of Darren Burgess, Andrew Hills, Shane Briers, Martin McMahon and Crowan Frayne.

Underwood didn't have time to get the bottle back in its drawer before Stussman and Dexter appeared.

'John. Oh, I'm sorry,' said Stussman. 'I should have knocked.' She looked embarrassed. Underwood cursed his stupidity, his clumsiness.

'Don't be silly. I have toothache. Whisky's the only thing that helps.' It was a transparently poor excuse.

'A dentist might be kinder on your liver.' Stussman smiled gently. She fancied a drink, too. Those pictures had upset her: she wasn't looking forward to turning out the lights later.

'Guv.' Dexter rode roughshod over his embarrassment, like a tank in a field of strawberries. 'Dr Stussman's car is outside.'

'Do you need me any more, John?' Stussman asked.

Underwood came around the front of his desk and shook her

hand. 'No. Thank you, Heather, thanks for coming down. Your comments were very helpful. Call us if you have any concerns or if he contacts you again.'

'Will do.'

'We're getting closer, Dr Stussman,' said Dexter.

'Or he's getting closer to us.' Stussman seemed worried.

'Either way, we'll nail him.' Underwood's words didn't sound very reassuring. Stussman nodded and left the office. Dexter stayed. 'What did you make of all that, Dex? You think he's getting sloppy?'

'Maybe. I feel like you do: the Drury thing may have been a rush job.'

'But why? What's his hurry? When we found the Harrington girl, I thought it would be weeks until he struck again. He was so careful. But here we are, three days later and we've got two, maybe four bodies. Not to mention poetry coming out of our fucking ears.'

'Perhaps we are getting close to him, sir. Maybe he's getting freaked out. What should we do about the other two possibles?'

'Nothing we can do, really. Unless someone's reported missing, that is. We shouldn't assume he's killed anyone else yet. He might have been in a fight or something.' There was a pain in Underwood's chest: he shifted uncomfortably. Mad images flickered in his mind like some terrible bonfire. He was finding it harder to push them aside.

Dexter waited for a second. She had to say something. She pushed the door shut behind her. 'Sir, about what you told me earlier. Outside the Drury woman's house. About your wife.'

Underwood retreated back under his shell like a frightened turtle. 'What about it?'

'I know it's not my business but is there anything I can do, sir? I couldn't help noticing the bottle.'

'There's nothing to say, Dex. It's not your concern.'

'With respect, sir, it is.' She was quietly insistent. 'If it's affecting your work it *is* my concern.'

'What are you going to do? Report me for being separated?' His tone was desolate, despairing. The light in his eyes had been switched off.

'Drinking won't help, sir. It won't help toothache and it certainly won't help this. I needed to speak to you last night and your mobile was switched off. I understand that Harrison couldn't get you this morning.'

'Your point, sergeant?'

'My point is that I'm overstretched. Things are getting missed. We can't afford to balls this up now.' Her gaze scanned his face for some expression, some flicker of recognition. Nothing. 'And on a personal level, sir, I am always available if you need a sounding board. I've knocked around a bit myself. I've been shat on so often I sometimes think I should have WC stamped on my forehead.'

Underwood nodded. 'Point taken. Thank you Alison.' He felt ashamed. Again. *That bitch Julia. How could she have driven me to this? I'll make her understand, her and her musical ponce wife-fucker boyfriend.*

Dexter was talking. He tried to tune in.

'. . . Of housebreakers. The list is down to eighteen. Harrison and Jensen are going to start looking them up. I'm going to check up on antique shops and other places that might sell old medical junk. The more I think about it, that case *did* look old-fashioned . . .'

Little Julia Cooper with her spoddy haircut and brace . . . goody-goody Julia Cooper and her angel voice . . . Julia Cooper, make-up smudged with tears when he'd proposed, laughing through the tears, holding his face . . . Julia Underwood big-eyed in her cream-white wedding dress . . . Mr and Mrs Underwood cutting the fucking cake, taking the first dance – Unchained fucking Melody . . . Julia Underwood hugging her lover in the shadows of a lamp lit doorway . . . Julia Underwood writhing with pleasure under another man, grunting like an animal . . . Julia Heyer hosting a dinner party for the fucker's friends . . . expensive haircut over expensive earrings . . . sing us a song, Jules . . . sing us a fucking song . . .

'. . . More about Drury. What's she's done, where she's been. He must have found her somehow. I'm sure he's using public information, we just have to figure out how . . .' Dexter continued. Underwood drifted out again.

Julia Heyer drives her children to school . . . older than the other mothers but just as pretty . . . she drives a big, flash Mummy-Jeep . . . she waves at the other mothers . . . her children have beautiful voices and big green eyes like their mother, their singing whore mother . . .

'. . . If that's all right with you, sir?' Dexter had stopped. He saw her suddenly, focused, watching him intently. He coughed.

'That sounds good, Dex. You run with it,' he improvised.

'Thanks, sir. How about you?'

'Me?' He thought for a second and an idea flared at him out of the bonfire. 'I'm going to follow up on that Heyer bloke. Remember the guy Harrison and I had in for an interview?'

'I thought he was a non-starter.'

'Probably. But it's probably worth checking where he was last night. His alibi for the eighth was a bit wobbly.' Underwood stood up and tried to look businesslike, reaching for his coat. He knew that his every movement shouted 'Liar!'

'Fair enough. Have you got your mobile, sir?'

'Right here.' He tapped his coat pocket and hurried out.

Dexter waited for a moment, until she was sure he had gone, then edged around his desk and withdrew the whisky from the drawer. She unscrewed it and poured a double measure into a plastic cup. It tasted fantastic: bad for toothache, bad for broken marriages, but good for concussion and the shakes.

43

Suzie Hunt got home just after four that afternoon. She had gone beyond tiredness and was operating on automatic pilot: turn key, take off coat, kettle on, biscuit from barrel. There was no sign of Katie anywhere in the house. Suzie flopped into her favourite armchair and dialled Katie's mobile for the tenth time in six hours. No reply. She was beginning to feel a pang of anxiety. Still, she reasoned, Katie was a big girl now, she'd stayed out nights before. You had to give youngsters freedom these days or they just took it for themselves and resented you for ever. She didn't want Katie to be her enemy. She didn't have that many friends. The kettle clicked off. Suzie squeezed the life from a tired-looking tea bag and collapsed back in her armchair. Her phone was ringing. She smirked: here come the excuses. Suzie had heard them all before: mainly from herself.

'Hello.'

'Is that Katie's mum?' A woman's voice, aggressive. Suzie felt a flash of uncertainty.

'It is.'

'I'm June Riley, Steve's mum. Is he there?'

'Here? No. I haven't seen him or Katie since they went out last night. I assumed they had stayed at yours.'

'Wait till I get hold of that dirty little bastard. He was supposed to call me.'

Suzie sat up in her armchair. 'Hang on a minute – do you think they're all right?'

Ten miles away, as the sky began to darken and birds aligned themselves blackly on telephone wires, Jimmy Jarrett drove his flat-backed van along Blindman's Lane out of Afton. He was in a bad mood: up at five in the morning, he should have finished an hour ago. He had got delayed at a farm near Evesbury, mending a cow gate. Replacing the hinge had been straight-forward but the wood of the gatepost had been rotten and it had crumbled when he'd screwed the new hinges in. That had meant a new post and a fifteen-mile drive to the timber mill on the outskirts of New Bolden.

One job left before Jimmy could put his feet up. It looked pretty easy, though: a quick waterproof-paint job on a rusting gate between two fields. He found the entrance to the meadow quickly and away in the distance he could see the gate connecting with the next field. He knew he shouldn't drive down there really but there were no animals about and the ground looked pretty firm. He drove down the slope and parked up near the gate. A quick inspection, and then Jimmy retrieved his paint-brushes from inside the van. A brook babbled happily in the background as Jimmy got to work, slapping the waterproof paint over the rustiest patches of metal. His mobile phone started ringing.

'Wouldn't you bleedin' know it?' he muttered as he trudged back and rooted around in his pockets for the phone. Eventually, he found it. It was turned off. Something else was ringing, though. He looked around, confused. Was someone hiding in the trees? He made his way in the direction of the noise: it drew him towards the trees, towards the brook. There were tyre tracks on the ground. Jimmy quickened his step, jogged to the edge of the brook and looked down the bank. He caught his breath.

Steve Riley's Fiesta lay against the bank of the gully, its nose in the water and its back end in the air. Jimmy couldn't see anyone inside. Katie Hunt's mobile stopped ringing.

'Jesus Christ.' Jimmy Jarrett scrambled down the gully, slipping and cursing in the mud until his feet were underwater. He was breathless. *Getting old, Jim.* 'Is anyone there?' He bent down and looked through the driver's open door, stretching into the car. What he saw would haunt him.

Suzie Hunt slammed her phone down. She had agreed with June Riley to keep trying Katie's mobile until six. Then June would call the hospitals and Suzie would call the police. Time crawled by and Suzie became increasingly agitated. She chewed her fingernails and sucked the last molecules of smoke out of a packet of ten. At half-past five, her house phone rang.

44

New Bolden's scene-of-crime officers were stretched: four murders in under a week had put their meagre resources under strain. Extra officers had been seconded from the Area Major Incident team at Huntington after the news of the murdered couple broke. He stood amongst the mêlée in the darkening field with a growing sense of frustration. He had now examined four bodies – all young and healthy people – in a matter of days and felt no closer to the killer. There was some trace DNA from the Drury woman but even though it might give them a preliminary match if they actually caught the killer, he shuddered to think what a good defence lawyer would do to it in court.

Leach stepped back as a crane began to haul Steve Riley's Fiesta from its muddy resting place. The chain creaked and groaned as it grappled with the car's inertia. Slowly and awkwardly, the car edged up until it juddered to a halt at the top of the bank. Not for the first time, Leach glumly considered the banality of death. *We exist as inexplicable complexities, the crest of the evolutionary wave, imbued with insecurities and aspirations, preconceptions and knowledge, affectations and delusions. And yet, we leave the world in lumpen, ugly banality. Car crashes, heart attacks, cancer, hypothermia: attached to a machine in a hospital corridor or lying in a puddle of glass on tarmac. Or sometimes brutally ripped from the world, like Kate Hunt and Steven Riley.* He held their personal effects in two evidence bags: a purse containing twenty pounds and a Connect card, a wallet holding ten pounds, a couple of credit cards and two unused condoms, and two mobile phones. What could be more banal than caving someone's skull in with a hammer?

Leach needed a smoke. He watched Sergeant Dexter walking towards him from the recovered car. Her face looked softer under the light of the SOC's halogen lamps; the harsh lights of the police station made her look like she was carved from granite. He realized that was an illusion. *More like marble, really*, Leach mused.

'What do you think, Doctor? Is it our man?' Dexter stumbled slightly on the uneven ground.

'Almost certainly. Similar pattern of blows to the back of the head, within two miles of the Drury woman, approximate time of death between ten and midnight yesterday. No obvious signs that they fought him. I'd say he surprised them.'

'Or maybe they surprised him?'

Leach nodded. 'Very possibly. There doesn't seem to be any damage to the eyes of either victim.'

'Poor bastards.' Dexter looked back at the car. 'Harrison's with the parents at the station. Common as muck, he reckons; they're already blaming each other. We can do the formal IDs whenever it suits you.'

'Tomorrow. I'll need to look them both over tonight, then we'll clean them up a bit. We can't let the parents see them like this.'

'Understood. I can't believe this is happening, Doc. I thought it was supposed to be quiet country up here. It's worse than London.' She looked tired and tried to stifle a yawn.

'A long day,' Leach observed as he placed the possessions of Katie Hunt and Steve Riley in a secure evidence box. 'Where's your guv'nor, by the way? No offence, I'm sure you are at least as capable as he is, but shouldn't he be here? It's his disco, after all.'

'He's chasing up a possible suspect.' Dexter wanted to believe that. 'I tried to call him but his mobile's switched off.'

'A difficult character, is Underwood. An enigma wrapped inside a monumental pain in the arse.'

'Impossible bloke.' Dexter let her guard drop. 'God, I'm knackered. Have you got time for a drink?'

Dexter updated Harrison over the phone and left the scene with Leach an hour later. They drove in a two-car convoy to the edge of New Bolden where they parked outside The Plume of Feathers and went in. It was warm and welcoming. Dexter suddenly felt exhausted.

'Double Scotch?' asked Leach, with the ghost of a smile.

'For starters . . .'

They sat in a quiet corner of the dark-timbered pub, the open fire licking at their heels. Dexter stared into the bottom of her drink and blinked away the bloody eyeball that stared back at her.

'How long have you been doing this, Doc?'

'Drinking, or my Dr Frankenstein bit?' Leach grinned. 'Actually, the answer is roughly the same either way: about twenty years.'

Dexter took a swig of Scotch: it seared straight to the centre of her brain. Fantastic.

'Have you ever seen anything like this?'

'Like this? No. The organization of the killer and the post-mortem mutilations on the body are extraordinary, in my experience.' He looked up at a framed certficate of beer-worthiness on the wall of the pub. 'We still haven't got any real idea why he's doing it. That's the most troubling thing, as far as I can see.'

'He's trying to recreate these poems, isn't he? Dazzle us with his wit, Dr Stussman reckons.'

'OK, so why the eyes of Drury and Harrington but not those of the Hunt girl?'

Dexter thought. 'The names are important to him. They are the names of people in Donne's intellectual circle, whatever that might be. His merry bleedin' men, I suppose.'

'But when he killed Riley and Hunt he broke his pattern anyway. So why not take their eyes and have done with it? Why kill them, then hang around in the area for another seven or eight hours risking detection just to get hold of Elizabeth Drury? As Underwood said, it's a massive risk.'

'Like I said, the names matter to him.'

'I think it's more than that. Harrington and Drury both had blue eyes, Riley and Hunt both had brown eyes.'

'Come on, Doc! You don't think this lunatic has a thing about blue-eyed girls, do you?' She laughed bitterly. 'Then again, why should he be any different to the rest of the male population?'

'What I am saying is that serial killers have highly specific fantasies that they act out. Now, if blue eyes are central to your killer's fantasy that is something specific that doesn't, on the face of it, have anything to do with the poetry.'

Dexter saw the point. 'The poems refer to eyes but not to blue eyes. It's more general stuff about tears and oceans.'

'Right. But in the two murders where the poetry was left behind, both the victims had blue eyes. Riley and Hunt both had brown eyes that he left alone.'

'So what are you saying?'

'Why would someone specifically want blue eyes as opposed to brown or green?'

Dexter got it. 'Maybe he thinks that the eyes refer to a specific person. Some fantasy woman he's created.'

'Problem is – ' Leach paused for a sip of his whisky, half for effect ' – he took the left eye in both cases. If you were creating a fantasy woman – you know, eyes that you could stare longingly into on those cold winter evenings – wouldn't you take a right eye and a left eye?'

'I would have taken both of Lucy Harrington's eyes,' Dexter replied. 'I had her all to myself, no chance of interruption.'

'Exactly. And she was an attractive girl: a fantasy figure, if you like.'

'But he didn't do that.' Dexter felt a twinge of excitement as pennies began to drop. 'He took double the risk to get Elizabeth Drury's left eye. Then, when he bumps into Riley and Hunt and knocks them off too, he multiplies the risks again.'

'And still hangs around for eight hours to get what he really wants,' Leach emphasized. 'Imagine staying near to a spot – a spot where you've just battered two people to death – for eight or nine hours: that takes incredible will-power. He must have really wanted that left eye.'

Will-power. The power of the rational will. Dexter remembered Stussman's phrase. She frowned. 'Why would anyone want two left eyes?'

Leach scratched his head languidly. 'You're the detective.'

45

Harrison was pissed off. It had been the worst day he could remember in his eight years in the CID. Three bodies, the local and national press baying for blood, a serial killer at large, distraught parents and no decent leads. He and Jensen had spent two hours trying to console Suzie Hunt and June and Duncan Riley before the counsellors from Huntington had turned up. Arguments, tears, recriminations: two hours of wasted time.

What did they have to go on after a week of legwork? No

fingerprints, some scratchy DNA evidence, a phantom white van, African violets and a list of eighteen housebreakers that nobody believed would be of the slightest value. It was demoralizing. As was being ordered about by little Miss Bossy-Dexter. He would love to stick it to her. He would give it to her hard – across the desk, maybe. That would shut her up. He would make her squeak in her stupid cockney accent. *Strike a light with that, darlin'.*

He wished all female coppers were like Jensen. You could have a laugh with her and she didn't mind putting it around a bit. He was planning to go round to her flat later: she only had a single bed but he didn't plan on doing much sleeping. There was always the couch for that.

Jensen walked back into the crime room, looking exasperated.

'Have they gone?' Harrison asked.

'Yes. Thank Christ.' She took a cigarette from Harrison's pack and lit it hurriedly. 'God, that was awful. The girl's mother says that they went out for drinks in Afton. I made some calls. The landlord of The Farmer's Boy says they were in there until after nine.'

'The parents are coming in at ten tomorrow for the IDs,' said Harrison. 'Dexter can do that. I'm through being a bloody counsellor.'

'Where is she, anyway?' Jensen asked. 'Shouldn't she be back by now?'

'Should be. Still cleaning up the crime scene, I guess. It always takes a bit longer when you have to use the AMIP team: different teams have different methods.'

Jensen slumped in her chair and rustled the bewildering pile of paper in front of her. 'This African-violet business is a waste of time.'

'Of course it is. You don't think that Dexter would have let you follow it up if it wasn't, do you?'

'I've called all the local flower shops and the nursery and none of them stock *Saintpaulia*-bleeding-*Ionantha*. Wrong time of year, apparently.'

'Our man must grow his own. Nice relaxing hobby.' Harrison laughed at the thought.

'Tomorrow I'll start the house-to-house on the list of burglars. I'm tired of shuffling the list about. We might as well start interviewing them all: getting alibis and that.' Jensen exhaled the blue cigarette smoke with a sigh of pleasure.

'That's gonna be another dead end. I tell you. This guy isn't a burglar, he's a cold-blooded fucking maniac. We won't get this boy until he screws up or we get lucky like Dexter did this morning.'

'Can we go? I fancy a beer. The pubs close in an hour.'

'We should wait for her to get back really.' Harrison thought for a moment. 'Oh, sod it. The guv'nor's not here. I'll treat you to a Babycham.' He stood and picked up his coat. 'And after that I will take great delight in examining you for evidence.'

'Returning to the scene of the crime, eh?' Jensen smiled. 'You're very meticulous. Maybe I'll pretend you're Inspector Underwood.'

'Maybe I'll pretend you're Sergeant Dexter.'

'Don't do that. I don't want you to go all floppy on me.'

'No danger of that, constable.'

'Pulling rank?'

'Whenever I can.'

Harrison held the door open for her. Jensen brushed past him a little closer than she needed to.

46

Suzie Hunt closed her front door. The house was empty and quiet. The police squad car pulled away outside. Through the frosted glass she watched its lights disappear. She was shaking but had no tears left to cry. Her little girl had gone. Gone. She hadn't even been able to say goodbye. She felt that Katie was standing behind her, shouting, screaming for her to help. *Little Katie alone in a vast dark night: just like her mother. Calling her, calling her. She was so young, so pretty.* Suzie Hunt collapsed, retching, onto her tired two-seater sofa and tried to think herself dead.

47

Underwood listened to Dexter's voicemail message without emotion. Another two bodies, another Spaghetti Junction of directionless leads. He was almost past caring. He had visited the offices of Heyer Properties late that afternoon. Heyer's secretary had given him her boss's phone number in Norfolk and Underwood had decided not to push for the address: no point in alerting Heyer that he was coming. The prefix to the phone number was '01263' and Underwood called Directory Enquiries to locate the area that the code covered. It was Blakeney in Norfolk: an hour up the A11, then the A1065 to Holt.

The drive had been easier than he had expected. The early-evening traffic had been light and he arrived in Blakeney just after nine. The tiny old medieval port was quiet as he drove in and pulled up in a car park overlooking the estuary. Across the water were the salt marshes and the bird watchers' sanctuary of Blakeney Point. It was a beautiful spot. *Nice place to unwind and fuck someone else's wife.*

There were two or three small restaurants close to the small front. He would find the happy couple eventually. It was just a matter of being patient. *The killer of Elizabeth Drury and Lucy Harrington is patient. He takes risks to achieve what he wants. He waits and wonders: grateful for the dark.* Underwood wound down his car window: the salty air was cold and unwelcoming but it heightened his senses. *I am the hunter. I will find you. I will bring you down.* The air made him hungry and he reached into his bag for a sandwich.

Time drifted by. Underwood became irritated. Sitting in a car park was pathetic. How else could he find them? *The car.* Underwood still had Heyer's car registration in his notebook. He reached into his jacket pocket and found the relevant page: blue BMW, S245 QXY. Blakeney was a small village with only three or four restaurants and a couple of pubs. Underwood climbed out of his car and walked through the car park. There were only a dozen or so cars and none of them belonged to Paul Heyer.

He began to walk along the front. Sea water slapped at the yachts to his left. A couple emerged laughing from a restaurant. Underwood felt exposed and pulled his collar up to shield his face. The village was well maintained, with a plush Georgian-style hotel as its architectural centrepiece. Were they staying there? It was the obvious place. Underwood found a telephone box and called the number Heyer's secretary had given him. No reply. It was unlikely to be the hotel, then. Perhaps they were staying with some friends of Heyer's – *that fucker* – or maybe they had got a cottage. A cottage seemed more likely, Underwood thought to himself: a bit of privacy for their sweaty little business.

Half an hour swept by and Underwood found no sign of Heyer's car. Maybe they had stayed in. It was the first night of their fuckfest, after all. Perhaps they couldn't control themselves. *Spoddy little Julia Cooper the sex goddess.* The thought almost made him laugh out loud. The air was breaking up the muck in his lungs and Underwood was beginning to feel uncomfortable: the mild pain in his chest was threatening to become more acute. He crossed a narrow cobbled road and headed for an ancient-looking pub: The Jack Tar. A brandy would help. After all, didn't doctors use alcohol to sterilize equipment? *Equipment. Lines of scalpels and bloody forceps. Rip their eyes out. Does he keep the eyes in alcohol? Do they float and bob in a jar, like pickled eggs?*

Underwood was about to open the black oak door of The Jack Tar when a BMW turned along the road ahead and parked. He paused for a second in the doorway of the pub, invisible. A hole in the night. The driver's door opened and Paul Heyer stepped out. Underwood's stomach clenched into a painfully tight ball and he edged closer, ducking into an alleyway. He could smell onions cooking. Heyer was about twenty yards ahead of him now, standing by the car, hands on hips. *Musical ponce.* Underwood caught his breath as Julia climbed out of the passenger seat. Her black hair was tied back into a neat bow.

She dyes her hair, mate, Underwood thought darkly. *I bet she hasn't fucking told you that yet. You'll find out, though. All her banal little secrets. Her smells and insecurities.* She shut the car door and smiled at Paul. He walked to the front of the car and took her hand, kissing her gently on the lips.

Underwood boiled with rage. He wished he had brought the hammer with him. He would have rushed out at that *oh-so-perfect moment* and smashed the back of Paul Heyer's head in as the adulterer violated Underwood's wife. Instead, he held back in the darkness of the alleyway and watched them walk slowly down the cobbles towards the tiny high street. Julia looked slimmer than he remembered. *All that screwing must have helped her to shed a few pounds.* She wore a dress he didn't recognize and heels that didn't suit her or the pavement. He recognized her perfume, though: *same old same old. Dress it up like a lady and it still smells like a tart.* He followed them at a distance until they entered the narrow doorway of a seafood restaurant.

Paul Heyer was beginning to relax. With New Bolden behind them, the quaint isolation of his friend's cottage seemed like an entirely different world. Julia had unwound visibly and looked beautiful in the outfit he had bought for her in Holt. The old worry lines still nagged at her brow but Paul was confident that a few days of fresh air and good food would iron those out. She had been through a lot, he reminded himself. He knew it would take time for her to shed her old skin of guilt and anxiety. He was prepared to wait. She was worth it.

A good meal would move things along nicely. 'Oysters' was a popular local restaurant and Paul was a big fan. The maître d' showed them to a window table that looked out across the estuary and Paul ordered two gin and tonics.

'It's beautiful here, Paul,' Julia breathed. 'It's so quiet.'

'They've got a great menu, too. The sole is fantastic. They also do a cracking lobster. Caught locally every morning.'

'I haven't had lobster for about ten years.'

'One of life's great pleasures. I had a New England lobster in

Boston once that I swear was hanging off the plate. It looked like an alien. I was actually quite scared of the thing in case it went for me.'

'I bet it was good, though.'

'Unbelievable.'

'I'd love to go to America.'

'I'll take you. If you survive a week of me in Norfolk, that is.'

'I'm coping OK so far.' She took his hand across the table. 'It's a long time since I've been on holiday.'

'Too long, Julia. That's behind you now. Let's look forward. Be positive.'

'Agreed.' Julia Cooper sat back in her chair happily, again the giddy schoolgirl. 'What about some wine?'

'You choose.'

'I'm hopeless. I don't know many wines. You're the expert.'

'Don't be silly. Positive, confident Julia starts today.' He nodded at the wine list. 'Give me your best shot.'

Julia scanned the list for something familiar. White wine with fish, obviously, but which one? There were so many. South African Chardonnay. That was a safe bet and easy to pronounce too.

'The Pine Forest Chardonnay,' she said boldly, folding the wine list shut with a flourish.

'An excellent choice, Madame,' said Paul in an affected waiter voice. Julia smiled and took his hand again as their gins arrived.

Underwood hurried back to his car in a daze of anger, hurt and jealousy. He was careful to walk past the back of the restaurant, taking the long way round to the car park. He would drive to a spot closer to Heyer's BMW and follow them. *Drive through the darkness, lights off, unseen. Careful to keep a distance. Careful to be anonymous. They are both on edge. They would both recognize me immediately. Must be on my guard. Must stay invisible until I am ready for them. Ready to show them myself: explain what they have created in me. Reveal the monstrosity I have become. Make them understand. Make them fucking understand.*

He paused at a street corner. He was at the car park.

Breathless and in pain, as if his lungs had burst in agony. He no longer coughed up slabs of phlegm but long strings of blood: the warmth clung in his throat. He hacked the strings into his mouth and pulled them out into his handkerchief. He was coming apart from the inside: dissolving into a shapeless bloody nothing. Underwood sat on a low wall and composed himself, brushing away the tears that felt so cold on his exposed skin. *For in a common bath of teares it bled,* he remembered, *yes, tears that freeze with blood. Lucy Harrington's one-eyed gaze; Elizabeth Drury's last breathless panic to escape; Julia Cooper tied to a bedpost, wild-eyed with fear.* Underwood wiped his face dry: every chilled tear was a horror.

Underwood's hand rested briefly on the bag of items he had brought with him. He had stopped at a garage in Holt to buy a few essentials: a roll of thick masking tape, some bin bags – and a hammer.

He was hungry again. The infection in his lungs was draining his body's strength, its ability and desire to fight back. He looked up. There was a fish-and-chip shop about fifty yards away. He ordered a bag of chips and two pickled eggs. Five minutes later, in the darkness of the car park, he slid half an egg into his mouth and imagined it was Lucy Harrington's eye. He rolled it gently around his mouth, cleaning it with his saliva. He could almost feel the gouges with the sensitive tip of his tongue, the ragged hood of flesh where it had been torn from the socket.

He placed the egg back in its bag and repeated the process with the other, this time remembering Elizabeth Drury: elegant even when floating in her own blood. He cleaned the egg with care, at one stage even taking the entire object into his mouth. It fitted perfectly. Suddenly he thought of Julia's soppy green eyes rolling in pleasure as she writhed orgasmically under Paul Heyer. Underwood bit down hard on the egg. He imagined smashing down through the lenses of Julia's eyes, snapping the ciliary muscles with his teeth. He relished the crunchiness of the cornea and the cold liquid of the aqueous humour that broke over his tongue like a liqueur. He swallowed hard.

*

The wine had been excellent and the lobster enormous. Paul Heyer and Julia Cooper had no room for a dessert so they settled for coffee. By eleven-thirty, the restaurant was nearly deserted and Paul finally got the message from the awkward-looking waiting staff. He left a generous tip, shook hands with the maître d' and walked back to his car, holding Julia's hand. He was well over the legal alcohol limit but knew that the area was pretty thinly policed and, besides, he was still in control of all his faculties. The BMW started first time and Heyer steered the powerful car gingerly along the narrow road that led out of Blakeney and edged along the cliffs towards Wells. He concentrated so hard on the black road in front of him that he did not notice John Underwood's Mondeo, following quietly behind him with its normally powerful headlights turned off.

48

Heather Stussman dined in the college hall. Although the prospect of another intellectual flaying at the hands of Dr McKensie filled her with gloom, she was tired of being kept prisoner in her own rooms. Besides, seeing the photographs of the murder victims at New Bolden police station had unsettled her: she wanted to be with people.

As it happened, McKensie and his coven left her alone during the meal. Perhaps the presence of a uniformed policeman at the door made them nervous: skeletons jangled in everyone's cupboards. After dinner, Stussman retired to the warmth of the Combination Room with a coffee and her battered edition of John Donne's *Songs and Sonnets*. The ancient room was almost empty and she sank gratefully into the security of a high-backed leather armchair in front of the open fire. A steward brought her the brandy she had requested at dinner and stirred the burning logs in front of her. Sparks flew high into the old stone chimney, glowing brightly orange before disappearing for ever.

She tried to organize her thoughts. It was hard: comfort

worked against her, it was seductive and distracting. She leaned forward in the chair and tried to simplify what she had spent her career complicating.

What are the major themes that Donne addresses in his poetry? she asked herself.

Love, Sex, Religion, Death.

His poetry reflects the uncertainties of the time. It attempts to fuse religion with science. The humanist obsession with classical philosophy was also important. Indeed, the killer of Harrington and Drury had asked her about the music of the 'spheares'. Donne was one of a number of writers who developed this notion from the early writings of Aristotle and Pythagoras.

A log hissed and spat in the flames. Stussman jumped, despite herself. She looked around the room. Only Professor Proctor and Dr Wuff remained: both seemed at best semi-conscious, their eyes losing focus under sagging lids. The brandy tasted good and she rolled its fire around her tongue with relish. Cambridge had *some* advantages.

So Donne's poems were essentially hybrids: fusions of ideas that often contradicted each other. The poet's own life had been something of a contradiction. Donne was born a Catholic, a descendant of the martyr Sir Thomas More, and yet he became a high-profile Anglican. Indeed, he ended up as the Protestant Dean of St Paul's Cathedral.

Was the killer religious, Stussman wondered? He had not referred to any of Donne's overtly religious works. And yet, religious uncertainty was central to understanding the poet he had selected. *Curious.*

She returned to her book and flicked to 'A Valediction: Of Weeping'. The killer had written a line of this poem – 'Draw not up seas to drowne me in thy spheare' – on Lucy Harrington's wall. Stussman shivered as she remembered the grisly photograph of Harrington's butchered face.

The poem is about separation. It's a valediction: a farewell poem. The conceit is based on the idea of reflection. The two lovers are reflected in each other's tears. The woman's tears reflect the poet's face and vice versa.

171

Stussman frowned as an idea began to germinate. She reread part of the first stanza:

> '*For thy face coines them, and thy stampe they beare*
> *And by this Mintage they are something worth*
> *For thus they be*
> *Pregnant of thee*
> *Fruits of much griefe they are, emblems of more.*'

It was a symbiosis. His tears are given meaning by her image. And conversely, his image gives purpose to her suffering.

'*Pregnant of thee . . .*'

Stussman remembered that other writers, contemporaries of Donne had used similar imagery: the idea that one appeared 'as a baby' in the eyes of a lover was not originally Donne's. She had never considered the image in depth before. However, the meaning was obvious: we feel emotionally vulnerable and dependent when we are in love. We need unconditional love in return; just like a baby does.

To whom do we show our vulnerabilities? To whom do we always appear as babies? Our partners, our parents – our grandparents, perhaps.

Stussman stared into the red-gold depths of her brandy and saw her own distorted image wobbling back at her. She thought of her father, how he had stewed his genius in a brandy bottle, turned his liver into a brick. 'Unravelling a poet's mind is like trying to knit with spaghetti,' he had told her once. She smiled at the memory. She missed him. She was always the baby in his tears.

The dead girl is the killer's conceit: the shocking imagery at the centre of his argument. In themselves, the victims have no other significance.

'If those women meant nothing to you,' Stussman whispered into her glass, 'then who are you really saying goodbye to? Who gave meaning to your pain?'

At the second murder scene the killer had left extracts from two poems: 'The First Anniversary' and 'A Feaver'. Stussman flicked through her book.

Both poems concern sick women: Elizabeth Drury is one of

them, the identity of the subject in 'A Feaver' is not known but may have been Donne's wife. Has the killer lost his wife? His mother, maybe? Is he trying to say goodbye to her? Are the murders some personal form of valediction?

Stussman turned between 'A Feaver' and 'The First Anniversary'.

Both poems suggest that the world will cease to have meaning should the female subject die. In 'A Feaver' Donne even suggested that the woman's disease would become a day of judgement for the world, that the very heat of her fever would consume the world in flames:

> *'O wrangling schooles, that search what fire*
> *Shall burne this world, had none the wit*
> *Unto this knowledge to aspire*
> *That this her feaver might be it.'*

There were similar apocalyptic references in 'A Valediction: Of Weeping' and 'The First Anniversary'. So there were quasi-religious undertones after all.

When is the world a 'carkasse'?

The question nagged at Stussman. The killer had asked it twice on the phone: it was clearly important to him. It seemed to imply a specific answer. Her head was spinning. Heather Stussman had always been better at understanding the structural and intellectual aspects of poetry than the emotions that underpinned it. She screwed up her eyes in concentration. She always told her students to focus on applying simple principles. If you don't understand a poem then stick to what you know it is, not what you think it might be. Who wrote it? Who is it aimed at? How many stanzas are there? How many lines in each stanza? Do they rhyme? Is the language colloquial or contrived? What imagery does the poet employ? What is the single most important defining feature of the poetry?

Wit.

Donne wanted to dazzle his coterie with his wit: persuade them of his intelligence. His poems set an intellectual challenge that his audience were invited to attempt. She was his audience. He was challenging her.

173

When is the world a carkasse?

She was missing something and it irritated her.

The candles flickered softly in the Combination Room. Faint shadows twisted and danced against the panelled oak, smudged and indistinct like cave paintings. Wind rumbled in the chimney and the fire began to wither and die. Proctor and Wuff had retired to bed. Heather Stussman downed her brandy and decided to do the same.

49

Whitestone Cottage stood alone on a clifftop about two miles outside Blakeney. A narrow, potholed track led from the main road to the cliff edge, bisecting a carrot field. The cliff itself was gradually tumbling into the sea, its soft red soil sloughing in great chunks down to the shingle beach two hundred feet below. There was a steep path, uneven and crumbling in places, that led from the field down to the beach. It was a lonely spot, desolate and cold. The black mass of the North Sea rippled vast and menacing beyond the square lines of the cottage. The buildings themselves would gradually fall into the waves below as salt water gnawed the ground from under them. However, for the moment the cottage was secure: its lights flickering weakly, like four burning cigarette tips trying to illuminate infinity.

Underwood could hear the roar of the water below, the hissing of the pebbles: the forces of nature smashing relentlessly against stone. Rocks become smoothed by exposure, polished by vicissitude; their surfaces flawless to the touch. Underwood ran a stone between his fingers. Life had eroded his own smoothness; instead, it had made him ragged and ugly, smashed him into terrible splinters and blown them into the bitter winds.

He waited twenty minutes for the lights to go off in the cottage. Then he returned to his car and collected his equipment. His chest seemed to have dried up temporarily: he no longer coughed up any blood or phlegm, although an uncomfortable cold sweat had broken out under his shirt. The digital clock in his car said 12:25. He slammed the door shut, crossed the main road quickly and hurried back along the track. There was a small shed at the back of the cottage and Underwood waited for a moment to catch his breath.

A freezing cold wind that smelled of salt and tasted of dirt whipped across the water and slammed into the side of the cottage. Underwood winced and huddled in on himself. He looked up at the top windows of the house. Julia was in there screwing Paul Heyer. His wife, screwing someone else. He craned his neck slightly into the wind, trying to filter her moans and whimpers of pleasure from the rushing wind and water.

'Oh my love you do me wrong'. Underwood's dustbin bag full of equipment flapped accusingly as the gusts grew in ferocity. The tumbling air shouted derisively at him: 'fucking your wife ... he's fucking your wife ... by the sea ... by the sea.' She was right there, behind the vulnerable glass and the patterned curtain. *Heyer's sweat on hers, Heyer's skin on hers.* 'To cast me off discourteously,' whispered the wind. He would sing her a new song now. He would make her understand.

Underwood made a dash for the kitchen door and crouched low, pressing against it. The sweat seemed to be freezing against his skin. It would be appropriate if he died here in this barren, dark wilderness; frozen against the door while his wife sweated and bumped against a sweating, heaving stranger inside. He looked into the keyhole. The key still sat in the ancient lock. He knew how to open it. 'Lucy Harrington, famous swimmer, eyeball ripped from its socket,' chanted the wind. The rhythm of the words pleased him 'Lucy Harrington, famous swimmer, eyeball ripped from its socket.' The key dropped to the floor and Underwood pulled it outside, under the door. He waited for the wind to die down for a moment and then quickly unlocked the door and stepped inside.

The kitchen smelled of flowers and faintly of coffee. Underwood froze, pain searing at his chest, sweat running in icy rivulets down his back. He strained to hear any tell-tale signs of movement in the old house: it creaked and groaned back at him. Perhaps the noises came from Julia's tired bones, Underwood mused, creaking as she worked them into new shapes of immorality. 'There's many a good tune played on an old fiddle,' he remembered: 'knees up, Mother Brown, knees up, Mother Brown, knees up, gotta get your knees up.' He looked around, afraid that his thumping heart might give him away.

Smart new pots and pans hung on the kitchen wall above a large Aga cooker that looked like it had never been used. In the middle of the kitchen stood a huge oak table on which nothing was ever carved. Underwood smiled as he imagined the cliff falling away beneath him. He saw the kitchen underwater: expensive saucepans clanging at the rocks, crabs crawling out of the Aga. A huge spray of flowers sat on the table: lilacs, roses and orchids. Underwood pulled the petals from a rose and rolled them between his index finger and thumb. He felt the fluid smear onto his skin like blood or ointment.

Paul Heyer had floated off to sleep immediately. He dreamed that the sea had stolen under the bedroom door, into the room, and was sucking them both away. They were falling. The ground beneath them was gone. He could see the waves reaching up for him, shouting his name, shouting his name. His eyes opened sharply. The phone was ringing downstairs. Julia stirred and mumbled something from the cusp of sleep and wakefulness. Paul rolled out of the bed into the chill room, pulled on a dressing gown and hurried downstairs. The living room had no carpet and the exposed boards felt freezing on his feet. The phone stopped ringing as he picked it up.

'Bollocks,' he cursed. He put the phone down and waited for it to ring again. It didn't. Angry now, Heyer dialled 1471 and listened to the caller's number as an electronic voice repeated it back to him. It was a mobile phone number that he didn't recognize. He pressed redial and waited for the connection to be made. To his surprise, the shrill beep of a mobile phone rang out directly behind him. Paul Heyer swivelled in shock and surprise – and found himself staring into the eyes of John Underwood.

'What the bloody hell?' He dropped the phone as a sharp

blow struck him squarely in the face. He fell backwards onto the sofa. Underwood was on him quickly, slamming the side of Heyer's head with the wooden grip of his hammer. Heyer slumped, bleeding, to the floor. Underwood gasped for breath in the heat of his triumph. The surprise in Heyer's eyes had been a joy to behold. He gathered his strength and hauled Heyer's wheezing body into the kitchen.

Julia Underwood had been vaguely aware of background noises, but the softness of the double bed had drawn her back into a deep sleep. Even the buffeting wind at the window and the muffled crashing of the sea didn't bother her. In fact, she found it comforting – hypnotic, almost. She turned over and dreamed of music.

Underwood tied Heyer's hands and feet tightly with rope and dragged him from the house. The spiteful air tore at Underwood's clothes as he hauled the groaning man to the cliff edge. It was only twenty yards but it required a monstrous effort: the sweat seemed to freeze against his skin like water frosting against glass. The pain was driving at Underwood's chest, seemingly growing more acute with every heartbeat. His thoughts scattered in all directions like chickens evading a fox. *Concentrate.*

Underwood pulled the prone form closer to the cliff edge, until Heyer's head hung – face down – over the precipice. Blood streamed from his head wound and fell in dark beads into the void. The terrifying drop made Underwood nauseous but his fury drove him on; the hissing of water on the rocks seemed deafening to him now. It was as if the taste of Heyer's blood had excited the waves into a fury of hunger; they were reaching for the wife-fucker, begging to pull him down with them and tear the flesh from his adulterous bones.

Underwood hesitated. The moment had come. He had to decide. He had the power to reduce Heyer to his elemental parts: smash him back into water, iron and carbon, reduce him to silt and fish shit. He could dissolve Heyer into the waves.

The thought was stimulating. When the sunlight evaporated the sea water, he would watch Heyer rise with the steam, he would deride the blackening clouds and mock the man that he'd imprisoned there. When the rain fell from the sky, he would stand agape and feel the droplets splash Paul Heyer onto his tongue. He would drink himself turgid and piss the bastard back into the sea, entomb him in the cycle for ever.

It would be easy.

Julia was in the house, warm and unaware. Julia Cooper, the little girl who made him cry. Julia Underwood, the woman who no longer loved him, reborn as Julia Heyer. She was shedding the unwanted skin in her sleep. How would she react to her lover's reduction, Underwood wondered. How would she regard his dissolution? Would she tingle at his cold touch whenever she swam in the sea? Would she howl her pain at the godless sky when she tried to hold her martyred lover and he ran uselessly through her fingers? Would she drink the rainwater with relish and draw the man inside her for ever? Would he swim in her saliva and linger in her tears?

Would the memory of the man be more potent than the reality? Underwood's heart burned in his chest and he sank to his knees on the yielding earth, close to exhaustion and uncertain of how to proceed.

He had become a stranger to his own mind, uncertain of its capabilities. His rational mind was like a frightened bird, floating on an ocean of anger and despair; unable to fly, too scared to dive. Memories flared at him, made acute by his pain, merging and folding until he came to confuse them with imagination. A marriage without love; a marriage without sex; a marriage without children. He was existing without living. Maybe he had died the night he and Julia had first met and had existed since then only in a terrible purgatory; scrambling blindly in circles unable to climb to the light.

So where was he now? On top of the mountain, perhaps, one short step, one killer blow from paradise. Would his guilt and despair die with Paul Heyer? The question surprised him: emerging without warning from a primitive part of his brain that hadn't yet learned to deceive itself. Why should he be stricken with guilt? Julia had betrayed him. She had disavowed their marriage; the holy fucking union. He had done nothing wrong.

He almost believed himself: the burden of half-invented evidence was almost compelling. Then, as the truth gradually broke through his inventions and contortions, somewhere far out on the surface of the churning water the bird broke free and started to fly. For a split second Underwood saw the terrible virulence of the lie and realized it had infected everything. The truth was that he had failed her; he had fallen short of her expectations. He had failed to return the love she had so willingly offered. The guilt didn't come from his failure. It came from his denial of responsibility. He was a horror to himself.

Paul Heyer could suddenly taste metal. Rusty metal. There was noise and he was cold, very cold. There was pressure on his chest. He had trouble breathing. His head pounded as he struggled to understand where he was. Something warm tickled at the corner his mouth. Blood. He remembered Underwood, standing right behind him – inside the cottage. He tried unsuccessfully to move his hands and then snapped open his eyes.

For an instant he thought he was dead and staring through the gates of Hell itself. Water smashed and snarled onto the rocks below, far below. Was he falling? Panic seized him. He clamped his eyes shut as the stones and foaming water suddenly seemed to rush up at him. He braced for the terrible impact: the crushing of his ribcage and rupturing of his organs, the dashing of his brains against the rocks. The Spartans threw their weakest children off mountain tops. Unnatural selection. Perish the thoughtful.

The pain never came.

The kitchen door crashed shut with an impact that shook the entire cottage and Julia Underwood sat up bolt upright in shock. Paul wasn't there. The bed was cold. Had he gone outside? She swung her legs out of the bed, her naked skin pimpling in the chill air, and pulled on Paul's dressing gown.

'Paul?' she called out from the top of the stairs, suddenly afraid. The old house rattled in reply as another gust threatened to tear it from its foundations. Julia cursed and hurried downstairs. The wooden floor felt freezing against her bare feet. She turned on the kitchen light. There was no sign of Paul.

Outside, Underwood saw the light and brushed away his tears as if embarrassed by the glare. He noticed Heyer was moving. He was alive, straining at the rope. This was the pathetic offspring his life of failure had produced. Throwing the child from the mountain top wouldn't lighten his guilt. It would be a further act of denial.

Underwood looked out across the black water into the very eye of time. He thought of a second of compressing time; of imagining every emotion, action, decision of his life crushed into a nanosecond. That would have been ideal. There would have been no time to become bored, no time to make mistakes, no time to become isolated. However, time passes slowly and agonizingly, lingering on failure and disappointment the way traffic slows to study a road accident. Life itself is a purgatory; a common bath of pain in which we struggle to purge the consequences of our mistakes. Guilt is the torture of the piteous.

Underwood could see Julia looking out through the kitchen window, straining her eyes to decipher the darkness. He remembered they had bought their first home together in the summer of 1983. The previous owner had been a widower. He had been in his late sixties, worn down by life and loneliness and with deep lines of sadness cutting across his face. He lacked the energy to maintain the house. John Underwood had pitied the old man, sensing his pain and resignation. He had been struck by the contrast with his own situation, then so full of promise. The old man had seen it as well. Eighteen years later and Underwood knew that he too now faced the void alone. There was always time enough to make mistakes, and to dwell on them.

'What the fuck's going on?' shouted Heyer above the screaming wind. 'Get me away from the edge.'

The only real sin is to sharpen the agony of others. Life is an agony, but a shared agony; a shared bath of pain. *For in a common bath of teares it bled. Which drew the strongest vitall spirits out.* Perhaps the agonies of fury and failure had drawn out the 'vitall spirits' of his brutality. He had been reborn in a bath of tears: now he was reaching for the light, gasping for air.

Underwood thought suddenly of Elizabeth Drury, suspended in a solution of blood and water: returned to a prenatal state in death. He hadn't thought of that before. Drury and Harrington had entered death as they had entered life. Except, he remembered, their eyes had been torn out. Two left eyes. Was the placement of the bodies in water intended to signify that they too had been reborn? Was the removal of the eyes some kind of rite that occasioned the transformation? Why would you need two left eyes?

'Listen to me,' Heyer gasped. 'This is crazy. Look at yourself. Look at what you're doing. Don't throw your life away.'

Underwood looked down at Heyer and then beyond him to the black hissing mass of shale and rock. The pain in his chest was growing ever more acute. An uncomfortable sense of his own fragility twisted at his guts. He felt a cold stab of panic. Walking into the night alone suddenly terrified him. Heyer tried to shift his weight away from the cliff edge. Underwood knelt on the man's back and entwined his fingers in Heyer's hair.

'My life?' Underwood shouted. 'What do you mean, my life? You have walked into my life and taken what you wanted. This is all that's left, my friend.'

'This won't help you,' Heyer gasped as Underwood's weight bore into him. 'She'll hate you.'

'Do you read the papers?'

'What?'

'Do you read the fucking papers?'

'What's that got to do with anything?'

'I've spent the week chasing some maniac who hacks women's eyes out.'

'Bully for . . . y – you.' Heyer spat the words defiantly as the air was squeezed from his lungs.

'And you, you've been screwing my wife – buying her clothes, buying her dinner, buying her a fucking holiday.'

'Fuck you.'

'Maybe I should hack *your* eye out.' Underwood squeezed the sides of Heyer's left eyeball with his thumb and index finger. 'You couldn't buy another one of those, could you? I could open you up so we can all see all the nasty conniving shit that goes on in the back of your head.'

'You're pathetic. If you were going to kill me you'd have done it by now. You're just a bully. Julia was right about you.' Heyer's head was throbbing, he was nauseous, the night was whirling disturbingly around him. 'You're just a coward.'

But Underwood wasn't listening. A terrible realization had sliced across the surface of his brain like a razor across skin. He struggled to follow its insane logic. *Why do you need two left eyes? What do you gain from having them – unless . . .*

Underwood stood and Heyer's chest heaved as the pressure on him was finally released. He dragged oxygen back into his desperate lungs. *Why do we have two of everything? Two kidneys, two lungs, two eyes.* Underwood watched the flickering lights of a passenger plane crawling towards him across the night. By some curious and terrible osmosis the idea was creeping into his consciousness.

What do we gain from having two of everything?

He dragged Heyer away from the cliff edge and hauled him to the beach path that uncoiled steeply downwards about ten yards away.

Insurance. If one kidney stops working, you still have another. Does the killer have one eye? Jesus – is he walking around with a ravaged eye rammed into an empty socket? How would you lose an eye? Maybe he's been in a car accident. Maybe he was a soldier. Underwood tried to concentrate his madness away. *The eyes were dead and useless: they were most likely terribly damaged. What use would they be? The killer is almost certainly male. If replacement is his motive, wouldn't he have chosen male targets? Were the eyes intended for someone else?*

He steadied himself against the wind. *Julia has two men. Why? Because one stopped functioning so she got herself another*. The simplicity of the equation made him feel desperately sad. Half of the double helix sloughed away in that moment: only despair remained. Maybe he could purge the guilt after all: progress through pain. Maybe she deserved the chance.

'Do you love her?' Underwood asked suddenly.

'Of course I do,' Heyer growled.

'Say it.'

'I love her.'

'Say it like you mean it.'

'I do mean it. She knows it. Now so do you.'

The weight had lifted slightly. Slowly, as though waking from a terrible dream, Underwood turned his back on Heyer and walked unsteadily towards the light.

Julia couldn't see anything, despite straining her eyes at the dark shadow of the clifftop. Her irritation at not being able to find Paul was rapidly being replaced with a profound sense of unease. The house was alive with strange sounds. She sat down in an armchair and gathered Paul's dressing gown tightly around her. *Where is he?* She turned on a reading lamp and felt the chill air rush at her ankles as the kitchen door clicked open. Relieved, Julia jumped to her feet and, stepping quickly over the cold wooden floor, came face to face with her husband. He stood motionless in the centre of the kitchen: ill, gaunt and broken-hearted.

Underwood tried to order his thoughts through the pain that was gnawing at his insides. Japanese soldiers placed hungry rats on the stomachs of Allied prisoners of war and then covered the rats with metal tins. The animals chose the path of least resistance and ate their way downward. He felt that pain now: hungry rats tearing through his flesh, scrambling furiously over each other in their frenzy to escape. He gasped for air and steadied himself against the kitchen table. *Blood in the bathwater signifies rebirth. Why do you need two left eyes? Dexter would know.*

Alison is clever. Ali is a star: sharp like salt on your tongue. Didn't Stussman call that wit? The killer would appreciate it.

Julia's gut twisted into a knot of fear and pity.

'John?' He looked at her, through her and behind her. 'What the hell are you doing?'

Underwood blinked away the madness and found his wife at the centre of his field of vision.

'Hello, Julia.'

'Where's Paul?'

Underwood turned his head slightly towards the kitchen window. 'Getting some air.'

'What have you done?' She was scared now. There was blood on his hands.

'I thought the two of you needed some space.' Underwood stepped in front of her as she made for the kitchen door. 'So I created some.'

'For Christ's sake, John.'

'I'm not going to hurt you, Julia.'

'If you've hurt him, I'll never forgive you.'

'You wouldn't, anyway. It makes it easier, doesn't it? Gives you a reason to hate me.'

'I've got plenty of those.'

'I think you feel frustrated, disappointed, let down, blah, blah, blah. But you don't *hate* me, Julia.'

'I'm working on it – and you're helping.' She tried to push past him again. He held her wrist, firmly but without malice. He wondered how long he could hold her. She was strong and his energy was bleeding away. The rats were in his head now, scratching and tearing at his brain.

'Do you remember what your mother said about me, when we got engaged?' he asked.

'John, let me go.'

'She said that one day I'd break your heart.' Underwood hacked agonizingly – dark strings of blood flew onto his free hand. He seemed surprised. The wreckage inside him was oozing to the surface. Julia watched in horror.

'You're ill. You've got to get help.'

Underwood swallowed the warm glue that hung in the back of his throat. 'Was she right, Julia?'

'What are you talking about?'

'Right at the beginning. She could see how much you loved me. She knew I could never live up to that. She knew that I could never love you unconditionally like you did. She saw that something was missing. And you know, after a time, I realized she was right. I couldn't.'

Julia felt tears of frustration and waste welling up behind her eyes, crawling up from the great cave of grief inside her. 'Why not? Why couldn't you? That's how I loved you.'

'That's why.'

'I don't understand.'

'I lied to you, Julia. I let you believe I was something, someone that I'm not. I made you love me. I didn't want to lose you. So I gave you the person you wanted for as long as I could.'

'Why have you never said this before?'

'If you could see into my head you'd know. It's a bad place to be.'

'But why?'

He fixed her with a sad, hopeless gaze. 'I don't know,' he said despairingly. 'The things I have seen; the things I think. You wouldn't want to go there. I locked you out. I didn't want to ruin you with it.'

'That's ridiculous.'

'If you really knew me, you wouldn't love me.'

'That should be my decision, not yours. Besides, I know you better than anyone.'

'Except me.'

A wave of anger washed over her. It was insulting of him to claim that she didn't know him. She had spent twenty years with him.

'You don't know yourself at all,' she said bitterly.

Underwood released his grip on Julia's wrist and immediately missed the urgent spring of her pulse against his fingers. He knew she was gone. She was dead to him now. He would never touch her again. He sat down. He was falling through the branches: there was no one to catch him. 'Four dead bodies,' he said quietly. 'Lifeless, mutilated things reborn in tears and blood. Two of them, two women, had a bad thing done to them. Can you guess what?'

'I don't want to know.'

'He cut their eyes out. One from each of them.'

'Oh God.'

'That's what I thought. Now, why do you think someone would do a thing like that? Do you think he collects them? Do you think he puts them in a jar as though they were pickled eggs?'

'For God's sake, John.'

'Me neither.' Underwood continued, 'If he did, he'd have taken both eyes: left and right. So ask yourself, why would you need two left eyes, Julia?

'Come on, Jules.' Underwood was crying too. 'Welcome to my head. I want you to understand.' He felt a sudden urge to ram a knife into his chest and tear his tormented lungs out.

'I'm trying to.'

'So.' He was coughing again. 'One more time. What would happen, if I'd – say – removed old Pauly-boy's eye, for example. Our killer likes poetry. Think aesthetics.'

She looked up in utter despair. 'I don't know.'

'He'd need another one, wouldn't he?' Underwood was breaking up; like a satellite re-entering the atmosphere, he was burning inside and out, falling apart. 'I wasn't there for you and you replaced me. Same difference, isn't it?'

'No.'

'I think it is.'

'I didn't replace you. I fell in love with someone else. It happens.'

'So does shit.'

'Now tell me where Paul is.' She was more confident now. Underwood was crumbling before her eyes but as the wave of her anger receded it fizzed on tiny fragments of pity.

'Tell me one thing,' he said. 'If you could live life again, compress everything into a split second where you felt every emotion, thought every thought, what would you remember most vividly?'

'John, I . . .'

'Tell me.' Beads of sweat gleamed on his forehead: some fell and spread miserably on the floor. 'What would you remember?' He tried to take her hand but she moved quickly away.

'Loneliness,' she said simply.

The eye of time focused on him suddenly. He felt pierced by its tragic gaze. 'Me too,' said Underwood, struggling for breath. 'For in a common bath of teares it bled. I understand that now.'

'I'm sorry.'

'Paul's on the beach path. I hurt him.'

'I'll get him. Please go now.'

'Yes.'

Underwood coughed hard as he stood up and a new flame burned in his chest. Harder, hotter than before. Blood spat from his mouth. He gripped at his heart, trying to tear out the agony. The chair fell backwards as he staggered against the wall while the room began to spin in nauseating circles. The ground seemed to fall away from under him.

John Underwood collapsed in on himself and fell awkwardly to the floor.

It was 2.04 a.m. Exhausted and shaking, Julia had called the Norfolk police and an ambulance. Then, afraid of what she might find, she stepped out into the freezing night to look for Paul Heyer.

50

13 December

Heather Stussman lay awake, waiting for the dawn. She was a poor sleeper at the best of times but bad dreams had torn her night horribly apart. Knowing that there was a policeman outside the entrance to her rooms hadn't helped. In fact, the rustling of his newspaper and the occasional squawk of his police radio had woken her several times.

She was concerned for her career at least as much as for her physical safety. It had been a long, arduous climb up the academic greasy pole. Getting funding for her doctoral thesis had been tough, researching it had been tougher. Dredging up the discipline to haul through volumes of stodgy literary criticism and ancient monographs had been akin to a labour of Hercules. Her book had been similarly painstaking but at least it had enabled her to cast off the shackles of deference and forelock-tugging that had compromised her PhD dissertation.

Reconstructing Donne had given Stussman a certain notoriety but it had closed as many doors as it had opened. She had almost become the academic equivalent of soiled goods. A successful fellowship at Southwell was vital to restoring her credibility. This was particularly vulnerable in the USA where the intellectual establishment tended to have long memories and fragile egos. She had avoided writing book reviews in the British newspapers, despite receiving a number of lucrative offers, and concentrated instead on researching her next piece for the academic journals. But now her association with the New Bolden murders was becoming quite widely known across the university: in Cambridge bad news spread like an airborne virus. They would be queuing up to demolish her career. She would not get re-elected at Southwell and would have to go back to Wisconsin worse off than when she had left. Then Stussman thought of Elizabeth Drury and Lucy Harrington and felt horribly guilty, sickened by her own selfishness.

She walked through into her kitchenette and made a cup of coffee. She was nursing a mild headache induced by cognac and insomnia and the hissing of the kettle grated unpleasantly. The caffeine smacked her satisfyingly between the eyes and she returned to her lounge in slightly better spirits.

It was still dark outside. Britain seemed to run out of sunlight completely by the end of November. Clouds rolled low across Cambridge from the east, threatening to engulf the spires of King's College Chapel. The reflected clouds would blacken the

Cam and turn it the colour of burned treacle. There had been a storm in the small hours and from her window Stussman could see that leaves and litter had been blown onto the lawn at the centre of the first quad. The trees in the college garden would be skeletal. Something was niggling at her. Was it something she had forgotten?

She turned on a desk lamp and slumped into her armchair.

She thought briefly of Underwood. He was an interesting character: polite and perceptive. She had registered his interest in her, too, had felt his eyes edging over her when he'd thought she wasn't looking. Dexter had grown on her slightly. The sergeant's brusque manner had annoyed her at first but Dexter had asked pertinent questions and made intelligent connections about the poetry. That was refreshing. Perhaps the friction had come from similarities between them, Stussman mused. After all, they were both outsiders in worlds that men dominated. Stussman wondered which one of them had been patronized and pissed on the most in their respective careers: it was a tough call.

The wind rattled her window and whined outside in the stairway. Four, maybe five months until spring: it was a depressing thought. Five months until colour and sunshine flooded back into the countryside. She had heard that Cambridge was beautiful in springtime: daffodils spreading in great yellow washes across the college garden. Bright cold mornings. Sunlight splashing onto the Cam. Life returning to the dead land.

When is the world a carkasse?

Stussman felt the tiny hairs on the back of her neck stand on end as the question suddenly snapped back at her. An idea. A distant corner of her memory began to fill with the light of recognition. Could it be?

She took her book of Donne's *Songs and Sonnets* and flicked impatiently to page twenty-one. There it was. 'A Nocturnall Upon St Lucies Day, Being the Shortest Day.' She tried to remain calm: had she guessed correctly?

It was a poem about loss, transformation and the author's longing for annihilation. However, it was the title and setting of the piece that had sparked Stussman's interest: both focused on a specific day. Carefully, anxious not to embrace any premature conclusions, she picked up a pen and began to read the poem, making notes on each verse as she went:

> 'Tis the yeare's midnight, and it is the dayes
> Lucies, who scarce seaven hours herself unmaskes
> The Sunne is spent, and now his flasks
> Send forth light squibs, no constant rayes

'Today is St Lucy's Day, the darkest day of the year, and there are scarce seven hours of sunlight,' Stussman scribbled onto her notepad.

> The world's whole sap is sunke
> The generall balme th'hydroptique earth hath drunk
> Whither, as to the beds-feet, life is shrunk
> Dead and enterr'd; yet all these seeme to laugh
> Compared to me, who am their Epitaph.

'The world is dry and lifeless, having drunk the life-giving balm that supports it. Life itself is shrunken, dead and buried.' Stussman's pen scratched against the paper.

> Study me then, you who shall lovers be
> At the next world, that is, at the next spring
> For I am every dead thing
> In whom love wrought new Alchemie
> For his art did expresse
> A quintessence even from nothingness

'I am every dead thing in whom love transformed ugliness into spiritual purity. Love, the great alchemist, extracted a quintessential life-force from me even though I am a nothingness.'

> From dull privations, and leane emptinesse
> He ruin'd mee and I am rebegot
> Of absence, darkness, death; things which are not.

'Destroyed by love, I am now reborn of things that are nothing: absence, darkness, death.' Did the killer think he was some sort of alchemist? Stussman was annoyed the thought hadn't occurred to her already.

190

> *All others from all things, draw all that's good*
> *Life, soule, forme, spirit, whence they being have*
> *I, by loves limbecke, am the grave*
> *Of all that's nothing.*

'All other living things have a form and a soul, but through love's limbecke . . .' Stussman paused for a second. What was a limbecke? She opened a reference book and sought a definition. There it was: a limbecke was the vessel in which the actual process of alchemy – the transformation of base things into gold – supposedly took place.

Did the killer think that the murdered women were the limbecke for his own terrible alchemy? Were they the vessels in which his basest thoughts were converted into something pure and valuable?

> *Oft a flood*
> *Have wee two wept, and so*
> *Drown'd the whole world, us two; oft did we grow*
> *To be two chaosses, when we did show*
> *Care to ought else; and often absences*
> *Withdrew our soules, and made us carcasses.*

'Whenever Donne or his lover thought of anything except each other, they cried a flood that drowned the world. They resembled the chaos that preceded the birth of the universe. Separation from each other turned them both into carcasses.'

Stussman noted the latest appearance of the notion of a flood drowning the world: there were similar references in each of the four poems that the killer had cited.

> *But I am by her death (which word wrongs her)*
> *Of the first nothing, the Elixir grown;*

'Donne distinguishes between an "ordinary nothing", meaning the mere absence of something and the "first nothing", the quintessential nothing that existed before the birth of the universe.'

> *Were I a man, that I were one,*
> *I needs must know; I should preferred*
> *If I were any beast*

Some ends, some means; yea plants, yea stones detest,
And love, All, all some properties invest
If I an ordinary nothing were
As shadow, a light, and body must be here.

'He outlines the order of nature below man: animals, plants and stones, claiming that even these lesser creatures are invested with properties such as emotion. If the author were an ordinary nothing he too would possess these characteristics.'

Enjoy your summer, all
Since shee enjoyes her long night's festival
Let me prepare towards her, and let me call
This houre her Vigill and her Eve, since this
Both the yeare's and the daye's deep midnight is.

'Donne says he has become a quintessential nothing: the absolute nothingness of pre-creation. He will not be renewed. So on the festival of St Lucy, the longest and darkest night of the year, he prepares to join the dead woman.'

When is the world a carkasse? When had death and grief sucked the very life from the soil itself? Now she knew. As far as Donne was concerned it was St Lucy's Day, the year's midnight: the night he mourned the death of his wife during childbirth. The very substance of the poem, its central conceit and argumentative logic, drew their strength from the day on which the piece had been conceived.

Timing.

Stussman checked her calendar: the longest night of the year was in December. She ran her finger along each of the days. There it was: 21 December. The beginning of winter.

'Eight days from today,' she said aloud, scaring herself.

She paused. 21 December. It didn't seem right. She had written critiques of the poem before and the date didn't sound familiar.

'Shit!' She suddenly remembered and, cursing her stupidity, turned to the back of the *Songs and Sonnets.* Stussman found the footnotes that accompanied 'A Nocturnall Upon St Lucies Day':

'Note 2. Saint Lucy's Day was regarded by Donne and his

contemporaries as the first day of winter and the shortest day of the year. Prior to the reform of the calendar in 1752, St Lucy's Day was 13 December, the day on which the sun entered Capricorn, the sign of the goat.'

13 December. Today. The world is a carkasse on St Lucy's Day. Today is St Lucy's Day.

Stussman felt a hot stab of excitement. She stood and pulled down her copy of *Brewer's Dictionary of Phrase and Fable* from a high shelf. On page 376 she found the entry she was looking for:

'St Lucy, the patron saint of people with eye afflictions.'

Stussman read on and the story came back to her. Lucy of Syracuse had been blessed with beautiful eyes. She had plucked them out to deter an eager suitor rather than break her vow of chastity. God had rewarded her with a place in paradise.

Stussman sat back in her chair, shaking with nervous excitement. She felt sure that the murderer of Elizabeth Drury and Lucy Harrington was going to kill himself.

51

He was not awake but he was cognizant. Spinning in his own head. There were noises around him. People speaking, clattering metal on metal, electronic humming. He couldn't open his eyes. A sheet of light lay across his eyelids. He was conscious; flailing his arms and legs. Voices. People holding him down. Fragments of memory nibbling at him: the cottage, the clifftop, Lucy Harrington. Disjointed thoughts and folded logic. Where was he?

Pain. He was aware of pain. So at least he wasn't dead. His head throbbed. There was a kind of bruised tightness in his chest. A needle in his wrist spread dull pain up the length of his arm. He was exhausted, swimming at the bottom of a bright white ocean. Creatures gnawing at him, eating him from the inside out. So much pain. Was he dying? Flailing now in impotent waking panic. People all around him again. A prick of pain on his arm. Injection. He relaxed slowly, thoughts swirling, eyes staring at him.

He could not move. He could not see. He could smell. There were different smells. Perfume, soap, antiseptic. Was he floating in a bath? Was he being reborn in this agony? Perhaps he had never lived at all and had merely dreamed his life from the womb. Perhaps his mistakes were merely flickerings of the foetal imagination. Perhaps he had been given another chance to start from scratch.

He knew the idea was absurd. New life could never be so lifeless. Every atom of his being felt jaded and polluted.

He couldn't open his eyes. Had they been torn from their sockets? No. There were changes in shade, flickers of bright and dark. Cooking. He could smell cooking: a distant, insistent greasy smell. And coffee. He could smell coffee.

Coffee in the kitchen. Coffee and flowers: yellows and reds, washes of colour. Wind noisy at the glass. Darkness, violence. Julia crying. Heyer's blood on his hands. Had he killed him? He had left him on the clifftop. Julia crying, beautiful even in her pain. An ambulance, people running around him. Machines beeping at him.

Hospital. He was in hospital. And Dexter. Dexter was in danger – he had to call her. Had to tell her.

Something over his mouth. He cannot speak. There is pain again. Torture in his chest, like a butcher chopping meat from the inside out. Chop. Chop. Make it stop. Make it stop.

Activity: people running, shouting. Machine beeping louder. Was he dying? Don't accept it. Fight it. Must speak to Alison. Danger.

John Underwood grunted something into his oxygen mask. Another needle pierced the skin of his arm. Darkness.

Part IV

Strange Connections

52

February 1945
Tottenham, London

Rose had laid on an impressive spread, considering the meagre resources. Violet Frayne crunched her third cucumber sandwich of the morning and washed it down with a gulp of sugary tea. It was a comfortable room. Neatly presented, without the clutter of ornaments that Violet always found so distasteful in the homes of others. Rose had bought a couple of prints since Violet's last visit: both were of composers, Mozart and Bach. They had been strategically placed above the piano. Perhaps Rose found inspiration in their black-eyed gaze.

Elizabeth had finally fallen asleep in her crib after squawking and yowling for over an hour. Violet found her baby exhausting sometimes and was grateful when her sister had the idea of placing a drop of brandy in the baby's milk. It had worked like a dream and Violet made a mental note to intoxicate Elizabeth whenever she played up in future.

Violet scanned Rose's book collection. It covered an entire wall and contained many first editions and beautifully bound collections of poetry and drama. Her own collection back in Bolden seemed rather threadbare in comparison. She chanced upon a copy of *Macbeth*, superbly presented in black leather binding and delicate gold-leaf lettering. It was her favourite play. She returned to her chair and began, with considerable care, to turn the pages. She jumped slightly as Rose returned to the room bearing a freshly baked Dundee cake.

'There we are, Violet, I know it's your favourite.' Rose placed the cake on the small table in front of her sister and cut off two generous slices.

'You shouldn't have, Rose.' Violet felt guilty. 'You must have wasted a week's rations on me.'

'Nonsense. I always have more than I need. And I've no one

else to cook for.' Rose winced as the words came out. 'Oh, I'm sorry, Vi, I wasn't thinking.'

'It's been nearly a year now,' Violet said. They left it at that.

'I see my little trick worked on Madam,' said Rose, looking over at the sleeping baby.

'She's dead to the world.'

'Oh! You found one of my Burlington Shakespeares.' Rose nodded at the book in Violet's hand.

'It's beautiful, Rose. Wherever did you get them all?'

'There's a shop, Forbes Books, in Charing Cross Road. They have a wonderful selection. Very reasonable, too.' She took a sip of tea. 'They bought all the stock of Burlington Publishing when the company went broke a year or two ago. You can pick up some real bargains. Nobody wants quality books any more. I think they make the room.'

'They do, Rose. I'm frightfully jealous.'

'Why don't you pop in there before you head home? You can pick up a bus on Seven Sisters Road. It would only take half an hour.'

'I might do that.' Violet turned back to the book. '*Hamlet* is masterly but I think I prefer *Macbeth* to all the other tragedies. The language is so compelling.' She read aloud from the text:

'Methought I heard a voice cry, "Sleep no more!"
Macbeth does murder sleep, the innocent sleep
Sleep that knits up the ravelled sleeve of care . . .'

Rose finished the quotation from memory:

'The death of each day's life, sore labour's balm
Balm of hurt minds, great nature's second course.'

Violet closed the book softly and smiled at her sister. 'Only two schoolteachers would meet for lunch and end up quoting Shakespeare at each other.'

'At least we put the emphasis in the right places.'

'You have to know your iambs from your trochees!'

Rose laughed. ' "Iambic pentameter is the building block of modern culture." Sound familiar?'

'Father.' Violet smiled too. 'I always thought that his monologues on classical literature were his revenge on us for being girls.'

'You may well be right.' Rose paused for a moment. 'Are you all right, Vi? I hope you don't mind me asking but sometimes I can't sleep for worrying about you and the baby.'

'We're fine.' Violet's eyes misted slightly but she wouldn't cry, she would be strong. As she had always been. 'We have the house and money's not really a problem.'

'That's not what I meant.'

'I know what you meant.'

'Losing someone like that. It must be a terrible thing.'

Violet swallowed hard. The tears were brimming up inside her. She fought them all back except one. She looked her sister directly in the eye.

'Talking about it doesn't help me, Rose. I have to get there by myself.'

'I understand. But I didn't want you to think that I didn't care, or that you can't speak to me if you have to.' Rose floundered for the right words. 'I just feel so helpless.'

Elizabeth suddenly started crying.

'She's hungry,' said Violet. 'Could you give me the milk bottle?'

'Shall I give her a drop more brandy?' Rose asked.

'No. But you can pour me one,' Violet joked despite herself.

'We'll both have one.' Rose hurried out to the kitchen to find some glasses.

Violet picked up her baby and cradled it in her arms. Elizabeth had her eyes: round and blue. She had her father's smile, though, when she chose to. Violet hushed the baby softly and stared out of the living-room window. It was a sunny afternoon, warm for February. Seven Sisters Road bustled with activity beyond the glass: men in uniforms, women with babies. Violet Frayne suddenly felt very small and very alone. 'Pull yourself together,' she remonstrated with herself as she started to cry again. 'Must be strong. Have to be strong.'

Rose walked them to the bus stop about an hour later. They kissed each other goodbye and promised to meet more regularly. Rose slipped Violet a small bottle of brandy as the bus trundled up. 'For whoever needs it,' she whispered. The conductor helped Violet to carry the pram onto the bus. She had originally planned to get off at Finsbury Park and then take the Tube to Liverpool Street via King's Cross. However, her mind wandered back to the bookshop that Rose had mentioned. Violet felt like she deserved a treat and she loved books. She decided to stay on the bus all the way to the West End and then walk down Charing Cross Road.

Central London was a friendly chaos. Violet Frayne pushed her pram against a seemingly endless tide of people. A group of American servicemen smirked at the shop girls in a Woolworth's store. One pressed his lips tightly against the window. A couple of them caught Violet's eye, then saw the pram and quickly looked away. She found their attention shaming.

Strange faces and accents milled around her. There were policemen, boiler-suited ARP wardens, couples holding hands, and children. Lots of children, running and shouting. Most of the evacuated children had returned to the capital over the previous few months as the threat of air raids receded. Violet enjoyed the distractions but she didn't like London any more: compared to Bolden it seemed dirty and noisy.

Bumped and jostled, she turned along Charing Cross Road and made her way south towards Leicester Square. The crowd gradually thinned and she began to pass the various second-hand bookshops. Finally she found Forbes Books. It had a smart dark blue awning and a small table of books outside the window. on the pavement. She ran her hand across a few of them. *Treasure Island*, Oscar Wilde, Thomas Hardy. None of them particularly inspired her and, in fact, many of them looked rather tatty. Perhaps exposure to the air had damaged them. She went inside.

The shop bell tinkled as she pushed her pram through the narrow doorway. A young man stood behind the counter. He wore severe-looking half-glasses over a thin, angular face. He watched her struggle for a moment before his expression softened and he helped her guide the pram into the centre of the shop.

'There we are,' he said. 'Plenty of room.'

'Thank you,' said Violet, her gaze drifting around the shop. It was an impressive sight. Row upon row of new and used books, some beautifully presented as Rose's had been, others worn and dusty with age. The room smelled of leather. Violet felt a sudden hunger for knowledge that had been absent from her for some time.

'Was there anything in particular, madam?' the assistant asked. 'We have a number of books on special offer.'

'My sister has some leather-bound editions of Shakespeare that she bought from you. I think they were published by Burlington's.'

'Indeed.' The assistant guided her to the back of the shop. 'We bought them as a lot. They're rather well put together. Burlington produced a whole series like that. English classics, you know: Shakespeare, Dickens, Hardy and so forth. Sadly, there're only a few remaining. They've proved rather popular.'

Violet looked at the shelf: there were six books bound in the same attractive black covers as Rose's copy of *Macbeth*. She scanned the titles: *Titus Andronicus* and *A Winter's Tale*. She didn't like either of those. *The Mayor of Casterbridge* and *Joseph Andrews*. She already owned a copy of the former and despised the latter. The last two books were more promising: *Great Expectations* and *Donne: Complete Works*. She took them both off the shelf as the shop assistant padded back to his chair at the counter.

Both were in excellent condition. She smelled the leather on them before opening each in turn and delicately turning the pages. *Great Expectations* was her favourite novel and Donne her favourite poet. She resolved to buy them both and handed over the seven shillings and sixpence for each with a warm glow of satisfaction. The assistant wrapped them carefully in paper and wished her a good afternoon before returning to his own copy of *An Ideal Husband*.

Violet tried to get her bearings as she stepped into the light.

The Underground was probably the quickest way to get to Liverpool Street but negotiating the stairs with a pram would be exhausting. Better to get a bus. She turned right and headed up towards Tottenham Court Road where she hoped to find a bus stop. She eventually found the correct stop and stood at the end of a queue. Boredom quickly overcame her and she turned to look into a shop window: the shop sold antiques and Violet gazed at a beautiful bracket clock.

It had been made by Frodsham of Gracechurch Street and was fixed in a highly polished mahogany case with a bright brass inlay and matching brass hands. It was in excellent condition. She guessed it had been made around 1820. It seemed a fair price. Had she been intending to buy it, Violet would have insisted on seeing the mechanism: the hands were frozen at half-past six.

The explosion came from behind her and to her right. There was no warning. The noise was vast and sudden, a terrible dull metallic crash. There was a tremendous rush of air and as Violet half-turned in shock she was blown against the shop window, which imploded and shattered in her face. The air was thick with flying glass. Splinters spat at Violet Frayne's legs and arms, and then, horribly, tore into an eye. She was aware of a terrible pain in the side of her face. Lying on a carpet of debris, she raised her hand to her face and felt a shard of glass jutting from her left eye. Her hands were warm with blood. She could hear people screaming, sirens beginning to wail. She reached out blindly for Elizabeth. The pram had been blown onto its side. Violet could hear Elizabeth crying.

It took an hour for her to be moved. She was taken by stretcher-bearers to the Middlesex Hospital and placed under heavy sedation. Her left eye was removed the following morning after it became obvious that it could not be saved. Two days later, Violet was moved to Moorfields Eye Hospital on the City Road. Here, specialist eye doctors cleaned her wounded socket and tidied up the emergency operation that had been performed at the Middlesex.

She had lost a lot of blood and was exhausted and trauma-tized. Violet lay for a week, half-asleep and dreaming morphine dreams. She was vaguely aware of Rose at her bedside, of her sister crying, of someone saying that Elizabeth was fine. Rose talked about books and read her poems: Donne and Shakespeare's sonnets. She talked about the V-2 attack. That people had been killed. That Violet was fortunate to be alive. Clarity gradually returned to her mind and Violet came to realize that she had been desecrated.

53

Alison Dexter drove to New Bolden Infirmary in a state of shock. Chief Superintendent Chalmers had called her to his office at 7.30 a.m. Accompanied by a senior officer from Huntingdon whom Dexter didn't recognize and Chalmers didn't identify, the chief superintendent told her that Inspector Underwood was in hospital recovering from a heart attack. He also told her that there were 'extenuating circumstances' and that, with immediate effect, Underwood would no longer be heading the investigation into the New Bolden killings. She would be in temporary charge until a new detective inspector from the AMIP office at Huntingdon could be brought in.

Dexter eventually found a parking space in the hospital car park and, on entering the main building, headed for Ward S6, the cardiac recovery ward. The lift was hot and crowded: Dexter felt a snake of sweat slither down her back. At reception on the sixth floor, a staff nurse directed her along a noisy corridor to a bay at the far end. John Underwood was asleep, surrounded by machines that monitored his pulse and blood pressure. Dexter checked the digital read-outs of the machines: pulse 68 b.p.m., blood pressure 180 over 90. That seemed high. She walked over to the bed and sat down. Underwood stirred, his head moved slightly and he half-opened his eyes.

'Dex.' It was no more than a croak, dry and rasping.

'Look at you, guv.' Dexter tried to be light-hearted. 'A right two and eight.'

'Been better.' His eyes closed again as exhaustion clamped them shut.

'You've been stupid,' she corrected him. 'You've been ill for weeks. It's too much for . . .'

'. . . For someone my age?' He coughed and pain seared at him. His heart rate jumped to 82 b.p.m. Dexter shifted uncomfortably.

'Shall I get a nurse?' she asked.

'No . . . no, I'm all right.' Images rolled across his mind like clouds: the sea, the wind rattling against windows, Julia cowering away from him in terror, Paul Heyer trussed like a turkey. He forced his eyes open and saw Dexter as the clouds began to dissipate. 'Dex . . . listen to me.' He gulped phlegm from his throat and the effort made him wheeze. 'I think you're in danger I . . .' He gasped for air at the edge of unconsciousness. 'He's not performing . . . not performing. That isn't the point.' His eyes closed.

A staff nurse walked up and checked Underwood's machines. 'He's very tired,' she told Dexter with a faint night-shift smile. 'Don't be long.'

'I won't,' Dexter replied as the nurse walked away.

Underwood drifted back from a fragment of a dream about drowning. The drugs had made him extremely drowsy, as if his limbs were filled with water. He focused on Dexter's sparkling green eyes as they fizzed over his face: *he could take them and put them in Julia's head to make her pretty again.*

'You said he's not performing, sir, I don't understand what you mean.' Her voice snapped him back: her accent was as abrasive as her personality. He summoned the strength to answer her: *the will.*

'The audience . . . he's not performing . . . he's educating, using Stussman.' He was nauseous now, the room was starting to spin gently away from him. *Got to concentrate.* 'You found him . . . he'll come for you.'

'Why didn't he kill me when he had me, then? Why let me go?'

'He wanted you to see the Drury woman . . . to understand

204

. . . to be improved by it . . . he killed the couple that found him . . . why not you – unless he wanted you for something else?'

'I'll be careful,' Dexter assured him. She wasn't convinced, besides she had green eyes, not blue. She had been told once that they were her best feature.

Only once.

'What about that Heyer bloke that you went to see? You want me to rattle his cage some more?' she asked.

A shadow flitted across Underwood's face. 'Waste of time. Leave him alone.' His eyes flickered and closed. Dexter wondered if he would live. She hoped so.

Underwood was speaking again: much softer this time, as if he was muttering something in his sleep. His words ebbed away as unconsciousness overtook him. Dexter's eyes moved instinctively towards the computer screen next to the bed: 65 b.p.m., 180 over 90. He was OK. Underwood breathed heavily in front of her. He was sleeping. Dexter watched him for a second and then left without looking back.

Dexter's head ached inside and out as she drove back to New Bolden police station. The morning traffic was thick and the journey was an irritation. Was she in danger? She touched the laceration on the side of her head where the killer had struck her. If he had wanted to kill her he could have done so already. He could even have taken her with him, she mused. If only she could remember his face. He was tall certainly, slim, white. What else? She racked her brain for something. What else did they know? He was clever.

'Fucking pathetic.' Dexter slammed her hands against the steering column and cursed the limits of her own imagination. Four people dead and all she could manage was 'clever'. The traffic began to clear ahead of her and she accelerated hard to vent her frustration. The thing that worried her most now was that she was in charge of the investigation – albeit temporarily. How would she feel if someone else was murdered now? Responsibility burned like the headlights of an onrushing truck.

She drove into the station car park and glided smoothly to a halt. Rain began to spatter on her windscreen. She thought of Elizabeth Drury. How had the killer found her? Dexter had located Drury from a two-year-old newspaper article. Surely the killer hadn't waited two years to kill her. The thought troubled her as she climbed the stairs to the crime room. Both victims had been mentioned in newspaper articles. That was the only link between them, apart from their names. It had to mean something. Did the killer have access to some database like the one at County Police Headquarters in Huntingdon that could search thousands of old newspapers for specific names? They were expensive systems. Dexter knew some banks and law firms had them. Where else?

Harrison was waiting for her. He looked tired. 'We're getting Inspector Tarrant from AMIP tomorrow. They're bringing him back from holiday.' Dexter gently closed the door to Underwood's office and walked through to the Incident Room. 'What's up with Underwood?' Harrison continued. 'Will he be all right?'

'Don't know. He doesn't look too clever.' Dexter paused in front of the pictures of Harrington and Drury on the board. *Educating us. Why is he educating us?*

'Word is,' Harrison whispered in Dexter's ear, 'he went cuckoo last night. Roughed up his wife and beat up her boyfriend.'

'Don't be ridiculous!' Dexter snorted. 'He's had a heart attack.'

'I'm just saying.' Harrison guided her into a quiet corner of the room. 'We heard a rumour out of Norwich CID. Jensen knows a DC there.'

'I'll bet she does,' Dexter replied acidly.

'He told her that our man Underwood was arrested, picked up from some arse-end-of-nowhere cottage and taken to hospital. His wife gave a statement saying that Underwood had broken in, tied up her boyfriend, smacked him on the head and dumped him on top of some cliff.'

'Bollocks!'

'I'm being serious. Guess who the boyfriend is?'

'I've no idea.'

'Paul Heyer,' said Harrison with a note of triumph in his

voice. He knew he had her now. He was wiping her nose in the shit trail her precious boss had left behind him.

'Heyer? The same bloke—'

'The same bloke who Underwood supposedly got an anonymous tip-off about, right. The same bloke that me and him interviewed a couple of days ago about Lucy Harrington. Don't you see? He made it all up, Dex. I've been up in the Chief Super's office taking the flak. This Heyer bloke filed a complaint about Underwood this morning. Assuming he stays alive, Underwood's up to his neck in the brown stuff.'

Dexter recoiled slightly in shock. She felt betrayed and angry. They had wasted time looking into Heyer: interviewing him, researching him and his company. Time that could have been better used elsewhere. Maybe Drury and the others would still be alive. Then she remembered Underwood, alone and heartbroken, wired to a machine. She banished the thought.

'If what you're saying's true, he's finished,' she said quietly.

'All hail, Inspector Dexter,' Harrison said, with the ghost of a smile. 'You shall be king hereafter.'

'Piss off.'

She walked back to the noticeboard. 'We'd better get cracking. What else have I missed this morning?'

'Jensen has taken a PC and started visiting the names on that list of local housebreakers. She's done two so far: one's got a gold-plated alibi for both nights, the other's in a wheelchair.'

'Brilliant,' she said bitterly. 'I knew that list was a waste of time.'

'Your doctor friend called for you this morning,' Harrison continued.

'Leach?'

'No, the American woman. Stussman.'

'Has he called her again?'

'I don't think so. She said she needed to speak with you.'

'I'll call her.' Dexter reread the names of Elizabeth Drury and Lucy Harrington for the tenth time. 'Get hold of that list Stussman did for us. We have to find out if anyone else with those names lives locally. We just concentrated on Elizabeth Drury before, now we need to follow up on the others.'

Harrison winced. That would take an age and Jensen was out. 'OK. I'll try and second some uniform grunts to help me out. It's such a slow fucking process. Anything else?'

'Get someone to look up local antique dealers on the Net. Cambridge especially. Leach reckons our man might have bought himself some Jack-the-Ripper doctor's bag. It might be worth a look.'

'I'll do that,' said Harrison. It sounded more interesting than trawling through the electoral register. 'What are you going to do?'

'I'm going to the library.'

'What for?'

'Underwood thinks that the killer is trying to educate us. I want to have a look at some books on Donne. The answer's in these poems somewhere. We can't rely on Stussman all the time. We need to get smart.'

'By the way, while you're there – ' Harrison lifted a piece of paper from his desk ' – you might want to check this out. Drury wrote a book.'

'What about?'

'Lard-arses. It's called *The Weight of Expectation.* Her secretary told me.' He handed her the slip of paper.

54

New Bolden library was a ten-minute drive from the police station. The rain and volume of traffic doubled the journey time. Dexter fumed silently. Everything seemed to take an age. London had traffic problems but it also had benefits. New Bolden still seemed very small to her.

She decided to hold off calling Stussman until she had learned some more about Donne. Half of what the academic said had gone over her head and, in any case, Dexter hated being out-flanked in conversation. She would ambush Stussman with her knowledge when she called her back. Harrison's comments about Underwood had upset her. The inspector had certainly been behaving strangely and he had confided to Dexter that his wife was seeing someone else. However, Dexter couldn't believe Underwood would manipulate his position to get at Heyer and then actually attack him. It didn't ring true. Maybe Underwood *had* lost it.

The library was almost empty and was gratifyingly warm. Dexter exchanged some uncomfortable pleasantries with Dan, the librarian she had briefly dated. She politely refused dinner and then hurried, as directed, to the literature section. She found the poetry shelves and scoured the titles for Donne. Nothing. She remembered that there had been some texts on Donne when she had visited a couple of days previously. Annoyed, Dexter marched past the newspaper and magazine section and found Dan again.

'Dan, sorry to be a pain, but all the books on Donne have gone.'

'They can't all have gone,' he sniffed. 'Some people don't put them back. Students, mainly. We get a lot of students from Westlands College. Messy sods. I bet your Donne books are lying about in a workroom somewhere. I tell you what.' He took her gently by the arm and led her towards the library computer system. She shifted slightly, uneasy that he had touched her. 'Have a look on this. It's our central database. If your books are here it will tell you. If they're out, it will tell you when they should be back.' Dexter winced slightly: Dan's breath smelled of stale coffee and constipation.

He leaned over the glowing console and typed in a few instructions. The screen changed. He stood up. 'There you go. That's the search page. Just type in the author you're looking for and you're away.'

'Thank you, Dan.'

'No problemo!' He grinned and headed back to his book stacks.

Dexter cringed. Nobody said things like 'No problemo' any more. And she had got off with the bloke: twice, in fact. What had she been thinking? She scratched her head thoughtfully and sat down in front of the computer terminal. She used the cursor to click the name 'Donne' into the on-screen keyboard. Lines of information appeared:

Search results: *Five matches*
First Match
Author: *Donne, John*
Title: *Complete Works*
Class Mark: 604.111' 282
Year: *1946*
Material Type: *Non-Fiction*
Language of Text: *English*
Copies: *1*

The other books were listed below. She selected the first entry and pointed her cursor at the 'Status' key at the bottom left of the screen. The computer paused for a moment, then displayed its results:

Copies: *1*
Copy in Library

It looked like Dan had been right. She repeated the process with each of the five entries and received the same response each time. According to the computer, all the Donne books were in the library. *Or they've been nicked*, she thought. Dexter glanced around: the workrooms were all upstairs, adjoining the reference section. She walked up the central stairway and moved through the reference area towards the three workrooms. A man and a woman were working at opposite ends of one room: both looked up at her as she entered. She smiled apologetically and closed the door again. All the other rooms were empty and there were no books lying around in any of them. She swore beneath her breath and returned down the stairs to the computer terminal. Dexter wasn't academically minded and the silent stillness of the building brought back uncomfortable memories of school and hot exam rooms. She undid the top button of her blouse and looked at the screen again.

This time she typed in 'Donne' as a search term rather than an author name and got twelve matches. She scrolled down the list, writing down their class marks. Most looked like academic studies of Donne and all were apparently in stock. She was pleased: someone explaining poetry in simple English was much better than trying to figure out the gobbledegook for yourself. Dexter was about to leave the terminal to seek her list of titles on the shelves when she remembered Harrison's passing comment about Drury's book.

She unfolded the note of paper he had given her. *The Weight of Expectation. By E Drury*. Dexter cleared the search results from the computer and called up the now-familiar on-screen typewriter again. She selected 'Author Search' and carefully pointed her cursor arrow at 'D'. She clicked her mouse. Then 'R'. She clicked the mouse again. It was a slow system. Something flickered on the screen and she looked up at it.

Drury, Elizabeth J appeared automatically in the prompt box.

Dexter paused. How had that happened? The computer was a mind-reader. She thought for a second and then cleared the prompt box. Again, she selected 'D' and then 'R' and again *Drury, Elizabeth J* popped into the prompt box. Dexter pressed 'select' and read the search results.

Search results: *One match*
Author: *Drury, Elizabeth J.*
Title: *The Weight of Expectation: Obesity and Self-Image*
Class Mark: 678.094' 081
Year: *1992*
Material Type: *Non-Fiction*
Language of Text: *English*
Copies: *1*

Dexter tried to marshal the thoughts that were flying at her. Dan was hovering nearby. She caught his eye and waved him over.

'What's up?' he asked through his yellow teeth.

'I have a question.' She was trying to keep a lid on her excitement. 'I'm doing an author search, right?'

'Right'

'So, I clear the box like so . . .' She clicked her mouse and deleted the text in the prompt box.

211

'OK . . .'

'And then I type in the name of the author I'm after.'

'Correct.'

'So here goes. D, then R.'

Drury, Elizabeth J appeared again in the prompt box.

'Why does that happen?' Dexter asked sharply. 'Why does a name appear in the box even though I've only typed in two letters? There must be loads of names that begin with D R.'

Dan nodded. 'It's a time-saving device in the software. It's a default setting. When you typed in DR, the program defaulted to the last name beginning with DR that a user entered. In this case Drury. You've been looking for books by John Donne, right?'

'Yes.'

'So watch this.' Dan cleared the screen and typed in D, then O. Immediately, *Donne, John* flashed up in the prompt box. 'Do you see what I mean? You were the last person to type DO into the author search. So the program automatically reverts to its last search command that began with the same letters. In case you're the same person coming back and repeating your search. Like I say: it's to save time.'

Dexter nodded but didn't speak.

'Anything else?' Dan asked. Dexter shook her head slowly. 'Don't worry, you'll get the hang of it,' he added as he walked away.

Dexter wasn't listening. She felt a cold rush of excitement and again typed in DR:

Drury, Elizabeth J.

She was struggling to organize her thoughts. *The system defaults to the last entry beginning with those letters. So someone was searching for Elizabeth Drury's book recently. It's a public database. Public information, like the newspaper articles. Has the killer used this terminal? All the Donne books are missing. Maybe he took them. He's clever. He's local. He wouldn't want his name and address in the library records. The killer used this library. He touched this terminal. Fuck. Can they lift off the keyboard or the computer screen? Jesus Christ. Think. Think. There could be dozens of partial prints on the terminal.*

But what if one matched a police record of violent offenders or housebreakers?

Dexter stood immediately and walked over to Dan. She told him to turn the computer terminal off and to stop anyone from using it. He did so and put dust covers over the screen and keyboard. Outwardly calm but shaking with nervous excitement, Alison Dexter pulled her mobile phone out of her handbag and walked out of the library's main entrance.

She pressed her fast-dial button for the police station and waited for a reply. Rain streamed off the canopy over the library's glass doors, rippling the puddles spreading on the pavement. She decided to finish the call before making a dash for her car. The line connected and Harrison answered.

'Incident Room.'

'Dexter here.'

'What's up, Alison?'

'Get a print team down to New Bolden library. I think the killer might have used the computer terminal they use to find books.'

'You're not serious?'

'I'll explain it later.' She squinted up at the clouds that tumbled unhappily overhead. 'There'll be lots of prints on the keyboard but we might get a partial. Our man might have a record. It's something.'

'I'll send one of Leach's boys down. We might have to bring the machine in to the lab.'

'Whatever.'

'Are you coming back now?'

'No. I'll hang around here until the print team turns up. I've got some calls to make.'

She hung up. Now she needed Stussman's phone number. Dexter reached into her bag for her notebook and rummaged among its contents. No notebook. She must have left it in the car. Rain hammered down hard on the concrete: it seemed to roar back at her. The noise reminded Dexter of standing outside Upton Park as a child and listening to the chants and roaring of the football crowd inside. If she ran to the car she would get soaked. Could she call Stussman later, when the rain had

213

stopped? That didn't strike her as very professional: she was running the investigation now, after all.

'Oh, fuck it,' she muttered and dashed out into the rain. The car park was at the back of the library and Dexter tried to use the side of the building to protect herself from the brunt of the downpour. It made little difference. She was drenched almost immediately and felt water running down the back of her neck. She hated that feeling. It made her shiver.

Her Mondeo was parked under an elm tree about fifty yards from the exit barrier, sandwiched between an exhausted-looking Fiesta and a white van. She fumbled with her keys at the driver's door. She could see the notebook on the passenger seat and swore at her stupidity. She would have flu now for sure: that was all she needed. Finally the car door opened and she leaned inside, stretching over the handbrake and reaching for her book.

Crowan Frayne stepped out from behind the Escort van. It was time. He seized the driver's door of Dexter's Mondeo and slammed it hard against her legs. Half inside the car, Dexter fell face down against the seat. The pain in her legs was agonizing and she felt a sudden surge of panic. She tried to extricate herself from the car but the door slammed again on her legs. She screamed for help: her right leg felt as if it was broken. It was bleeding, too: she could feel blood flowing warmly against her chilled skin. *Got to get out . . . got to get out.* Crowan Frayne was quickly inside the car. Dexter felt his weight against her back: the pressure was intense and she thought her spine might snap. She shouted for help but Frayne pushed her face into the upholstery. She couldn't move. She steeled herself for the blow that she knew was coming.

'It's the yeare's midnight,' said Crowan Frayne softly.

Dexter, using her last vestiges of strength, twisted her head sideways and for the first time stared the killer of Lucy Harrington and Elizabeth Drury in the eye.

'You fuck . . .' she gasped. 'I'll fucking kill you.'

Crowan Frayne tightened his grip on her neck. 'I am every dead thing.' He pushed Dexter's face into the seat and punched her hard, twice, in the side of her skull. He knew that the cranial shell was at its thinnest by the temples and he had aimed his blows with precision. Dexter's body went limp. Crowan Frayne got out of the car and looked around. The car park was empty. The rain had kept everyone inside. He opened the back doors of his Escort van and dragged Dexter's unconscious form along the side of her car. With an effort, he hauled her inside before climbing in himself and slamming the van doors shut behind him.

He crouched over her. Dexter was groaning softly, her leg bleeding onto the wooden floor of the van. Frayne reached into his toolbox and withdrew his roll of masking tape. He gagged her and bound her hands and feet. He then rolled Dexter onto her side and pushed her into a foetal position. He looped a length of washing line around her neck and tied the ends tightly to her ankles and her wrists. If she moved her hands or legs the cord would tighten around her neck. She was a cop and Frayne did not plan to take any chances with her.

He touched the wound on her leg. The blood felt warm. He held his hand up to the light and watched the fluid form into a droplet and hang in the air. Frayne thought of the millions of dead compressed into the tiny red stalactite. Just as all matter had burst from a tiny particle, infinitesimally small, so had the memories and goodness of a thousand generations of life been fused and dissolved into Dexter's blood. He would bind them with his own in an infinite multiplication: a beautiful amplification of their intelligences. Frayne suspended the pendulous droplet above his open mouth, watched it ripen and bulge, then felt it drop onto his dry tongue.

Frayne savoured its metallic taste spreading in his mouth. He sensed electricity as he drew the goodness up into himself like his favourite laburnum tree.

Once he was satisfied that Dexter had been immobilized, Frayne climbed into the front seat of the van and reversed out of the parking berth. Following Dexter had been considerably easier than he had originally imagined it would be. He had noted her car and registration number outside Elizabeth Drury's house after their first meeting. The thick traffic had slowed Dexter's car and he had trailed her from the station to the hospital, back to the station and then to the library without incident.

Frayne swung his Escort 1.8d onto the large roundabout opposite the library and headed for the east side of town. Home.

55

Heather Stussman was angry and panicky. It was well after nine now and no one had called her back. She had called New Bolden police station three times already that morning and had still failed to speak to either Underwood or Dexter. She was confident that she had discovered something. That she had answered the killer's question: when is the world a carkasse?

It is the yeare's midnight today, she thought. *The world is a carkasse now. Today is St Lucy's Day. Someone is going to die today. Maybe the killer. Maybe me.*

Was she going mad? Maybe she'd been mad to come to England in the first place. Heather Stussman had never really known fear before: a certain nervousness when her academic articles were published, maybe, but nothing like this. She had taken a small carving knife from her kitchenette and placed it in the pocket of her cardigan as a precaution. She held it with her right hand. The steel felt cold against her skin. There was another knife under the pillow of her bed. They didn't reassure her. Neither did fresh-faced Constable Dawson who sat reading the newspaper outside the door to her rooms. In the US cops carried guns.

The college clock bonged once outside her window: it was nine-thirty. She would give them an hour. Then she would call again.

56

February 1967
New Bolden

Elizabeth Frayne died in childbirth. She had a weak heart that collapsed on her during labour. No one had known of its weakness and the doctors had been unprepared. One said it was a miracle that they managed to save the baby. Elizabeth was unmarried: she had kept the identity of the child's father a secret.

The funeral was simple and immediate. Rain whipped bitterly across New Bolden Cemetery, whirling grit around the grave. Droplets of water gathered on the funeral casket, merging and rolling off the sides like tears as Violet watched. The open ground yawned in front of her. Violet wished it would suck her down in her daughter's place. The ceremony was over in a matter of minutes. Two of Elizabeth's friends from the library attended. Violet did not invite them back home afterwards.

She collected her baby grandson from her neighbours and took the boy inside. He was big: over nine pounds at birth and much heavier now. He burbled as she nursed him. How would she manage? Twenty-two years of struggle and she was back where she started: holding a baby and wondering what on earth she could do. Twenty-two years and she had made no progress. God had a dark sense of humour, heaping grief upon grief on her shoulders. She looked at the baby and thought for an instant that it was no more pathetic, no more vulnerable and helpless than she was: a molecule of water in a vast directionless tidal wave. She banished the thought.

She had agonized over whether to have the baby adopted. She was middle-aged, she told herself; she didn't have the energy to start over again. She had faced disaster three times before: when she had become pregnant with Elizabeth, when Arthur had been killed and when she had lost her eye. On each occasion she had looked deep into the abyss and, from somewhere, had summoned the will to fight on.

The baby started to cry and she stroked his brow softly. When Arthur had died she had come to believe that there was no God. However, her logical schoolteacher's mind quickly argued her out of that position. If there was no God then all life was meaningless – Arthur's existence and death had been meaningless. But she knew that in the happiness they had shared, there was meaning. There had to be meaning here too, she reasoned as she stared down at her grandson. Perhaps she hadn't been tested enough. Perhaps this was another test of will and belief. She would fight again. She would defy her interfering God.

She thought of her daughter, dead and gone. No way to say sorry, no way to say goodbye. They had grown apart. Violet had got married some nine years previously. It had proved to be a mixed blessing: an arrangement born more of necessity and mutual convenience than affection. Elizabeth had hated her new father, his coarseness and the smell of alcohol that followed him around the house, his rages and his brooding, his alternating gentleness and violence. A week after her eighteenth birthday, Elizabeth had left home and started work at the Bolden library. Violet felt a sudden rush of guilt and loneliness. Elizabeth was gone.

Violet carried the baby into the kitchen and rested him in his cot. She could hear her husband snoring in the lounge. She imagined the newspapers and the mess of food and dirty plates. Bill Gowers had been a merchant seaman during the war. She had met him at a Remembrance Day service in Bolden. They had become friendly and started meeting for drinks. Bill had worked on the Atlantic convoys during the war, just as Arthur had done. Violet sat quietly and listened while Bill drank whisky and told his stories: of U-boat attacks, of black Atlantic skies strewn with glittering stars, of storms and of waves that smashed down upon the decks as if they were the wrath of God Himself, of burned and lost ships, of friends with daft nicknames, of fear and resolution.

She realized years later, lying in the darknesses of their marriage, that Bill's stories had made her feel closer to Arthur;

for a while, they closed the gap that his death had opened. They had allowed her to enter an imagined world, where she could seek out the only man she had truly loved. When she finally realized that Arthur wasn't hiding behind Bill's reminiscences, the stories became a horror to her and she punished her new husband with a coldness that he couldn't understand.

A name. The baby had to be given a name. The reality dawned on her out of the blue. It was her first responsibility. She sat on a hard kitchen chair and rocked the cradle as she thought. 'Arthur' was her first choice but Bill would not appreciate that. He knew a little about Arthur. There was no point turning her husband instinctively against the baby.

Violet considered the names of some English kings: Richard, Henry, George. They were all possibilities but none of them appealed particularly. Then an idea dropped into her head. Arthur's surname had been 'Crowan': Able Seaman Arthur Crowan. She had never told this to Bill. She had been half worried that Bill might actually have known him personally: Violet hadn't wanted Bill intruding on her imagined world. Arthur's blood was in the baby, it was only right that his name was used. 'Crowan Frayne': she liked that. It fused her with Arthur.

Once she was dead, Crowan Frayne would be the only proof that her happiness with Arthur had meant anything, or had even taken place at all. She decided that Crowan was the meaning, the purpose that was hidden in her sadness. She resolved to throw her heart, mind and soul into the child. His success would be her revenge on a vengeful universe.

57

Marty Farrell, the New Bolden scene-of-crime officer, approached the front desk of the library and asked for Sergeant Dexter. He carried a standard police fingerprinting kit and water ran off his waterproof jacket onto the floor. The young female librarian looked at him blankly for a second and then remembered.

'Oh, you've come about the computer terminal.'

'That's right. Is Sergeant Dexter around?'

'You should speak to Dan, really – he was dealing with her.' Dan was standing guard over the newly covered keyboard and computer screen. Farrell nodded and walked over.

'I'm Marty Farrell from New Bolden police.' He waved his ID at Dan. 'I understand you've been dealing with my sergeant.'

'Alison,' said Dan. 'Yes, although I don't know where she's got to. She told me to isolate this terminal and keep it covered up. Does that make sense?'

'Probably.'

A small group of curious onlookers had gathered to watch. Farrell looked around for Dexter. *Where the hell was she? The useless tart. Doing her bloody make-up, most likely*. He couldn't work under these conditions. Besides, it was boiling hot in there. He made a quick decision.

'I'll need to take this terminal back to the station with me.'

Dan looked surprised. 'Is it evidence? Has there been a crime?'

Farrell ignored him. 'Is there a back entrance to this building? Like a delivery entrance?'

'Absolutely. Access is from the car park.'

'OK. I'll bring my van right up to that entrance. I don't want to compromise the computer by getting it wet – and it is pissing down out there. I'm going to disconnect the terminal and then bag each component part individually. Then we'll take them to the delivery door and we'll put the bags straight into my van. Understood?'

'No problemo.'

Farrell knelt and opened his box of equipment. He took out four large plastic evidence bags and put them on the table next to the computer. 'Did Sergeant Dexter say when she would be back?'

'No, she just ran out with her mobile about forty minutes ago. I haven't seen her since. She's like that, isn't she? Impulsive, I mean.'

Farrell ignored the question and handed Dan a typewritten

220

form. 'This is your receipt. I fill out the top section but you'll need to sign it before I leave. We'll contact you when we've finished with the item.'

'I'll have to get the chief librarian. I'm not an official signatory,' said Dan sadly.

Farrell took a deep breath and turned his attention to the computer. It took him fifteen minutes to secure each of the major items: the screen, the keyboard and the hard drive. He also bagged the mouse and the mouse mat. Dan helped him carry the bags to the back of the library and Farrell made a dash for his van across the rainswept car park. Backing up to the entrance, he saw Dexter's car parked opposite the back wall of the library. The driver's door was open.

Farrell quickly loaded the evidence bags into the airtight containers inside his van and then jogged over to the car. It was definitely Dexter's. Blue Mondeo. T69 MPF. He always remembered her licence plate as its initials were MPF, like his own: Martin Peter Farrell. Farrell looked in the driver's door and then looked around; Dexter was nowhere to be seen. 'Dozy bird,' he muttered to himself and was about to slam the door shut when he noticed blood on the driver's seat and on the inside of the door.

58

June 1978

He was an intelligent child; a quick learner. He had an aptitude for language and music that Violet knew had come from the Fraynes. He had a shock of dark hair that shone when it was brushed and furious eyes that constantly sought connections and explanations. Crowan received good school reports, although some teachers expressed a concern that his quiet nature had made him something of an outsider. Violet wasn't concerned. Her grandson was intelligent and healthy: he had ideas and interests that were beyond his years. They would sit together reading at night, while Bill Gowers watched television and drunk himself to sleep. They would read Shakespeare, each taking different parts and performing to each other.

Crowan liked the 'seven ages of man' speech from *As You Like It*. He particularly relished the infant 'mewling and puking' in his nurse's arms. Crowan spat the words out with such venomous clarity that Violet couldn't help but smile. She taught Crowan to play the piano that she had inherited from Rose and gradually guided him through her sister's book collection. He was too young to enjoy Dickens and Hardy and his sallies into *Nicholas Nickleby* and *Jude the Obscure* never lasted longer than a couple of chapters. However, he enjoyed the rhythms and colour of poetry: the rhymes made the poems easier to remember. *Old Possum's Book of Practical Cats* was his favourite, although Violet steered him gently but insistently towards Wordsworth and Donne.

Donne grabbed his attention. The language often confused him but he liked the simple images at the centre of some of the poems. He could recreate the picture in his mind and then work the language around it. Violet understood this and deliberately chose poems with a vivid conceit at their heart to help her grandson understand more rapidly. Crowan especially liked 'The Flea'. Its simple, colourful images became rooted in his mind and he listened rapt as Violet explained the poem to him. 'The poet is annoyed with his girlfriend because she won't kiss him. So he points out a flea to her and says that she let the flea bite her so she should at least allow him to kiss her! Like this.' Crowan giggled and retracted as Violet pursed her lips and tried to kiss him. '*Marke but this flea, and mark in this/How little that which thou deny'st me is/ Mee it suck'd first, and now it sucks thee/ And in this flea our two bloods mingled be.*'

Violet made some unpleasant sucking noises for dramatic impact.

'So do fleas suck blood?' Crowan asked.

'Yes. It's their food.'

'Like chips?'

'Just like chips. So, you see, because the flea has bitten both

Donne and his girlfriend, their two bloods are mingled together inside it.'

'Like a baby.'

Not for the first time, Violet Frayne was surprised at her grandson's perceptiveness. His mind was so quick to make connections, to find the meaning behind text and ideas.

'That's right,' she said softly, 'and Donne says to the girl that if she kills the flea by crushing it, then she will actually be killing the three of them: *Though use make thee apt to kill mee/Let not to this selfe murder added bee/And sacrilege, three sinnes in killing three.'*

Bill Gowers appeared at the kitchen door. 'You'll make a poofter out of that boy,' he hiccoughed and opened the fridge.

Violet tensed. 'Don't you dare speak like that in front of him.'

'What's a poofter?' asked Crowan Frayne.

'A pansy. A shirt-lifter. Where's the bleeding cheese?' Gowers rummaged in the fridge and eventually found some Cheddar. He cut a hunk of bread from a half-loaf and slapped on some margarine.

'A pansy's a flower, isn't it, Granny? Like a violet.' Crowan was confused.

'That's right, darling,' Violet replied. 'It's a little flower.' She fired a withering look at Gowers as he added a slab of cheese to his doorstep of bread.

Gowers snorted with derision. 'Hah! Flowers! That's right. Little flowers they are. We had a load of them in the Navy and didn't they smell pretty?' He bumped into Crowan Frayne as he turned. 'Get out of my fucking way, you're always cluttering.'

'Don't you touch him, you drunken oaf,' Violet snarled, 'or, God help me, I'll—'

'What?' shouted Gowers. 'What will you do? I've been blown up and sunk. Splashing about in the Atlantic in the middle of the bleeding night with the skin burned off me hands. There's not much you can do that'd scare me.'

'Just go away.' Violet felt a cold fury at the man. 'Let us be.'

Gowers showed his hands to Frayne. The boy had seen the burns before but they still made him shiver. 'See these, nancy? Adolf Hitler did that and he didn't bloody scare me either.'

Gowers returned to the lounge and slammed the door behind him. Violet shuddered as she heard the television volume increase.

'Don't cry, Granny,' said Crowan Frayne. He wondered why she only seemed to cry out of one eye.

'I'm all right, darling.' Violet brushed the tears from her face and swallowed her pain. 'Right, then. Where did we get up to?'

'The second stanza,' said Crowan helpfully, looking again at his book of poems, beautifully bound in black leather. 'He's just told her not to crush the flea.'

'Thank you. Let's finish this one off, then.' Violet continued explaining the poem to Crowan but by now he was only half listening. He was thinking of ways to kill Bill Gowers.

That night Crowan Frayne dreamed that he was trapped inside a flea – swimming in different kinds of blood. Ladies' blood smelled of pansies: men's blood smelled of whisky and feet. It washed over him, pouring into his throat. His hands banged against the walls of the flea's stomach; *cloistered in these living walls of jet.* He was like a baby, floating in blood. Nancy baby. But he couldn't be born because he didn't have a mummy. He felt a great force lift the flea in the air. Blood and fluid swilled against him and his head smashed against the flea's stomach lining. The flea was being crushed – he couldn't breathe. The sides of the flea ruptured and a great pressure bore down on him. *Cruel and sodaine hast thou since purpled thy nail in blood of innocence?* He had been crushed, he had lost his shape. Now he was just blood falling through the air. And he didn't smell of anything.

After leaving the Merchant Navy, Bill Gowers had worked at Bolden station until it was demolished and rebuilt as New Bolden Parkway in 1965. Gowers was still fond of the railways and each morning would take a long walk along the edge of the track to the South Bolden signal box. He enjoyed talking to the engineers and often stopped for a cup of tea and a bun with

Albert Faulks, the signalman. Crowan Frayne often asked Gowers if he could walk with him but Gowers always refused. So Crowan would follow him. He would wait in bed until he heard Gowers slam the front door. Then he'd dress quickly and follow the old man outside.

It was about a four-mile round trip and it took Gowers over three hours, including his stop for tea. Crowan would stay back about a hundred metres: he knew that Gowers's eyes were bad and he was unlikely to spot Crowan at such a distance. The route took them through the old village allotments, then past the cemetery and on to the railway line. Crowan liked the railway: the rush and energy of the trains, the scrunch of granite shale underfoot. He watched Gowers's awkward, laborious progress and wondered what it would be like to push the old man under a train. Would he fly into the air or be pulled underneath and sliced apart?

The June morning was bright and fresh but Crowan preferred the security of darkness. He felt conspicuous in the daylight. He held back further, often losing sight of the old man as the footpath twisted through, around and behind the allotments. Crowan wasn't concerned. There was a film of dew on the leaves like droplets of pearl, or tears: '*Blasted with sighs, and surrounded with teares/Hither I come to seek the spring*'. He liked Donne's 'Twicknam Garden'. Crowan ran his hand softly against the wet leaves, feeling the cold water evaporate against his skin. He rounded a corner in the path and came face to face with Bill Gowers.

'What are you doing, you little bastard?' Gowers snarled.

'Nothing.'

'You're following me. I'll brain you with me stick.' He waved his walking stick angrily at Crowan. 'Can't you give me any peace? Haven't you messed my life up enough?'

'I'm going home.' Crowan turned and started to walk away. Gowers lashed at the back of his leg with the stick. Crowan Frayne felt a rush of pain as he fell to the tarmac.

'I could kill you, nancy boy, and no one would know. I could tie you to the rails in the tunnel and let the train have you and no one would know. They'd only find bits of you. A leg in Bolden, an arm in Evesbury, and your miserable little head at Liverpool Street.'

'I'm telling Grandma what you said.' Crowan Frayne scrambled to his feet. 'You're a fucking nancy.'

Gowers cracked his stick at Frayne's right knee and the boy fell over again. 'Tell her,' he snorted. 'Maybe I'll do for her as well. I'd be rid of the both of you then. I might get some peace. I could line you up in the bleedin' cemetery with your mother: be a nice family get-together, wouldn't it? Now fuck off home and if I catch you sneaking about behind me again I *will* do you. Understand?'

Crowan Frayne stood awkwardly, the pain stabbing at his knee. His face was red with childish fury and he tried to hobble away. He didn't look back as tears began to course down his face and Gowers snorted behind him.

'Go on, cry, nancy boy. See what good that does you!'

Crowan Frayne stumbled back along the path that ran parallel to the railway. A freight train clattered angrily past him and he started with fright. He thought of his mother. He knew that he didn't have a mummy: that his mummy had died when he was born. Somewhere inside he had always hoped that this was a lie and that one day she would come back for him. But Gowers had said she was in the cemetery, she was in a place under the ground. She wasn't coming back for him. The path snaked alongside the graveyard. Frayne paused and looked at the hotch-potch of grey and black headstones, the small statuettes and the white bulk of the war memorial. His mummy was in there. She was somewhere. Why hadn't they told him before? He made a decision and climbed through a gap in the hedge.

It took Frayne nearly an hour to find the headstone. The text on many had faded with time and rain and were hard to read. Elizabeth Frayne's headstone was black with gold writing. The plot itself was neat and well looked after, in stark contrast with some of the overgrown graves that surrounded it. He read the inscription: *Elizabeth Maureen Frayne, 1944–1967. Gone to seek Thee, God.* This was the place. She was here. Hiding beneath the flowers and the soil. She had gone to seek God. A rush of thoughts almost overwhelmed Crowan Frayne: frustration, loneliness, disappointment. She had given him life and then deserted him. It would have been better if she had killed him and lived herself. She had left him behind. He hated her.

Violet made egg and chips for lunch. It was Crowan Frayne's favourite but today it made him want to retch. An egg was like a baby. Was the yolk the brains and the white the body? A baby with no mummy. Like him. He felt sick and pushed the plate away.

Gowers ate loudly and hungrily, eyeing the boy. Crowan hadn't said anything to Violet about the morning's confrontation. His grandmother slept in on Saturdays and had still been asleep when he had returned. His knee throbbed uncomfortably.

'I think I'll sit in the garden this afternoon,' Violet said. 'It's a beautiful day.'

'Good. The racing's on at two,' Gowers replied between mouthfuls. 'Take the nancy out with you. I could do with some quiet.'

'Would you like that, Crowan?' Violet asked, ignoring the jibe. 'We could do some sketching.'

Crowan Frayne nodded silently without looking up. Gowers smirked and returned to his *Sporting Life.*

By two o'clock it was hot outside. The garden hummed with light and colour. Violet had set up a small table and brought out some sketching materials. The air smelled thick and sweet with honeysuckle and lilac. Crowan watched bees hop from flower to flower.

'Do bees bring food to the flowers, Granny?'

Violet smiled. 'No. The other way around. Bees drink nectar from inside the flowers. Bees pick up pollen from one flower and carry it to other flowers. It's how they reproduce.'

'So how do flowers get food?'

'They draw up nutrients, goodness from the soil, and they use sunlight.'

Crowan Frayne went quiet. 'Goodness from the soil.' He knew what that meant.

They started to draw the laburnum tree at the end of the garden. Violet's depth perception was poor and she drew as much from memory as from what she could actually see. She sensed that Crowan was unusually quiet but stopped herself from asking him why. Sometimes he was best left alone. She looked over at his drawing.

'That's good, darling, but don't try and draw every leaf and twig. You'll go mad trying. Think about the light: the shapes it makes as it shines through the leaves and branches. Light and dark: simplicity.'

'OK.' Crowan Frayne was only half listening. He was thinking of how many dead things had their goodness inside the tree: thousands, probably. One day he would draw them all: people's arms and legs tangled into branches, flowers and plants twisted and sucked into leaves, dead animals' bodies bound into roots, Bill Gowers's tired face gnarled into the trunk.

'I am every dead thing,' said the tree softly. Crowan Frayne nodded. He understood.

Violet paused for a moment. She was getting a headache.

'Crowan, be a love. Could you go and get my glasses from my bedroom? They're in the chest of drawers. Third drawer down.'

Crowan walked back to the house. He was careful to go by the kitchen door rather than the French windows. He did not want to disturb Gowers. The television blared out an excited horse-racing commentary and he could hear Gowers barking encouragement at his bets. Crowan climbed the narrow staircase and went into Violet's bedroom. It was cool and dark inside. There was no carpet and the two single beds stood on exposed floorboards. He had rarely been in the room before.

The chest of drawers was in the far corner, next to the beautifully made bed that he knew had to be his grandmother's. There was a neatly aligned row of expensive-looking books on the top surface of the dresser. He ran a finger along them as he walked past: Shakespeare, Hardy, Dickens, Keats, Wordsworth, Austen, Brontë. The names were becoming increasingly familiar and each conjured images, characters, stories and rhymes to him.

Reaching his destination, Crowan knelt painfully and opened the third drawer down. Its contents were carefully arranged: a diary, a photo album, some writing paper and envelopes, an eyeglass case and a small wooden box. He touched the box with a finger: it felt beautifully smooth as he traced the grain of the wood. 'V. Frayne' was stamped on the lid of the box.

Curiosity overcame him. He stood up and lifted the lid. Three glass eyes stared back blankly at him; his face reflected in their blue corneas and fixed black pupils. Crowan Frayne recoiled in shock and dropped the box. It clattered against the edge of the dresser. Two of the eyes fell to the floor and shattered immediately against the floorboards. Then the box hit the floor with a crash. Crowan tentatively crouched and turned it over. The final eye was cracked in three pieces inside the box, its jagged shards resting against the purple lining. It leered horribly at him. Crowan Frayne was sick.

He heard laughter behind him. Gowers stood at the door. 'You've done it now, you silly little bastard!' He turned slightly and shouted down the stairs. 'Violet! Violet! Come and see what the nancy's done.'

Frayne was shaking. He had no idea what had happened. He felt he had violated a dark, private place. Glass fragments lay strewn across the floor. Violet appeared at the door and raised her hand to her mouth.

'Look at that!' shouted Gowers triumphantly. 'He's only gone and smashed your eyes, up the little bastard. What Hitler started he's finished. Mind you, the Nazis only got one of your eyes – he's done three!'

Violet pushed past him and picked Crowan Frayne up from the floor. She sat him on the bed and knelt to start picking up the larger pieces of glass. She said nothing. She felt ashamed; as if a great deceit had been exposed.

'I expect he done it on purpose.' Gowers beamed. 'He's a vindictive little so-and-so. Now what are you going to do?

Them's expensive things now. And I ain't paying for a new set.' He rubbed his chin in glee. He had scored a great victory. 'You'll have to wear dark glasses now, like Ray Charles.'

Frayne flew at Gowers across the bed and threw a childish punch at the old man's mouth. 'Fucking shut up! Fucking shut up!' he screamed. 'I'll fucking kill you.' The surprise and the momentum of the assault knocked Gowers back against the wall. He quickly recovered his footing and hit Crowan hard on the chin: the boy fell backwards and banged his head against the dresser. He started to bleed. Gowers picked him up and held him by the throat.

'You think you're man enough, do you? Have a go, then. I'll do you, I swear it. Maybe I'll tear your eye out to replace the ones you've buggered. See how you like it. How about that?'

Violet pushed Gowers away. Crowan fell back onto the bed. 'Go away, Bill,' she ordered him firmly. 'Go away and leave us alone.' She leaned closer to him and whispered, 'And if you ever lay a finger on that child again, I will finish you. Do you understand?'

Gowers stared at her. '*He* attacked *me*, in case you didn't notice. Ain't it bleeding fair, eh? I was just defending myself. I'm an old man.'

'And he's a child. You should know better. Now go away.'

Gowers grunted and turned away. Violet sat down next to Crowan on the bed and put her arm around him. He was shaking, sobbing without tears. Blood trickled warmly from the back of his head. The boy nodded silently as she explained to him: about the war, the explosion, the glass, her eye. But Crowan Frayne wasn't really listening.

He was suddenly on a desert planet. It was the first time he had been there. There were no footprints on the sand except his own.

The sand is black and the mountains have eyes: the rocks talk when the sky replies.

He decided to stay a while.

59

Marty Farrell bounded up the central staircase of the New Bolden Police Station and was panting for breath by the time he reached the third floor. Harrison was waiting for him outside Underwood's office.

'What's all this about Dexter?' Harrison asked.

'Her car was at the library but I couldn't find her.' Farrell paused to catch his breath, 'The librarian said she went outside and didn't come back in again. Her car door was open. There was blood on the seat.'

'Fucking hell.'

'That's what I thought. There's another SOCO and a couple of plods working on the car and taking statements.' Farrell looked Harrison straight in the eye. 'You reckon he's got her?'

'I hope not. But she found him before. Maybe she found him again.' Harrison was starting to feel a depressing sense of resignation. 'We've tried her mobile. There's no reply.'

'I must have missed him by minutes,' said Farrell.

Harrison thought for a second. 'Look, Marty, she wanted us to lift prints off that computer. We should get moving on it ASA-fucking-P.'

'It's in the lab now.'

'Good. You call me if we get a match with anyone who's got a record. I don't care what for. This might be our only chance of finding him.'

'And Dexter,' Farrell added.

'And Dexter.'

'There'll be a lot of prints. This might take time.'

'Start by looking at the keys he was most likely to have used. If he was looking for books by John Donne or by Elizabeth Drury he would have had to type their names in.'

'Understood. Lots of people could have used the keyboard after him though.'

'True. But some of the letters are fairly uncommon: "Z" and "H", for example. We might get lucky.'

'All right. I'll call you.' Farrell pushed open the double doors and headed back down to the Forensic Laboratory.

Harrison felt paralysed for a second, wondering what he should do. What if Dexter was already dead? He discounted the idea. The killer could have bashed her brains in at the Drury woman's house but had decided not to. Maybe he wanted her alive. But what for? A secretary leaned out of the door of the Incident Room and spotted Harrison.

'Sir?'

He turned towards her. 'What's up?'

'That American doctor's on the phone again. She's getting a bit stroppy.'

Harrison returned to the Incident Room and picked up the phone. Stussman was on line two.

'Dr Stussman? This is DS Harrison.'

'What is going on down there?' Stussman sounded furious. 'This is the fourth time I've called this morning and no one's called me back.'

Harrison held the phone slightly away from his head. 'Sergeant Dexter was going to call you but she's – erm – indisposed.'

'Look, sport, I have information about your killer that might be very important. Shall I tell you or shall I just take out an advert in a newspaper?'

Harrison scrambled around his desk and picked up a pen. 'Go ahead.'

Stussman took a deep breath. 'OK . . . When I last spoke to him he asked me, "When is the world a carkasse?". He asked me twice, so I guessed that he figured it was important for me to find out.'

'Go on.' Harrison couldn't see where this was going but he was getting desperate.

'The answer is today. 13 December. He referred to a Donne poem called "A Nocturnall upon St Lucies Day". I won't trouble you with the details but St Lucy's Day used to be regarded as the longest night of the year. In Donne's time that was 13 December – today.'

'What's the poem about?'

'It's about mourning the death of the loved one. And it's about suicide,' said Stussman.

'You think he's going to kill himself?'

'I think it's on his mind. He's lost someone close to him; a mother or a sister, I'd guess. Or a daughter, maybe.'

Harrison was scribbling notes, trying to make sense of Stussman's comments, trying to link them in with Dexter's disappearance.

'Where is Inspector Underwood?' Stussman asked.

'He's ill, Doctor.' Harrison didn't see any point in lying. 'He had a heart attack. Sergeant Dexter has disappeared. We think that the killer might have taken her.'

'Oh my God,' Stussman breathed.

Harrison put down his pen. 'Look, Doctor Stussman, if this bastard makes another attempt to contact you, call me immediately. If you're right about the date, we don't have much time.'

'Agreed.' She sounded scared.

'You still have police protection there, don't you?' He asked.

'Yes, I do.'

'You're perfectly safe. This guy is very methodical, cautious. He's not just going to walk up and knock your door down.'

'I hope you're right.'

'If you think of anything else . . .'

'You'll be the first to know.'

Harrison put the phone down and looked around the room. It was chaotic with activity and gossip: phones were ringing unanswered, paper was strewn everywhere. He looked up at the photographs of Lucy Harrington and Elizabeth Drury pinned against the board and thought of Alison Dexter.

Part V

The Children in the Oven

60

September 1995

The feeling still thrilled him. Standing in a strange house, enshrouded and empowered by the darkness, Crowan Frayne felt a curious sense of belonging. He enjoyed the strange smells and decorations; the feel of unfamiliar furniture; the rush of power and control. Sometimes he took things, things that might prove valuable when the time eventually came. However, for the most part he just stood, masturbated and absorbed the darkness.

It was useful practice, too. He worked on a variety of houses. He knew that gaining experience and knowledge would prove invaluable when the time came to execute his conceit. This would be his fifth house. It was a large Edwardian building: part accommodation and part veterinary surgery. There was a burglar alarm: he would need to be careful. The surgery might contain equipment that he could use; drugs, even. The back of the building was approachable only via a narrow alley. It was a bottleneck: it made him uncomfortable.

The security light made him feel worse. He accidentally triggered it as he entered the alley. He froze and waited for darkness. There were no further lights at the rear of the house and Frayne moved quickly. He withdrew a spray can from his pocket and sprayed 'Wanker' in red paint on the brickwork: better to be thought a vandal than a burglar in New Bolden. He traced an electric cable that powered the burglar alarm down the line of the wall. He used his Stanley knife to slice through the cable. The alarm didn't ring. Frayne started work on the back door.

The alarm had a silent trigger to the New Bolden police station. A police squad car half a mile away received the alert call almost immediately. The surgery had been identified as a possible target for drug abusers and the car was outside within two minutes of Frayne cutting the cable. He still hadn't managed to open the security lock on the back door of the house when he heard footsteps and saw torchlight in the alleyway. There was nowhere to run. He threw his equipment bag over the nearest fence, took a deep breath and sprinted out of the darkness at the two policemen in the alleyway, spraying paint into their eyes as he did. One of them fell, the paint burning at him, but the other caught Frayne around the neck and hauled him to the floor. They struggled and Frayne almost managed to escape when the other policeman regained his vision and kicked him hard in the stomach, driving the breath from Frayne's lungs. He gasped as they rolled him onto his stomach and pulled his hands up behind his back. The plastic handcuffs were extremely tight and cut into his skin. One of the policeman called him a 'junkie cunt.'

Frayne gave the address of his temporary lodgings in New Bolden and claimed to have no living relatives. He had no desire to break Violet's heart again. He was charged and convicted in November 1995 for criminal damage. His legal-aid lawyer explained to the court that Crowan Frayne was unemployed and resentful of affluence. His vandalism was merely a confused act of expression. This was nonsense, of course, but it served a purpose. Frayne was ordered to pay costs of five hundred pounds to the veterinary practice and did not receive a custodial sentence. The judge recommended that Frayne see a social worker.

Frayne didn't bother.

Violet Frayne didn't ever find out about her grandson's conviction. He kept it a closely guarded secret, paid the fine himself and destroyed all the free local papers when they fell through Violet's letter box. It was an unnecessary precaution. By this time Violet Frayne's vision had deteriorated so much that she was unable to read any newspaper print without a magnifying glass and she rarely bothered. Much to Frayne's amusement, Bill Gowers had died of liver cancer the previous Christmas. In a way this was unfortunate, as Frayne had already developed his own plan for Bill Gowers. He had intended to inject concentrated sulphuric acid into the old man's stomach if Violet had died before her husband. No need now. Nature had devised a far more uncomfortable and drawn-out torture and Bill Gowers was now just another contortion in the bark of the laburnum tree.

Frayne had escaped prison but at a cost. He now had a criminal record. When he came to realize his great conceit he would have to be extremely cautious: eyes would be upon him. Mistakes would prove very expensive. Planning would be crucial and the experience he had gained would be useful. Timing would be the variable. He would know when the correct moment arrived. Until then he was content to wait, to prepare.

And to dream.

61

Dexter was suddenly conscious. Her pain centres were firing messages across her brain. She was lying on her side in total darkness. Pain everywhere. She tried to move but something tightened against her neck. Where was she? She couldn't see. Had he taken her eyes? Had he blinded her? No. Her eyes were stinging with dust. She struggled to remain calm and forced her body to relax. Her hands and feet were bound and there was cord around her neck. She had tape across her mouth. Again she tried to move, again the noose began to choke her. She got the message and lay perfectly still.

Think rationally. She tried to brush aside her discomfort and focus on where she was. The floor was cold and she guessed it was concrete. It was dusty too and her eyes were starting to water now. Was he watching her? Was he standing in the blackness, staring at her? She desperately tried to distinguish shapes and listened for tell-tale noises such as breathing. Nothing. She could see his face in her mind clearly enough. Thin and bony: well-defined cheekbones and a shock of dark hair. He had looked pale, as if his angry eyes had drained the life and colour from his skin. He looked like a ghost.

Where could she be? Concrete floor. Total silence. A warehouse, maybe? A garage? She didn't think so. The room didn't smell of oil or machinery. If anything, it smelled of old books: dry and musty. There was no draught. He had gagged her, so he must have been concerned that someone might hear her cries. She found that strangely reassuring. There must be people nearby. Somewhere above her, away in the distance, she heard a car start and slowly accelerate.

Maybe she was in his house. On a residential road. If she was in a house she had to be in a cellar or a shed. She guessed it was the former. Dexter sensed there was a low ceiling above her: the room was tight and airless.

Underwood had been right. The killer wanted her alive for something. What had the inspector said? He wasn't performing, he was educating. Why had he chosen to educate her? Her mind sought explanations. She had found him at Elizabeth Drury's house; surprised him. Hadn't Stussman said that the metaphysical poets valued unexpectedness as a form of wit? Perhaps the killer valued her intelligence or appreciated the stream of connections that she must have made to find him so quickly. Did that mean that he wasn't going to kill her? She doubted it.

The bindings on her hands were slightly less painful than those around her ankles and Dexter gradually began to move her wrists in an attempt to loosen the tape further. The cord tugged at her neck as she did so but she persevered. It would take time but she was confident that eventually she could work her hands free. She also used her tongue to lick the inside of the masking tape that sealed her mouth. It tasted disgusting but it slowly began to loosen as she moistened the adhesive with saliva. It was exhausting, sweaty work and she had to rest for breath every thirty seconds or so.

She was confident that she was alone in the room. Why had he left her? A car had just driven off. Was it the killer? If so, where had he gone? How long did she have? *Concentrate, Alison.* She began to work her wrists once more.

62

Heather Stussman's telephone rang at three p.m. The noise smashed through the tense silence like an exploding hand grenade. She sensed bad news.

'Hello?'

'When is the world a carkasse?' said Crowan Frayne.

The voice chilled her to the marrow. 'Today,' she replied. She looked out of the window across the old quad. She had an instinctive sense that he was close: as if the hairs on the back of her neck had all suddenly stood on end. There was nobody in sight. Most of the students were at lectures.

'Why?'

'13 December is St Lucies Day. The yeare's midnight.'

There was a pause. Frayne seemed to be digesting the information. Eventually the voice came again: dry and rasping.

'Are you looking out of your window?'

She froze in horror. 'Why do you ask?'

Crowan Frayne took a deep breath: it sounded like a wave whispering against dry pebbles. 'See how the thirsty earth has withered and shrunk as to the beds feet?'

Stussman understood the reference to the poem. Hippocrates said that a dying man will huddle at the foot of his bed. Donne had used it in his St Lucy's Day poem. She looked again at the quadrangle. There was no one there: he couldn't possibly see her.

'I suppose you're every dead thing?' she replied after a moment.

'So are you.'

'Is that meant to frighten me?' She tried to hide the tremor in her voice.

'No. To help you. Listen to the dead inside you. We are only

241

animations of forgotten souls. Listen to their cries, their anguish. They will give you perspective. They will teach you pity.'

'What do you want?'

There was another pause. Stussman wondered what he was doing: playing with himself, maybe. 'What's the matter?' she added. 'Can't you think of anything scary to say?'

'Are you acquainted with Detective Sergeant Alison Dexter?' he asked softly.

Stussman hesitated. 'Yes.'

'Alison Dexter has short dark brown hair and green eyes that glower like a cat's. Her blood tastes of sugar for a second; then of rust.'

'Is she with you now?'

'She is.'

'Let me speak to her.'

'I don't think I can allow that.'

'Is she alive? Have you hurt her?'

'Sergeant Dexter has the ability to make extraordinary connections,' said Crowan Frayne. 'I'm sure she is doing so as we speak. She is unable to do much else.'

'Listen to me.' Stussman was trying frantically to think of an angle. 'Killing a cop is heavy shit. You think you're in trouble now. If you kill her they will tear you apart, mister. No trial, no jury. You won't make it as far as court. They will crucify you. Every policeman in the country will want your head.'

'With your cooperation, Sergeant Dexter need not come to any lasting harm.'

'My cooperation?'

'I want you to come to the war memorial in New Bolden Cemetery.'

'Why?'

'I will explain it to you when you arrive.'

'I don't think so, buster.'

'Alison Dexter has pretty green eyes, fiercely intelligent. She also has surprisingly delicate hands for a policewoman.'

'Don't threaten me.'

'Similarly, if you are not at the war memorial in New Bolden cemetery at five o'clock today I will tie Sergeant Dexter to a table and cut out her left eye. While she screams into her gag, I will tell her that you refused to help her. She may pass out with the pain, of course: I imagine peeling back her eyelids will cause considerable distress. But then, Sergeant Dexter strikes me as a particularly strong-willed individual. She may remain awake for some time. She may even have the unique privilege of seeing her own eye pulled from its socket.'

'You are a very sick fuck.'

'I will then send the eye to a national newspaper – probably a lurid tabloid – with an accompanying note explaining that my actions were inspired by your radical text *Reconstructing Donne* – rather in the way that The Beatles apparently inspired Charles Manson – and that you had the chance to save Sergeant Dexter but refused. I am uncertain how the university would react but your celebrity would outlive both of us. If I am arrested as a result of your actions I shall instruct my solicitor to post a parcel that I have prepared and entrusted to him, again to a major tabloid newspaper. It will have a similar effect.'

Stussman was being backed into a corner. If Frayne meant what he said, she'd be ruined.

'How do I know that you won't hurt me?' she said. 'I'd be crazy to swap my life for Dexter's.' She would play along with him, then call the police.

'That may not be necessary. If you trust in your knowledge, if you are confident in your own work, if you are certain of the arguments you put forward with such intellectual force in your book, then you will not come to any harm.'

'That isn't very reassuring.'

'If you contact the police, I shall know. If you are accompanied or followed to the war memorial I shall know. In my house I have a large flask of concentrated sulphuric acid. If you attempt to deceive me in any way I will remove Sergeant Dexter's eye and then drop acid into the socket, using a pipette. I will then apply the acid to her face, her hands, her nipples and Lord knows where else. I guess that her heart will eventually succumb to the agony but who knows how long that will take?'

'If I come you'll kill me, won't you?' She was floundering now.

'Once I have finished with Alison I shall visit you in any case. Do you understand?'

'I understand.'

'This is your opportunity to live. If you try and fuck me around I will show you every dead thing that crawls around inside you, shits behind your eyes and slithers in your blood. I will take great pleasure and much time in showing you. When you leave the college today, you should assume that I am watching you all the way. I shall know if you are playing with me and I promise that I will find agonies for you and Sergeant Dexter that will burst your brains.'

'I get the picture.'

'And I am rebegot,' said Crowan Frayne, 'of absence, darkness, death, things which are not.'

The line died suddenly and Stussman put the phone down. Her hand hovered over the receiver. She knew she should call the police. But what if the killer was nearby? What if he was a policeman? The idea made her shiver: there was a policeman outside her door. *If you are accompanied or followed to the war memorial, I shall know*, the killer had said. That meant he must already be in Cambridge, unless he was just trying to frighten her to make sure she'd comply.

He had said that he was planning to visit her. That this was her chance to live. Calling the police would be a huge risk. He would kill Alison Dexter for sure and offer Stussman's name to the tabloid press. She could not let that happen. Heather Stussman had built her academic reputation piece by exhausting piece. It had been a tortuous process, driven only by her instinctive desire to succeed, like a salmon swimming against the flow of a thick black river. It was her entire life. Without her reputation what would she do? Go back to Wisconsin, probably, but then what? She would be unemployable and, worse than that, she would be notorious.

If you are certain of your arguments then you will not come to any harm. He would say that, though, wouldn't he? Stussman mused. She thought again of 'A Nocturnall on St Lucies Day'. The killer had quoted from it again as he hung up: *'And I am rebegot of absence, darkness, death, things which are not.'* He was obsessed with annihilation, self-destruction, nothingness. If, as Stussman had previously suspected, he planned to kill himself, perhaps she could encourage him in the act. She sat down at her desk and wrote on a piece of college notepaper:

'Murderer of Harrington and Drury asked me to meet him today at five p.m., New Bolden Cemetery, War Memorial. He has Sergeant Dexter and has threatened to kill her if I do not attend. I believe he plans to kill himself.'

She folded the note carefully inside an envelope, sealed it, addressed it to Sergeant Harrison, New Bolden CID and wrote the phone number of the Incident Room at the top edge of the envelope. It wasn't much of a contingency plan but it was better than nothing. Stussman opened the door of her rooms and smiled down at her blue-uniformed sentry.

'I'm going to drop this letter at the porter's lodge,' she said. 'Then I am going to the college library for an hour or two. I'll be quite safe. It's within college grounds and there will be plenty of students there.'

'I'm supposed to stay with you, Dr Stussman.' PC Jarvis was young and eager not to screw up.

'There's really no need. No offence, but I won't be able to work with you sitting next to me. Wouldn't you be better off here? In case he calls or turns up, I mean. He's not likely to attack me in the library in front of the entire college.'

'I guess not. All right, Dr Stussman, but please don't leave the college site without telling me first. Would you like me to walk with you to the lodge?'

'You're very kind but there's no need. I'll leave the room open. Help yourself to tea.' She smiled her most dazzling smile at him and PC Jarvis melted like hot butter.

Stussman hurried down to the porter's lodge. The air was bitterly cold. Tiny flakes of snow drifted across the stone quadrangle like ash from a distant bonfire. The newly refurbished lodge was centrally heated and the warmth enfolded her as she stepped inside. Johnson, the head porter, was hanging room keys on the board behind the front desk.

'Johnson, can I ask you an important favour?'

The head porter twisted the right side of his mouth into a sardonic knot. He put down his pipe on the wooden counter. 'That's why I am here, Dr Stussman.'

She handed him the envelope. He read the name of the addressee with interest.

'I have to leave the college for a couple of hours on police business. You've heard the rumours, I'm sure.'

'Every one of them.'

'Good. You'll understand the importance, then.' She looked Johnson in the eye, using her toughest stare. 'Listen. If I have not called you by six p.m. today I want you to call Sergeant Harrison on the number I have given and read him the contents of the envelope.'

'Open it, you mean?'

'Obviously. This is a matter of life and death, Mr Johnson. I wouldn't bother you otherwise.'

The head porter nodded and carefully placed the envelope in the breast pocket of his blazer.

'What about the young police gentleman on your staircase?'

'He's in my room. We . . . we are expecting the killer to call.'

'Very well, Dr Stussman.' He tapped his pocket and winked at her. 'I shall wait for your call.'

'Thank you, Mr Johnson. I knew I could depend on you.'

'Always, madam.'

Stussman nodded at him and then stepped back outside. Into the oven.

63

Marty Farrell had been lifting prints from the New Bolden library computer for nearly four hours. It was a painstaking process. The machine was covered with dozens of latent prints. He started with the keyboard, carefully dusting and brushing black non-magnetic powder onto the surface of each of the keys to highlight the tell-tale oils in the fingerprints. He lifted the prints from the surface by pressing adhesive tape against the powder. Farrell then used a special camera to photograph the imprints on the tape. The procedure took time and he knew that time was a critical factor now. There were some faint latent fingerprints that the powder was unable to clarify. On these he used a small laser that caused the perspiration in the prints to glow a mysterious yellow. These too were photographed.

The problem was not so much finding the prints as separating them. The library computer was used by the general public and dozens of greasy-fingered people had used it. The fingerprints were smudged and overlaid on top of each other on many of the keys. The smudging was so bad on the mouse buttons that lifting individual prints was virtually impossible. Still, Marty Farrell persevered and by 4.30 p.m. he had lifted and photographed seventeen reasonably uncorrupted partial and whole prints.

He knew that attempting to identify each of them in turn could take hours so he acted on the suggestion that Harrison had made to him that morning. On a piece of paper Farrell wrote down:

ELIZABETH DRURY
JOHN DONNE

He then cross-referenced the constituent letters of the two names with the locations where he had found each of the prints. This allowed him to prioritize more effectively. He would concentrate his attention on the more uncommon letters from which he had lifted a fingerprint. He decided to start with Z, H, D, R, and Y. In total, he had taken nine partials from those letters. He might not be able to secure the court-required sixteen-point match but at this stage that wouldn't be necessary. At this stage he just needed a name. And a break.

Marty Farrell scanned the photographed prints from Z, H, D, R and Y into his computer and, brushing the sweat from his brow, began to look for possible matches in the police fingerprint records with the two whorl-patterned prints he had lifted from the Z key. The clock marched inexorably towards five o'clock.

64

December 1999

Violet Frayne's final act had been to kiss her grandson's forehead. She fell back and breathed a last, tired breath: her grey hair was spread out on the pillows of her hospital bed. Then she was gone. Crowan Frayne watched her closely. He had hoped to see her spirit quit her body with that final resigned breath. Instead he saw nothing and felt only the gradual relaxation of her grip on his hand. He was alone, absolutely without meaning. A nothingness without form or direction.

He leaned forward and brushed his grandmother's hair back from her face. Beside the bed were the flowers and plants that he had brought her. Crowan Frayne pulled some petals from the African violet and scattered them softly over the pillow. He reached for her treasured leather-bound book of Donne and turned to the page that he had selected for this moment. *Sotto voce*, below the hum of machines and the clatter of the ward, Crowan Frayne began to read from 'The Extasie':

> *'Where like a pillow on a bed*
> *A Pregnant banke swel'd up to rest*
> *The violets reclining head*
> *Sat we two, one anothers best*
>
> *'Our hands were firmely cimented*
> *With a fast balme, which thence did spring*
> *Our eye beames twisted and did thread*
> *Our eyes upon one double string.'*

To his frustration, he could read no further. Tears welled up in his eyes and he squeezed them back, swallowing the pain in deep acid draughts as he always had. He had disappointed her in death as he had failed her in life. She was the intelligence: the angel that had moved his physical and intellectual cosmos. She had given the spheres their strange and beautiful music, put poetry into his darkest, most senseless thoughts, bound his thoughts with hers on one double string. Violet Frayne had fired the alchemy that was glowing now in his soul: Frayne could see the divine in the mundane, music behind the terrible vastness of space and time, celebration in desecration, the yoking of opposites. Wit in horror.

Like a billion burning magnets, his thoughts sought connections. Some were unusual and disturbing, as if terrible predators swam in the dopamine and serotonin that connected his neural transmitters and receptors. Monsters hid between his cells and in the electrical pulses of his thoughts. What if they were the spirits? *'As our blood labours to beget, Spirits . . . that subtile knot that makes us man,'* Donne had written. The spirits lived in human blood and communicated the brain's instructions to the body. What if monsters, abominations of time and evolution, deformed and malignant, were the binders that united his mind with his body?

The thought dug like a scalpel at the matter of his brain. Could he marshal those monsters to celebrate her? Could he use their alchemy to convert the banality and ugliness of the life she had endured into the rarefication of beauty that she deserved in death? When he had smashed the glass eyes he had turned her agonies inside out. He had snagged the monsters that dwelt in her blood and hauled them writhing to the surface. She had injected beauty into his soul and he had revealed her ugliness in return. He despised himself for that. He would make amends.

Crowan Frayne kissed his dead grandmother's hand and promised he would make her beautiful again.

65

'You're a sick man, Mr Underwood,' said Dr Barozzi as he read the inspector's charts. 'You are lucky to be alive.'

'I know.' Underwood's head still swam with exhaustion and

traces of drugs. Clarity was beginning to return, however, like fresh air circulating in a dark stuffy room.

'You have had a minor heart attack. Your signs are now stable.'

'Thank you.'

'You have a severe infection of the pleural membrane in your left lung. This has put a huge strain on your cardiovascular system. How long have you had this lung infection?'

'A long time.' Underwood's throat was dry and painful. It hurt to talk.

'Six months?'

'More.'

'A year?'

'Perhaps.'

Dr Barozzi shook his head slowly. 'Your left lung is a mess. It's dog meat, to be blunt. You have let this go much too far. Men of your age have to take care of themselves. You have put your heart under terrible strain through your own negligence. It's like taking the pin out of a hand grenade, then jumping up and down with it in your breast pocket.' Barozzi smiled at his own imagery.

'I understand.'

'We have put you on a course of powerful antibiotics. These will attack the infection in your lung but you will feel tired for some time. Your heart is weak and the strain of fighting this infection will take it out of you.'

Underwood was floating away. He could feel exhaustion crawling through his veins like water through tissue paper.

'I will be back to see you tomorrow.' Barozzi reattached the chart board to the foot of Underwood's bed. 'I've left some papers by the side of your bed in case you feel like reading.'

Underwood drifted off to sleep for a couple of minutes. He dreamed of his parents; less distant now than when they were alive. 28 September 1988 and 3 March 1989. Gone within six months of each other. He woke suddenly. Would he have killed Paul Heyer? Would he have kicked him over the cliff edge and watched him smash onto the rocks below?

The killer of Lucy Harrington and Elizabeth Drury was giggling at him, pulling the strings in the back of his head.

He opened his eyes and looked over at the bedside cabinet. There was a small pile of newspapers: The *Independent*, the *Daily Mail* and the *New Bolden Echo*. Underwood reached over for the local newspaper. It was a week old. Lucy Harrington's smiling face looked back at him from the front page: 'Local Girl Strikes Gold' boomed the headline happily.

The killer was local, thought Underwood. *He read this story. It surprised him and occasioned his actions. Why? The name. The killer liked John Donne. Lucy Harrington was a member of Donne's coterie. He saw the name and got the idea. Why now, though?* Underwood remembered that serial killers built and adapted their fantasies over time. *Lucy Harrington didn't give the murderer his idea. She occasioned it. Something about the story occasioned his fantasy. Occasioned his need to educate and explain.*

He tried to read the article that he had already read ten times at the station over the previous week. But his eyes failed him and he drifted away again, drugs lapping at his consciousness like waves on a lonely shore. Underwood dreamed he was walking with his parents on a pebbled beach. He threw pebbles into the sea, watching them skim across the waves. None of them sank into the water. They bounced over the wave tops until they faded out of sight, over the horizon. He looked at the pebble in his hand. It was an eye.

66

Dexter lay half-asleep in bloody exhaustion. She had loosened the bindings slightly but at a cost. Her wrists bled painfully and she felt no closer to manoeuvring herself free. She had been in the darkness for what seemed like hours. No one had come for her. Had the killer left her in the basement of a deserted house to rot and starve to death in the dark? The thought terrified her. A blow to the head would end things quickly. She would prefer that. She was brave, always had been. Crying alone and soundlessly in the dark terrified her. It was the terror of waiting to be born.

67

Heather Stussman took a taxi from Southwell College to Cambridge Station, then boarded a local train to New Bolden. She was alone.

Crowan Frayne had watched Stussman board the train and had then driven at high speed, but within the speed limits, to New Bolden station. He beat her train there by five minutes. Stussman stepped out into the unfamiliar environment of New Bolden and immediately climbed into a minicab. Frayne followed at a distance, two cars back. He knew that she would be expecting him. No other cars appeared to be following her. Perhaps she would go through with it. He dared to dream.

Once he was confident she was heading for the cemetery, Crowan Frayne accelerated past the minicab. He knew a short cut and found a quiet place to park his van. Following Stussman from Cambridge meant that he hadn't checked the cemetery. He would do that now.

Stussman climbed from her minicab at the main entrance to the cemetery. She shivered in the dry cold of the gathering darkness. The driver had told her that the war memorial was in the centre of the site, a two-minute walk from the road. The red lights of the car flared briefly at her as the minicab braked, turned right along Station Road and disappeared. She was alone. She felt the cold steel of the carving knife in her coat pocket and walked through the cast-iron gates into New Bolden Cemetery.

There was a path lined with imitation gas lamps that led into the heart of the graveyard. Stussman stepped briskly along the hazy yellow trail, her shoes crunching the gravel underfoot. It seemed to stretch endlessly into the darkness: there were black outlines of headstones all around that seemed to lean towards her, throwing strangely shaped shadows against the murmuring grass: angels and carved flowers, open Bibles and crosses. The wind moved silently through the naked trees and chilled stone. She looked behind her and ahead. She could see nobody. Fear pricked at her skin, together with the crisp air. He was out there, moving with her like a shadow in the textured blackness. She was illuminated like a good soul in hell.

The war memorial loomed suddenly. Stussman's heart hammered at her chest. She would give him five minutes. A train rattled and moaned in the near distance. She stood with her back against the cold marble of the monolith, felt the carved names of the dead press into her back. It was disrespectful, but at least it meant that no one could creep up behind her. If he came at her it would be from the front or the sides and she would have a second or two to draw the knife from her pocket.

She knew that she had to be mad. Coming to this place was a terrible mistake. She checked her watch: 5.15. Johnson would call the police in forty-five minutes if she didn't call. It seemed like a long time now. She could be fifteen or twenty miles away in forty-five minutes. What would she do if he appeared? She hadn't really constructed much of a strategy except self-defence. Stussman suspected that the killer might be suicidal and she hoped she could play to that if they started a discussion – encourage him, even.

'Good evening, Dr Stussman.'

The voice came from directly in front of her. Out of the darkness. Heather Stussman jumped in terror and gripped the handle of the carving knife in her pocket. As she tried desperately to make out a face or a form, she half withdrew the knife in case he ran at her.

'Who's there?' she said. It sounded pathetic, reedy and shrill in the vast openness of the cemetery.

'I think you know,' the voice said.

'What should I call you?'

'Nothing.'

Her eyes were becoming accustomed to the dark. She thought she could make out a figure, straight ahead of her in the shadows. He was clever. He had chosen this spot carefully and deliberately. The same lights that illuminated her and the war memorial blinded Heather Stussman to the area beyond the pathway.

'I am alone,' she said.

'So it seems,' said Crowan Frayne. 'Who did you tell? Not the police.'

'I haven't told anyone where I am. However, I have left a sealed envelope at Southwell College. It contains details of the arrangements for our meeting. It will be opened if I do not call in during the next half an hour.'

'Very resourceful of you.' Crowan Frayne stepped from the shadows onto the pathway. She could see him now: tall and lean, silhouetted. A hole in the night.

'Where is Sergeant Dexter?'

'Safe.' He didn't move.

'I want to see her.'

'You will.'

Heather Stussman shivered. There was a terrible calm about the man.

'I would like you to come with me.'

'Where to?'

'There is a grave plot some twenty metres from here. I would like you to see it.'

'Why?'

'It's important. Step out onto the pathway and walk. Please.'

'You're going to kill me.'

'If you don't do as I say, I surely will.'

Stussman stepped away from the war memorial and onto the gravel pathway. The killer stood some two metres from her now. She could see his face more clearly: thin and gaunt, gouged with deep lines of sadness. His eyes appeared black – as if they weren't there. He gestured to her to start walking. He stayed a couple of paces behind. Stussman kept her right hand in her pocket.

'Let me guess,' said Crowan Frayne from behind her. 'A screwdriver or a Southwell College cheese knife?'

She cursed quietly. She could hear him smiling. 'It's a carving knife and if you screw with me I will stick it into your dick.'

'That won't be necessary. Turn left here.'

They had arrived where two pathways crossed. Stussman did exactly as she was told. There was a cluster of small gravestones to her right. They had walked about ten yards when she heard Frayne step off the gravel. She stopped and looked around. He was standing looking down at a grave. *So, Stussman thought, you have lost someone and now you want to join them.* How could she use that to her advantage? She took a step towards him.

'Someone who was close to you?' she asked softly.

'She *is* me. She penetrates my every thought and action, every molecule that holds me together. Just as a tree draws up the dead in its sap and its leaves, in the yellow and white of its flowers, so she is drawn up into me. See her blossoming beauty.' He stretched his arms to the sky.

'Who was she?'

Crowan Frayne gestured to her to approach him. Stussman did so and turned to look at the inscription on the headstone. Frayne shone a torch on the stone. She read aloud, *sotto voce*:

'*Violet Frayne 1908–1999, beloved mother and grandmother. One short sleep past, we wake eternally, and death shall be no more. Death, thou shalt die.*'

Frayne stood absolutely still as Stussman read. She paused and turned to him. She was close now, dangerously close.

'It's from the "Holy Sonnets". Death be not proud, for though some have called thee mighty and dreadful . . .'

'Thou art not so,' said Crowan Frayne.

'Were you very close?'

Frayne ignored her and raised his eyes to the sky. The stars blinked and sung back to him. He relaxed his grip on the torch and its light drifted over onto the next headstone. Stussman read it to herself. '*Elizabeth Frayne, 1944–1967.*'

'Is this your mother?'

'She facilitated me. She was fortunate to work such an alchemy.' Frayne knelt at Violet's grave and scooped up a handful of dirt. He stood and placed it in his mouth, turning to face Stussman. She took an instinctive step backwards. Soil fell from Crowan Frayne's mouth as he chewed.

'Aristotle believed that stones and plants, animals and men all had souls. Am I correct, Dr Stussman? I suck their souls from the earth. These flowers – ' he pulled up a clump from the ground ' – are rich with my grandmother's colour and spirit. Her intelligence gives their simple cell divisions and chemical reactions a breathtaking musicality.'

Frayne tore off the leaves and petals and ate them vigorously. 'A year ago today my grandmother died under the same sky, these same stars. Her spirit was engulfed by the soft cadences of the *Harmoniae Mundorum* – the same pitches and rhythms that we hear now, infusing this place.' He raised his hands to the vast celestial orchestra, as if he was conducting their strange and terrible music: the music of time, separation and creation that had triangulated across the infinities and sharpened to a white-hot point in his brain. 'And yet she remains incomplete, an abomination.'

Stussman watched him, uncertain whether to run away as his attention plummeted through the dark pools of his imagination. But he would catch her, she knew. Besides, she was lost in an unfamiliar place. He turned back to her.

'Life is an ugliness, Dr Stussman. My grandmother defined beauty and yet she was herself an exhibit of ugliness. I was born in ugliness; the ugliness of loss and agony. My life has been an ugliness and yet I scale the heights of beauty and wit.' He moved his hand in a sudden, flicking movement and hurled dirt and grit into Stussman's face. She staggered back, her hands at her face, trying to push away the scratching, dirty pain in her eyes. 'Do you feel the salty sting of my wit, Dr Stussman?' he asked as he advanced on her. 'Do you roast in the flames of unexpected genius? Do your eyes burn as if they had seen the very face of God?'

Stussman fell backwards over a gravestone and in a second Crowan Frayne was on her. He put his foot against her throat and quickly took the knife from her pocket, flinging it into the anonymous distance. He hauled her, kicking and writhing, back to Violet Frayne's grave and, rolling her over, pushed her face into the dirt. Stussman panicked as the pain seared at her eyes and she struggled for breath.

'Take a long, deep, luxurious mouthful, Dr Stussman. Let the elemental dead crawl across your tongue and infuse your consciousness with music and colour.' He pushed her harder into the soil. Mud forced its way into her mouth. She felt sick as it tickled her throat. 'This is the taste of death, Dr Stussman. Relish it. There is transcendent beauty in its ugliness. The earth is enriched. *I am every dead thing/In whom love wrought new Alchemie/For his art did expresse/A quintessence even from nothingness.*' Frayne pulled Stussman's face from the mud. She was coughing and retching. 'Tonight, Dr Stussman, we will complete my grandmother's ascent back to beauty. We will become the burning soul of wit. Through the alchemy of our intelligence, the chanting voices of the dead that we draw together and amplify, we will forge angels in the oven and rise into infinity like smoke on the wind.'

Crowan Frayne struck Heather Stussman on her right temple with the butt of his torch. Then he struck her again.

68

Harrison called Marty Farrell at six-fifteen that evening. He had just received a call himself from the Head Porter of Southwell College and had learned that Heather Stussman had met with the killer an hour previously. A squad car had been dispatched to the cemetery immediately and had found nothing.

Farrell picked up the phone on its fourth ring. 'Lab.'

'Marty, it's Harrison.'

'No joy as yet. The only clean match I've found so far is Dexter's right index finger.'

'Fuck. It looks like he's taken someone else.'

Marty groaned. 'Who?'

'Stussman, the lecturer.'

'Jesus.' Marty was already exhausted and the pressure had just been upped another notch.

'I don't need to tell you, Marty, that it's going to be a long night. You might be our only chance of finding this fruitcake.'

'I realize that. You need to understand something, though.' Farrell took off his glasses and rubbed the bridge of his nose. 'I have started with the less common letters in the two names you gave me. I've looked at D, R, J, T, H, and U, and haven't found any matches in our records except Dexter. I'm about to do Z, B, N and Y now. It's taken me six hours to get this far. Most of the prints are partial and overlaid with others. Getting the computer to match smeared partial prints with our files is virtually impossible. If I have to broaden the search and check every print on the keyboard I shall be here all night. And some.'

'That might be too late, Marty.'

'I'd better get on with it, then.'

'Call me. When you get something.' Harrison hung up.

Marty Farrell sighed and tried to clear his head. He was beginning to think that this was a wild-goose chase. Not so much looking for a needle in a haystack as looking for a specific needle in a room full of needles. The thought of dusting and analysing every key on the computer filled him with gloom. There had to be a way he could short-cut the process. He swallowed the remains of his cup of coffee and frowned in concentration.

Z, B, N and Y. He had lifted five partials from those keys. It could take two or three hours for his computer to process them. Could he prioritize those in some way? He thought about the software that the library computer used. He knew it was a basically just a search program. The same kind of format that he used to access files on the Cambridgeshire Police mainframe. How did that work? It was easy, he remembered. You just typed the name of the person you wanted to find and pressed the 'Return' key. He made a mental note to dust the 'Return' key of the library computer. However, that didn't seem very promising: everyone who used the system would have pressed 'Return' at some point. There would be dozens of prints, all of them smudged beyond recognition.

What else, then? Separation. You separated the forenames and surname of each subject with a comma. The same problem applied, though. Every user would have touched the comma key for precisely that purpose. He needed to isolate a key that only

258

the killer had used. *Forename and surname.* The thought niggled at him. Why didn't that sound right? In the back of Marty Farrell's head an idea began to germinate. Suddenly he closed his eyes and cursed at his own stupidity.

The principal search term was always the subject's surname. You typed the surname first, then the comma, then the forename. In fact, on many of these systems you didn't even need to enter a forename: the database presented a list of subjects with the same surname and you could just click on the one that you wanted.

Marty looked again at the letters he had already checked: D, R, J, T, H, and U. Dexter's prints had turned up on D and R but not on U. What did that mean? Dexter had typed in the first two letters of 'Drury' and the computer had defaulted to the name typed in by the killer. Dexter hadn't needed to type in the woman's full surname. But the killer must have done. The U key was smeared with a number of prints so fragmentary and corrupted that he had been unable to lift any usable prints from it.

Z, B, N and Y. He thought for a second. The killer must have typed in 'Drury' in full. He had to have pressed the Y key. Y was a less common letter than U. Marty called up the partial print he had lifted from the Y key on to his computer screen. It was a fragment: about a third of a full print. Right index finger, most likely: classic loop pattern. He decided to take a chance. He selected the print and ran for matches. The system began sorting through its files. This was the tedious part of the process; the time-consuming part.

Marty stood and walked out of the laboratory area and into the toilet. He splashed some cold water on his face. He was annoyed with himself. He had wasted so much time concentrating on the wrong letters: he should have realized that the letters making up the surnames of 'Donne' and 'Drury' were potentially the most useful targets. Marty dried his face on a paper towel and walked round to the coffee machine. The coffee was nearly always awful but he needed some sustenance. He chose a cappuccino with extra sugar and walked back into the laboratory.

A light blue dialogue box had appeared on the centre of his

computer screen. Marty put his coffee down carefully. The box said: *Print Search: One Possible Match*. He tried to contain his excitement and clicked on the dialogue box. It took a second for the next screen to appear:

Eleven Point Match: Probability 68.75%

Subject Record Loading

Please Wait.

Marty Farrell tapped his finger against the Formica surface of his desk. It took a minute for the file to upload. He wrote down the details as they appeared on the screen:

Subject Name:	*Frayne, Crowan*
Date of Birth:	*11 February 1967*
Address:	*Flat C*
	Beaufort House
	Ravenswood Estate
	New Bolden NM6 8QJ
Arrested:	*5 September 1995, Brierly Veterinary Practice, NM*
	Suspected Breaking and Entering
Arresting Officers:	*PC Woods & PC Hillgate*
Conviction:	*Criminal Damage & Resisting Arrest*
	17 November 1995, NM Magistrates Court

Marty Farrell picked up his phone and dialled the Incident Room. He had a name and an address. *Suspected breaking and entering.* The words sent a chill down the length of his spine. Marty allowed himself a smile as Crowan Frayne's picture slowly materialized on the screen.

69

Dexter started at the noises above her: a thud, footsteps and a door slamming. She strained her eyes, peering into the darkness. More footsteps, then a door opened. A blinding shaft of light blazed into the room. She tugged frantically at the binders on her wrists and the cord tightened again around her throat. He was here. This was it now. She was going to die. Her eyes quickly adjusted to the light and she looked around her. It was a basement, piled high with books. There were books everywhere. It was like the storage room under a library. There was a heavy old-fashioned wooden table in the centre of the room and three chairs arranged around it.

A torch shone in her face from the top of the stairs. She was dazzled by its intensity and yellow spots floated in front of her eyes. The light went away. She squinted hard. There were two figures on the stairs. Alison Dexter tensed again as the cord choked her. She was no longer alone.

'Sergeant Dexter.' A man's voice, his voice. 'I believe you know Dr Stussman.'

Dexter could see more clearly now as her eyes grew accustomed to the light. The killer had sat Heather Stussman in the chair next to the table. He was in the process of tying her hands behind her. She had a black plastic bag over her head. Once Frayne had secured her to the chair he untied the bag and pulled it from her face. Stussman's head lolled drunkenly to one side. She was swimming in and out of consciousness, mumbling to herself. Satisfied that Stussman was secure, Crowan Frayne walked quickly around the table and dragged Alison Dexter up from the ground.

'I apologize for leaving you alone. But, as you can see, I have had a busy afternoon.'

Dexter swore at him through her gag and coughed as the cord cut across her windpipe. Frayne placed her in the chair opposite Stussman and loosened the line around her neck. Then he left the room, bounding up the stairs like an excited child and slamming the door behind him.

The room plunged into darkness and Dexter sat at the table in frightened confusion, listening to Heather Stussman's soft moans. She started work again on her wrists. The pain was acute, gnawing at her flesh like an insistent, hungry animal. She drove herself on with the thought of what she would do to her captor's face if she managed to work herself free. When the pain became almost too much to bear, she thought of what *he* might do to *her* face if she couldn't get free.

Five minutes passed and he returned. The room was again bathed in light. Crowan Frayne stepped and clanked awkwardly down the wooden stairs, carrying a large metal barrel. It looked like an oil drum. Dexter watched him place it next to a stack of books and go back into the main part of the house. When he re-emerged Frayne was carrying a large brass candlestick that resembled a short metal tree with eight small wax candles attached. He put the object on the table between Dexter and Stussman and lit each of the candles in turn. Their flickering light illuminated Stussman's face: Dexter could see that she had been bleeding. Crowan Frayne sat at the table and placed his black leather box of antique medical instruments in front of him.

The gaunt lines of his terrible face creased into an abomination of a smile as he looked at Dexter.

'Now then,' he said, clapping his hands together. 'Shall we begin?'

70

Three squad cars raced through the centre of New Bolden, a whirl of blue flashing lights and noise. Harrison was in the lead car. In all, ten officers accompanied him. He would have liked some firearms specialists with him but there hadn't been time to call in the team from Huntingdon. Harrison hoped that surprise and the weight of numbers would be enough to overwhelm Crowan Frayne.

The Ravenswood estate was an unpleasant sprawl of local-authority accommodation on the northern outskirts of the town. It took fifteen minutes for the cars to cut through the evening traffic. As they approached the estate from the south, the car sirens and lights were switched off. Beaufort House was a square, grey oblong in the centre of the Ravenswood. Harrison ordered that the cars park out of sight of Beaufort House and his team ran the final hundred yards. Surprise would be everything.

Flat C was on the first floor. There was no light on. Harrison ordered two officers to wait at the foot of the stairwell and two more at the entrance to the lifts. He led the remaining officers up the piss-smelling stairs to the door of Flat C. Barker, a heavy-set uniform sergeant came forward with a large sledge hammer and, at Harrison's signal, smashed open the front door.

The team piled in, shining torches into the darkness. The flat smelled stale and dirty. As soon as Harrison breathed the dead air, he knew Frayne wasn't inside. It was the smell of neglect and absence. He had recognized it immediately. It reminded him of the smell he had encountered in the houses of old-age pensioners who had died of hypothermia and been left to decay in their own beds. His officers kicked open the doors to both bedrooms and the kitchen. The living room was barely furnished. There were no books or ornaments. There was no television.

Harrison sat down in a threadbare brown armchair and looked at the shelf in front of him. There were eight glass flasks arranged in a neat line. He shone his torch at them. Each contained two or more eyes. They varied in size and colour from small yellow-centred pebbles that Harrison presumed had been taken from cats, to large scraggy-looking dog and sheep eyes.

'Practice makes perfect,' Harrison muttered to himself.

Sergeant Barker flicked on the living-room light and started in shock as a row of floating eyes glowered back at him. 'Stone me!' he cursed as he jumped. 'He's not here, guv. There's no sign.'

'Check all the drawers and cupboards. Bag everything,' said Harrison. 'If you find any envelopes or forms with another address on them let me know right away.' Frustration smacked him sharply in the face and he slammed his fist against the dusty arm of the chair.

'Fuck!'

He thought of Dexter and Heather Stussman. They were dead now, for sure.

71

The ward was nearly empty now, apart from the duty nurse and the male orderly who was chatting quietly to her. Underwood had woken ten minutes previously as the last dinner trays had been collected and taken away, clattering. He had not eaten and wasn't hungry. In fact, he felt so nauseous that he thought he might never eat again.

He picked up the *New Bolden Echo* lying on top of the cabinet next to his bed. He was faintly annoyed that no one other than Dexter had come to visit him. Then he remembered that he didn't have anyone other than Dexter. Once Paul Heyer and Julia recovered, Underwood knew that he would receive lots of visitors: solicitors, the Chief Super, Norwich police. He tried to sort through the fragments of memory and madness that still littered his brain. It was painful to walk there.

Lucy Harrington stared at him accusingly from the front page of the newspaper. He remembered the gaping hole in her face, the corruption of her beauty. She had been a strong, successful athlete, butchered for no reason. She left behind a devastated family who had supported and encouraged her in life. Now they would mourn the idiocy of her death. Underwood almost envied her. Who would mourn him? He had been cut adrift on an ocean of uncertainty; smashed against the dark edges of his personality. *The people around us define us and bind us together. When those people fall away we are left alone to unpick the fabric of ourselves as if it were the only way to fill the silences.*

Underwood's attention drifted back to the newspaper. He couldn't bring himself to read about Lucy's achievements again. He turned the pages slowly and with little interest. Most of the stories were tedious local news items about old ladies being mugged and pets winning awards at shows. He didn't read them. Had the killer bothered to read the rest of the paper?

The date on the newspaper was 1 December, just over a week before Lucy Harrington had been murdered. The killer had called the author of the article – George Gardiner – the morning after he had killed Lucy Harrington. He had read this paper and found something he hadn't expected: a name that resounded with significance. *A Providence, if you like,* Underwood mused, *a catalyst.* If finding Lucy Harrington had been unexpected, had the murderer been looking for something else? What would you look for in a local paper? What would a local man look for in a local paper?

Himself, perhaps. Or someone he knew, someone he was close to. *The people around us define us and bind us together,* Underwood thought again. *When they fall away we pick ourselves apart. The killer values the wit of strange connections. He connected Lucy Harrington with something else he was looking for.* Underwood looked at the rain thumping on the window; he thought of Julia, of his parents. *When they fall away we pick ourselves apart.*

'Jesus Christ,' he whispered to himself. He turned to page seventeen of the *New Bolden Echo*: the page that contained birth, marriage and death announcements. His tired eyes scanned the page quickly. He discounted births and marriages, concentrating instead on the death announcements. The first two obituaries didn't seem appropriate: they were written in the clipped middle-class prose that announced deaths as if they were changes in a cast list at an amateur-dramatics evening. The third obituary in the column grabbed his attention, though:

Violet Frayne, d. 13 December 1999, beloved mother and grandmother. Shee by whose lines proportion should be examin'd, Measure of all Symmetree, Whom had that Ancient seen, Who thought Soules made of Harmony, He would at next have said, That Harmony was she.

Underwood knew he had him. He recognized the dedication. It was from Donne's 'The First Anniversary': the poem that the killer had written on Elizabeth Drury's ceiling. This woman, whoever she had been – mother, grandmother – had died a year before this edition of the newspaper had been produced. So that was it. The killer had been commemorating the first anniversary of the death when, by chance, Lucy Harrington's beautiful round eyes had illumined his grief.

Underwood reached over for his mobile phone and dialled the Incident Room. A woman answered.

'Dexter?' he asked.

'No,' said a weary voice. 'This is Jensen.'

'Jensen, it's Inspector Underwood.'

'Hello, sir.' She sounded surprised. 'How are you feeling?'

'Listen to me, Jensen. I think I have the killer's name. His surname, at least. I won't bother you with the details but tell Dexter that I think his name is Frayne, F-R-A-Y-N-E.'

'We think so too, sir. We lifted the prints of a Crowan Frayne from the computer terminal at New Bolden Library. Harrison went to his flat with a team about twenty minutes ago. There's no one there. Harrison reckons the flat's been deserted for some time. I was just trying to dig up some more information on Frayne. Job records, relatives and so on.'

'Look for a Violet Frayne. I think it's his mother or grand-mother. She died a year ago but I think she lived locally.' Underwood paused for a second. 'Did you say Harrison had gone after the killer?'

'That's right, sir.'

'Where's Dexter?'

Jensen bit her lip. *He didn't know . . . how could he know?* She took a deep breath and briefly told the inspector the story of Dexter's abduction, of Dr Stussman's meeting with the killer and subsequent disappearance and of how she, DC Jensen, had been knocking on doors all day and had missed virtually all the excitement. By the end of the story Underwood had stopped listening. He knew that Dexter and Stussman were dead. And

266

he was truly alone. He hung up before Jensen had finished speaking.

Annoyed by Underwood's hanging up on her but focused on the task in hand, DC Jensen tried to call up the name of Violet Frayne on the New Bolden electoral roll. The database was two years old so if the woman had died twelve months ago she should still appear on record. It only took a couple of minutes to find her: Violet Frayne, 12 Willow Road, Hawstead, New Bolden. Jensen called Harrison's mobile on her way out of the Incident Room.

72

The candles smoothed shadows across Crowan Frayne's face as he read from memory. Heather Stussman's eyes were open now and her gaze was fixed upon Dexter in fear and expectation. Dexter watched Frayne and worked at her bindings as he spoke. Frayne had been reciting 'A Nocturnall upon St Lucies Day, Being the Shortest Day'. His dry, rasping voice rose and fell like a boat on an ocean as he drifted through the last verse.

'But I am None; nor will my sunne renew
You lovers, for whose sake the lesser Sunne
At this time to the Goat is runne
To fetch new lust, and give it you.'

The candle flames bent and sparked slightly as Frayne's breath cut across them. Dexter looked around the room. There were great piles of books everywhere, some ancient and expensive, some falling apart at the bindings. She tried to piece together the jigsaw. The oil drum concerned her. It seemed incongruous, an ugliness. What was he trying to achieve?

'Enjoy your summer, all
Since shee enjoyes her long night's festival

Let me prepare towards her, and let me call
This houre her Vigill and her Eve, since this
Both the yeare's and the daye's deep midnight is.'

Frayne paused for a second and then turned to face Heather
Stussman, wild-eyed, gagged and seated at the table. Frayne
opened his box of medical equipment and stared at the glittering
rows of scalpels and scissors. His hand hovered over the box
like a sparrow hawk until he selected one of the heavier-looking
scalpels. He stood and walked around the table to Heather
Stussman.

'Dr Stussman, I am going to remove your gag now. If you
scream or attempt to scream I will insert this instrument into
Sergeant Dexter's left eye. Do you understand?'

Terrified and shaking, Heather Stussman nodded her agree-
ment. In a swift movement, Frayne sliced the masking tape gag
from her mouth and returned to his chair.

'So, Dr Stussman, lecturer in English at Cambridge University,
tell me about "A Nocturnall upon St Lucies Day, Being the
Shortest Day."

Stussman frowned. Sweat streamed from her brow into her
eyes. She tried to blink it away. 'What can I tell you that you
don't already know?'

'It's what *you* don't know that I am interested in,' said
Crowan Frayne as he replaced his scalpel into its holder and ran
a gentle finger across his other instruments.

Stussman breathed deeply. 'It's a poem about bereavement. St
Lucy's Day was regarded as the longest, darkest night of the
year.' She looked over at Dexter, 'December the thirteenth.
Today.'

Stussman paused. What did he want her to say? She decided
to keep it simple and apply her own basic critical model. 'The
poem is probably about his wife Ann. She died in childbirth.
There are five stanzas, each with nine lines. The rhyme scheme
is fairly standard and straightforward: ABBACCCDD. The rep-
etition of rhymes at the end of each stanza is deliberate.' She
dared to look in Frayne's direction. He nodded encouragement.
'It is calculated to enforce the sense of despair: the rhymes are

268

heavy and ponderous, like "drunk" and "shrunk", "laugh" and "epitaph", "absences" and "carcasses".'

'What about the conceit?' Frayne took another blade from the box and held it to the light.

'Donne says that by the woman's death he has become a quintessential nothing. The nothing that predated Creation. An absolute nothingness. He says that even stones and rocks have some kind of spirituality.'

Frayne smiled at Dexter. 'Aristotle.'

'Yes, it's an Aristotelian idea.' Stussman started speaking more rapidly as Frayne stood and began to walk around the table. 'Then he resolves to join with the dead woman, he yearns for annihilation, to become nothingness on the darkest, longest night of the year.'

Frayne walked around the table to Dexter and stood next to her, blade in hand. Stussman desperately groped for something else to say. 'It's an interesting theological point explored by Augustine and Aquinas: can a man wish to become nothing? If being nothing is better than his present state then surely it must be *something*. Now, in my opinion—'

Frayne cut her off in mid-sentence. 'Suddenly a man may wish himself nothing, because that seems to deliver him from the sense of his present misery.' His eyes rolled in his head, like a shark biting down on its prey, as he remembered the remainder of the quotation. 'But deliberately he cannot; because whatsoever a man wishes, must be something better than he hath yet; and whatsoever is better is not nothing.' He reached down and cut away Dexter's gag. 'Donne's *Sermons*, yes?'

'Yes,' said Heather Stussman.

Dexter gulped air into her dry mouth. 'Listen to me,' she said to Crowan Frayne. 'This is madness. Let us go. There are people who can help you. I can arrange that.'

Frayne frowned at her, curious. 'You think I need help, sergeant? Do you think I am a monster? Or a madman like the tramps who drink lighter fuel by the bus station and think they can fly?'

'I didn't say that.' She struggled to find neutral language, 'I don't think that you're mad but I *do* think that you need help. I am prepared to help you.' The tape was loosening slightly on her wrists. If she could stay alive for a couple more minutes . . .

'You make an interesting point, Alison.' Frayne moved away from her. 'You have the ability to make strange connections about people. What is the essence of that, do you think?'

'I don't understand the question,' Dexter replied. *Keep him talking* . . .

'Let me rephrase, it then. What do you think that Dr Stussman here missed in her analysis of the poem?'

'I am not an expert,' said Dexter. 'I don't understand poetry.'

'I think you understand people, though.' Frayne picked up a roll of black masking tape from the floor. He tore off a long strip and wrapped it around Stussman's mouth. 'Let me help you. The poem is a man's response to bereavement, to the loss of his wife and daughter. Dr Stussman talked very lucidly about the structure of the poem, of the devices employed by the poet to attain his ends. She even entertained us with a snapshot of the theological tensions that underpin man's desire for annihilation.'

He moved his left hand across Stussman's face, feeling the smooth ridges of her cheekbones, the elastic perfection of her eyeballs. 'What's missing?'

Dexter saw where he was driving her. 'She didn't talk about the pain. The man's emotions.'

'Correct!' Frayne seemed pleased as he drew the hair back from Stussman's face. 'The word is "pity". It is a concept that I am sure Dr Stussman understands but she is afraid to apply. You see, sergeant, "pity" is a literary term. Tragedy is meaningless unless you pity the protagonist.'

'I don't understand.'

'Unless his condition arouses pity in the audience, feelings of compassion that arise from empathizing with his desperate condition, his redemption has no more meaning than his suffering. Dr Stussman is a literary electrician. She understands circuitry and technique in language. In many respects she is original. However, unless one has the honesty and the courage to embrace one's own agonies, how can we understand the pain of others? Dr Stussman's ivory tower is in her head. Poetry is not mathematics, you see, Alison: it grows from the agonies of the soul.

It bleeds. If Dr Stussman had the capacity to feel pity, her logical structures would be beautiful.'

'Did you pity Lucy Harrington and Elizabeth Drury, then?' said Dexter angrily, despite her fear. 'Or those two kids that you beat to death and pushed into a stream?'

'No,' said Crowan Frayne. 'But I pity *you*, Alison. Your cleverness has made you lonely like me.' He pulled back Stussman's chair so he could get around in front of her. 'And I pity you, Dr Stussman. So I am going to help you both. I am going to show you that beauty can come from ugliness – and once we have each attained beauty we will become angels together.'

With his left hand Crowan Frayne held Heather Stussman by the neck. With his right hand he sliced the four letters that spelled 'PITY' into her forehead with his scalpel. Stussman screamed noiselessly into her gag as blood streamed down her face. Crowan Frayne stepped back to admire his handiwork.

'Now, Heather, you are beautiful,' he said happily. 'You are complete. Pity should arouse pain.' He wiped the scalpel against his trousers and replaced it in his equipment box.

'You bastard!' Dexter shouted at him. 'What kind of sick fucker are you?'

Crowan Frayne held a finger to his mouth and shushed her. He walked over to a bookcase and picked up a small wooden box. He placed it on the table between Dexter and the sobbing Stussman.

'Guess who?' he asked as he opened the box.

Dexter saw the two bloodied eyes staring back at her and thought she might be sick. Lucy Harrington and Elizabeth Drury glared angrily at her.

'What do you suppose, Alison Dexter?' asked Crowan Frayne. 'Is she not beautiful?'

'Who? All I can see is a bloody mess that you created.'

'You're closer to the truth than you realize, Alison. As I said, you have the ability to make strange connections. Sometimes you do it in ignorance of yourself. Donne would regard you as a wit. Remember that beauty is born of ugliness. Worthiness is born of failure.'

'We learn from our mistakes?' Dexter snarled at him. 'Is that the best you can do? That doesn't strike me as especially witty. More like a big bloody cliché.' She stopped herself from saying anything else: there was still one empty space in the eye box.

'I was born of an ugliness, Sergeant Dexter. Unwanted and unloved, an accident that killed my mother as surely as if she'd walked under a bus. I was born in death. Infused with its ugliness at a subatomic level. But my grandmother created beautiful structures in my soul. She was an alchemist where Dr Stussman is an electrician. She refracted darkness and made it light, catalysed music from white noise, drew poetry from the billion dead voices shouting in my head.'

'What has that got to do with us?' Dexter shouted at him. She had a sense that events were beginning to accelerate. A reckoning was approaching.

'Everything. You see, she hid her ugliness, the darkness of her times and her life. She kept her pain in a wooden box in her bedroom. I found it. The tiny universe of pain and experience she had compressed into this box, into three glass eyes. How fragile and corruptible beauty is. I exposed her horror to the world. It overwhelmed her. I took her placid beauty and made her abhorrent to herself. She saw herself in my eyes and finally knew her own ugliness.'

Stussman moaned in pain, her face a curtain of blood. Dexter had almost worked her hands free. Now she just needed an opportunity. Frayne moved to the foot of the stairs and rolled the oil drum to the centre of the room.

'So I resolved to become the alchemist, Sergeant Dexter. I decided to take the ugliness I had created, the base matter if you like, and restore it to beauty.'

'You're replacing her eyes?' Dexter asked, playing for time.

'I am creating poetry, Alison. I am reaching beyond physics and religion, plugging the gaps in the glistening spider's web that is man's self-knowledge. Let's get Dr Stussman here to help us now she's had a rest.' Frayne peeled the tape from Stussman's mouth. She groaned in agony.

'Doctor, what are the basic characteristics of a metaphysical poem? If you fail to answer I will have to molest Sergeant Dexter's eyes.'

Stussman tried to look beyond the pain, to concentrate the agony away. 'Intellectual rigour, sexual or religious imagery, conceit . . . performance.' It was all she could manage. Stussman's head fell forward and dark spots of blood dropped onto the wooden table.

'You might say, Sergeant Dexter, that the last week has been my own valediction. You must admit it has approached poetry. The rigorous transubstantiation of ugliness into beauty: the bold and bloody imagery, oceans of tears drawn from sightless eyes. Wasn't my conceit confusing to you at first? Have you not gained knowledge and understanding as it unfolded through Harrington and Drury? Has my performance not entertained and engaged the chosen audience? Has it not dazzled you all with wit and invention? The generation of beauty out of baseness. Violet Frayne's beauty reborn from the same blood and destruction that once took it from her. It's alchemy, Alison. It's the very essence of man's struggle out of ignorance.'

'So what are you going to do now?' Dexter asked. 'How does your poem end? I suppose you'll cut my eye out and bash my head in. That doesn't strike me as poetry, though. That strikes me as exactly the kind of pig ignorance you say man has been struggling to crawl away from.'

'Why do you think I contacted Dr Stussman? Why did you think I chose women with such specific names? I meant you all to understand, Alison. I took it upon myself to educate. To educate myself and my coterie. To make you worthy. Do you read the Bible, Alison?'

'No.'

'The Book of Daniel interested Donne. The writing on the wall at the murder sites? Does that not seem reminiscent of the writing on the wall at the Palace of Nebuchadnezzar prophesying the fall of Israel?'

'No. To me it is reminiscent of a maniac with a big fucking ego.'

Frayne smiled and turned to Stussman. 'I'm sure the piteous Dr Stussman is familiar with the Book of Daniel. Tell me, doctor – ' Frayne shook Stussman violently until her eyes rolled open and her stare fixed on him ' – are we not as Shadrach, Meshach and Abednego?'

Dexter started. She remembered her first encounter with Frayne: 'bedtogoto bedtogo'. *Abednego.* She hadn't dreamed it.

'What?' said Stussman, blinking through the blood that was starting to dry in crusts around her eyes.

'Are we not worthy now? Have I not made us worthy? I have achieved alchemy, you have found pity and Alison has her mind full of strange connections. Together we are the essence of metaphysics.' Frayne unscrewed the top of the oil drum, 'Kind pitty chokes my spleene; brave scorn forbids/Those teares to issue which swell my eyelids.'

Stussman heard the words rise above her pain. The opening couplet of 'Satyre of Religion'. What did they mean? What was he thinking? She tried to think of his loss, his madness, to put herself in the centre of the inferno that raged inside Crowan Frayne's mind. *Shadrach, Meshach and Abednego.*

'We've got to get out of here,' Stussman croaked at Dexter across the table.

'I'm working on it.' Dexter had one hand free now.

'We're all going to die.'

'Not if I can help it.'

'Shadrach, Meshach and Abednego. Donne called them the children in the oven in his "Satyre of Religion". He used them as imagery.'

'What oven? What are you talking about?' Dexter was getting annoyed.

'In the Book of Daniel, Shadrach, Meshach and Abednego are cast into a burning furnace to test their faith in God. God saved their lives because of their faith and worthiness.' Stussman's wounds were starting to dry and they cracked painfully as she spoke. 'He sees us as the most worthy.'

Dexter watched in horror as Crowan Frayne tipped the oil drum over and spilled petrol over the floor. He lifted the container and poured the remainder over the book piles, over the table and finally over himself. He then returned to his seat and pulled a cigarette lighter from his pocket. He placed it on the table and took two vicious-looking skin clamps from his box of medical equipment. With her left hand, Dexter frantically picked at the tape that bound her right wrist to the wooden chair. She needed more time. *Must talk to him.*

'So now what?' she asked. 'Burning the house down isn't poetry.' The smell of petrol was everywhere. The room was as dangerous as a powder keg. It smelled of death.

'The conceit has almost unfolded, Sergeant Dexter. This process has been educative for us all. You have become a worthy audience and I have become a worthy poet. Are we not poised to become angels?' With that, Crowan Frayne placed the two eye clamps on the skin above his left eyebrow. Then he ignited his lighter and threw it into the nearest book stack, which promptly burst into flames. The wall of heat hit Dexter in a second. She only had moments to get out before the whole room exploded into flames. Crowan Frayne let out a high-pitched scream as he drove his scalpel into the ciliary muscles at the side of his left eye.

Dexter was panicking. The glue on the tape was melting onto her hands, burning at her skin. A final wrench and both her hands were free. The staircase was on fire now and Dexter was gasping for air. She tore at the tape around her ankles. Flames were spreading quickly up the wall. They rolled across the floor in a blue and yellow tide, eating at the legs of the table. Crowan Frayne dropped his scalpel onto the table and pulled a pair of metal forceps from his equipment tray. Dexter tried not to watch as he forced the claws of the instrument into his eye socket and begin to pull on it.

Finally she was free. She ran around the table to Stussman and desperately tore at the lecturer's bindings. Fire burned at her feet and her ankles, melting her tights against her skin. Crowan Frayne screamed again as fire washed over his chest and back. With a final terrible effort, he pulled his left eye from its socket and dropped it on the table in a dark pool of blood.

'Is this not the triumph of the will, Sergeant Dexter?' he screamed.

The fire was roaring now. She had to get to the staircase fast. Dexter quickly reached across the table, grabbed a scalpel from Frayne's box and slashed violently at the tape around Stussman's ankles. It finally came away and Dexter dragged Stussman to the foot of the stairs.

'Look, Alison!' Crowan Frayne shouted through the flames. 'Love has wrought new alchemy. I have forged beauty from ugliness. She is beautiful again.' As flames engulfed him, Crowan Frayne held up the highly polished purple-lined box that now contained three eyes.

Dexter hauled Stussman up the burning staircase with her last vestiges of strength. At the top she turned the door handle and pushed hard against the wooden door. It was locked. For the first time that night, Alison Dexter screamed for help.

73

Jensen heard the screams and smelled the smoke rising from the house. There was a large stone urn in the front garden. She grabbed it, groaning under its weight, and smashed it through Violet Frayne's living-room window. The broken glass tore at her skin as she climbed through. Three squad cars pulled up in the street outside.

'Sergeant Dexter?' She shouted into the smoke. 'Dr Stussman?' She heard a muffled scream in response.

Jensen hurried into the hallway and opened the front door. She saw Harrison running across the road and turned back inside, staggering blindly through the smoke in the direction of he cries. She found the door to the basement in a few seconds. The handle was red hot. The door was locked. She looked desperately around for a key. Harrison had joined her.

'We're going to have to force it,' she shouted.

'All right. On three.'

'Stand back inside.'

They charged at the door together and it fell open, hanging inwards as the rotting frame gave way. The wall of smoke and heat hit them immediately. Jensen crouched, coughing, and reached blindly into the smoke. After a second she felt a body.

Part VI

The Glass and the Water

Two months later . . .

74

Paul Heyer's BMW purred to a halt outside the house. The spring sun was bright and hard. He could still see the moon, slowly receding from the morning sky. The light hurt his eyes. He flipped down the car's sun visor and turned to Julia.

'Are you sure you want to do this?' he asked.

'I'm sure.'

'I don't like leaving you alone with him.'

'It'll be all right. He's had a heart attack, Paul. I don't think he's up to a fight.'

Heyer shook his head. He still bore the scars.

'You've got your mobile phone?'

'In my coat pocket.' Julia tapped against the soft material of her new jacket.

'If he tries anything – or if he looks like he's losing it – just press your speed-dial button for my mobile. You won't have to talk to me. I'll come running as soon as I see you calling.'

'I'll be fine.' She hesitated for a second. 'You'll be right here, though?'

'At the end of the road.'

Julia clicked open the car door and stepped outside. The house looked scruffy and exhausted, the garden overgrown. She took a deep, cold breath and walked up the garden path as Paul gently pulled away behind her. She pressed the doorbell. It didn't ring. She knocked at the door. It opened almost immediately.

John Underwood wore a jacket and tie. He was clean-shaven and had a smudge of toothpaste on his tie. He smiled at Julia and gestured at her to come inside. The house had recently been hoovered. Julia could smell furniture polish.

'You've tidied up,' she said as they entered the living room.

'Just starting to,' he said. 'I've been back a week.'

'The garden . . .'

'Is next on the list.'

Julia sat down in what had been her favourite armchair. She looked strangely beautiful in the sunlight. It glowed on the side of her face. Underwood remembered her standing by the bonfire twenty-something years ago. He squashed the thought as it dug at him.

'Tea?' he asked.

'No, thanks. How are you feeling now?'

'Better. Back up to seventy-five per cent, I'd say.'

'Have they given you drugs for your heart?'

'Oh yes.' Underwood waved vaguely at a row of pill bottles on the sideboard. 'Two of the green ones with breakfast and dinner – they're for my heart. One yellow and one blue one every morning for my chest. They seem to be working, although my water's gone a funny colour.' He risked a smile.

Julia looked at him closely. 'And you, John, how are you feeling in yourself?'

He paused for a second. Should he tell her about the nightmares, about the panics and depressions that rolled through him like storm systems over the North Sea? What was the point? He was too tired to try and score points. The endgame was over. He had lost. 'I see Jack Harvey once a week,' he said simply. 'Do you remember him? He's the police psychologist in Huntingdon.'

'Vaguely.' She didn't.

'The disciplinary committee insisted I see him. They like to keep embarrassing episodes like this in-house. I . . .' He fumbled for the right words, 'I want to thank you and Paul for not pressing any charges. It helped. It helped a lot.' It hurt him to say that. He felt the rage rise slightly in his throat but this time it passed quickly; blown like smoke into the wind.

'It was Paul's decision,' she said abruptly.

Underwood smiled. He knew it must have been a bit more complicated than that.

'Thanks, anyway.'

'Will you go back?'

'That depends, really.' Underwood's eyes tracked a sparrow as it darted past the window. 'I am suspended for six months. Well, they've called it sick leave. In June I will have a full psychiatric evaluation and on the basis of that they'll decide whether I can go back. I doubt CID will have me. Maybe they'll put me on the cones hotline.'

Julia smiled faintly. John was in there somewhere. Underneath the crumpled, tired face and the sunken, haunted eyes, there was a spark of someone she recognized.

'John. We might as well get this over with.' She opened her handbag and withdrew a piece of paper. She handed it to him. 'This is the name and address of my solicitor. He'll be sending you a letter next week about the house, the mortgage and so on. It's really just paperwork now – making sure everything gets agreed, signed and exchanged.'

'I understand.'

'Have you looked at any other houses?' She floated the question tentatively; uncertain of how he would respond.

'I've been looking at some flats advertised in the newspaper. Prices have gone mad here since they built the high-speed link to London.' He tried to mask his concern. It was going to be a tough ride over the next few months.

'I'm sorry, John, I really am. But it has to be for the best.'

'That's what I keep telling myself.' His eyes had misted over slightly. 'It's got to hurt to work, right?'

Julia nodded. She was upset but she wouldn't cry. She had cried enough.

'Sometimes we have to change to move on,' she said. 'I suppose I should go really. Paul's waiting outside.'

Underwood's brow furrowed slightly. He still hadn't reconciled himself to Paul Heyer. '*Alas my love you do me wrong,*' the voice in his head sung sadly, '*to cast me off discourteously.*' He suddenly realized that the tune no longer infuriated him. The voice wasn't his.

'Well,' he said briskly, 'we can't keep him waiting.'

He walked her to the front door. For the first time he noticed her hair. It was shorter, tidier than he remembered. It suited her. She opened the door and turned towards him.

'I suppose this is it, then,' she said.

'I suppose it is.'

Julia leaned forward and kissed John Underwood on the cheek for the last time. He closed his eyes for a second, drowning in memories. Then he remembered.

'Oh, I've got something for you.' He coughed away the tears and hurried back into the house, returning with a book in a small paper bag. He handed it to her. 'I thought you might enjoy these. Don't open it now.'

'John. I . . .'

'Just take it, please. I . . .' He paused. 'It would mean a lot to me.'

Julia Underwood took the book and walked out of the life that had become a torture. She didn't look back, not even when the door closed behind her. Paul drove up and parked just out of sight of the house.

'How was it?' he asked as she climbed in.

'Fine,' Julia replied. 'He seems a bit better.'

'I've been looking at some of the houses in the street. It's a nice area. You might get a quarter of a million for the old place if he tidies it up a bit.'

Julia looked at Paul coldly but said nothing. For the first time, she felt a shiver of doubt and trepidation. They drove to a service station and Paul jumped out to fill the car with petrol. While he was away, Julia strolled to the edge of the forecourt, opened the bag and took out the book. It was a book of poetry: *John Donne's Songs and Sonnets*. There was a bookmark at one of the centre pages. She opened the book and read:

> *'Break of Daye'*
>
> *'Stay, O Sweet, and do not rise*
> *The light that shines come from thine eyes;*
> *The day breaks not, it is my heart*
> *Because that you and I must part*
> *Stay or else my joys will die*
> *And perish in their infancie.'*

Julia didn't make it to the second verse. She closed the book and walked hurriedly towards the open door of Heyer's BMW.

75

Heather Stussman lay in only mild discomfort in Ward C5 at New Bolden Infirmary. She hated hospitals: the smell, the noise, the invasiveness. 'Hell is other people,' Jean-Paul Sartre had once written. She now knew exactly what he had meant.

It had been a painful eight weeks. Eight weeks of bandages and embrocation. The burns on her legs were the worst. The fire had seared through her trousers as Dexter had frantically tried to cut her free from the hell that was Crowan Frayne's basement. The scars on her forehead were horrendous but improving. She had only looked 'Pity' in the eye once. It would take time and the agony of skin grafts before she could face the pity of other people.

'Have you spoken to John Underwood?' asked Stussman.

'Not for a few weeks. He's got other things on his mind,' Alison Dexter said flatly, trying to conceal her guilt. 'He's not well.'

'You should go see him.'

'Maybe. I owe him a call.'

'Are you feeling better?'

Dexter shrugged. 'It takes time, right?'

'Nightmares?'

'A few,' Dexter said tightly.

'It's hardly surprising.'

'They're less frequent since they put Mr Frayne in the ground.' Dexter hesitated. 'Well, what was left of him.'

'Not much, I imagine.'

'You don't want to know.'

There was a brief silence. Both women knew how close they had come to joining their tormentor. Dexter felt uncomfortable and coughed the moment away. Stussman watched her closely.

'You know, Alison, we got off on the wrong foot . . .'

'Forget it,' Dexter replied without emotion.

'I was cold towards you.'

'I'm used to it.'

'So am I. That's why I should have known better.'

'It's ancient history.' Dexter's hard green eyes watched the food trolley rattle past. The nurse had bobbed red hair. She was pretty. Dexter looked away.

'I've had a lot of time to think while I've been lying here,' said Stussman.

'Thinking's dangerous.'

Stussman didn't smile. It hurt to smile.

'People like you and me . . .' she said carefully, pausing to find the right words. Dexter shifted in her seat. She sensed where this was going. 'We have no reason to be dismissive of each other. There's no logic to it. In different ways we are fighting for the same thing.'

'And what's that?'

'Respect.'

'Go on.'

'We're driven by common elements. The characteristics that we value most in ourselves we often find repellent in others.'

Dexter nodded, suddenly ashamed of herself. 'You look tired. I should go.'

'Do you think about it much?' asked Stussman abruptly.

'I try not to, but yes, thinking about it is unavoidable. It's necessary, isn't it?'

'I suppose so.' Stussman's head was stinging again and she adjusted her bandage as it became uncomfortable. 'You know, in *The Divine Comedy*, after Dante leaves Hell he arrives in Purgatory. An angel writes "P" on his forehead seven times. It stands for "Peccatum," which is Latin for sin.'

'Seven deadly sins, right?'

'Right. As Dante repents his sins each "P" is removed from his forehead until he can enter Paradise.' Stussman's gaze explored the clear sky beyond the grimy hospital glass. 'I guess I have a way to go yet.'

'It's funny. The thing that bothers me now . . .' Dexter paused, then went on. 'Now it's over and I've had time to think it through – why did he burn all those books? I would have thought that he loved books.'

284

'I've been thinking about that, too,' Stussman said. 'He talked a lot about every dead thing living inside him . . . about how he could hear the dead speaking to him. Maybe he thought the dead spoke to him through the books, too. Books are just thoughts on paper. Perhaps he thought that by burning the books he was performing some kind of fucked-up alchemy on them. You know: the ideas in the books become flame and smoke, he becomes flame and smoke, you and I become flame and smoke. We all become one big beautiful bonfire of ideas.'

'Bloody hell.'

'Donne wrote in "Air and Angels" that angels assume a physical reality, just as air condenses into clouds or fog.'

'He talked about *us* becoming angels.'

' "Then as an Angell, face and wings/Of air, not pure as it, yet pure doth weare/So thy love may be my loves sphere." Stussman smiled faintly at Dexter. 'Perhaps he thought we were worthy of becoming angels with him; with faces and wings of smoke. A smoky ecstasy of angels and ideas, worthiness and knowledge.'

'Doesn't sound so bad when you put it like that. It's a less attractive idea when your arse is catching fire in a basement, though.'

Stussman let out a tired sigh. 'The metaphysical poets tried to fill the gaps between recognized science, religion and logic. The Renaissance was a time of great uncertainties and intellectual conflict. Donne and his colleagues took these uncertainties and inconsistencies and catalysed them into a new mode of expression.'

'Strange connections,' said Dexter quietly.

'Absolutely. Let's take the case in point. Newton's law of matter says that nothing is ever destroyed, it merely changes form. It's not too much of an intellectual leap to say that ideas and memories don't die, either. Maybe Mr Frayne thought that the fire would turn the knowledge buried in the books, the ideas and abilities that you and I have, and his own intelligence into something unitary, beautiful and complex.'

'That's mad.'

'Alison, the Catholic Church believes that a wafer and a glass of wine are transubstantiated into the body and blood of Christ during Mass. There's not a huge difference in the two positions. At least Frayne's position is based on logic.'

'You'll burn in Hell, saying things like that.'

'I doubt it. Let me ask you something now. Underwood said that these killers have a fantasy life that they live out through their killings.'

'Some do. I guess our man Frayne fell into that category. They're called Visionary Motivated Killers. They dream, they plan, they develop a fantasy that they gradually escalate and refine until they are compelled to act it out.'

'Poets plan and fantasize, Alison. Donne is a very good example. He would plan and build a logical argument, then dream up a fantasy or an image that came to represent and extend that argument, and he would perform his work for the gratification and education of a selected audience.'

'Like Crowan Frayne,' said Dexter.

'We live in uncertain times too, Alison. Donne said, "The new philosophy calls all into question." That, in a nutshell, is the paradox of the modern world. Science has done an effective job of destroying our confidence in established religion without creating anything to replace it. We are drowned in information and starved of knowledge. We live in a free society but our freedom is dependent upon the forces that value it least. Maybe Crowan Frayne saw some of these inconsistencies and uncertainties and thought he could hammer them into a new mode of expression.'

'Can we talk about something else?' said Dexter.

Dexter stayed for another half an hour and although Stussman was worn out she appreciated the company. Southwell College had given her a term's sabbatical to recover from her injuries. She wondered what McKensie and his henchmen would make of her new-found celebrity. There'd probably be a series of bad jokes followed by an overwhelming vote not to renew her research fellowship. Stussman wasn't looking forward to her first night alone back in her rooms, though, or to the first time her phone rang. Staying in Cambridge at all might be difficult for her now. Suddenly the open spaces and quietness of Wisconsin didn't seem as dull to her as they once had.

Fortunately, her mother was coming over the following week and the two of them were planning to take a holiday in Europe together. Thank God for family. Isolation from her family had been hard. She thought for a second of Crowan Frayne, trying to give his dead grandmother back the beauty that had been torn from her. Heather Stussman felt a sudden flash of emotion. Perhaps it was Pity.

Inspector Alison Dexter stepped out of the hospital foyer and paused for a second in the cold sunlight. She felt curiously empty. She should be happy; at least she should feel relieved. She paused for a moment. The wind hissed and rippled through the delicate branches of the newly planted saplings that lined the hospital car park. Out of the blue, she suddenly remembered a question she had been asked at college, years previously: 'If a tree falls in a forest, does it make a sound if nobody is there to hear it?' She pushed the thought aside.

Ambition had driven her this far. Ambition had earned her the respect of others. Respect had earned her promotion. She was an inspector; she had achieved her dream. Why, then, did she feel so hollow? So utterly numbed by the whole experience?

Dexter walked across the empty car park, hunting for an answer. If she had fallen, there would have been no sound.

She was alone.

76

The garden was already overgrown. The dead cannot be contained.

Violet Frayne's laburnum tree was awash with beautiful yellow flowers. They fluttered and danced for the sun under the benevolent sky.

Tangled roots divided and stretched down into the crowded soil, pushing aside stones, sucking in water and nutrients, drawing in the elemental goodness that would fuel the tree's blind reaching for the heavens. Oxygen, water, carbon dioxide: salts and sugars and memories.

77

They drove around the edge of the town centre. New Bolden became impenetrably clogged with shoppers on a Saturday morning. Dexter was wise to this and swung her Mondeo around the ring road as if she was some mad comet circling the sun. She spoke continuously: she found the silences trying. She spoke and John Underwood listened. Dexter talked about Crowan Frayne, about how she had made the connections that led her to the computer terminal and about how she had been a few seconds from becoming a barbecued sausage – or an angel.

Underwood was only half-interested. He found himself drifting in and out of focus. Sometimes he was absorbing the details of Dexter's recital, sometimes he was walking in the Yorkshire Dales with Julia and sometimes he was at the bottom of the blackest hole his mind could conjure. The sunlight glanced brightly off the car windows as Dexter turned off the ring road and headed towards the cemetery. His mind was cluttered with images.

Take a glass of water. That is a symbiosis that neither party understands because neither party has the capacity to understand. Squint, limit your field of perception and the glass of water appears as a single entity. A dog will just see a hole in its field of vision. Take the glass and pour out the water. Its molecules never mix with the glass but some cling to it: thick viscous blobs that hang like barnacles.

Why do some linger like memories and others fall away? All matter exploded from an infinitesimally small particle. All the atoms in our flesh, in the ground we walk on, in gas giants a billion light years away, in comets and the red-hot centres of planets, once coexisted in a single whole. Perhaps the atoms in the water recognize atoms in the glass that they were once bound to, once torn apart from. Perhaps they don't want to let go again.

Underwood didn't want to let go.

Dexter parked at the entrance to the cemetery and they both got out.

'Are you sure you don't mind, sir?' she asked.

Underwood shook his head. 'No, it's a nice day. The exercise will do me good.' He placed his mobile phone on the passenger seat and slammed the car door shut behind him. 'I'm not sure I understand why you want to do this, though.'

Dexter walked alongside him, more slowly than usual. 'I want to make absolutely sure the bastard's in the ground.' It was half true. She also wanted to scare Underwood into looking after himself. She hoped the grim finality of the headstones might help.

Birds swooped and cut the sky above them as walked. It didn't bleed, as he thought it might.

'Magpies?' asked Underwood.

'Don't ask me,' Dexter laughed. 'My bird knowledge begins with the pigeons in Trafalgar Square and ends with turkey on Christmas Day.'

'When did they bury the body?'

'Three weeks ago,' Dexter said. 'It's not really a body any more, though.'

'I can imagine.'

'He hacked his own eye out.' The memory still made her uncomfortable. 'He said "Is this not the triumph of the will" as he did it.'

'Imagine the will-power it takes to cut your own eye out.'

'You sound like you're impressed.'

'Frightened is closer.'

'Try being there.'

Underwood smiled thinly. 'You've done well Dex. You'll be Chief Inspector in a couple of years. You're an irrepressible force.'

'What about you?'

'They might make me a sergeant, I suppose. If they don't lock me away in some funny farm.'

Dexter frowned. 'That's only going to happen if you lose the plot. You're feeling better, aren't you?'

'I don't know. At the moment I feel pretty shitty. It's like every mistake, horror and bad memory happening at the same time.'

'Will-power, sir. You have to make yourself better. You have to want to fight.'

Underwood laughed humourlessly. 'Fight? Why? What for?'

'For yourself.'

'I'm not sure I'm worth the effort.'

'You are.'

Underwood looked at her but Dexter stared straight ahead. She was getting angry with him. She had heard the rumours: that Underwood had lost it, that he was on a diet of happy pills and was seeing the police shrink at Huntingdon, but this was the first time she had seen the evidence at first hand. Her concern just outweighed her irritation.

'Are you religious, sir?'

'You don't have to call me "sir" any more.'

'Are you religious?'

'I'm not a Mason, if that's what you mean.'

His joke fell flat. 'You know what I mean.' She was quietly insistent.

'No. I'm not religious. I do not believe in God. I do not believe in heaven. I believe that this – ' he gestured vaguely around and at himself ' – whatever the fuck it is, is it.'

'Then that's why you have to survive,' Dexter said simply. 'Because there isn't any point in you dying.'

Crowan Frayne's headstone was plain: black text on granite. 'C. A. Frayne 1967–2000.' There was no inscription.

'Who paid for the headstone?' Underwood asked, ever suspicious.

'Some distant relative. A cousin, I think.'

'Not much of an epitaph,' said Underwood, looking at the grey stone.

'Not much of a person.'

'I guess not. So Heather Stussman thinks he was writing a

kind of poem. A celebration of beauty, an argument that ugliness could be transformed into beauty.'

'Something like that. It's mad shit.'

He had changed Julia into an ugliness. She had been beautiful in body and spirit. He had made her ordinary and afraid. Mad shit. Somehow, Paul Heyer had made the ugliness beautiful. Underwood knew that he had become a monstrosity: half alive and half sane. His mind bounced like a ball on a piece of elastic; flying at impossibly absurd trajectories before rolling back to stasis. Your thoughts have no value. Do not pass go. Go directly to jail. Do not collect two hundred pounds. Mad shit. Mad shit.

'Look at this, guv.' Dexter gestured at him to come over. She was kneeling by a headstone a few yards away. It was plain grey marble. The black text read: *William Eric Gowers, 1917–94, Rest Eternally.* Underneath the engraving a four-letter obscenity had been aerosoled onto the stone.

'Gowers was married to Violet Frayne,' she said. 'Not much of an epitaph, is it?'

'I don't suppose she sprayed it.' Underwood managed a smile.

They waited for a minute or two and then walked back slowly towards the car. They didn't say anything.

Underwood felt a sudden rush of anxiety. What if Dexter was right? What if this was it? What if there really was nothing else? What would his epitaph be? They passed a young woman carrying flowers. She looked them over with soft, sad eyes.

The sun seemed exceptionally bright now. Underwood sought order in his thoughts:

Life is a tightrope of perception with darkness on either side, darkness behind and darkness underneath.

He had hacked most of the rope from underneath him. Maybe Dexter was right. Maybe staying on the tightrope was the only point. The darkness had seemed appealing, a relief from the hard light of reality. Sometimes he had wanted to let go, to embrace the peace of annihilation. But maybe his spirit was like the water in the glass. Maybe he couldn't let go. Suddenly, Underwood was uncertain and afraid.

'Survive,' said the Magpie.

Dexter unlocked the car and they climbed in. Underwood picked up his mobile phone from the seat before he flopped down.

'I'm hungry. Do you fancy some lunch?'

He thought for a second, pushing the darkness to one side. He had to take his heart pills with food. 'That'd be nice.'

'Fry-up?'

'I shouldn't, really.'

'Neither should I. How about scrambled eggs as a compomise?' Dexter asked.

'Good enough.'

Dexter ground through the gears and they accelerated towards the town centre. There was a greasy spoon behind the police station. Scrambled eggs with Alison: the simplicity almost overwhelmed him.

Underwood looked at the LCD display on his mobile phone and saw that there had been a missed call. He pressed a button and the phone displayed the identity of the caller: 'Julia'.

Survive.